MW01131402

SEEING BEYOND THE SHADOWS

William Clark

WestBow Press books may be ordered through booksellers or by contacting:

WestBow Press
A Division of Thomas Nelson & Zondervan
1663 Liberty Drive
Bloomington, IN 47403
www.westbowpress.com
1 (866) 928-1240

ISBN: 978-1-9736-8671-2 (sc)
ISBN: 978-1-9736-8670-5 (e)

Printed in the United States of America.

WestBow Press rev. date: 03/26/2020

This book is dedicated to all the people, who gave their lives, to make America a nation and to keep it one nation, under God.

"A house divided against itself cannot stand."
Abraham Lincoln
Springfield, Illinois
June 15, 1858
(from the words of Jesus Christ in
Matthew 12:25 KJV)

Foreword

My younger cousin, Andy McGraig, could beat me in a game of chess by the time he was five, and I was ten. I was the chess champ in my school, which was in the next county north of Andy's home county. Ever since that first defeat, I was aware of how bright my mom's nephew is.

Andy's family is as exceptional, as Andy's intellect is. It's hard to believe that Andy is as humble, as he is talented. Andy became an all-star basketball player in Indiana, and the best player in Purdue's history.

By the time, I went to college in the late 1950s, a number of professors were questioning their students' faith in God. I found it ironic, because one of the main readers in nineteenth century public schools was the McGuffey Eclectic Fourth Reader. It contained many Bible chapters, verses and the Sermon on the Mount.

By the 1960s, it was hard to believe that the New Age Socialist Party became one of the main political parties in America. I believe that God blessed Andy with unique spiritual gifts, so he could help bring healing to our nation. God can also bring healing to any nation, even if they're tormented with a border crisis, terrorism, and subversion within the government.

Anderson McCollister

Contents

1

Andy's Family

The little bungalow at 1137 W. 5th Street stood with the other bungalows like snug rows of neatly, decorated wooden huts, with eye-catching flower boxes placed below the front windows. They house mostly families of hourly laborers, who work at two neighboring factories; an auto plant and a card table and chair factory. The table and chair factory had been converted to manufacturing bombs for the World War that ended just three years ago.

Outside of freezing, snowy weather, most of the men walk to work; day or night. Andy's dad, Owen McGraig, a good looking man in his early thirties, just completed his second shift work. He walks in the dimly lighted darkness by two blocks of the 700 to 800 sf bungalows that were mostly built in the 1920s. He enters through his back door into the kitchen at 11:40 p.m. He sets his black, metal lunch pail on the counter top. He takes out the thermos and rinses a few drops of coffee from the cup and the thermos.

Owen's wife, Davina, a charming and pretty lady, comes in the kitchen and greets her husband with a loving kiss. "How was work, honey?"

Owen replies, "Not bad; the last hour I was mainly thinking of you and the kids. How are they doing?"

"Real well. I read an Uncle Arthur's Bedtime Story to them, and Judy fell asleep before I finished the story. Andy was a little restless, but he fell asleep right after we prayed. Can I get you anything before I go back to bed?"

Owen answers, "No thanks, sweetheart. I'm going to take off these grimy clothes and freshen up. I'll be there in a few minutes."

Owen throws his outer clothes on the checkered green and white asbestos linoleum in the kitchen, near the basement door. (Davina finishes laundry before 2:00, since Owen leaves at 2:45 for the second shift.) He goes in their small bathroom and takes a nickel bath. He puts on a pair of red and white striped pajamas. He makes sure the night light is on; turns out the overhead light, and quietly gets into their full size bed, so he doesn't wake Davina.

Andy wakes up, when his dad comes out of the bathroom. He knows everyone is now in bed, and he notices how quiet it is. He sees that the night light is on, in case nature gives a late call. His two year old sister, Judy, is sound asleep in her twin bed; close to Andy's bed. Andy tries not to think of the shadowy creatures on the wall, that he usually sees at this time of the night. He sees them on the left side of the short hallway wall and the ceiling. As he tries not to think about them, he starts to get sleepy, when he notices some shadows forming on the wall and moving up to the ceiling. When several snake-like creatures are moving around on the wall and the ceiling, he cries, "Mommy!"

Judy remains asleep, but Andy's sleepy mom gets out of bed to check on her distressed five year old. She comes in his room and says, "What is it, Andy?"

Andy sobbingly replies, "The creatures are back, Mommy. I don't like them!"

"Now, Andy, you know that we sometimes imagine things. God will protect you, so don't worry. Go back to sleep, and I'll say a prayer with you." Davina recites, "I lay me down to sleep. I pray thee, Lord, my soul to keep. If I die before I wake, I pray thee, Lord, my soul to take. Amen." Before Davina finishes the prayer, Andy falls to sleep. Davina goes back to bed. Owen is snoring, and oblivious to his son's recent encounter.

Morning comes early at the McGraig household. Davina makes coffee and fixes breakfast for Andy, who has morning kindergarten at 8:30. Davina tunes in their Motorola radio on the kitchen counter top. She listens to music and the news on an Indianapolis AM station. Andy is just finishing his Cheerios and orange juice, when Owen comes in the kitchen to fix breakfast for Judy. Davina says, "Andy will be ready to leave for school in a few minutes. Help yourself to the coffee."

Owen replies, "Thank you, sweetheart. I'll get some coffee and wake up Judy in a minute." He rubs Andy's head and says, "How is my son this morning?"

Andy says, "Just fine, daddy."

As Davina helps Andy with his coat, she says, "It's the first day of December, Andy, and it is already getting cold. I'll get my coat, and we'll walk to school."

They walk out their front door onto the short concrete path to the neighborhood sidewalk. After they pass a few houses, their street curves around to a busy road with an old general store on the corner. Once the last car rushes by, the patrol boy, dressed in his white shoulder belt, steps out to the center of the cross walk to make sure that any oncoming traffic stops. Davina takes Andy's gloved hand, and they cross the street. The sidewalk continues along a run-down neighborhood. They pass a house that has an old refrigerator in the backyard. It's been set out in a junk section of the yard. The door has been left on the refrigerator. Davina and Owen have talked about reporting the safety hazard to the city sanitation department.

Right after the run-down neighborhood, they cross over an old train track that is not in use. Once they get to the next corner, Andy's school is in front of them. Davina walks with Andy to the big front door of the old school building. She leans down and kisses Andy on the check. "Have a good morning in your class. Daddy will pick you up at 12:00."

Andy replies, "Thank you, mommy."

Davina walks swiftly back home in the brisk weather. The sky is totally overcast with steel grey clouds. She walks through the front door into a refreshing scent of coffee that permeates the little bungalow.

It seems to Davina that the morning is rushing by. She makes the beds and dresses Judy. Owen goes into the kitchen to where the basement door is installed in the kitchen floor. Owen lifts up on the sturdy metal ring and pulls up the door. He leans the door against the kitchen wall and goes downstairs to do some work at his workbench. While the basement door is open, Davina keeps her eye on Judy, so she doesn't wander into the kitchen.

In an hour, Owen comes back upstairs, and says, "Davina, since the basement door is open, do you want to do laundry while I watch Judy?"

Davina says, "Yes, honey. I can be done with it early and watch Judy, while you meet Andy at school." Davina decides to do a light load. Owen only has two pairs of work clothes, so she washes his dirty pair and a few other things. Since she can't hang the clothes outside to dry in cold weather, she'll hang them up in the basement, and Owen's clean work clothes will be ready for the next day. Her wash tub has an open top with an agitator, that runs by electricity. Her rinse tub has a mounted wringer that she cranks and feeds the clothes through with her other hand. After she wrings the excess water out, she hangs the clothes to dry.

She comes up the stairs, and looks at the clock. She goes in the next room to find Owen and says, "The timing was good. It's about 11:30. I'll start to get lunch ready, when you leave to get Andy."

Owen says, "Good deal. I may find out at work today, if I can apply soon for the toolmaker apprenticeship. When I get the application, I can confirm, if I'll be making $1.00 more an hour, when I become a journeyman."

Davina replies, "Wow, honey. That's about $2,000 more a year! How many years do you think it will take to save for a bigger house?"

"The toolmaker journeyman program takes at least a year to complete. If I get in the program and complete it, we could have enough money for a bigger house in about four or five years after that. I better grab my coat and be on my way."

Davina says, "I will have lunch ready, when you and Andy get back. Do you want me to pack anything special for your supper?"

"No thanks," replies Owen. "The usual will be fine."

When Owen steps outside, he thinks, "It still feels like it's in the mid-thirties." He wastes no time in getting to Andy's school. He opens the sturdy wood door and walks down the wooden staircase to Andy's class. He's a few minutes early and waits near the classroom door. He can hear the children talking and laughing, as they get ready to return to their warm homes. Owen thinks, "I hope they all have comfortable homes to go to."

The door flies open, and over twenty little five year olds burst from their classroom of beginning knowledge. After the last one exits, Owen peers into the colorfully, painted classroom, looking for Andy, when his teacher, Miss Alexander, comes to the door.

She says, "How are you today, Mr. McGraig?"

"Just fine, thank you."

Miss Alexander asks, "Do you have just a few minutes to come in and talk?"

Owen says, "I would be glad to."

Miss Alexander looks at Andy and says, "Andy, please wait at the door for daddy."

Andy looks at his dad, and Owen smiles at him and nods his head.

Miss Alexander looks at Owen and says, "Let's sit down at my desk."

As they sit down, Owen admires the water color paintings that the children must have just turned in.

Miss Alexander says, "The class did these water color paintings today. Let me show you Andy's and a few others."

After Owen looks at several paintings, Miss Alexander asks, "After seeing several paintings, do you see any difference in Andy's?"

Owen replies, "It looks like it has been done by an older student."

"Exactly. Andy is emotionally and mentally ahead by a minimum of two or three years. He's the most mature student I have, and he interacts with the other students exceptionally."

Owen says, "I've noticed for a good while that he is a bright kid."

Miss Alexander asks, "How long has he been reading?"

"Since he was four. At times he reads a bedtime story to his sister and mother."

Miss Alexander asks, "I want to talk with the principal about Andy taking an IQ test. Before I talk with Miss Pittenger, I would like to get permission from Mrs. McGraig and you."

"I'll talk with my wife. When would the test be given, and how long would it take?"

"I can arrange with Miss Pittenger to have it taken during class time. For Andy's age, the test will take roughly thirty to forty minutes. There is a small, adjoining room by the principal's office, where Andy can take the test. The test could be administered after the Christmas break. Your wife, you and I can tell Andy about the test, so he will be at ease taking it."

"Thank you for your interest in Andy, Miss Alexander. He stands up and shakes her hand. I will talk with Davina about it, and she can let you know soon."

Andy is waiting patiently at the door, and Owen asks, "Are you ready for a hot lunch, Andy?"

Andy replies, "I sure am." They walk up the basement stairs and cross the wide hallway on the main level to the front doors."

At home Davina serves the family hot, home-made vegetable soup and grilled cheese sandwiches. Over lunch Owen says to Davina, "Andy's teacher would like him to take an IQ test after Christmas break."

Davina replies, "That sounds like a tall order for a five year old."

"She said the test only takes thirty to forty minutes. He can take it in an area next to the principal's office during class time. Miss Alexander said that Andy does very well in a class. She believes he is ahead of his age group."

Davina says, "Well, letting them give him the test may be okay, but I don't want him in a class with older kids."

Owen replies, "I'm neutral about it. If you're alright with the testing, it is fine with me. If you don't want him in an older class, that's also fine with me."

Davina looks at Andy and says, "You haven't told me, Andy, what you want Santa to bring you for Christmas."

Andy says, "I saw a parking garage at Woolworth's. It comes with two cars and two trucks, and a ramp that takes them from the first level to the second level. It also has a filling station by the first level. I didn't notice the price."

Owen says, "Don't worry about the price, son. I'm sure Santa will be good to you." Owen enclosed the front porch last summer, so the kids would have more room to play.

Andy says, "Thank you, Daddy."

Owen says to Judy, "And young lady, what do you want for Christmas?"

Judy chatters some, but she says the word, "doll".

Owen laughs and says, "Ok, babe, I bet Santa can handle that!"

Davina looks at Owen and says, "Honey, after lunch look at Judy's right leg. Even though she has thin legs, the right one looks thinner than her left leg and not as strong."

"Okay, sweetheart, I'll look at it."

It's even colder outside than it was in the morning. Andy stays in and colors in an activity book and reads another book. Judy plays with some paper dolls after Owen looks at her leg.

After 2:00, Davina starts making Owen's supper for his 7:00 supper break at work. Owen comes in the lighted kitchen and says, "I looked at Judy's leg. I see what you mean. If you're still concerned about it next week, you can call the doctor. Tomorrow is Friday already, and Saturday we'll be busy with the kids, shopping, house cleaning and getting ready for church on Sunday."

Davina replies, "That is fine with me. I was looking in the refrigerator for leftovers and came up short. I made you a P&J sandwich. We have some oranges, celery and carrots. I could cut them for you."

"That will be plenty. If I get hungry before I leave work, they have vending machines in the break room with nickel items like candy bars, chips and pastry."

Davina replies, "I'll also make coffee now for your thermos."

"At 2:45, Owen grabs his lunch pail; kisses Davina and says, "Thanks for the supper, sweetheart."

Davina says, "Be safe at work. Love you."

It's dark already by 5:30, and Davina and the kids finish with supper. She gives Judy and Andy a bath. After they get on their PJs, they go in the living room, and Davina turns on the Zenith console radio. She tunes into an AM station that plays the Amos and Andy broadcast at 7:00. While they listen to Amos and Andy, Davina and Andy laugh heartily, and Judy is on Davina's lap laughing with them.

2

Only Seventy Years Ago

When Davina and Andy step outside Friday morning, it's lightly snowing. Fortunately, the walks are not covered, so they can get to school a little quicker. Davina leaves five minutes early, so she can speak with Andy's teacher about the IQ test.

As they walk into the classroom, it is beginning to fill with the high, excitable voices of several children already there. Davina walks up to Miss Alexander and introduces herself. Miss Alexander says, "Good to see you, Mrs. McGraig. I remember you from orientation day."

"It's good to see you again. Andy's dad told me about the IQ test. We are okay with Andy taking it. When would he take it, and when would we get the results?"

Miss Alexander replies, "I can ask the principal to administer it by January 15th, and you should get the results by January 30th."

Davina says, "I want to make sure the test and results are confidential. I also want to make sure Andy won't be under stress or pressure from taking it or from the results."

Miss Alexander says, "I can assure you it is confidential, and no pressure is put on the student."

Davina is relieved; smiles and says, "Thank you, Miss Alexander. I know it's about class time."

"Thank you, Mrs. McGraig. You're blessed with a gifted son."

"Yes, he is," says Davina. She sees Andy in the classroom and waves at him.

Davina goes home to give Owen a chance to rest before he goes to work. She watches Judy, while she irons and washes the dishes. Owen catches up on some reading as well as the news and sports. After a restful morning, he picks up Andy at school. He gets some pointers from Miss Alexander about Andy's test, so Andy won't feel anxious.

After lunch they start talking about their Saturday plans. Saturday is usually a big day for the McGraigs, as well as for most working class families. Davina tells Owen what she needs to buy at the grocery store and makes a list. She makes sure they have enough in their budget to buy meat for the freezer. She sorts through the coupons that she's been saving, and she sets out her green stamp book.

Before they go to bed, everyone gathers around the Zenith radio in the living room. Davina turns to a 50,000 watt channel that has good reception in the evening. They enjoy country, ballad and gospel music on "The Nashville at Night Show". They especially love listening to The Mills Brothers and Eddy Arnold. At 7:30 "The Adventures of Ozzie and Harriet" follows "The Nashville at Night Show". Little do they realize that in four years, they will enjoy the Nelson family on a new medium called, "television".

At 8:00, Davina announces the bedtime call for brushing teeth and a bedtime story. When Davina tucks in Andy and Judy, Andy asks her, "Are we going to Woolworth's tomorrow?"

Davina replies, "We can go there, and you can show Daddy the parking garage and filling station, so he'll know what you're asking Santa for."

Andy says, "Mommy when I see the creatures at night, I'm trying to pray instead of calling for you."

Davina replies, "I will be praying for you. If you need me, just call." Davina kisses Andy and Judy goodnight and turns off their bedroom light.

In the morning, Andy wakes up to the smell of bacon with the good fortune of scrambled eggs. After Andy comes out of the bathroom, Judy gets up, and they go into the kitchen to enjoy breakfast with the family at the kitchen table. Davina and Owen talk about their shopping plans today.

After Owen and Davina clear off the table, Owen says, "I'll open the garage doors and warm up the car for you, when you're ready. I'll stay home with the kids, while you get the groceries."

About an hour later, Owen walks out to the back yard; past the bare cherry tree to the twenty year old, one car garage. He goes to the back of the garage which faces an alley that runs between his street and the neighboring street. He unlocks the padlock that secures the two large, wood doors, and then swings them open to the right and to the left. He steps inside on the dirt floor and gets into the aging, 1940 black Chevy Sedan. He starts up the 6 cylinder engine, and lets it idle several minutes before Davina leaves.

About five minutes after Owen starts the car, Davina comes outside wearing her mid-calf length, brown wool coat and carrying her beige purse. Owen bought her coat at J.C. Penny's four years ago for $8.95. Owen steps outside, while Davina pushes down the clutch and puts the sedan in first gear. As Davina leaves on the two mile trip to the local A&P, Owen closes the garage doors.

Davina pulls into the A&P parking lot and pulls on the emergency brake after she turns off the engine. Davina gets her grocery list and coupons out of her purse and goes inside the brightly, lit A&P. Davina has listed most of the prices: a head of lettuce, 10 cents; apples, 5 cents per lb.; ground beef, 29 cents per lb.; one box of Cheerios, 39 cents; two loaves of bread, 29 cents; one gallon of milk 25 cents; a six pack of 8oz. soda bottles, 25 cents and a large can of coffee, 79 cents. Along with several other items she has not priced, she estimates her grocery bill will be about $4.00 after she uses several coupons. (No one in Indiana has heard of a sales tax on groceries.)

Before she pays for her groceries, she goes down the coffee aisle one more time. She loves the smell of the coffee that mainly comes from all of the Eight O'clock Coffee, and people grinding coffee beans. After she pays for the food, and they're put in large paper bags, she sees that she has 25 cents left to give to the Salvation Army Bell Ringer. The cashier gives her the receipt and her green stamps. When she gets back home, she honks so Owen will help her carry in the groceries. Andy watches Judy, while they put the groceries up. Davina tells Owen, "After I used the coupons, the total was $4.28." Before Davina fixes a light lunch, they all take a nap. She plans to have supper ready by 4:00, so they can go downtown by 5:00.

During supper Davina says to Owen, "It looks like the gas war is continuing in Muncie. Right now we can get gas for 23 cents a gallon, and the tank is half empty."

Owen replies, "We'll stop for gas on the way to town."

Davina says, "I'll do the dishes, when we get back. If we're about ready to go, we'll take turns in the bathroom, then I'll bundle up the kids."

Owen says, "Alright, let's make our pit stops and all systems will be go!"

After they get their coats, caps and gloves on, they get in the Chevy sedan, and stop at the Standard Oil filling station, which is the closest station to their house. The attendant comes out to the driver's door and Owen says, "Fill her up, please. You can clean the front windshield and check the oil, but you don't need to check the tires."

The young attendant replies, "Yes, sir."

It takes less than five minutes for the attendant to finish his routine. He comes back to Owen and says, "That will be $2.30 for the gas."

Owen pays him and they're off to the center of downtown, which is only a mile away. They park across the street from J.C. Penny's. It's almost dark, but the main part of downtown has plenty of lighting. A lot of people are already bustling about doing their shopping in a happy Christmas atmosphere. The city workers have hung white lights and snowflakes from the street lamps. The ground is barely covered with snow and all of the sidewalks and crossings have been cleared. Its 34 degrees and fairly mild weather for late autumn in central Indiana. Owen takes Andy's hand, and Davina holds Judy's hand.

Davina says, "I don't need anything at Penny's. I guess the first stop will be Woolworth's. Andy wants to show you the parking garage and filling station that he likes."

Owen says, "Sounds good." He looks at Andy and says, "Does that sound good to you, son?"

Andy replies, "It sure does!"

They walk into F.W. Woolworth's Five and Dime. The air is filled with the tempting smell of mouth-watering popcorn. Owen says, "They have large bags for a nickel. On the way back to the car, we'll stop and get two bags. At home we can have it with some pop."

Davina says, "That's my favorite Saturday night treat!"

Andy directs his family to the toy section and hopefully, to his special, Christmas morning gift. When he sees his favorite toy, he says, "There it is, mommy and daddy."

Owen says, "Wow! That's a humdinger alright! I would be thrilled to get that, if I were eight years old."

Andy says, "Now you know why I would like it for Christmas."

Owen says, "I know you're a good boy, so I would say that your chances of getting it are better than average."

Andy's face lights up with a big smile. He can envision it sitting under the tree on Christmas morning.

When they leave Woolworth's, they wait for the red light at the first crosswalk. Andy looks at the city police officer near the corner. To Andy, he looks like a giant with a huge Billy Club on his side. Owen says to Andy, "He looks big, doesn't he? We have some big officers." As they cross the street, Owen continues, "Muncie use to be called little Chicago. There was a lot of prostitution, bootleg liquor and gambling in the 1930s. Muncie was also a hideout for John Dillinger."

Most five year olds probably wouldn't grasp all of what Owen shared, but Andy caught the gist of it. Davina wants to go into Sears and look at some children's clothing on the second floor. They walk into Sears and to the elevator. In a minute, the elevator operator opens the gate, and they step inside. They say, "Hi" to the nice-looking young operator, who lives just down the street from them.

Davina gets some ideas for Christmas gifts, as she goes through some sale items of boy's and girl's clothing. She looks at Owen and asks, "Do you want to do some window shopping at Montgomery Wards before we head back to the car?"

Owen replies, "Yes, for just a few minutes."

When they walk out of Sears onto the crowded sidewalk, they see the beggar that they have seen many times during their trips to downtown. He has no legs and sits on a padded piece of plywood that is mounted on four casters. He moves the dolly along with his hands. He holds a cup of pencils for the public. Owen doesn't take a pencil, but he drops a dime in his cup and says, "God bless you, brother."

The beggar says, "God bless you, sir."

Inside at Montgomery Wards, Owen looks at tools for just a few minutes, and then looks at Davina and the kids and asks, "Are you ready to get some popcorn?"

In unison, they say, "We sure are!"

They go back to Woolworths, and Owen gives the female clerk a dime for two large bags of popcorn. Owen and Davina each hold a bag of popcorn in one hand and hold their children's hands with their other hand. As they walk to the parking lot, it begins to snow lightly.

Owen says, "It's probably getting closer to 32 degrees."

By the time they get inside their warm home, it is 7:00. They take off their wraps; turn on the radio in the living room and sit down to enjoy the popcorn and pop. Andy makes a comment about the husky police officer.

Owen says, "Andy, you might be big and strong, when you grow up. How will you feel, if you're big like that?"

Andy replies, "I'll help people."

Owen says, "Good for you, Andy."

A little before 8:00 Davina says, "Kids, we need to start getting ready for bed. Tomorrow is church and morning will be here soon."

Owen says to Davina, "While you help Judy and Andy, I'll do the dishes."

Davina replies, "Thank you, honey."

After they get their pajamas on, Davina reads to them and prays. Davina kisses them and turns out their bedroom light. They fall asleep in a couple of minutes. Davina and Owen stay up another hour, and they get ready for bed. Once again, when they finish in the bathroom and go to bed, Andy wakes up.

In a little while, Andy sees the shadowy creatures reappearing on the hallway wall and ceiling. He does his best to pray. He is thankful they're going to church tomorrow. The inspiration that Andy gets at church helps him with his challenges.

3

The Christmas of 1948

The McGraigs get up early on Sunday morning. Owen and Davina both help with the breakfast and getting Andy and Judy ready for church. It takes extra time for everyone to get on their Sunday best. Once teeth are brushed and the neckties and shoes go on, Owen goes to the garage to warm up the car.

Their evangelical church is a little over three miles. To get there, they go across the tracks; through the western edge of downtown and pass several businesses, churches and neighborhoods. Their church is located just several blocks from the outskirts of the Ball State Teachers College campus.

They have Sunday School at 9:30 and Worship begins at 10:45. At 9:15 the traffic is light. As they begin to leave the downtown area, Andy asks, "Why is that big wall around that church?"

Owen is driving, so Davina asks, "What wall, Andy?"

Andy replies, "Its real tall, mommy."

Davina looks at Owen, "Did you see a wall around the church we just passed?"

Owen says, "I didn't notice one."

In another minute they pass another bigger church and Owen asks Andy, "Do you see a wall around that church, Andy?"

"Yes, Daddy. It's tall also."

About a half a mile before they get to their church, they pass a smaller church.

Owen asks, "Andy is there a wall around that church?"

Andy replies, "Yes, but it's much shorter."

Davina asks Owen, "What do you make of this?"

Owen replies, "I don't know, but where Andy saw the big walls are at older, bigger churches."

After Owen parks the sedan on the street, about a block from their church, Owen asks Andy, "Do you see a wall around our church?"

Andy says, "Yes, a short one."

Their church has a large front entrance and a side entrance that the McGraigs enter. Owen and Davina take Judy and Andy to their Sunday school classes downstairs, then they go to their class on the second story. In fifty-five minutes, they leave their class a couple minutes early to get Andy and Judy.

An usher is by the side entrance to the sanctuary and greets them and gives them a church bulletin of service information and activities. As they go in, they say, "good morning" to a number of people before they come to their favorite pew. With just three Sundays remaining before Christmas, the sanctuary is decorated with red poinsettias, small wreaths and white Christmas candles on the window sills below the beautiful stain glass windows.

The organist is finishing her prelude of "Jesu, Joy of Man's Desiring", by Bach. Even though Davina and Owen especially like southern gospel music, they made this church their home, because the people are exceptionally friendly, loving and caring. They also enjoy the traditional hymns that they hear every Sunday.

The song leader has the congregation stand to open the service by singing, "What a Friend We Have in Jesus". After the song, the congregation is seated, and the Sunday School Superintendent reads the church announcements. The pastor then goes to the pulpit; welcomes everyone and gives prayer requests before a time of prayer.

Andy is enjoying every word. Judy is sitting on the pew and drawing on the back of the church bulletin. After the prayer, the congregation stands again and sings, "The Old Rugged Cross". The morning offering is taken, and then the choir sings a medley of Christmas songs. Traditionally, they will be singing all Christmas songs for the next three Sundays.

The pastor comes back to the pulpit and announces the scriptural text and his sermon title, "The Importance of America's Traditional, Christian Values". He gives a prayer, then reads the text before he delivers the morning message.

After the service concludes, everyone is shaking hands and talking.

The attendance and offering board shows that 190 people attended the morning worship service last Sunday. Owen tells an older toolmaker friend that he is applying for the toolmaker apprenticeship at his auto plant. His friend, Carl, is glad to hear the news and says, "Owen, I'll be praying that you get the apprenticeship." He and his wife, Thelma, are good friends of the McGraig family. Carl greets Davina, as she talks with Thelma. He looks down at the kids and says, "How are Miss Judy and Mr. Andy this morning?" He looks at Andy and reaches behind his ear, and with sleight of hand produces a nickel. "Look there, Andy, did you know that you have an extra nickel?" Andy laughs and thanks him. Andy admires Carl and likes the attention.

The McGraigs talk with several other church friends. Owen looks at his watch and says to Davina, "What time are we expected at your brother's?"

Davina says, "1:00", and she looks at her watch. "Oh, wow. We should go home right away. I put a chicken in the oven. We'll pack it and leave for Hartford City. If we leave home around 12:30, we should get to Edward's about 1:00." Uncle Edward and Aunt Ella's 10 year old son is Anderson McCollister, Andy's cousin. Andy especially likes it, when they invite him on their trips to the Smoky Mountain National Park

They hurry home and load the Indiana baked chicken. Uncle Edward's house is 19 miles. On HW 3 North they pass the country home of John Dillinger's girlfriend. In the rearview mirror Owen looks at Andy and says, "Do you see any walls, son?"

Andy replies, "Just some farm fences."

Owen laughs and says, "There certainly are plenty of them and cornfields."

After a delicious Sunday dinner at Edward and Ella's home, Andy plays Anderson in a game of chess. Andy always likes looking at their old Story & Clark piano and their grandfather clock that chimes on the hour. After the dishes are done and the pleasant conversations are over, Andy gets his coat out of Anderson's bedroom. He goes up to his 6'2 uncle (Andy's mother is 5'9") and asks, "Uncle Edward are you going back to the Smokies soon?"

He looks down at Andy and says with a big smile, "Are you going with us?'

Andy replies, "I sure would like to."

His uncle replies, "Alright then. We'll wait for school to let out, and we'll go before the end of June."

Andy says, "I hope we see Clingmans Dome again."

"We'll see that and a lot more."

They say goodbye to their favorite relatives and head back to Muncie. They talk about Christmas and Davina's brother's family. It's getting late in the afternoon and it's almost dark, when they pull up to their one car garage.

The coming week is a busy one. Owen applies for the apprenticeship program. Davina casually mentions Andy's upcoming test, so he won't be anxious. By the end of the week, Davina makes a local doctor's appointment for Judy. The week before Christmas, school closes for two weeks during the holidays.

Right before the Christmas break, Davina takes Judy to the doctor while Andy is in school. Owen stays home, so he can meet Andy at school. After the doctor examines Judy, he orders some tests. He tells Davina that if any of the tests come back positive, he wants Judy to see a specialist in Indianapolis. He tells Davina if she is bathing the children together, refrain from that until the diagnosis is complete. The doctor explains that his office will be closed a week during Christmas. He wants Davina to bring Judy back the first week of January, so he can go over the test results.

Owen and Davina make their final preparations for Christmas. They've completed decorating their home for Christmas. They have a snow blanket under the Christmas tree for special gifts from Santa. Because the McGraigs prefer ham over turkey, they made up a Christmas poem, "The night before Christmas and all through the house, the smell of baked ham dances by, as the family reclines on the couch". Judy and Andy are excited about Christmas morning. Davina reminds them that they have to go to bed after their favorite radio programs end.

As the kids get ready for bed, they continually talk about Santa; what time they will be getting up and what they hope Santa will bring them. After Davina tucks them in; reads a bedtime story and prays, Andy is too excited and preoccupied to think about nighttime shadowy creatures.

Davina and Owen are still in bed at 7 am, but Andy and Judy have been awake and talking for several minutes. Andy can tell through his window blinds that daylight is beginning to break, and it's just too much for a five year old and two year old to stay in bed after 7:00 on Christmas morning.

Davina hears the children get up, and she nudges Owen. He's still sleepy, but he faithfully gets up with his wife to share the festivities. They get on their robes, and Andy is patiently waiting by the living room doorway and holding his sister's hand. Davina says, "Andy, thank you for waiting on Daddy to give the Christmas prayer blessing."

Owen prays and thanks God for giving His son to all mankind. He thanks God for Christmas and the true meaning of celebrating His son's birthday. He says, "As we enjoy receiving these gifts, may we remember the greatest gift of all."

As soon as Owen finishes the prayer, Davina says, "Andy, will you start and open that big gift with your name on it?"

Andy runs over to it; slides on his knees, and starts tearing off the wrapping paper. It's the parking garage and filling station! Andy is delighted and says, "Can I watch Judy open her gifts?" Judy's gifts are given to her. They're a Shirley Temple Doll, a dress, some socks and some paper dolls. Besides the parking garage, Andy opens gifts that include Legos, a long sleeve shirt and a pair of pants. Owen and Davina share their gifts. Owen especially likes his portable power saw, and Davina especially likes her beautiful pearl necklace.

Andy goes to bed Christmas evening thinking about the wonderful celebration with his family today. He is not aware of Christmas celebrations at big hotels; at mansions; at country estates; at vacation resorts or at downtown apartments. Andy knows that the joys of Christmas are with his family in their cozy home on West 5th Street.

4

WINTER OF 1949

At the outset of 1949, the McGraigs are expecting some important responses that will have major impacts on their lives: Owen's acceptance or rejection in the toolmaker apprenticeship; Andy's IQ score and Judy's exam results. 1948 had been a happy year, especially the Christmas season. Just after New Year's Day, Davina is thinking about the reports they will be getting before the end of January. She is hoping for good news; especially when she returns to Judy's doctor's office this week.

She has set Judy's appointment for Friday. Owen stays home again, so he can pick up Andy. Davina hopes that she and Judy will be back home by 1:00. At 11:00, the nurse ushers Davina and Judy into the doctor's exam room. Within a few minutes, Dr. Hill comes into the room with a file of papers and x-rays. To Davina, he seems to be too cordial and patient.

Dr. Hill says, "How are both of you doing? Is the office warm enough for you on this cold day of January?"

Davina replies, "We're doing well. Yes, I think we're both warm enough."

The doctor sets down his stack of papers and x-rays. He puts one of the x-rays of Judy's legs on the x-ray screen. He says, "As you know, I examined Judy last month, and we took a blood sample and several x-rays. My findings are not conclusive, so I am going to refer you to a specialist in Indianapolis."

Somewhat impatiently, Davina asks, "What did you find, doctor?"

Dr. Hill clears his throat; hesitates a second then quietly says, "I believe Judy has polio."

Davina gasps and puts her hand on her chest as her heart sinks. For a few seconds she sits in a trance-like state.

Dr. Hill says, "Mrs. McGraig are you alright?"

Davina finally says, "I think I am, but I don't know what to say about Judy."

Dr. Hill is serious, but faintly smiles and says, "Mrs. McGraig, I think the polio that Judy has is comparatively mild."

Davina says somewhat bluntly, "What does that mean?"

He replies, "One of the worst case scenarios is when the polio virus attacks the lungs, and the patient needs the assistance of an iron lung. Judy appears to have a more mild case, where the polio has attacked the muscles in her right leg. It appears that there is not extensive muscle damage. I want you to see the specialist as soon as possible to make sure."

Davina says, "Do you know, if the specialist can see Judy by the end of the month?"

Dr. Hill says, "I'll be right back." He goes to his nurse, so the call will be made immediately. He goes back into the exam room and says, "We should know in a few minutes. This month there is not much to do to help Judy. The polio virus is contagious. Make sure the children bathe separately and check the lavatory, tub and commode daily for cleanliness. Use Comet or another cleaner with bleach in it. If the specialist measures for a leg brace, I can fit the brace on Judy in this office. There is one more thing. I want you to bring her brother in for a blood test. Adults usually do not get the virus, because their bodies are fully developed."

Davina asks, "When can I bring Andy for the blood test?"

Dr. Hill says, "See Miss Johnson, our office lady, before you leave, and schedule Andy about a week before you leave for Indianapolis."

As Davina leaves with Judy, Dr. Hill's office manager says the specialist, Dr. Ziegler, can see you and Judy on January 18th. Is that okay with you at 11:00?"

Davina replies, "That is fine. What date can you see my son? He gets out of school at 12:00."

She says, "Can you bring Andy in at 1:00 on January 8th?"

Davina says, "Yes. Thank you." At the moment she is only thinking about Judy. She hasn't thought about how she will share the shocking news. After they walk out of the doctor's office and get in their sedan, Davina looks at Judy and says, "Do you want me to pick up some Nestle Quick and extra milk, so we can enjoy hot chocolate at home?"

Judy with her auburn curls and white winter coat looks like a little angel, when she says, "Yes. That's good."

Davina stops at the grocery store, and they make it home before Owen and Andy return from school. With the Nestle Quick and milk, Davina makes hot chocolate for everyone to warm the spirit after a disappointing diagnosis.

Owen and Andy come in, and as they take their coats off, Owen asks, "What's the occasion? Did you get good news?"

Davina in calm composure says, "The hot chocolate is ready. Let's sit down first and enjoy it, before it cools down." She gets the marshmallows from the cabinet, and puts them in the four cups of hot chocolate, as they sit down at the kitchen table.

After they talk about Andy's day at school and drink the hot chocolate, silence prevails for a minute over the family table. Owen becomes serious and asks Davina, "What did the doctor say about Judy?"

Davina for a few seconds looks past Owen and stares at the kitchen wall. She quietly says, "She has polio."

Owen echoes the insidious word, "polio?"

Davina looks at him and says, "The doctor still wants her to see a specialist in Indianapolis. Dr. Hill says it's a more mild case. He said that it is not in her lungs. He also said that the polio has not done extensive damage to her right leg muscles."

Owen replies, "So what are we to do?"

Davina says, "We go to the specialist, Dr. Ziegler, in Indianapolis to get a confirmation of Dr. Hill's findings and prognosis."

Owen takes a deep breath and a moment of silence. He looks at Judy, then at Andy. He smiles at them and says, "Do you want to see, if we can talk mommy into another round of hot chocolate?" The children are elated and a heavy atmosphere, that seemed to hover over the kitchen table, has dissipated. Davina gets up and says, "I can't let you down. It will be ready in a few minutes."

After the hot chocolate and some light-hearted family conversation, Owen begins to get ready for the second shift at the auto plant.

On July 8th Davina takes Andy to Dr. Hill's office for the blood test. In a few days they find out the test is negative. The results are a great relief for the McGraigs, and Andy begins to think about the IQ test. Even though there are no psychologists around Andy, a professional observer would probably notice Andy psyching himself up for the test. On January 14th he takes the test at school without any noticeable signs of anxiety. After the test, Miss Alexander tells Andy that they should have the results by January 29th.

January 18th arrives before they know it. The whole family piles into the 1940 sedan at 9:30 in the morning to make the hour drive to Indianapolis. Muncie and Indianapolis got about five inches of snow a few days ago. Now it has turned to slush that the other vehicles on the road involuntarily splash on their sedan. Semis they pass seem to bury them with flying slush.

They arrive at the doctor's office on N. Meridian St. a few minutes after 10:30. They have ample time to answer the receptionist's questions and to fill out a small volume of paperwork. They are surprised to learn that Dr. Ziegler, an aging man in his late sixties, is patient and good-natured. He meets with the family for about thirty minutes. He has already studied Judy's file. He examines her and measures her for a right leg brace. Dr. Ziegler says, "The brace is taken off at bedtime, and she will want to have breakfast and dress before the brace is put on. The brace will take pressure off the muscles, and it should diminish the effects of polio. Just keep an eye on her. She may not have further problems, and by the time she is grown, she may not need the brace. Dr. Hill will fit the brace on her in about two weeks. It will be shipped to him."

After Dr. Ziegler answers the few questions they have. They shake his hand; thank him and bundle up before they step outside. Owen and Davina enjoy looking at the Indianapolis downtown skyline, and going to the Indiana State Fair in Indianapolis every August. As they get in their sedan, Davina says, "Can we take the time to go farther south on Meridian, so we can look at the downtown skyline? If we have the time, let's take Meridian to Monument Circle to drive around the Soldiers' and Sailors' Monument."

Owen replies, "Sure, honey, we're not in a hurry. After we leave

Monument Circle, we'll stop at White Castle before we get back on highway 67."

The kids also enjoy the drive to downtown Indianapolis. The highlight of their day is seeing the 284 foot Soldiers' and Sailors' Monument. A close second is stopping at White Castle.

As they leave Monument Circle they pass some huge office buildings. When they go by one of the largest buildings, Andy says, "Look, there are different kinds of traps around that building. Do you see them? Some look like quick sand and tar pits?"

Davina and Owen look at the building Andy is pointing to, but they don't see anything unusual. Davina asks Owen, "What building it that?"

Owen replies, "It's one of the biggest businesses in the country. It's the BS&S building. It's owned by the Broadcasting Systems and Sales Corporation."

On the way home, Andy nor his parents say another word about the company and what Andy saw. They keep in mind these things, including what Andy saw around the churches and on the wall from his bed.

January passes by quickly. The week after their Indianapolis trip, Owen gets wonderful news that he has been accepted into the toolmaker journeyman program. After the excitement wears down in a few days, Owen and Davina get anxious while waiting for Andy's IQ score. January 29th rolls around and when Owen picks up Andy at school, he meets with Miss Alexander and Miss Pittenger in the principal's office. A teacher's assistant watches Andy, while his dad is in the brief meeting.

Miss Alexander looks at Owen and says, "Andy's test results are remarkable. His IQ is 159. He is not only a genius, but he is on the borderline of the few, exceptional geniuses."

Owen is somewhat stunned by the news and at first, doesn't know what to say. Miss Pittenger says, "Miss Alexander told me, Mr. McGraig, that you and his mother don't want to put him in a higher grade. We recommend he finish the year in his kindergarten class, but if you did decide on advance placement, Andy is qualified academically to be in the third or fourth grade, when the new, academic year begins."

Owen is still astonished, but finally says, "It is just so impressive. It's difficult to make a comment. Are there things educators recommend to help advance him at home?"

Miss Pittinger says, "Good question. Sometime gifted children have more understanding than many adults realize. The most important thing is to be supportive of the child. I'm sure that you and Mrs. McGraig will encourage him, and do what you can to help him."

Owen emphatically replies, "Absolutely! This is such great news!"

Miss Alexander says, "Congratulations, Mr. McGraig. Andy will be able to do virtually anything he wants to do. Whatever he sets his mind to do, he will accomplish it exceedingly well."

Owen gets up with a big smile on his face, and with warm gratitude he thanks Andy's teacher and the principal.

When Owen walks out of the office, he sees Andy reading to the teacher's assistant. He greets the teacher, and says, "Andy, are you ready to go home?"

Andy replies, "Yes, and I want to find out how I did on the test."

His dad says, "How about I share the good news at home with you and mommy?"

Andy says, "Sounds good."

Even though it is another cold, winter day walk, the sun is out, and the sunshine and the test results lift their spirits. They're talkative when they come into the knotty pine enclosed porch. Davina greets them near the front door and says, "By the levity, it sounds like you're happy with the test results."

Owen looks at Andy and puts his hand on his shoulder and says, "Mrs. McGraig, you have a very intelligent son."

Davina laughs and says, "I already know that!"

They go in the kitchen and sit around the table. As they sit down, Owen says, "It feels like I need to throw some more coal in the furnace. I'll go downstairs, when we get done. What is Judy doing?"

"She's in her room playing with her dolls."

Davina is anxious to hear the results and she fervently says, "Come on; let's hear it!"

Owen says, "I was stunned when Miss Alexander said Andy's IQ is 159."

Davina exclaims, "159! Isn't the average score about 90 to 110?"

Owen replies, "I think so. Miss Alexander or Miss Pittenger said that 159 is borderline, exceptional genius and 130 is the genius threshold."

Davina says, "It is just so hard to imagine." She looks at Andy and says, "Andy, God has greatly blessed you. We're very proud of you."

Andy says, "I feel blessed. I'm grateful to know God and to be in this family."

Owen comes down on the table with his hands, as he gets up and says, "Get Judy and we'll have a round of hot chocolate with marshmallows before I leave for work!" He goes in the basement and gets more coal from the bin. He stokes the furnace, while Davina warms up the milk for the hot chocolate.

The rest of the 1949 winter is fairly mild for central Indiana. The lowest temperature is 9 degrees, and the biggest remaining snowfall is only six inches. Judy is getting use to her new leg brace before Andy finishes kindergarten.

Davina's brother, Edward, calls Davina to make plans to take Andy to the Great Smoky Mountain National Park in June. It has become the most popular national park in America. They leave on an early summer day and spend four days in the Smokies, Gatlinburg and Sevier County. They hike, swim and do a lot of sight- seeing. Andy especially likes Clingmans Dome, Cades Cove (the old Indian trail), the settlers' cabins and Abram Falls.

During the summer at home, Andy enjoys outings with his family to the fire station and to the train station. There isn't a nice park or nice playground nearby, but Andy loves to go to the fire station. He likes looking at the shiny red fire truck and the firemen's big hats and protective gear that line the wall in the station. They have an ice chest where they stock ice cream sandwiches, ice cream bars, popsicles, sundae cups and push up orange rockets. Mostly kids and their friends and families come in for the ice cream treats that sell for a nickel an item.

The fire station is only three blocks from their house, and the train station is only another three blocks toward downtown. When the steam engines are rolling in, they stand by the station to watch. Most of the trains don't stop at the station, but when a passenger train stops, Andy and his family watch the passengers arriving and leaving. They also watch the porters loading and unloading cargo at the station dock.

When the trains aren't coming in and Andy and his dad have extra time, they walk another eight blocks to Muncie's downtown library, The Carnegie Library. By the time Andy is in third grade, he is checking out classics like John Steinbeck's "Grapes of Wrath" and Nathaniel Hawthorne's "House of the Seven Gables".

Andy and his dad pass a record shop, when they walk to the library. As Andy gets a little older, he asks his dad, if they can go into the record shop. From the radio he knows some of the singers and songs. Before the end of his first grade year in 1950, they get a Sylvania television. The black and white programs have some singers on shows like Milton Berle's Texaco Star Theatre. The first two 45 rpm records that Owen buys for Andy are "Tennessee Waltz" by Patti Page and Mockin' Bird Hill by Les Paul and Mary Ford. Judy and Andy first started playing children's records on a portable turn table that they both received for Christmas in 1949. By 1951 Davina's favorite TV show is "Queen for a Day" and Owen likes "The George Burns and Gracie" show. The entire family enjoys the "People Are Funny" show with Art Linkletter.

In the spring of 1951, Andy is finishing 2nd grade. When he begins 3rd grade, right after Labor Day, Judy begins kindergarten. Since she has kindergarten in the morning, Andy walks her to class, and Owen picks her up at noon.

Since Judy started wearing a leg brace, Andy has been spending more time with her. When she starts kindergarten, Andy also becomes more protective of her. There are a number of children who walk the same route to school that Andy and Judy take. Andy had never noticed a 5th grade boy until he started taunting Judy and Andy. He walks on the other side of the street, but he starts regularly yelling at them and demeaning Judy and her brace.

Even though Andy is a third grader, he is already bigger than most of the fifth grade boys. (He's probably stronger too, but Andy doesn't realize that.) Andy says very little to the boy, but with time he resents it more. His main concern is seeing that Judy stays safe.

One Saturday, about two months before school lets out for the summer, Davina sends Andy to the corner general store to get bread. When Andy turns the corner to go into the store, there is Judy's tormentor. Without thinking, Andy jumps on him and knocks him to the ground. He starts pummeling the boy, when two of Andy's friends who are inside the store, see what is going on. They run out and pull Andy off of the bloodied fifth grader.

Nothing is ever said about the incident. In weeks to come, Judy wonders why she doesn't see the annoying boy again. By 4th grade Andy is regularly following national and world news. He also starts reading U.S. News & World Report every week, from cover to cover.

Jonas Salk improves his polio vaccine in 1955, and by the fall of 1955 both Judy and Andy receive the polio vaccination. Judy's condition remains stable, and her doctor said she may not need the brace, when she starts high school.

The summer that Andy turns eleven, he helps his dad with his part-time work. Two sweet, elderly sisters have a big home that has three big cherry trees in their large back yard. Andy helps his dad paint their house, and in mid- June they pick cherries for the sisters. The sisters are partial to Andy. Almost every time he is there, they give him their homemade cookies or candy, including salt water taffy. The sisters also give Owen and Andy some of the cherries they picked. Davina has a special knack with homemade cherry pie.

Andy saves most of the money he earns. He has a fondness for popular music, so he spends a few dollars in 1954 and 1955 on several hits. Four of his favorites are "Sh-Boom" by the Crew Cuts;" Shake, Rattle and Roll" and "Rock Around the Clock" by Bill Haley and His Comets and "Maybelline" by Chuck Berry. Disc Jockeys start calling it Rock and Roll by 1955. Andy notices that some of his friends and acquaintances criticize the music, especially adults.

Before he starts 6th grade, he starts playing a lot of basketball. He is big for his age, and he seems to be a natural. In 6th grade, Muncie has an inter-city school league, and Andy plays starting center for his school. When their season ends, the best two players in the city are Andy and Don Bonan. Andy has no problem playing against Don, but Don is a terrific shooter.

After Andy's basketball season ends, he and his family are at Uncle Edward's house one Sunday. His Aunt Ella and his mother are talking about something in the kitchen after they do the Sunday dishes. Ella says, "Davina, have you noticed how remarkable Andy's appearance is?"

Davina replies, "Yes, he is a good-looking boy."

Ella says, "He is going to be a heartbreaker. He is already as big as eighth grade boys. His good looks are uncommon. It's not just his thick, dark blonde hair and general good looks. His striking blue eyes have an aura mixed with perception and courage."

Davina replies, "Wow! I never thought about all of that!"

Ella laughs and says, "I should have been an artist!"

5

The Mahican Years

For five years after Owen became a journeyman toolmaker, he saved enough to buy a bigger house. In May of 1955, he receives an offer to fill a retiree's toolmaker position at a big auto plant in Mahican, Indiana, near Lafayette and close to the Wabash River. The McGraigs move from a house that is barely 800 sf to one that is over 1400 sf. Judy now has her own bedroom. They have a bigger and more modern kitchen, two bathrooms and a two car garage with a concrete floor. They even have a natural gas furnace instead of coal.

With the move to Mahican, Owen's annual income increases from \$5,100 to \$5,950. Fortunately for Andy, they moved just one month after he finishes sixth grade. In September he will begin 7th grade at Harrison Jr. High in Mahican. He finds out through his former sixth grade coach that Harrison has a competitive basketball program.

When school begins, one of Andy's favorite classes is history. He finds out from his own reading that a new magazine, the National Review, started by William F. Buckley Jr. has favorable, critical reviews. He wishes that he could take a civics or government class. He decides he'll ask the school librarian and the city librarian, if they carry the National Review.

Andy has learned that it is better not to share the visions that he sees. As he gets older, he doesn't see the shadowy figures on the wall at night. He still sees walls around a lot of churches and government buildings, and a lot of snares around many corporate buildings.

Andy spends his free time playing basketball and reading magazines and newspapers from the library about current national and world events. He is looking forward to trying out for the 7th grade team. Since his 6th grade season went well, he is curious what he can do this season.

Andy is surprised that try outs for the team start just two weeks after the beginning of school. When he shows up for the first day of try outs, he finds out that he is a head taller than most of the boys. Andy is 5'8" and most of the boys are around 5'2". During practice he doesn't have much competition. A boy named Tim, who is 5'1", is a good guard and shooter. Most of the boys trying out know the game fairly well, but he doesn't see a lot of talent.

After three try out sessions, the basketball coach tells Andy that he is the starting center. They play 7th grade teams, mostly between Mahican and Kokomo. After 12 games, their record is 10-2. Andy and Tim carry the team and do most of the scoring. Andy averages 23 points a game and Tim averages 18. Andy averages 19 rebounds per game. Through the school year, they become friends with three boys from the team, who improve their game considerably.

By the time he finishes 7th grade, his frugal parents realize that they have worn out their 1940 sedan. At his dad's plant, they can go on a waiting list for a one year old dealer's car. Andy doesn't know that his dad put his name on the list right after they moved.

Owen is now on the first shift, and he gets home about 3:30. He pulls up in front of the house. He gets out of the car, in the eighty degree, sunny day and finds Judy, Andy and Davina in the house. He is all smiles and doesn't say a word. For a few seconds they just look at him, then Davina smiles and says, "What's on your mind?"

Owen replies, "A 1955, two tone, blue and white, Chevy Bel Air!"

They all jump out of their chairs and rush outside. They stop in the yard for a second and just admire the gleaming, like-new Chevy that is now theirs.

Davina looks at Owen and exclaims, "Oh, honey, it's just beautiful!"

Owen says, "Hop in, and we'll go for a ride."

As they get in, Owen says, "It has all the options except a V8 engine and has only 9,200 miles."

They drive to the local Dog N Suds and get a root beer. Even the car hop says to Owen, "What a beautiful car!"

Andy never forgot experiences like their outing to Dog N Suds, and all the simple things they enjoyed, like watching people board the old passenger trains.

In the summer of 1956, Andy continued to help his dad at home and with part-time jobs. They also volunteered to help paint the inside of the fellowship hall at their church. In his free time, he played basketball with Tim and their three friends from the team: Bruce, Gary and Doug. They all got better as a team. All five had grown. Bruce and Gary were now a good size for forwards, and Tim was three inches taller, when they started 8th grade. Doug played as a guard and was a couple inches taller than Tim. When Andy was measured at their first eighth grade try out session, he was 6 feet.

Their coach, Mr. Zimmerman, was impressed with how much Andy and his four friends had improved. He named all five to the starting five. They had a perfect season and won the 8th grade championship. Andy had a game high record of 35 points and 24 rebounds. Tim had a game high record of 12 assists and 24 points.

During the eighth grade year, Andy continued to read U.S. News & World Report cover to cover, and checked out the National Review from the library. He also watched regularly the Huntley-Brinkley Report. His appetite for current events and the national political system seemed to be insatiable.

His closest friends are from his church and the basketball team. He likes the attention that girls are starting to give him. They are mostly eighth graders and some are ninth graders. Andy still checks on his sister a lot. In September she will be in sixth grade. He is very thankful that her leg is getting better.

Before the eighth grade year ends, his science teacher, Mr. Townsend, approaches him about a science project next year. He says, "Andy you're a bright student, and you're doing well in science. Next school year you can enter a science project in the regional science fair at Purdue."

Andy replies, "I will consider it, Mr. Townsend. I wish they had the same kind of fair for government and political affairs."

Mr. Townsend says, "Yes, I've heard of your interest in that. Well, think about a science project, and let me know if you're interested in the regional fair."

Andy says, "Okay. Thank you, Mr. Townsend."

Even though Andy briefly thinks about the suggestion, he stays focused on current events and basketball. 1956 was a soul searching year for Andy. It was heartrending, when he read about Russia's takeover of Hungary. He just didn't understand why his country would let Russia invade them; imprison many and execute their leaders. After the shock of how Russia took over Hungary, Andy started reading about how Russia took control of Poland, East Germany, Czechoslovakia, Albania and Bulgaria.

In the summer of 1957, Andy continues to work for his dad and play basketball with his friends. By the time his freshman year begins at Harrison Jr. High, Andy is 6'3" and a muscular 220 lbs. Andy's massive shoulders are built like a Mac Truck. Andy has big hands and a muscular frame, but he is agile on the basketball floor. He begins lifting weights and before basketball season is over, he is bench pressing 350 lbs. He hears that his old competitor, Don Bonan, in Muncie is playing well for a junior high team there.

Andy and his friends are the starting five again, and they have a perfect season. They don't play any Muncie teams in 9th grade, but only Jr. High teams in the Mahican, Lafayette and Kokomo areas. They win the championship for their region. Andy is awarded the MVP for their playoffs.

Even though Andy is very bright and a conscientious student, he misses earning a 4.0 GPA, but he is third in his class of 204 students. The evening before their graduation, Andy and his basketball friends go to their favorite restaurant equipped with a soda fountain and juke box. Of course, their special female friends are there to join in the celebration. Their hamburger, fries and chocolate shake orders cost them 50 cents each.

The next day after graduation, Owen has to work overtime, and Davina asks Andy to help her with a trip to the hardware store. Davina says, "Andy can you help me with the 80 lb. bags of compost and mortar that I need to pick up for your dad?"

"Sure I can. I have my learner's permit now, can I drive?"

Judy gets in the back seat, and Andy and Davina get in the front of their esteemed 1955 Chevy.

The Mahican Hardware Co. is on the edge of town and a couple miles from them. Right before the hardware store is the farm co-op, and on the other side of the store are cornfields.

Andy backs into the area where the bags of compost, fertilizer and mortar are stacked up. After Davina pays for two bags of compost and a bag of mortar, Andy loads them with little effort. The three of them are still outside the car, when they see their neighbor, Sue, who lives a block down from them.

When Sue gets out of her car, Davina says, "Hi, Sue, how are you and your husband?"

Sue seems a little nervous and replies, "Charlie hasn't been well. He has been overworked as a construction foreman, and he's hurt his back."

Davina says, "I'm sorry to hear that. Come by and let me know how he is doing."

Sue says, "I will. It's good to see you, and it looks like your son is even bigger than the last time I saw him."

Davina laughs and says, "He has always eaten a lot of Cheerios."

After they get in their car and pull out on the road, Andy says, "Mom, what she said about her husband isn't true."

Davina looks at Andy and says, "Have you heard otherwise?"

Andy says, "No, I can just tell that it wasn't true about his back or about being a foreman."

Davina doesn't say any more about their neighbor to Andy.

After her kids go to bed that evening, she mentions the incident to Owen. Owen says, "We can't worry about why Andy said that. We both know that Andy is honest. With the things Andy has experienced in his life, it's possible that he has some kind of special gift."

Davina replies, "I've wondered about that. I never said anything, but I wonder if it has to do with discernment."

Owen says, "It could be. I think we should just pray that God leads him. It could very well be a spiritual gift."

Davina finds out by the end of summer, that Sue's husband is an alcoholic, Davina is also told that he is trying to get disability."

Andy has a busy summer. He works for his dad part-time; helps his mom and dad with the yard work; goes to a church youth retreat, spends time with Judy and swims, plays basketball and lifts weights with his Jr. High team and friends.

High School begins for Andy immediately after Labor Day. Mahican Central High School is one of the largest high schools north of Indianapolis. Mahican has three large Jr. High Schools and only one Sr. High School. Andy's entering sophomore class has 578 students.

Andy is glad to find out that he can take civics in his junior year. Right now he is satisfied taking history, and he hopes that his teacher likes current events. He also makes inquiries about a high school debate team. Basketball try outs start soon, and Andy is anxious to try out for the team.

Andy works hard and breezes through the cuts. He makes varsity. His four friends from Junior High, Tim, Doug, Gary and Bruce, make the junior varsity team. The residents of Mahican love their high school basketball teams. The junior varsity plays right before the varsity team plays.

After the cuts are finished, Coach Tallman meets one on one with each varsity player. Before the end of September, the coach meets with Andy.

Coach Tallman says, "Andy, your coach from Jr. High told me about your ability. It looks like you've added some more height and weight. At 6'4" and 227lbs you're one of the biggest players on our team. The Mahican Cougars are proud to have you."

Andy says, "It's an honor and pleasure to be part of the team, coach."

Coach Tallman says, "Andy, our starting center, Mike, has done a good job for us, and our big forward, Rick, has done a good job also. They are both seniors now, and our record last year was 22 wins and 8 losses. I believe we can improve that record this year. We won the sectional, and I believe we can win the regional this year. The Kokomo Wildcats have a good team again, and they will be our main competitor in the regional."

Andy says, "I hope I will be a good addition to the team."

Coach Tallman says, "I know you will be, and I want to talk with you about that. You are probably the strongest player on the team, and one of the tallest. Mike is 6'6" and Rick is 6'4". You weigh as much as they do, and you have a lot of strength. Do you know what you can bench press?"

Andy replies, "About 400 lbs."

Coach Tallman says, "That's excellent. I want you to continue to run and build up your endurance. When we start the season, I will give you a lot of minutes, but I want you to sub for Mike and Rick. They will be stronger in the game, if they get adequate breaks. My guess is that you will be playing about as many minutes as they do. When our opponents have a strong center, you may get more play time than Mike. When our opponents have a strong power forward, you may get more play time than Rick. When they're evenly matched or have the upper hand, you will still get plenty of play time. I want to start you by next year, and the play time will give you the experience you need."

Andy says, "It sounds good to me. I'm looking forward to every game."

The coach says, "Me too, Andy. Take care of yourself. Get plenty of rest; eat nutritious food and do well with your studies. Be on time for our practices. Any question?"

Andy says with compassion, "No, sir! It's great being with the team."

"Okay, Andy. Have a good weekend, and I will see you at 3:30 Monday for practice."

"Thank you, coach." Andy is elated as he walks out of the coach's office. He thinks to himself, "Wow, a varsity player for the Mahican Cougars!"

Andy likes his new high school classes. He finds out that debate club practice begins by February, and they have meets between March and May. The basketball season begins quickly for Andy. He plays hard and by Christmas break, they have a record of 20 wins and 3 losses. So far, they have only lost to Kokomo, Muncie Central and the Wyandot Eagles.

Judy is excited about Christmas, and she likes going to Harrison Jr. High. Andy enjoys the real reason for the season, but he is unsure about asking for anything.

On Christmas morning, Judy receives a large gift bag promoted by "Teen Magazine" for a year's subscription and a large variety of cosmetics and hair products. Because Andy has a great interest in current events and debate, his parents give him a new, 1959 Olympia Deluxe Burgundy typewriter and an extra ribbon. He thinks to himself, "Good, I don't have to use the antiquated Woodstock anymore."

Before Andy prepares for joining the debate team, he focuses on the remainder of the season and the playoffs. Their biggest win of the season is over Lafayette Jefferson, 80 to 79. Andy scores 25 points and has 16 rebounds. Their season record is 25 wins and 5 losses. They win the sectional, but lose the regional to the Kokomo Wildcats. Andy's average for the season is 22 points and 14 rebounds.

Debate Club meets after the semester break. One of the main debate topics that will be used through May is North Viet Nam's invasion of Laos. Andy starts making all the notes he can find from U.S. News & World Report and from the National Review.

In Andy's first semester he starts developing a friendship with Linda Ulrey, who is in his English class. She is an intelligent student with a captivating personality. She's a stunning girl with coal black hair, brown eyes, a radiant olive complexion and an unmistakable figure, that should be classified information. Before the second semester convenes, Linda starts calling Andy regularly at home.

Soon after the second semester begins, he gets a call from Linda at home. He is studying at his desk in his bedroom, when Judy comes in and says, "Andeeeee, Lindahhh is calling." Andy gets up, pats Judy on the cheek and says, "Thank you, Sis, hold my other calls."

Andy picks up the receiver and casually says, "Hi, Linda."

Linda says in kind of an alluring voice, "Say, Andy, you and your basketball friends are at Good Times, when my friends and I come in. Why don't the two of us go there?"

Andy clears his throat; fidgets a little and says, "Why shouldn't we? I think it's a good idea."

After Andy gets silent a couple seconds, Linda says, "How about sometime Friday or Saturday?"

Andy's mom is sitting in the living room reading a "Better Homes and Garden", when Andy says, "Just a second, Linda." He holds his hand over the mouth piece and says, "Mom, is it alright if Linda and I go to Good Times from about 6 to 8 pm this Friday?"

Davina replies, "Sure you can."

Andy says, "Linda, can we meet there at six Friday? I still have my learner's permit and maybe mom or dad can pick us up about 8:00 and take you home."

Linda says, "That's perfect. I'll look forward to seeing you there!"

Andy says, "Me too. Have a good night, Linda."

Andy hangs up the phone and takes a deep breath.

Davina says, "Andy, you look like you're sweating a little."

Andy laughs and say, "Yea, I guess I'm not use to those things."

Encouraging Andy, Davina says, "You'll get use to dating. It takes time. There is no rush."

Andy says, "Thanks, mom."

As Andy is busy with classes, debate club and getting to know Linda, he continues to support Judy as she attempts to conquer polio. She is becoming a good pianist, and as she gets ready to go to her piano recital at the local YWCA, Andy says, "Judy, you look beautiful in your red and black checkered skirt and white blouse."

Judy blushes and says, "Aw, Andy, you're just saying that because I'm your only sister." Andy bends down and kisses her on the cheek, then looks at her and says, "No, sis, I'm saying it, because it's true."

Judy hugs him, and the McGraigs get in their 1955 Bel Air and head to Judy's recital.

As Andy gets into the debate club season, he tries his hand at extemporaneous and impromptu speaking. One of their meets is at Notre Dame, where he is given the topic, "If you had been President during the 1956 Russian occupation of Hungary, how would you have allowed or not allowed the Russian takeover of Hungary?"

Andy cherishes the opportunity to speak on the topic. He has thirty minutes to study any notes he has and to prepare an outline and notes for his speech. After the debate rounds and the impromptu and extemporaneous speeches, the Mahican Central Debate Team defeats three other high schools in the Notre Dame tournament.

Andy's top honors at the debate tournament make him feel as good as his best game during the 1958-59 basketball season. The second semester seems to fly by, as he and his friends gear up for a summer of fun and working out. Besides playing basketball with his friends during the summer, Andy works out in the weight room four days a week. His only break from the weights is a four day church youth retreat near Brown County State Park, close to Bloomington.

On Labor Day, after Andy and his family grill out in their back yard, Owen says, "Let's go inside for some watermelon." They walk into the kitchen and Davina says to the three of them, "Have a seat in the living room, and I'll bring the watermelon to you." When they go in the living room, Judy says, "What's in these three boxes on the floor?"

Owen kiddingly says, "What three boxes?"

Judy says, "Dad, I guess I'm seeing things!"

As Owen is laughing, Davina brings them the watermelon

Davina says, "Let's eat this good looking watermelon, and then you can open the boxes."

Judy gobbles it down, and Andy says, "Judy, do you like the watermelon that well?"

Judy replies, "Come on, Andy. You're curious too about the boxes."

Andy continues, "I'm not curious, if mom and dad got us pet snakes."

Everyone is laughing and Owen says, "Okay, Andy here is my pocket knife. Cut them open, and let Judy see if the first box has a pet snake."

Andy cuts the first box open and says, "Okay, Judy close your eyes and stick your hand in there."

Judy pulls out one book; looks at her mom and dad and says, "Is this a whole set of World Book Encyclopedias?"

Davina says, "Yes, they're for you and Andy, and the 1958 Year Book is also in there. We ordered Year Books to go through 1965."

Andy and Judy thank their mom and dad. Andy shakes his dad's hand and leans down and kisses his mom on her cheek.

When Andy's junior year begins, he is bench pressing 500 lbs. At the first basketball tryout, he weighs in at a lean and muscular 235 lbs. and at a bare-footed height of 6'5". After tryouts are over, his team members start calling him Avalanche Andy. He dominates the floor with his strength, size and skill. His friend, Tim, from his old junior high team makes varsity. The former starting guard graduated in 1959, and Tim takes his place as starting guard.

After their last practice before the season begins, Andy says, "Tim, we're going to have a real good team this year. All five starters are juniors. Even though we lost Mike and Rick to graduation, we have a 6'7" center and a 6'4" forward."

Tim says, "Yes, the season looks promising. I just hope our new center and small forward develop the skills that Mike and Rick had."

Andy says confidently, "I think they'll catch on real fast. We've seen them play, and I think they have at least their potential. We also have a new talented guard, who is going to be a contender for everyone."

Tim laughs and says, "I hope so. You and I know about Don Bonan and Jack Damber at Muncie Central. I heard that Jack is now a 6"3" guard."

Andy taps Tim on the shoulder and says, "I bet we've got them worried!"

One morning Tim is talking with Andy in the school hall before their first class begins. Three of the football team starters walk up to Andy and the 6' 250 lb. tackle says, "Hey, McGraig, how come you haven't come out for football?"

Andy replies, "Basketball season starts soon, and I have a lot of activities." The stocky tackle says sarcastically, "Really? Well, I say you're chicken, and I'll prove it." He throws a punch at Andy, and Andy catches his fist with his big hand. The tackle tries to move his hand, but he can't. Finally, he says, "Okay, man, let go."

He walks away with his two friends, and one of them looks at the tackle and says, "Dude, are you stupid? Andy can bench press 500 lbs."

Tim looks at Andy and says, "I wonder what got in to him?"

Andy says, "I think adults would say a combination of poor upbringing and teenage hormones."

As basketball season gets under way, the whole community starts yelling, "Avalanche Andy, Avalanche Andy," when Andy gets the ball. When the crowd starts the chant at home games, they play, "Great Balls of Fire", over the sound system. Most games at home, Andy starts scoring over 25 points and making over 16 rebounds.

Most Friday evenings, Andy spends with Linda at Good Times. On the Juke Box they always pick, "Twilight Time" by the Platters and "Lonely Teardrops" by Jackie Wilson. Sometimes on a Saturday evening, they double date with Tim and his girlfriend. Their favorite date is the drive-in movies with Nehi pop and buttered popcorn. Their favorite movies, they've seen together are "The Fly", "The Blob" and "Ben Hur". Tim and Andy take turns driving. Andy borrows the family's '55 Chevy, and Tim drives his dad's older car, a 1950 Mercury.

Andy is looking forward to the Christmas break. It will give him a chance to relax before the end of the basketball season and the sectionals.

On a slow Saturday afternoon, Judy asks her dad to take her to a friend's house to listen to records. Davina is at the kitchen table counting her green stamps, and looking at their catalogue.

Andy comes in the kitchen and sits down by her. Davina asks, "Are you bored?"

Andy replies, "Not really; I've been reading. I wanted to share something I've been thinking about."

As Davina puts down the catalogue, the sunlight through the kitchen window settles on her lush, strawberry blond hair and kind face. Andy notices a purity and honesty that radiates from his mother. Davina smiles at Andy and says, "What have you been thinking about?"

Andy says, "Well, you know that my English teacher is really into the classics, and he has us reading a good bit and taking quizzes."

Davina asks, "Is he requiring too much?"

Andy replies, "No, that's not the problem. Almost every day, he is telling us a war story; supposedly from his World War II experiences." Andy gets Davina's undivided attention. Andy continues, "I don't think I can explain how I know, but most of his personal war stories are not true."

Davina with a look of conviction says, "Andy, please remember that you never need to explain to anyone how you perceive something. In the future, don't let anyone drill you about it. Just remember how Delilah wore down Samson. Some things are just between us and the Almighty."

Andy nods his head and says, "I understand. I guess I'm disappointed in my teacher's dishonesty."

Davina says, "I believe that people have different reasons for making up stories and for exaggerating. One common reason is low self-esteem. They want people to be impressed with them."

Andy says, "I've been noticing things more and more, but sometimes I just have to clear my mind and focus on what I need to do."

Davina says, "In your shoes, I would do the same thing."

Andy asks his mom, "Why do you think I know things like that?"

Davina says, "I think you have a special gift."

During Christmas break, Andy was introspective except for the time he spent with Linda. Judy's bad leg improved, as she prepared to complete her first semester in eighth grade.

As school resumed after the break, Andy continued weekly to read the U.S. News & World Report and the National Review. When he wasn't loaded down with school work, he would read the magazines daily. He would be absorbed with the evening news, whether he listened to it on television or radio. He never tired of listening to national and world events.

Even though he hates to see the ending of basketball season, he looks forward to the playoffs and to debate club for the rest of the school year. By the end of basketball season, Andy averages 25 points a games and 17 rebounds. Sports writers throughout Indiana have begun to write about Andy's basketball skills and strength. The Mahican Cougars win their sectional and beat Lafayette in the regional. Andy wins the MVP for the sectional and the regional.

The day after the regional tournament, Owen comes back home with the Lafayette newspaper. After supper he gets out the paper before his family gets up from the table. He announces, "I want to read a statement that is in the Lafayette paper about our hometown hero." Davina, Andy and Judy are all smiles as Owen reads, "Last evening it was a no contest as Andy McGraig and his Cougars pounced on our beloved team, who gave a valiant effort. What do you do with a player who drives to the basket and parts players, like Moses parted the Red Sea? McGraig deservingly won the regional MVP." The family applauds for Andy at their kitchen table. Andy says, "Any MVP that I might award would go to my family."

Unfortunately, Mahican loses in the semi-finals to the number two team in the state, the Indianapolis Attucks. Muncie Central is ranked number one and has had a perfect season. They are favored to win the state.

Only one month after Andy's junior year in basketball ends, the debate team starts practicing. He also practices for impromptu and extemporaneous speaking. The main debate and speaking topics for the season are: "The Presence of Communism and Fidel Castro in Cuba"; "Is the Russian and American Space Race Consequential?"; and "Based on the current presidential candidates, who should be the next president in 1961?".

After his first debate practice, he goes home and finds out that his mom and dad are planning a trip to the Smokies with Uncle Edward's family in June. Andy asks, "Is Anderson going?"

Davina replies, "I'll ask Ella. Isn't Anderson finishing at Purdue?"

Andy says, "He has one more year. I'm glad Anderson and his family came to the regional."

Davina says, "Me too. They're real proud of you. Do you have any suggestions about where you want to go in East Tennessee?"

Andy replies, "We always enjoy Clingmans Dome and Cades Cove. They're developing Gatlinburg more."

Davina says, "I read about a young country singer, Dolly Parton, who is Judy's age. She has already appeared on the Grand Ole Opry, and she is performing in Knoxville, when we're going to the Smokies."

Andy says, "I think we would all enjoy that."

The debate season goes well. Andy wins several firsts for debate, impromptu and extemporaneous. As the weather gets warmer, Andy spends more time painting with his dad. Owen pays him $2.00 an hour, which is a dollar an hour more than he would make at a gas station, restaurant or store.

After school is out, Andy signs up as a volunteer with others from several churches in the county to help those in need with painting, remodeling and repair. A friend from his church and Tim from his basketball team also sign up as volunteers for the month of July. Andy is glad he can work with his friends. He'll have weekends off, so he'll be able to lift weights; catch up on reading; see Linda and catch a couple movies at the local Ski-Hi drive-in.

When the McGraigs and McCollisters return from Tennessee, they all agree that it seems like they just left. Andy feels a tinge of melancholy from the vacation ending, but he has a lot to do during the summer.

After he does a week of volunteer work, he reads good reviews about a new novel that has just been released, "To Kill a Mockingbird". He is anxious to get it, and the new issue of National Review. He started subscribing to U.S. News & World Report, so he wouldn't have to wait for the new issues at the library. Just a weeks before Andy's senior year begins, he gets a new, non-fiction book that has just been released, "The Rise and Fall of the Third Reich".

Even on the first day of school, students are already talking about the possibility of their basketball team going to the state finals. Andy learns that their big contender, Muncie Central, has a new transfer from Indianapolis. Mac Davies is 6'8", and he is one of the best centers in the state. Now Muncie Central is a triple threat with Don Bonan and Jack Damber, who are in their senior year.

Starting with their very first game against Marion, college scouts are coming out to watch Andy play. Before the opener begins, Coach Tallman says, "Andy, I know that Kentucky and IU have scouts here tonight; there may be more."

Andy replies, "Thanks, coach."

The coach says, "Stay focused on the game, and do your best."

Andy says, "Yes, coach, I will."

Andy is fouled with four seconds left on the clock in the fourth quarter. Coach Tallman calls a time-out with Mahican 99 and Marion 78. The coach says, "Great game, guys. Andy, do you think we'll break a 100?"

Andy says, "Yes, coach. I'll try to put both of them in."

The game ends 101 to 78. Andy finishes with 32 points, 19 rebounds and 4 blocked shots. The coach says, "Great game, Andy. I bet Kentucky and IU will be talking with you soon."

"That sounds good to me!" replies, Andy.

When Andy gets home, he tells his mom and dad about the scouts at the game. Owen says, "That was a great game tonight, Andy. You'll be in good standing with them. Are you interested in Kentucky or IU?"

Andy says, "I don't know yet. I like IU, Purdue and several others."

Owen replies, "Don't be too quick to decide. You have about six months before they'll want an answer."

Andy's next big challenge is the SAT and the National Merit Test. He qualified for the National Merit by taking the PSAT last year. When he takes the SAT, he shows up with just two sharpened #2 pencils and a slide rule. Before Christmas break, Andy receives a 1570 out of a possible 1600 on the SAT, and he receives a full tuition National Merit Scholarship.

During the first half of the basketball season, Andy knows that scouts have also come from Cincinnati, Purdue, UCLA, Oklahoma, North Carolina, Michigan and Ohio State. Most sports writers in Indiana are saying that Andy and Don Bonan of Muncie Central are the best players in the state. By Christmas break, Muncie Central has a perfect record and Mahican has only lost one; to Muncie Central.

By Christmas break, Judy gets the good news that before she starts high school, the doctor believes he can take the brace off her leg. Andy continues dating Linda, but he senses that she is getting bored with dates at Good Times and the occasional drive-in movie dates with Tim and his girlfriend.

At Good Times, one Friday evening, Linda says, "Andy, you're doing wonderful with all of your good test results and with all of the scouts coming to your games."

Andy replies, "Yes, I'm fortunate. What about you? Are you still interested in modeling?"

Linda says, "I'm thinking about going to college, and I'm also looking into a modeling school that is in Indianapolis."

Just as she says, "Indianapolis", in walk several of Andy's teammates, including Tim. As they are talking loudly and laughing, they say in unison, "There's, Avalanche Andy!"

They come over to their table joking around and laughing with Andy laughing with them. Linda feels like she's sitting on the bench.

Tim finally says, "Okay, you guys, let's leave these two lovebirds alone."

Andy asks Linda, "Do you want to hear "The Twist" by Chubby Checker?"

Linda says, "Sure. Will you also play "Georgia on My Mind" by Ray Charles?"

As Andy walks over to the juke box, there is a chorus of, "Hiiii, Andeeee!" by several girls from his high school.

Saturday morning, Andy wakes up from a dream. He can't remember what it was about. He only remembers that he was in the hall at school and three or four girls were talking to him.

Andy spends a pleasant Christmas with his family; his cousin Anderson and his family in Hartford City. Andy always enjoys the wit of his Uncle Edward and the games of chess that he has with Anderson. At twilight, on their way back to Mahican, they pass through Fairmount, the hometown of James Dean. Andy didn't follow James Dean career (he was only twelve when Dean passed away), but Andy senses a sadness as they pass through the area.

Two days before Christmas break ends, Andy works out with Tim at their local gym. Tim asks, "Do you think we have a shot at winning the state?"

Andy replies, "I think it's a possibility. There are four other real competitive teams: Catawba, Muncie, Indianapolis Attucks and the Wyandot Eagles. Bonan and Damber at Muncie Central are NBA caliber players, and Davies will probably get a basketball scholarship."

Tim says, "In my book, you're as good as Bonan. If we had two other NBA caliber players, we would win the state title. Sometimes I think I let the team down."

Andy says, "Are you kidding, Tim? You're the best guard in the county. You also have a good chance of being valedictorian or salutatorian of our class. You don't take a back seat to anyone! Wouldn't it be great, if we can both rank in the top five of our class?"

Tim replies, "Absolutely!"

The end of basketball season is around the corner, and the college scouts escalate their efforts to draft Andy. IU, Purdue and Kentucky are at the top of Andy's list. Owen asks Andy, "Are their offers similar?"

Andy says, "Yes, since tuition will be paid by the National Merit Scholarship, all three colleges have offered scholarships that pay room and board and college related expenses, including expenses, when I travel with the team. Dad, confidentially, I'm more interested in their political science and international affairs programs than their basketball programs. I want to play varsity, but my top priority is not a national championship or a top draft pick by a NBA team."

Owen replies, "I totally understand, Andy. I admire you for

putting your career interests first. Basketball is temporary for most players. Even a lot of players in the NBA only play for a few years."

Andy says, "I love the game, but I'm more interested in national and world events."

Owen says, "I'm proud of you. I admire you for doing a great job with your team as well as your studies."

Andy smiles and says, "I think I take after a hard working toolmaker and painter."

Owen laughs and says, "That may be true, but your intelligence comes more from your mom."

Andy says, "I'm going to enjoy the playoffs. I still have a couple months to decide after the playoffs are over."

At the end of the season, Mahican's record is 28 wins and 2 losses. Catawba High is 29 and 1; Indianapolis Attucks are 28 and 2 and Muncie Central has a perfect season of 30 wins. Mahican Central wins their sectional and their regional.

In the first semi-final game at Butler Fieldhouse in Indianapolis, the Mahican Cougars play the Wyandote Eagles; the Eagles are 27 and 3 for the regular season. Andy, Tim and the rest of the team are fired up. Every time the ball is touched by Andy, his fans start yelling, "Avalanche Andy, Avalanche Andy, goodness, gracious, Great Balls of Fire!"

In the first half, they are back and forth and within three points of each other. At the end of the third quarter the score is Mahican 71 and Wyandote 67. At the beginning of the fourth quarter, Andy and Tim put it in the next gear. Andy ends up with 35 points and 21 rebounds and Tim scores 26 points. Its Tim's highest scoring game. Mahican wins 103 to 94. In the earlier game Muncie Central won, which puts them in the last of the semi-finals with Mahican Central.

Andy gives the night game his best effort against Don Bonan and Muncie Central. Andy ends with 31 points and 20 rebounds and Bonan ends with 33 points and 15 rebounds. Unfortunately, Jack Damber scores 25 points and Davies has 22 points and 18 rebounds. The final score is Muncie Central 98 and Mahican 95.

Four days after the semi-finals, Wabash College offers Tim a basketball scholarship, which completes his needs, since he also has a

National Merit Scholarship. Just one week after Muncie Central wins the state final against Catawba High, Andy declares Purdue to be his choice. All of the Indiana sport writers are covering Andy's decision, as much as they covered the winner of the state final.

Andy is voted on the first team of the Indiana All Star team along with Don Bonan and Jack Damber of Muncie Central. Two weeks after Andy chooses Purdue; Bonan picks IU. To Andy's surprise and delight, the 6'3" guard, Jack Damber of Muncie Central, chooses Purdue. Andy thinks that decision will clinch Purdue to be in the NCAA playoffs.

6

The Boilermakers

Andy rounds out his senior year at Mahican by placing first in the state in Impromptu Speaking with the National Forensic League. One of the finalist judges comes up to Andy after the event and congratulates him. She said, "You have a gifted voice and delivery. Your voice is clear and prominent like rushing water."

Andy's debate team wins the regional competition. Tim is salutatorian and Andy places fifth in his class. Andy is looking forward to living on the Purdue Campus. He decides not to pledge a fraternity, because he wants to focus on his majors, political science and international affairs, and basketball.

He doesn't see Linda during the last month of summer, because she enrolled in the modeling school in Indianapolis. She calls Andy just two days before he leaves for Purdue. She says, "Andy, I will still see you on breaks and some weekends. I still want to go to Purdue, but I probably won't be able to for another year."

Andy says, "Well, take care. I wish you the best."

Andy leaves for orientation at Purdue two weeks before Labor Day. His dad drives Andy to Lafayette with his sister and mom. On the way there, Andy says, "Judy, does your doctor check your leg Monday?"

She excitedly says, "Yes, and he expects that I can take the brace off before I start high school."

Andy replies, "That's wonderful! I wish I could be there. I will be praying for you."

Judy says, "We want to come to your first game at home."

Andy says, "No problem. I will mail three tickets for you, mom and dad."

Owen asks, "Do you think you'll be a starter this year?"

Andy says, "I talked to the scout and to the coach by phone about that. Of course, we still have try outs to see who makes first team. The coach says I have a good chance to play a lot of minutes. It might be like my first year in high school, where they have me sub for the center and the power forward."

Davina says, "I know that Anderson was in the School of Business at Purdue, but has he given you any pointers for your first year?"

Andy replies, "He gave me some general advice. He said that it's better not to pick the difficult electives the first year. He also told me to call him, if I have any questions or any problems."

Owen asks, "I know Tim is going to Wabash College, but do you have any other friends going to Purdue?"

As Andy says, "I know several from my class, who enrolled at Purdue," they arrive at the campus and are impressed with how appealing and colorful it is. There are many beds of lavender and purple hydrangea, black-eyed susan and geraniums. The large oak trees give ample shade on the green lawns. Soon they find Andy's dorm and a space near the front of the stoic building.

They unload Andy's luggage, typewriter, a small bookcase and enough snacks to get Andy conditioned to the cafeteria food. After they carry everything to Andy's new dorm room, they descend the stairway and go back to the car.

Owen says, "Do you have any plans for the rest of the day?"

Andy replies, "Not really. I'll probably walk over to the gym to see if it's open. Orientation starts at 9 in the morning, and I think on the first day it lasts until later in the afternoon. I know I'll meet other freshmen today, and I hope to meet some of the basketball team. I know that Jack Damber will be here for orientation."

Davina says, "I'm sure you'll have new friends real soon. It's a beautiful campus, Andy. Look at the virgin maple trees that have been left on their manicured lawn."

Andy says, "It's a nice looking campus."

Owen says, "Okay, Andy. Do you have everything?

"Yes, dad. I saw the phone in the dorm, so I can easily stay in touch."

Davina and Judy have tears welling up in their eyes.

Owen hugs Andy and says, "We'll all miss you, but we'll be back in less than two weeks to pick you up for Labor Day Weekend."

Andy gives his mom and sister a kiss and a hug. He says, "I'll miss all of you. I love you. It's a big change, but I think I'll enjoy the classes and my new team."

Davina says, "We all love you a lot, Andy," as she wipes away some tears.

As they get into the blue and white Chevy, Andy watches them as they head back to Mahican. He waves until their car is a block away. He thinks, "I'm kind of sad that my life in Mahican is behind me, but I'm looking forward to my new experiences on campus."

The freshman orientation starts flying by. Andy meets Jack Danber in person, when the team meets before the Labor Day weekend. Jack says, "Andy, we've known each other from the basketball floor for several years. I've always admired you and your basketball skills."

Andy replies, "The same here, Jack." All through high school, I thought you were the best guard in the state. I'm glad we're finally on the same team."

Jack says, "Me too. By the end of this season or next season, Purdue should have one of the best teams in the country. In Muncie, Don Bonan and I played basketball together, since we were young kids. We became good friends. Besides us being teammates now, I hope we become friends."

As Andy replies, he pats Jack on the shoulder and says, "I'm sure we will."

The coach comes out of his office and calls the players in one by one. He calls Andy next. Coach Bud Brown shakes Andy's hand and says, "Andy, we're very happy that you decided on Purdue. Based on your reputation, I have to ask how much you are bench pressing now?"

Andy says, "Well, first of all, I'm glad to be at Purdue, Coach. This summer I got up to 600 lbs."

"Wow! Very Impressive! From your physical report, it says, you're at 237 now and 6' 5 ½". Are you still running regularly?"

Andy replies, "During the summer I ran about twice a week. I'm close to running a ten minute two mile."

Coach Brown says, "Good. I want all of the team to stay in good running condition. We can't have a good team with players gasping for air."

Andy says, "Yes, sir."

The coach says, "I looked at your high school record and talked with Coach Tallman. He says that your first year with him you played a lot of minutes by substituting for the starting center and the starting power forward. We might sub you some for center, but will probably rotate you between small forward and power forward at the beginning of the season."

Andy smiles and says, "I'll be glad to, Coach."

"Our first practice is one week after you come back from Labor Day. Here is a welcome kit for you, which includes team information like travel and team rules."

Andy thanks the coach; gets up and shakes his hand. When he goes out the door, he spots Jack Danber and says, "Jack, the coach wants to see you next. Have a good Labor Day weekend."

Jack replies, "You too, Andy. See you by first practice."

Andy goes back to his dorm room; packs his luggage for the weekend and walks to the front of the dorm to wait on his dad, who is due by 5:00. When his dad pulls up, he throws his luggage in the trunk. He and his dad shake hands, and Owen says, "Your mom is going to cook for us this weekend, but to give her a break, Judy requested that we go to Pizza King this evening."

Andy laughs and says, "It sounds like Judy has a good excuse to go out for pizza."

On the way home they talk about Andy's new team and classes. He tells his dad that he signed up for two requirements, Biology and History. He also signed up for International Economics and American Foreign Policy. He says, "Three of the four courses are four credit hours each, so he'll have fifteen credit hours for his first semester. They will also give me some Phys. Ed. Credit for being on the basketball team. I also met Jack Danber from Muncie Central. He seems like a really nice guy."

His dad says, "I know you're glad he's on your team, instead of an opposing team. We're due back to pick up your mom and Judy about 6:30. Do you need anything first?"

Andy says, "No, let's go straight home."

They pull up in front of their house right at 6:30. Andy gets out to announce their arrival, when Judy comes running out of the front door, and with no leg brace, she jumps in Andy's arms. Andy gives her a kiss and says, "Now you can be part of my weight lifting routine. What does it feel like to be set free?"

Judy replies, "It has been wonderful!" Davina reaches up and gives Andy a kiss.

They take off for Pizza King and full court pizza.

When they get home, they play a few rounds of euchre with Nehi Cream Soda and popcorn. The phone rings, and Judy tells Andy that Linda is on the phone. He picks up the receiver and says, "How are you doing, Linda?"

"I'm doing fine, Andy. How are you?"

"Things are going well. I just got home at 6:30. Are you home now?"

She says, "No. I was hoping to come home for the weekend, but there are some special events here. I'm going to stay in Indianapolis this weekend with some of the modeling students."

Andy says, "I wish you could make it here." They talk for about five minutes and hang up.

Andy comes back to the card table, and Davina says, "Was that Linda?"

He replies, "Yes, and she's not coming home for the weekend."

Owen says, "Well, let's finish the game. In another hand or two, your mom and I might beat you and Judy."

It's 9:00 when they finish and Judy says, "I think I'll hit the sack." She goes over and hugs Andy and says, "It's good to have you home."

Andy says, "Sis, it's always good to be with you."

Owen says, "I'll put the card table and chairs away, so we can relax and talk in the living room."

Davina asks, "Andy, do you want some coffee or hot tea?"

Andy replies, "I'll take some green tea, if you have some."

When Owen comes back in the room, Davina is finishing with the tea. Davina sits with Owen on the coach, and Andy leans back in the big easy chair.

Davina says, "Tell us about Purdue!"

Andy smiles and says, "Of course, you know that classes haven't started yet. I told dad today that I signed up for International

Economics, American Foreign Policy, History 101 and Biology 101. I talked with Coach Bud Brown. I think he'll be a good coach. I met Jack Dunbar, and we hit it off. I've met a lot of freshmen in the dorm and got familiar with the school library and gym."

Owen says, "Tell me about the team."

Andy replies, "I haven't met everyone yet, but I know that three starters are back and two have graduated. It sounds like we have a good, freshman center. He's almost 7 feet, and his high school team in New Jersey won the state title."

Owen says, "Wow, the team sounds real promising."

Davina asks, "Andy, I haven't asked you for a while, if you have had any visions or seen anything special?"

Andy laughs and says, "I didn't see a wall around Purdue!"

They all laugh, and then Andy get a serious look.

Davina says, "What is it?"

Andy says, "It's interesting that you asked this evening, because I could tell that Linda was fabricating a story about her weekend stay in Indianapolis."

There's a brief lull in the conversation, then Owen asks, "Confidentially, Andy, do you want to tell us what she said?"

"She fabricated her reason for not coming home. She said that she was staying with some other modeling students for the weekend to attend some special events. I could tell that it is not true that she is staying with other modeling students, and there is something about the special events that is also fabricated."

Davina remarks, "Wow, when you find the right woman, Andy, she will have to be an honest one!"

Davina's remark lifts a grey cloud, and the conversation goes back to the weekend. Davina says, "Your dad invited his sister and family over for a noon cook-out on labor day."

Andy says, "Good deal. Is Anderson coming?"

Davina says, "Yes. Your dad has to work Tuesday morning. Judy and I would like to ride with you and your dad to Purdue."

Andy replies, "Why don't we leave around 4:30, so Dad can be back home by 8:00?"

Owen says, "That's a good plan. I'll tell Ella to come by 12, since we have to get ready for Lafayette about 4:00."

On Saturday morning, Tim and Andy get together and play some round ball, and they have lunch at Good Times. Later in the afternoon, Andy takes Judy to Mahican's largest park where they walk on the scenic trails. They talk about high school, basketball, church and childhood memories.

After church on Sunday, the McGraigs pack a picnic lunch and go to Turkey Run State Park, which is forty-five minutes from their house (Mahican is less than fifteen minutes from the Illinois state line). On their way back home from Turkey Run, Andy says, "I love driving this car."

Owen looks at Davina in the back seat and smiles. He asks Andy, "Do you know how long we've had this car?"

Andy says, "Sure. You got it in 1956, so we've had it five years."

Owen says, "Recently, I got on the waiting list for another dealer's car. By the time they get to my name, it will probably be a 1961 Bel Air or Impala."

Andy says, "That's great. What are you going to do with this car?"

Owen says, "Your mom and I have been talking about trying to find a worthy college student to give it to."

Andy looks at his dad and says, "Are you putting me on? You mean you're talking about giving me The Babe?"

Owen smiles at Andy and pats him on the shoulder, "You deserve it, son."

Andy honks the horn and lets out a shout. He says, "I don't know what to say except, thank you. You and mom are the best."

Owen says, "Just remember that I don't know when they will get to my name. It could be next spring or summer."

"I'm not worried about that, dad. We've always taken care of The Babe."

The rest of the way home, Andy (and probably the rest of the family) thinks about the tranquil creeks and rocky cliffs of Turkey Run. When they get close to Mahican, it's not quite sunset, but the haze of summer begins to fill the sky over Mahican.

They pull their car into the garage, and when they walk into the living room, the lamp with the automatic timer has already come on. Davina says, "The day has gone by so fast." Owen and Andy put away the picnic accessories in the kitchen. Judy brings Monopoly into the living room. Andy says, "Oh wow, Sis, it has been at least fifty years since we've played Monopoly."

Judy replies, "Oh, sure. I know we played it during Christmas vacation."

Andy continues to tease her, "We did, when you were five years old."

Davina says, "Ok, kids, enough with Act I. I'll fix popcorn, and we'll have pop and Monopoly with it."

They play Monopoly for over an hour; laughing about embarrassing moments from years gone by and talking about how much they're looking forward to the cook-out with the McCollisters.

Andy says, "Anderson called me yesterday, and wanted to know the professors I got, and the courses I'm taking. He said the professor I have for International Economics, Dr. Krause, is the same professor that he had for an economics course in his business major. He said the professor has been an advisor for the State Department."

Owen replies, "Wow, son. That is very impressive."

Davina says, "Yes, it is. If Judy gets any more houses and hotels, she is going to control the economy."

Owen says, "I'll see what's on the one-eyed monster." He gets out the TV Guide and says, "Ed Sullivan is over. Do you want to watch The Dinah Shore Show?"

Davina says, "That's good. When it's over, we should get ready for bed. We have a big day tomorrow."

Lights are out by 10:30, and this night, there are no shadows on the wall.

In the morning, they get an early start for the holiday. Judy and Davina clean the bathrooms and the kitchen, and Owen and Andy straighten up the rest of the house. While the ladies work on the salad and other food preparations, the guys prepare the grill and set up the chairs, tables, badminton and ring toss in the back yard.

Edward, Ella and Anderson arrive exactly at noon. They start with grilled hamburgers and hot dogs with a salad that has a cornucopia of raw veggies. They have watermelon for dessert, and they continue to visit after bellies are filled. Next they hit the badminton and ring toss court, then Andy and Anderson slip off to the living room and set up the chess board.

Andy's three favorite relatives wish him the best at Purdue and give him hugs, as they leave by 4:00.

Labor Day evening is a busy day on the Indiana roads with people returning home and others going to their college campuses. The McGraigss take the country roads pass many high cornfields, ready for harvest. They stop at a red light and turn north on Highway 25. Even though it's late afternoon, the sky is a bright blue with few clouds, and everyone in "The Babe" is in good spirits.

Owen says, "Now that we're on the highway, we'll get to the campus sooner than I want to."

Andy says cheerfully, "I understand, dad, but I have classes in the morning, and your department at the factory is counting on you being there."

Owen laughs and says, "You're spot on, son."

Davina says, "I promise not to be all teary eyed this time. I think the first time we left you at Purdue was the hardest."

Judy says, "That's right. Now we want you to work hard and be on the best basketball team in the country!"

Andy laughs and says, "I will work hard, but you have to promise to keep making your leg stronger."

Judy smiles and says, "It's a deal!"

Soon they're at the front of the dorm, and they say their goodbyes. As they get in the car, everyone waves, and Andy makes a bee line for his room. He wants to get settled and find a TV in the dorm, where he can catch the nightly news. Once he gets everything packed away in his room, it's about 6:30. He thinks, "I've got 30 minutes to find a TV and get a lock-in for the Huntley-Brinkley report."

In a few minutes, he's in the dorm lounge and only two guys are stretched out watching TV. Andy sits down and says, "What's happening?"

A tall, slim young man says, "We're just hanging out and talking. If we're still here at 8:30, we'll probably watch The Rifleman and maybe

The Andy Griffith Show after that. Didn't we meet during orientation? Aren't you on the basketball team?"

"Yes. I'm Andy McGraig."

"I'm Guy Richards, and this is Matt Talbot. Are you wanting to watch anything special?"

Andy replies, "I like the Huntley-Brinkley Report, which starts at 7."

Guy says, "You got it, my friend. We'll jump anyone who tries to change the channel."

Andy laughs and says, "Thanks."

Matt says, "We might grab a snack after 7, but we plan to come back later."

Andy says, "I think we'll have more people in the lounge after Labor Day. I won't have time to watch the news every evening at 7, but I will try to tune in, when I can."

Guy says, "Once they find out you're on the basketball team, they'll probably turn to Huntley and Brinkley, when they see you."

Andy laughs and says, "That would be nice."

Matt says, "Do you lift weights? I'm only 160 lbs. but I'm starting to work out with 150 lbs. on the bench press."

Guy laughs and says, "Andy probably lifts that much with one finger. So, can you tell us how much you lift?"

Andy says, "Okay, I'll tell you only because you seem like good men. Don't tell anyone, but I lift 600 lbs."

Matt says, "Are you kidding?"

Andy says, "No, I don't kid about weight lifting."

Guy says, "I think you'll own the Huntley-Brinkley Report! Well, Andy, it's great talking with you. We might get something to eat now, and it's almost time for the news."

Andy says, "See you soon; good talking with you."

As they leave the dorm to go to the Student Center, Guy says to Matt, "Man, Andy sure is imposing physically!"

Matt says, "I wouldn't want to be on a team playing against him."

Andy turns to the Huntley-Brinkley Report. Tonight is a 15 minute segment of world and national news. Andy's undivided attention is on a controversy between the Traditional American Party and the

New Age Socialist Party. During the early cold war days in the late 1940s, Congress passed a bill requiring all communists and members of the American Communist Party to register with their local police departments. David Brinkley in D.C. is reporting that leaders of the American Party met over the weekend to make plans for enforcing the legislation. The Socialist Party heard about their plans, so they are doing what they can to block their action on Tuesday.

During the news coverage, they show four interviews; two members of each party are interviewed by the media. When a Socialist Party member from the National Security Committee is interviewed, Andy could tell that he is misleading the media and the country. Tomorrow Andy decides to follow up with the report by seeing what U.S. News, The National Review, the Wall Street Journal, the Washington Post and the Chicago Tribune have to say.

After the fifteen minutes of the regular news report, Andy checks his dorm mail box before he goes to his room. He sees a letter from Purdue Boilermakers Basketball. As he walks to his room, he opens the letter, which announces a team meeting at 4:00 tomorrow. He walks in his room and gets out his calendar book. At 9 in the morning he has International Economics for an hour; History 101 at 11:00 and American Foreign Policy at 2:00. He adds, "Team Meeting at 4:00".

Andy decides to kick back and relax the rest of the evening with one of his favorite books, "Essays on Practical Politics", by Teddy Roosevelt.

His first official day as a Purdue student goes well. Each professor took most of the class time introducing their course; explaining how they grade the course and chatting with the students. One of the political science professors welcomed Andy to Purdue Basketball. He kidded with Andy and the class by saying, "We'll see if Mr. McGraig performs as well in class as on the basketball floor." The class and the professor might be surprised to see how well Andy excels.

By 4:00 he is sitting with his new team, and Coach Bud Brown starts promptly on the hour. He welcomes the starters back and the freshmen. He talks about the team qualifying for the NCAA playoffs. He says, "Our record last year was 19 and 15, and two teams, who had worse records than that, were in the playoffs. Men, we do not want to qualify by just the skin of our teeth; do we?"

The team in basic training unison yells, "No, Sir!"

"Alright then!" In silence, he takes a minute as he looks at every player. He asks, "Are we Purdue basketball men, or are we a knitting class?"

They yell, "Purdue Basketball men!"

The coach says, "We have one pre-season game before the end of October, but I want you game ready by this Friday, when we will start our first practice at 4:00. I expect each of you to be in good condition during our first practice. The next two days, I want you running and lifting weights each day. Do you understand me?"

"Yes, Sir!"

I will know, if you haven't followed my instructions, and that affects playing time for you. I don't want any of you slacking off between now and the end of the playoffs. I don't want slackers on this team. Are there any slackers here?"

In unison, "No, Sir!"

"Okay, men, before we dismiss I want everyone to introduce yourself and tell us your hometown and state, and year in college. We welcome all of our freshmen. Upper classmen, including fraternity people, I want you to help and not hinder the freshmen. I better not hear otherwise. Do you understand me?"

All of the upper classmen in unison yell, "Yes, Sir!"

The coach says, "Okay; to make it simple, let's start in the back row from left to right and continue that way to the front row. One more thing, we have welcomed a few Purdue students as walk-ons, but anyone can be cut after our initial practices, except for the basketball scholarship players."

As they introduce themselves, each player gets applause. When the three star freshmen players introduce themselves: Larry Quarles from Jersey City, New Jersey, Jack Danber from Muncie, Indiana, and Andy McGraig from Mahican, Indiana, each player gets an exuberant welcome.

After the meeting Andy and Jack greet each other and talk with Larry from Jersey City. Andy says, "It looks like we could make the playoffs this year."

Larry says, "I believe we will. I've heard about both of you. Andy, I heard a sports announcer in New Jersey refer to you as the linebacker of high school basketball."

Andy and Jack laugh. Jack says, "That's true. I've played against him enough. Ron Bonan and I always had a workout, when we played Andy. I've heard about you too. Did your high school team list you at 6'11?"

"They did. My dad always said that I should have eaten more Cheerios."

Andy says, "That's funny. I grew up on Cheerios."

Larry replies, "I can tell."

Andy says, "It's good talking with you guys. I'm going to do a quick workout before supper, then hit the books."

Larry says, "See ya Friday at 4."

Andy has his workout and supper done by 6:15, because he wants to find the newspapers and magazines at the school library to read up on the congressional bill and activities that the Traditional American Party and the New Age Socialist Party are arguing about. He finishes at the library by 7:30, then he walks to his dorm to work on his first day assignments, which are easier than future assignments.

It's close to twilight. The five minute walk is pleasant, but it is still a little humid for a late summer evening. When Andy gets in his room, he lays down to take a five minute rest. He wonders if he'll have a roommate this semester. The dorm officials didn't say; one way or the other. He wonders if he is a single occupant, because of his size and being on the team.

Andy is satisfied with his first four days of classes. He thinks the biology class might be a little more difficult than he expected. He arrives at the gym about 30 minutes early to suit up and to talk with some of his teammates. He gets to talk with all three of the returning starters, who are now seniors. Bill from Austin, Texas, played small forward and is 6'4. Bobby from New Castle, Indiana, is 6 feet and played shooting guard. Michael from Charlotte, North Carolina, played center and power forward and is 6'9. All three of their starters told Andy that they saw him play during the high school playoffs.

Coach Brown proves to be a disciplinarian. He spends the first five minutes with stretching exercises. He has the team run sprints up and down the floor. He has one on one drills with a guard and shooter. He has drills to test dribbling, passing and shooting. After an hour of drills. He has the team huddle, and says, "We might have a few cuts within a week. This month we'll practice twice a week, and once a week you'll meet as a team to improve your weight lifting and running. The first week of October we start practicing Monday through Friday at 4:30."

He calls six names to stay a few minutes and dismisses the rest of the team to the showers. The coach says, "The six of you: Michael, Bobby, Bill, Andy, Jack and Larry, we are going to build the team around. I already know about your skills, but I had to check out your conditioning today. This month I want you to rotate running with weight lifting; at least three days of running and two days of weight lifting."

He continues, "By coincidence we have three seniors and three freshmen. Everyone is important. Seniors, we also have to think about the future of the team. Every one of you will get your playing minutes, if you keep developing your skills and stay in condition. Michael, starting out, Larry and you will be sharing the center and power forward positions, and you will also be sharing the power forward spot with Andy. Bobby, you will start out as the shooting guard and Jack will be the point guard. After the season starts, we might switch those positions. Bill, you will start out at small forward, but Andy will also be sharing your position. We are deep with talent, except for the guard positions. I'm watching the other players for a good, third guard."

The coach dismisses them, and they take a quick shower, because they're more than ready for supper and for a short break over the weekend. After they walk out of the locker room, Jack asks Andy, "What are your plans for the weekend?"

Andy says, "The usual: study and working out."

Jack says, "There's a theater at the edge of campus. At 7:30 this evening, they're showing "The Hustler" with Paul Newman. They only charge college students 50 cents."

Andy says, "Let's do it. Isn't the Student Center between your dorm and mine?"

Jack says, "Yes. Let's meet in front of the Student Center between 7:10 and 7:15, and we'll be inside the theater by 7:30."

They're both at the Student Center by 7:10. When they get in line at the theater, there are only about 15 to 20 co-eds making eye contact with them. Once they get seated with their soda and buttered popcorn, Jack says, "I can't decide between blonde, brunette and red-head."

Andy laughs and says, "You don't have to worry about it tonight."

They walk to their dorm rooms about 9:30. As they get close to the Student Center, Andy says, "Thanks for telling me about the movie; it was good. Tomorrow I'm running, and Sunday I'm lifting weights. I might see you at the gym this weekend."

Jack replies, "Sounds good. Thanks for going with me."

Andy hits the sack about 10:30 and reads a little. As he turns the lights out, he thinks, "I need to call the family in the morning."

After Andy gets up and takes a shower, he goes to the cafeteria for breakfast. When he comes back to the dorm, he calls home. Davina answers.

Andy says, "Mom, how are you this morning?"

She says, "Hi, Andy. Why didn't you call collect?"

Andy replies, "My basketball scholarship covers all college related expenses. They reimburse me once a month for these kind of expenses on campus. How is everyone there?"

Davina says, "Everyone misses you a lot; especially Judy."

Andy asks, "Where is Miss Enthusiasm now?"

"They went to the record store. She still loves the Hit Parade music. I think you influenced her, when you started buying records by Chuck Berry and others. Her dad spoils her at times and buys her one or two 45s. She still uses the same turn table that we bought for both of you years ago."

Andy says, "We should try to get her or the family a Hi-Fi."

Davina says, "I'll look into that for Christmas. I saw one at Thelma and Carl's house."

"So what songs does she like right now?"

"She likes "I Fall to Pieces" by Patsy Cline and she loves Ricky Nelson. I think she wants to find his new hit, "Travelin' Man". How are things on campus?"

"Real good. We had our first practice yesterday. In the evening Jack Danber and I saw "The Hustler" with Paul Newman. I need to call Tim sometime and tell him about hanging out with Jack. Tim use to guard him, when we played Muncie Central. It was probably Tim's hardest game."

Davina says, "I'm sure Tim will be glad that you won him over."

"There's something I'm looking into, concerning the national political scene. Once I finish my research, I'm thinking about talking with Dr. Krause, since he's my professor, and he knows Anderson."

His mom says, "Good idea, Andy. Remember, it is probably a good idea to not divulge how you know these things. If Dr. Krause or anyone asks you how you know, just say something like my insight has a good record."

Andy replies, "It would be a general comment; like insight or a dream."

She says, "I'm glad to know that. It may save you a lot of heartache later on."

"Today, I'm going to run, study and do more research on what we were talking about."

Davina asks, "How is the food there?"

Andy replies, "Not near as good as yours! They do have a decent variety with some vegetables and fruit."

"It sounds like you're taken care of."

Andy says, "Yes, I believe that I made the right decision. Give dad and Judy my love."

Davina says, "I will. Take care; I love you."

Andy says, "I love you, mom."

Andy has a busy weekend with working out; studying; researching on his own and hanging out with some of his new friends, including some that he just met at the church by the campus. One of his main priorities for Monday is getting an update in the evening from the Huntley-Brinkley Report.

7

Affairs of State

Monday evening Andy goes to supper before 6:00, so he can be back at the dorm around 6:30 to get ready for the 7:00 news report. He had a chance to read the Monday edition of the Wall Street Journal at the library, but he didn't get much new information about the communist registration policy.

When he walks into the lounge area at his dorm, Guy and Matt are watching TV. Andy sits down near them and says, "Are you going to guard the Huntley-Brinkley report for me?"

They look over at Andy and Guy says, "Hi, Andy. We sure will. Matt and I will tackle anybody that walks up to the TV."

Andy smiles and says, "How do you like your classes?"

Guy says, "I like mine, but we think Bowling and Square Dancing might be challenging."

Andy replies, "Bowling and Square Dancing!"

Matt laughs and says, "Believe it or not, you can elect them to go toward your Phys. Ed. Requirement. But I don't recommend that you quit the basketball team to take Square Dancing."

Andy says, "You can count on me staying in basketball."

In a few minutes, Guy says, "It looks like you're in the clear for Huntley and Brinkley. I'm going to hit the books. You guys have a good night."

Matt also gets up and says, "I should get my studying out of the way."

Andy says, "Have a good night."

The news starts out with Chet Huntley in New York. After they switch to David Brinkley, he reports that Russia just tested a hydrogen bomb; the largest bomb ever exploded. Before the end of his report, he does say that in Congress the New Age Socialist Party is still disputing the American Traditional Party's plans to enforce the communist registration bill.

At the end of the fifteen minute report, Andy decides he will still search a few papers and magazines for more information. He also gets up to finish his studies for the evening.

By the end of the week, Andy has run three times and lifted weights twice. He completes the two basketball practices with flying colors. It looks like the top three drafted freshmen will get as many playing minutes as the three returning seniors. The coach and players found out that Andy, Jack and Larry are very competitive with the three returning starters. There's a feeling in the air that the team will make the NCAA playoffs this season. Coach Brown is also very impressed with a walk-on guard, who took a year off from school. He was a starting guard for Catawba High School in southern Indiana.

Andy and most of the students enjoy the arrival of the fall season and the cooler weather. At the beginning of October, Andy's team is practicing five days a week. On a week day evening while listening to the Huntley-Brinkley Report, Andy gets a big surprise. David Brinkley in D.C. announces, "Today in Congress, the majority agreed that it is lawful to require members of the American Communist Party and other communists to register with the local police. Many of the Socialist Party members booed, when the Speaker of the House announced the decision."

After the report from Congress, a news reporter interviewed a congressional member, who supported the decision and another member who was against activating the congressional bill. Andy goes directly to his room to make some notes. He puts a brief note in his calendar book, and some detailed notes on the news report in his own record.

He puts his notes aside and starts studying. He thinks that he's beginning to get a handle on his biology class; it's not taking as much study time as it did. He does the biology assignment first, so he can get into American Foreign Policy and International Economics. He has been enjoying both classes, especially Dr. Krause's economics class.

Andy is done with his assignments by 10:00. He gets ready for bed and reads from the gospel of John before he turns out the lights. As he drifts off to sleep, he thinks about the differences in views that the two congressmen had about communist registration.

It seems to Andy that the night had not passed, when he notices a strange light coming through the blinds on his window. He looks out through the window and sees many people yelling, as if they're protesting something. He puts on his pants, jacket and shoes and goes outside.

He sees some of the people holding flags and banners that say "The New Age Socialist Party" and signs that say "Down with Tyranny". Andy doesn't know what tyranny they're talking about, but he continues to watch the crowd.

To his side and across the lawn, he can see that some protestors are confronting and assaulting people walking down the street. It also looks like they're throwing something on some of the people. Beyond where the protestors are, he can see flashes of light behind the immediate college buildings. It looks and sounds like the flashes of light are from explosions and fires.

The longer Andy watches, the more the conflict seems to escalate, then Andy's alarm goes off. For a second, he feels startled. Until a couple seconds pass, he doesn't realize why he's still in bed. He gets up and looks out the window. Everything appears to be calm.

His day seems to go normally. He doesn't notice anything unusual around him. He enjoys his 4:00 basketball practice, and he has supper with Jack and Larry in the cafeteria. During supper, he asks Jack and Larry, if they caught the news last night, and they said they didn't.

Andy says, "Did either one of you notice anything unusual last night?"

Larry shakes his head and Jack says, "Why?"

Andy nonchalantly says, "I guess I had a dream that seemed like the real thing."

Larry says, "That happened to me in my last year of high school. I was playing a game in front of a fieldhouse full of people, and I was naked as a jaybird."

Andy and Jack laugh, and Jack says, "Don't get any funny ideas, when we play our first game here."

Larry says, "No, kidding. When I first woke up, I thought it had really happened."

Andy says, "I understand. I guess it happened to me this morning, when I first woke up."

Larry asks, "What was it about?"

Andy simply says, "Brother, it was confusing and depressing. I don't think I can describe it right now."

Larry says, "That's okay. I didn't want to think about me being naked in front of hundreds of people."

Jack smiles and says, "We don't want to think about that either."

Andy says, "Well, guys, I've enjoyed it, but its 6:30 already, and I want to watch the news before I crack the books."

The three friends get up and put their dinnerware and trays in their designated spots. The students left in the cafeteria watch the men go out the door, like three trees walking.

During team practice on Friday, the Boilermakers find out that their pre-season game is with Ball State on Friday, October 27th. On their way out of the gym, Andy asks Jack, "Do you know anyone playing for Ball State?"

Jack replies, "There was a senior on our junior varsity team thinking about going there, but I don't know what he decided. I knew a few people in my class, who were planning to go to Ball State, but they didn't play high school basketball."

Andy says, "We moved from Muncie after I finished sixth grade. I don't know about their players either."

Jack says, "It's a home game. We should win by a good margin. I will buy you a movie ticket, if we win by 15 or more."

Andy says, "Make it by 20 or more, and it's a deal."

Jack replies, "It's a deal then. What are your plans for the weekend?"

Andy says "After supper tonight, I'm going to call home. In the morning I'm going to lift weights. I could use a spotter."

Jack says, "I should work out too. What time are you thinking about?"

Andy says, "9:30 or 10:00."

Jack says, "Let's make it 10:00. When we get to the Student Center, I'm going to change and meet a friend for supper."

Andy asks, "Is she blonde, brunette or redhead."

Jack laughs and says, "She's a new friend, but I think she's auburn."

When they get to the Student Center, Andy says, "Have a good time. See ya at 10:00 in the morning."

After supper Andy feels compelled to watch Huntley and Brinkley before he calls his family.

After the news, he crosses the hall, and opens the door to the small room that has a table, chair and phone. He dials home and Judy answers. Andy says, "Watta ya say, sweet pea?"

"Avalanche Andy! Are you bored this Friday evening?"

"No, but you might be glad to know this evening that I will have your ticket soon and mom's and dad's for our first game."

Judy's voice gets louder and excitable, "When is it?"

Andy says, "It's Friday, October 27th. The game starts at 7:30 in our arena against Ball State."

Judy says, "Ball State! Our former church in Muncie was near Ball State."

Andy says, "I know. I was going into 7th grade, and you were going into 4th grade, when we moved. How are things at school?"

"School is going well, and my leg is getting stronger."

Andy says, "Excellent! Take care, sweet pea. Let me speak to dad."

Owen comes to the phone and says, "Hi, Andy. Judy just told us about your first game. How is the team doing?"

Andy replies, "It's a good team. It looks like Jack, Larry, and I will be getting as many minutes as the seniors."

Owen asks, "How do you think the coach will play you and the other starters for your first game?"

Andy says, "I'm guessing that the senior will start at center, even though Larry is probably a little better. I'm sure Larry will get as many minutes. I think the coach will start Jack at point guard, because he was use to starting the senior at shooting guard. He will probably start me at power forward or small forward and put the senior in the other position."

Owen says, "I'm looking forward to being there for the game. Your mom and I pray for you every day."

Andy replies, "Thanks, dad. I pray for you and mom every day."

Owen says, "Have a good weekend. I'll put your mom on now."

Davina answers, "It's good to hear from you, Andy."

Andy says, "Hi, mom. I guess you know about the game now. I would get to the arena fifteen to twenty minutes early. It will be more crowded by game time."

Davina replies, "I think we'll leave by 5:30 that evening, so we can be in the arena parking lot by 7:00. How is everything there?"

Andy says, "I'm happy with my classes and the team. Jack has become a good friend, and we're also friends with Larry, who played on the championship team in New Jersey. Mom, I want to talk with you about something related to the last time we talked. Do you remember me saying that I would probably be talking with Dr. Krause, who teaches my International Economics class.?"

"Yes, I remember that."

Andy continues, "Well, I will be talking with him soon, because something else has come up. My political concerns have proven correct, and I also had a dream that seemed as real as you and me talking now."

Davina says, "Tell me about the dream."

Andy says, "I think you know that the New Age Socialist Party has morphed into an extremist party. They are giving conservative leaders, especially the President and Traditional American Party members, a hard time over the required registration of communists. I really thought that a disturbance was taking place outside the dorm on Wednesday night. I looked outside; got dressed and went outside. There were loud, aggressive protestors on the dorm's front lawn, and to the side, on the walk that goes to the Student Center. There were other protestors assaulting people who were walking by. In the distance, on the other side of the buildings that I could see, there were fires and huge explosions. When the alarm woke me up, I realized in a couple of seconds that it was a dream."

Davina says, "Wow, it was a powerful dream. Has anything else convinced you to go ahead with your plans of seeing Dr. Krause?"

"Yes, it started with listening to a reporter interviewing a leader of the Socialist Party after Congress voted to enforce the law requiring communist registration. I could tell that the Socialist was misleading the public by lying about what the Constitution says and by inciting Socialist party members and others to resist and protest. I have also read about violence caused by Socialist protestors in several cities. I can tell, mom, that this problem they're causing is going to greatly escalate."

"Andy, I agree that you should talk with Dr. Krause in confidence. Have you been discerning anything else?"

"Yes, but it is not too big of a load. When I notice other things, I block most of them out, unless I think it is significant."

"I'm glad you're going to talk with your professor. When do you think, you'll meet with Dr. Krause?"

"On Monday, I'll make an appointment with him. How is everything with dad, Judy and you?"

Davina says, "I'm doing well, and your dad is happy with things at the factory. Judy is doing well, and we're so thankful that her leg is getting stronger."

Andy says, "She sounds good. After the pre-season game, I'll come home with you, if I can. I could stay Saturday, and Sunday morning, if you could get me back by 5:00 on Sunday evening."

Davina replies, "We would love to. I'll tell your dad."

Andy says, "Enjoy this October weather. I'll mail the three tickets to you, and I'll call you several days before the pre-season game."

Davina says, "It's good to hear from you. Love you."

"Bye, mom. Love you."

As Andy hangs up, he feels content, but loneliness sets in for just a few minutes, as he heads to his room to study. Just a few days ago he found an FM station from Indianapolis that plays classical and other easy listening music. He tunes in the channel for background music while he reads.

Saturday morning he meets Jack at the gym, and Sunday morning he goes to church, where he meets the most beautiful girl he has ever seen. After service they talk a few minutes. Andy is taken by her personality, and is amazed at the beauty of her blue eyes, blonde hair and complexion. After a minute of small talk Andy says, "I'm Andy McGraig. My hometown is about 90 minutes from Purdue."

She says, "I'm Lydia Van Ark from Holland. I came here on a

foreign student scholarship. I've seen you on campus. Are you on the basketball team?"

Andy says, "Yes. We have a pre-season game on October 27th. I hope you can come to the game."

Lydia says, "I'll have to put that on my calendar."

Andy smiles and for a second doesn't know what to say. He chokes up a little and says, "It's a pleasure meeting you. I hope I'll see you soon."

Lydia smiles and says, "I hope to see you, Andy."

Andy walks out of the large church foyer into the pleasant, October sunshine. He feels a little embarrassed. His next thought is Linda. He thinks, "I know Linda is preoccupied and not truthful, but I need to call her. I need to make sure there are no commitments now." He decides to call Linda this evening, and looks forward to making an appointment with Dr. Krause tomorrow.

Andy's talk with Linda went as he expected. She mainly talked about her modeling work. When Andy asked if she was seeing someone, she said, "no", but Andy could tell she was lying. He said that he would call her sometime to see how she was doing. Before Andy went to sleep, he started thinking about a first date with Lydia.

After his International Economics class, Andy approached Dr. Krause. As Andy began to talk, he noticed Dr. Krause's sophisticated look with his hair greying on the sides; his small, round glasses and his neatly trimmed mustache. "Dr. Krause, I've been studying a current events issue, and I would like to make an appointment with you, so we could discuss it."

Dr. Krause was all ears, because Andy was doing well in the class, and he noticed he is very bright. "I have my calendar book here. Do you want to meet this week?"

Andy says, "That would be good."

After Dr. Krause opens his calendar book to the right page, he looks up at Andy and says, "How about Thursday at 3:00?"

Andy says, "Yes, that's a good time. I appreciate you taking the time."

Dr. Krause replies, "Glad to do it; that's what I'm here for. See you Thursday."

Andy thanks his professor. As Andy walks out of the classroom, he is especially glad that he can share in just three days what has been on his mind. He continues to watch The Huntley-Brinkley Report most evenings. He also makes some brief notes for his meeting with Dr. Krause on Thursday. On Wednesday evening, his thoughts are mostly on the 3:00 meeting.

Dr. Krause's office is in the same building as his class with him. When Andy walks into the office, it seems like the most academic environment he has known. Two of the walls are filled with books on shelves from floor to ceiling. Dr. Krause is sitting behind a large, cluttered desk. He says, "Come in Andy, and have a seat. Are you playing in the pre-season game this month?"

"Yes, sir. I think I will be playing during most of the game."

Dr. Krause replies, "Good. I'll plan to be there. Tell me what's on your mind."

"I would like to start by giving you my references, so you'll know that I've made a comprehensive study. They are the "National Review", "U.S. News & World Report", "The Wall Street Journal", "The Washington Post", "The Chicago Tribune" and The Huntley-Brinkley Report."

Dr. Krause says, "That's an impressive list of references."

Andy continues, "The matter that I'm concerned about is the New Age Socialist Party's objections and ramifications to the required registration of communists in America. What they call profiling is the need for national security. I have also looked into how their party is promoting free access to our country for illegal immigrants. I have also looked into the rise of crime by illegal immigrants, including a proliferation of drug crimes. I didn't know about the existence of sanctuary cities, until I read about their increased population in cells of Socialist Party domination, including Baltimore, San Francisco, Berkley and Chicago. I read that there are now over sixty sanctuary cities in the states, and it is expected that there will be considerably more."

Dr. Krause said, "That's correct. I've read some of the same things, and I realize not all of it is covered by the televised news networks. Do you have any other concerns on the subject?"

"Yes, sir. I have strong inclinations that their stance and practices will lead to violent protests, increased crime and even severe civil disturbance. With Congressman Charles Hummer and billionaire Jordan Sorontine leading the socialist's resistance, I think the country may experience a national crisis. I believe that we will soon see some violent protests from this movement."

Dr. Krause says, "Andy, I believe that you have an astute evaluation of that movement. Why do think that there are violent protests on the horizon?"

Andy replies, "Dr. Krause, I am not being arrogant by saying that I have good intuition."

Dr. Krause asks light-heartedly, "Are you saying you are like a Jeanne Dixon or Edgar Cayce?"

Andy laughs and says, "I wish I could say that I'm more like a Nathan or a Samuel."

Dr. Krause nods and says, "I know who you're talking about; the Old Testament prophets."

Andy smiles and says, "Yes, sir."

Dr. Krause stands up and shakes Andy hands, "Thank you, Andy, for sharing these things. I will keep in mind what you said."

Andy thanks his professor, and feels a weight lifted as he walks out of Dr. Krause's office.

Andy has a rigorous basketball practice Thursday and Friday evenings, as the Boilermakers prepare for their pre-season game with Ball State. Friday evening Andy catches The Huntley-Brinkley Report and finds out that there is a large scale protest in New York City. The reporter says they are promoting the socialist agenda. On Saturday evening, Andy hears that in upscale business districts of Los Angeles, there is wide spread violence by protestors and gangs. The report says that socialists are involved with protests that led to looting, arson and assaults.

Andy is saddened by the events. The next morning he finds solace in church and has the opportunity to speak with Lydia again. Outside the church, he says to Lydia, "I've been busier lately with preparing for the first game, but if you would be interested in a soda and ice cream some evening, we could meet at the Student Center or the Sweet Shoppe just off campus."

Lydia says, "I would love that." As she writes down her phone number for Andy, she smiles and says, "The Student Center would be fine."

Andy says, "That's great. I'll call you early this week, and we'll set a time."

Andy spends most of the day with studies, and takes a break by going on a three mile run.

Monday morning rolls around fast. As he walks into his International Economics class, Dr. Krause greets him and hands him a folded note. The note says, "Andy, please see me after class. I want to ask you something." After class Andy walks over to Dr. Krause.

Dr. Krause says, "Andy, I thought about our conversation after the disturbances over the weekend. I would like to talk with you for just a few minutes in my office. Could you meet me there at 3:00 today?"

Andy says, "I would be glad to." Andy is somewhat anxious during his next two classes, since he is wondering why Dr. Krause wants to see him.

Andy is at Dr. Krause's office at 2:55. Dr. Krause asks him to take a seat. He says, "Andy, after our conversation Thursday, and after the events of the weekend, I knew that I needed to ask your permission for some inquiries."

Andy asks, "What inquiries?"

Dr. Krause replies, "I'm not at liberty to say just yet what is on my mind, but you may know through your cousin, Anderson, that I have been an advisor to the State Department."

Andy says, "Yes, Anderson told me."

Dr. Krause continues, "I want your permission to talk to Anderson about some things in general. For instance, I would like your permission to look at your academic record. I can tell that you're very bright. The only reason that I can give now is that I believe the State Department will be interested in our meeting last Thursday and the fact that the protest events took place after the meeting. If you allow me to talk with Anderson and to check your academic record, it could give me the green light to call the State Department."

Andy says, "I don't see any harm in it. As long as it doesn't affect my education and two scholarships, you have my permission."

Dr. Krause smiles, "On the contrary, Andy; these inquiries may give you even more opportunities in the future. For now, keep the nature of our conversation confidential."

They get up and shake hands. Dr. Krause says, "I hope to get back with you in about a week. Meanwhile, just keep your focus on your studies and basketball."

Andy replies, "I will, Dr. Krause. Thank you."

Andy leaves his office feeling that he has done the right thing by conferring with Dr. Krause.

By 4:30 Dr. Krause is at the Registration Office to access Andy's records. He finds out the Andy is an exceptional student, who graduated in the top one percent of his high school graduating class. He also sees that he has an extremely high IQ of 159. Besides his basketball scholarship, Dr. Krause finds that Andy also has a National Merit Scholarship. He thinks to himself, "That answers Part One; now I'll get Anderson McCollister's number for some answers to Part Two."

That evening, he calls Anderson's last known number, and gets his current number. He dials the number, and Anderson answers. "Anderson? This is Dr. Krause."

Anderson says, "What a pleasant surprise. Are you trying to enroll old students?"

Dr. Krause laughs and says, "No, I'm calling, because your cousin, Andy, gave me permission to make this call about him."

Anderson says, "Even though he is five years my junior, he usually beats me at chess. What can I help you with?"

Dr. Krause says, "You probably know that Andy is very bright and also quite perceptive. Do you know of any special gifts that he has like insight or discernment?"

Anderson says, "What you say about him is true. I'm not sure what to say about gifts. You may already know he is an exceptional basketball player and very strong. He's NBA material."

Dr. Krause says, "I've heard about his basketball skills. Do you know who might know about any other gifts he has?"

Anderson says, "The only ones that come to my mind would be his mother and father."

Dr. Krause asks, “Could I get their number?”

Anderson gives him the number, and lets him know that it is good hearing from him.

Davina answers his call.

“Mrs. McGraig? This is Dr. Krause at Purdue.”

Davina replies, “Yes, I know who you are. Andy said he was going to talk with you.”

“He has, Mrs. McGraig. Andy is an exceptional student, and we had a productive conversation. Andy shared some things that got my attention. Can you tell me, if Andy has any special gifts?”

Davina is silent for two seconds and then she says, “What do you mean by special gifts?”

“I was wondering, if he has special insight or discernment.”

Davina says, “He is a gifted person. His dad and I realize he is very talented. I can’t tell you about any certain gifts, but I do believe he has special insight.”

Dr. Krause says, “I believe that too. He seems to be a very special person, since he is very bright and has exceptional insight.”

Davina says, “Are there reasons for your inquiry?”

Dr. Krause says, “In confidence, Mrs. McGraig, I think the State Department will be interested in hearing about Andy’s talents. Please keep our conversation confidential.”

Davina replies, “It won’t go further than my husband and me.”

“Thank you, Mrs. McGraig. Have a good evening.”

After the evening news, Andy decides to call Lydia to go ahead and set a time with her.”

As he dials her number, he can’t believe he’s feeling nervous.”

Lydia answers.

Andy says, “Hi, Lydia, this is Andy.”

“Hi, Andy. You’re punctual. When do you want to meet?”

Andy replies, “Most any evening after 6:30 is good for me.”

Lydia says, “How about tomorrow evening at 7:00? The campus is fairly well lighted in most areas, but since it will be dark, when we finish, can you come to my dorm, and we’ll walk to the Student Center?”

Andy says, “Sure.” Lydia gives him directions to her dorm.

Lydia says, "I'll be just inside the front door by 7:00. After we finish at the Student Center, you'll walk me back, won't you?"

Andy says, "I'll be glad to. See you at 7."

When he hangs up, he has butterflies in his stomach. He thinks, "I can't believe that I get to walk her to the center and back."

8

FIRST DATE AND HEAD OF STATE

During the day on Tuesday, Andy is mainly thinking about meeting Lydia at 7:00. Dr. Herbert Krause is thinking about talking to Jonathan Abernathy, Secretary of State, about Andy. Mr. Abernathy returns Dr. Krause's call a little after 5:00. When Dr. Krause answers his phone, a booming voice says, "Herb, how are you these days?"

Dr. Krause says, "I'm still teaching full-time at Purdue."

Abernathy says, "Wonderful. Tell me about your new student, who you called me about."

Krause says, "Johnathan, no matter what you will think about the conversation I had with Andy McGraig, I believe he would be a great asset for the State Department. Andy's IQ is 159, and it appears the one thing he likes as much as basketball is government and international affairs."

Abernathy says, "So far, he sounds promising. I'm curious about why you mention his love for basketball."

Krause says, "He was one of the best high school players in the nation. He just started his college career, and he will probably be one of the best college players in the nation. He is unusually strong and athletic."

Abernathy says, "What is his size?"

"His record says he is 6'5" and 237 lbs. I heard that he bench presses 500 to 600 lbs."

Abernathy says, "Remarkable! We could also train him as a special security agent."

Krause says, "If you can recruit him, he probably won't come cheaply. He is NBA material."

Abernathy says, "We'll do what we need to do. Tell me what prompted your call about him."

Krause says, "He is also well read and intuitive. I have him in my international economics class. He wanted to see me last week, and we made an appointment. He seemed well informed about the current problem with the Socialist Party, concerning the required registration of all communists in the country. He gave me his references, and they are excellent resource materials. Jonathan, here is the icing on the cake. You may not believe this, but during the conversation, he made a comment, which prompted me to say, "Are you a Jeanne Dixon or Edgar Cayce?" Johnathan, FDR was close to Cayce. It is a possibility, I have a type of Edgar Cayce in my class."

Mr. Abernathy replies, "Yes, yes. Go on."

"After he shared his concern about the Socialist Party's reaction, he virtually predicted violence and civil unrest from what they're doing. He said that on Thursday, and by the weekend we know about all the violence that occurred."

Abernathy says, "Herb, you have a strong point. Whether his prediction was coincidence or not, he does sound like an excellent candidate for the department. Does he seem to be set on finishing his college career at Purdue?"

Krause says, "I would say very much so."

Abernathy says, "I will think about it for a few days. I have some important things to do this week, then I will call you next week. Herb, we don't want to let him slip through our fingers. It sounds like you're on good terms with him."

Krause says, "Yes, and Andy McGraig has an excellent disposition. It sounds like he is open to a future with the government."

Abernathy says, "Good. I'm sure that I will want to meet him soon. There is something on my calendar for that area next month. I think the meeting is in St. Louis or Chicago. Give him your best support, and I'll call you next week."

Krause says, "Thank you for your time. I know you won't be disappointed." When they hang up, Dr. Krause thinks, "I knew he would be interested in Andy."

Andy starts out for Lydia's dorm at 6:45. At the moment, Andy has no clue what is coming over the horizon, except for Lydia. His long stride takes him at a fast pace across the campus. As the sun sets,

Andy notices the rays peering through the branches. He enjoys the many trees on the campus. It's already cooler than two hours ago. He wears his grey Boilermaker sweatshirt and looks very much like a top collegiate athlete.

Lydia's dorm is part of the new dorm complex on campus. He finds the Emily Charles Dorm, and as he walks to the front doors, he sees Lydia coming out. He can't believe how beautiful she is. Her bright smile radiates through the shadows that are falling on campus. Her lustrous blonde hair is even more beguiling with her forest green Chenille sweater and her navy slacks. Andy is so taken that he only comes up with, "You look nice."

Lydia laughs and says, "You look good too."

Andy is too self-conscious to hug her or to tell her how good she really looks.

Lydia breaks the ice by saying, "So, how tall are you, Andy?"

"Sometimes I feel a lot taller than I am, but I'm 6'5".

Lydia says, "I understand. If I were 6'5", I would feel taller than everyone."

Andy says, "That's another good thing about basketball, because some of the players are 6'7" to 7 feet."

Lydia says, "Wow, that's hard to imagine. My dad is 5'10"; my mom is 5'3" and I'm 5'4"."

Andy smiles and says, "5'4" is good. I like your height."

"Well, frankly, Andy, I like your height too. You probably know that a lot of Dutch people are tall, but the height doesn't run in our family. I guess I've always noticed tall people."

Andy says, "Yeah, they're hard to miss."

They arrive at the Student Center in time to go through the line and pay for soda and ice cream. Lydia says, "I'm glad we could order the ice cream tonight, instead of getting it from the cooler."

Andy says, "You've got that right. It's hard to beat vanilla and chocolate mixed together. It looks like you also like cherry cola."

Lydia says, "I sure do, big boy."

Andy thinks to himself, "A pet name; that's a good sign." He says, "When we met this evening, I really meant to tell you that you look real good."

Lydia laughs and says, "I thought so. I could see it in your eyes."

Now Andy is thinking, "She must like me." He asks, "What does your dad do?"

Lydia replies, "He Is a pastor at a Dutch Reformed Church in Rotterdam, where I'm from. He went to the Theological University of the Reformed Churches in Kampen, Holland."

Andy said, "Church has always been important to my family. In Muncie, where I was born, and in Mahican, where I'm from, we have always gone to an evangelical church."

"Are both towns in Indiana?"

Andy says, "Yes, they're both in Central Indiana. My dad is a toolmaker in an auto plant. You probably guessed that most of my ancestry is Scottish. My last name, McGraig, is Scottish and Welsh. My first name and my parent's names, Owen and Davina, are Scottish."

Lydia says, "Yes, when I met you, I thought your name was Scottish. I wanted to tell you, Andy, that two of my friends at the dorm and I plan to see your pre-season game."

Andy replies, "That's great. My parents and sister will be there. I'm going to ask them to wait around in the arena, and I'll meet them on the floor after I finish in the locker room. Maybe you and your friends could do the same. I'm planning to spend the weekend with my family, but I'll be back late Sunday afternoon."

Lydia says, "I would like that. It will be nice to meet your family. We have almost two weeks left before the game. Will I see you again before the game?"

Andy lights up and says, "How often?"

As Lydia laughs, Andy thinks, "I've never seen such a beautiful woman." Lydia says, "Well, not every evening, but we'll work it out."

Andy says, "Tell me about your college plans and after college."

"At church, I think I told you that I'm considering teaching. I'm using my freshman year to look at my options. I've thought about teaching kindergarten or first grade. I've also thought about being a school counselor."

Andy replies, "Those are good goals. Some day you might be a principal of an elementary or secondary school. Are you thinking about going back to Holland or staying in America?"

Lydia says, "I plan to stay here. My parents love America. They haven't seen it yet, but my dad refers to the United States as the greatest country in the world. He tells everyone that America saved the Netherlands and the world from Nazi Germany."

Andy asks, "What was your dad doing, when the Nazis occupied Holland?"

Lydia says, "He was 21 and had just enrolled at the seminary in Kampen. The Nazis started occupying the Netherlands in May of 1940. They gave dad and some of the other seminary students a choice to be a medic in the Netherlands for the German troops and the conscripted Dutch troops or prison. He chose not to go to prison, but he became part of the Dutch underground. They were involved with Dutch resistance and helped save up to 25,000 Jews from the German Nazis."

"I know you're proud of your dad. The war was a terrible thing, but there were a lot of heroes. My dad volunteered for the army, but he was deaf in one ear from a mastoid, childhood ear infection. He made bombs in a converted factory, near our neighborhood. My dad is the same age as your dad. Since it's a school night, I shouldn't keep you up late, but could you tell me more about your parents on the way back to your dorm?"

Lydia says, "Sure I will."

As they walk out of the Student Center dining area, Andy holds the door for Lydia. Outside Lydia says, "Mother is a beautiful and caring lady. She mostly cares for the family, house and yard. She is very supportive of my dad and me. She is also a very active volunteer at our church. Sometimes the church puts her on part-time payroll, because they are short of help. Mom and dad don't know if they will stay in Holland, when they retire, or come to America. They assume that I will become an American citizen."

Andy says, "Do a lot of people in the Netherlands feel about America the way your father does?"

Lydia says, "Most people I know feel the same way. Dad says that Great Britain and Russia would not have won against Germany and their ally, Japan, without America. He is emphatic about America being the reason that Germany and Japan were defeated.

He believes that America is great, not only because of their victory over Germany and Japan, but also because of their mission work and charity throughout the world. I agree with him. It really is the land of opportunity."

Andy says, "That's right. Our ancestors, who became legal immigrants, believed the same thing. I'm concerned about the growing number of illegal immigrants crossing the southern border. We don't know who they are, and there is an increase of drug contraband and other crime."

Lydia says, "I briefly heard about that."

They approach the front of Lydia's dorm, and Lydia stops walking before they get into the brighter lights close to the front door. She looks up at Andy and says, "Andy, I'm surprised you didn't hold my hand on the way back to the dorm."

Andy blushes and is speechless for a second. Lydia laughs and says, "I'm just kidding with you." She steps toward Andy and leans up, and he bends over, and while they hug, Lydia kisses him on the cheek. She says, "Thank you for a very nice evening."

Andy gets out, "You're welcome. Thank you." He watches her as she walks to the front door. Just as she opens the door, she turns around and waves at Andy. When she enters her dorm lobby, a friend of hers is watching television. She asks, "How was your date?' Lydia says, "He was a perfect gentleman."

As Andy walks toward his dorm, he thinks, "I'm totally infatuated with her." He looks up at the stars and says, "Thank you, God, for letting me meet Lydia."

When he gets back to his room, he reaches for his calendar book before he finishes his studies. On today's date, he writes: first date with Lydia. He flips through a couple pages to October 27th, when they play their first game. He sees that the first game is less than two weeks away. He thinks, "I can't believe that it will be just a week from Friday."

Even though it's 9:00 already, he only has two reading assignments left. He's finished with them by 10:00. He turns out the lights and goes to bed. The only thing he can think about is Lydia. As he falls asleep, he thinks about seeing the blue orb of light around Lydia, when he talked with her this evening.

After Andy showers and eats breakfast, he starts thinking about the game being less than two weeks away. His International Economics class is first today. After class is over, Dr. Krause asks Andy to wait a couple minutes. After the class room clears, Dr. Krause says, "Andy, I had a conversation with a State Department official about you and what you told me. This official has to come to this general area in roughly a month on business. Before he goes back to D.C. he wants to meet you. Keep the details confidential, as I update you."

Andy is stunned; he says, "Really?"

Dr. Krause says, "I think he is interested in you. Anytime you have questions or want to talk, call me at one of these two numbers. Also, you may want to read up on the State Department."

As Andy takes the two numbers from Dr. Krause, he says, "Well, all I can say now is thank you for your interest."

Dr. Krause says, "You're quite welcome. Just remember, if anything is on your mind, I want you to call me."

Andy walks outdoors into the crisp and sunny October day. He feels honored that Dr. Krause and the State Department show an interest in him. Since he doesn't know any details yet, his mind is on the approaching game and Lydia. He has already mailed the tickets to his family, and Lydia is getting her tickets with her friends. He doesn't want to forget anything, because he'll be busy with practice and studying. He decides to call Lydia this evening.

Practice still begins at 4:00. Andy and his teammates work hard. It seems to Andy that Larry, Jack and he are stepping up in anticipation of the game. After practice he tells Larry and Jack, "Good job, guys. We have eight more practices before the first game, but I think we're almost ready."

Larry says, "Man, Ball State is gonna be feelin' Purdue."

Jack laughs and says, "That's my sentiment as well."

The three of them have supper at the Student Center, and they have a good time talking about their team and their high school glory days. As they get ready to go back to their dorms, Andy says, "Don't get so excited about the first game that you forget about your studies."

Larry says, "Did you have to remind us?"

On the way back to his dorm, Andy decides to call Lydia first thing. It's already 6:30. He figures he'll still have time to catch Huntley and Brinkley. He walks into the dorm's phone room, and talks with Lydia until almost 7:00. Before they hang up, Lydia says, "My friends and I are looking forward to seeing you play next Friday."

Andy says, "I hope you're not disappointed."

Lydia laughs and says, "You haven't disappointed me yet."

Andy says, "Let me continue my good record with a date before the weekend."

Lydia says, "I'm counting on that. Maybe we can get together a couple times before next week."

They say goodnight, and Andy is beside himself. He thinks, "Now I understand the expression of falling for someone. It's like a force that knocks you to the floor." He has a few seconds to spare, when Huntley and Brinkley come on the air.

Andy is glad that the next few days go by quickly. He has plans to see Lydia on Friday. After seeing a new movie, "The Absent Minded Professor", Lydia says, "What a hoot; I always liked Fred McMurray. I've seen him in Holland."

Andy says, "What a funny movie!"

They take a walk on campus. It's a clear night and sweater weather. After they're a block from the theater, Andy takes Lydia's hand, and she looks up at him and smiles. When they get to a more scenic part of the campus, there are a few benches and hardly no one is walking by. Andy says, "Do you want to sit here for a few minutes? Lydia says, "Sure."

After they sit next to each other and talk a minute, Andy puts his arm around her. Lydia stops talking and just looks up at him and smiles. Andy leans over and kisses her. He feels like he has reached a milestone in his life. Andy says, "I could do this the rest of my life." Lydia snuggles close to him and says, "Maybe we can."

The Student Center is open late on Friday night. They get some ice cream, then Andy walks Lydia back to her dorm. They stop in the same area as the first night. While they hug each other, Andy says, "I'll call you tomorrow, so we can make plans by Sunday." He kisses her, and Lydia hugs him another minute. They say goodnight, and Andy walks back to his dorm. He thinks, "I'll always remember October of 1961."

After church on Sunday, Andy and Lydia go on a picnic. They prepared everything on Saturday. Fortunately, one of Lydia's friends at her dorm has a car. Her friend, Tracy, wants to go hiking on the nature trails after church. She offers Lydia and Andy a ride. The park in West Lafayette is connected to the nature trails. When they get to the park, Andy says, "Tracy, have lunch with us before your hike."

Tracy says, "No, I'm not hungry now. Save me some leftovers, and I'll be back in an hour. If I'm not back by 2:00, come and look for me." Tracy takes off for the trails, and Andy and Lydia enjoy their picnic with a red and white checkered tablecloth and all the trimmings.

After they start eating, Andy says, "Are you familiar with Chevrolet at all?"

Lydia says, "Yes, we have Chevrolets in Rotterdam."

Andy says, "Do you happen to know what the 1955 Bel Air looks like?"

Lydia says, "Do I? My dad has a parishioner that has a blue and white one; it's beautiful."

Andy says, "That's exactly like my dad's car. He is getting a new car through his factory by spring or summer, and he's giving me the '55 Chevy!"

Lydia exclaims, "What do American's say….? Blow my socks off?"

Andy laughs and says, "That's the right expression".

Before they know it, an hour goes by, and Tracy is back; hungry and sweaty. She says, "Do you have any leftovers?"

Lydia says, "Dig in, girl."

They laugh about how hungry Tracy is. Andy says, "I'll get your drink."

By 2:30, they pack up and head back to the girls' dorm. Andy thanks Tracy, and Andy and Lydia find a semi-secluded bench near the back of the dorm. They talk and kiss a few minutes, then Andy says, "Yesterday I lifted weights and studied, but I need to get back and run two miles, and finish my studies."

Lydia says, "Will I see you before the game?"

Andy asks, "Can we get together Wednesday evening?"

Lydia says, "I'll be waiting on you."

Andy kisses her again and walks her to the front door.

Andy purposely has not told Lydia anything about the State Department, since he doesn't know any details himself. He decides to call his mom this evening, and just tell her that he has an important meeting next month.

Monday through Thursday, Andy, Jack and Larry are especially focused during the practices. After the Thursday practice, the coach even tells the three that they're doing well. Coach Brown tells Andy that he is planning to play him for most of the game as power forward and small forward. The coach tells the team to report to the locker room just before 6:30. He says anyone that walks in after 6:30 will be fined. He explains that they will have a short meeting, then warm up with stretches and shooting.

Andy walks to the cafeteria, and thinks about his date with Lydia last night. He also thinks about getting to rest until game time. Andy is glad there is no working out tomorrow. He thinks, "The game will be a great workout."

Andy meets with the coach and team by 6:30. The coach has a short meeting with them, then they dress for the game. They go out on the floor and do stretches. They practice foul shots; driving to the basket and perimeter shots. By 7:15, the Boilermaker Arena starts filling up. Andy's team and the Ball State team go to their respective benches by 7:20. Coach Brown goes over general strategy and a few key plays. He starts Andy at small forward and the senior at power forward. He starts Jack at point guard and the senior at shooting guard. He starts the senior at center with the understanding that Larry will be playing for at least half the game.

The Purdue band plays after they introduce the Boilermakers. The announcer welcomes the Ball State team and announces the starting five of each team. Ball State has a fairly good center, and they get the tip. They miss their first shot, and Andy tears down the rebound. The crowd gives a thunderous cheer.

After two minutes of play, Purdue leads by five points. Andy plays like a fine tuned machine. He dominates in every way. He rebounds, dunks, blocks shots, assists and scores nine points by the end of the first quarter. The coach rests him for two minutes at the beginning of the second quarter. When Andy is put back in the game at power forward, Purdue is ahead by six points. Every time Andy gets the ball, the crowd roars. Right after the coach puts Andy in, he puts Larry in at center. Larry is able to keep the Ball State's 6'10" center from scoring much, and Andy is at the top of his game. By half time, the score is Purdue 44 and Ball State 31. The crowd goes wild, when the Boilermakers go to the locker room. They start yelling, "McGraig, McGraig, McGraig". Jack smiles at Andy and says, "They like you."

Andy says, "You're doing well yourself."

During the second half, the coach plays Larry as much as the starting senior. He keeps Andy at power forward, and has the senior play small forward. Andy, Jack and Larry dominate the game. The final score is Purdue 93 and Ball State 68. Jack scores 21 and Larry scores 17. Andy has a triple double; he scores 28; has 14 rebounds and has 10 assists. Andy becomes an overnight sensation for the Boilermakers.

The team goes to the showers, and the coach congratulates the whole team. He says, "I'm looking forward to a great season. Keep it up."

Lydia notices where the team exits after the game. She tells her friends that she is going to try to catch Andy, when he comes back. She waits at the exit, and when she sees Andy, she runs and hugs him, and gives him a kiss. Lydia says, "Purdue has a new hero." Andy just laughs.

He says, "Thanks for meeting me here. Let's look for my family. He looks and says, "There they are; on the other side of the floor." He yells at them, and they walk across the floor to greet each other. Andy hugs his mom, and his dad pats him on the back, and says, "You did a great job, Andy."

Judy hugs him and says, "You're the best."

Andy has Lydia by his side and says to his family, "I want you to meet Lydia. Lydia, this is my mother, Davina; my dad, Owen, and my sister, Judy."

Judy says, "You're beautiful."

Lydia laughs and says, "You and your mother are beautiful too, and your dad is handsome."

Andy looks at Lydia and says, "I know my family will want to get home soon. May we take you to the dorm?"

Lydia says, "Thank you, but Tracy and Jean are going to walk back with me." Lydia points to them at the sideline.

Andy looks at them and waves. Tracy yells, "You were wonderful!"

Andy yells, "Thank you, Tracy."

Andy looks at Lydia and says, "Thanks for coming. I'll see you Sunday evening."

They hug each other, and Andy goes back to Mahican with his family.

It's 11:30 when they get home, and Judy wakes up after sleeping most of the way home. When they get in the house, Owen says, "I'm getting ready for bed, then I'll say goodnight to Judy."

Andy says, "Goodnight, dad. Thanks for coming to the game."

Owen says, "You were on fire. I thoroughly enjoyed the game."

Davina asks, "Andy, do you want some coffee or anything?"

Andy says, "I'm still hungry from the game."

Davina replies, "I'll make you an egg sandwich." She also makes a small pot of coffee.

Andy sits down at the kitchen table and says, "Mom, even though I can't say much about the meeting next month, I will tell you in confidence, who it is with."

Davina says, "Is it with someone from the State Department?"

Andy says, "How do you know?"

"Dr. Krause told me, and he said it is confidential. Only your dad and I know, and that is all we know."

Andy says, "I don't know much more."

Davina says, "They're interested in you and your gifts. Not to rehash, Andy, but don't say anything specific about your gifts."

Andy replies, "I won't, mom, and I don't mind you reminding me."

Davina says, "If you're interested in the State Department after the meeting, please finish college first."

Andy says, "I plan to. I'm enjoying Purdue. I want to stay four years."

Davina wisely says with a smile, "Do you enjoy Purdue more, since you met Lydia?"

"Definitely."

Davina says, "She's a beautiful girl and seems like a nice person."

Andy finishes the egg sandwich and says, "She's very nice, and has a great personality. After I finish this cup of coffee, I need to go to bed. I'll tell you about her and her family tomorrow." Andy picks up his cup of coffee and kisses his mom on the check.

Davina says, "Good night, son. It's wonderful having you here this weekend."

After a restful night, Owen comes in Andy's room and says, "Breakfast is ready; it's almost 8:00."

Andy opens his eyes and thinks, "I can't believe I slept eight hours." He smells the bacon and immediately gets up and heads to the bathroom. He comes out to the kitchen and says, "My favorite: bacon, eggs and toast." Davina says, "Have a seat, and dad will say the prayer."

Davina serves the breakfast, then sits down and says, "How would everyone like to go to Hartford City and go bowling with Edward, Ella and Anderson?"

Andy says, "Anderson will be there?"

Davina says, "Yes, and Ella says that they have a special announcement."

Andy says, "Are they going to adopt Judy?" Everyone laughs and Judy says, "Only if you're part of the package."

Davina adds, "We're going to bowl about 11; after the leagues finish. When we leave the bowling alley, Ella and Edward are going to take us out to eat at Richards Restaurant."

Owen says, "It must be a big announcement for Ella not to cook."

Davina says, "After breakfast we need to hurry, so we can leave by 9."

On the way to Ella's and Edward's in Hartford City, Andy tells his family about Lydia and her parents in Holland. He says, "When I first saw her at church, I knew she was special."

Owen says, "Outside of your mother, she's the most beautiful woman I've seen."

Andy says, "Exactly, dad." As they drive through the country on highway 26, the majestic fields of tall, light brown corn stalks are ready for harvest. The fall colors of gold, brown, red and yellow have filled the trees and given the McGraigs a pleasant autumn trip.

They pull in front of 909 E. Franklin by 11:00. Ella and Edward walk out to meet them, and behind them are Anderson and a young woman they haven't met. By the gate of their white picket fence, they hug each other and Anderson says, "We couldn't wait any longer to make the announcement. This is Ruth. We met at Purdue, and we've been dating two years. We just got engaged!"

Ruth is all smiles. She has a demure persona. She's a cute brunette and appears to be a very kind and considerate person. The McGraigss hug her and welcome her to the family.

When they arrive at the bowling alley, a lot of the people in the bowling league are already getting in their cars. When they rent their bowling shoes, Andy gets a size 13, and Anderson gets a size 12 ½ to support his 6'3" frame. As they put on their shoes. Anderson looks at Andy and says, "Cousin, are you still growing?'

Andy laughs and says, "I'm still eating Cheerios."

After bowling three games, Ella and Edward buy everyone dinner at Richards to celebrate Anderson's and Ruth's engagement.

During their drive to Carl and Thelma's house in Muncie, they talk about their relatives, and Andy says, "I'm looking forward to seeing my old friends at church tomorrow." The rest of the trip, Andy thinks about Lydia.

On Sunday morning they park on the street, near the church. Ball State crosses Andy's mind, since the heart of the campus is less than a mile away. While they walk to the side entrance of the church, Andy says, "Do you think any die hard Ball State fans will shoot me, when I walk in?"

Judy laughs and says, "When they see you, they'll probably run. While they greet their friends, several of his friends congratulate Andy on his win. Paul, one of his older friends and the church custodian, says, "Andy, you played a great game. I'm proud of you." Andy thanks Paul, and thinks that he and his wife, Desi, are two of the sweetest people he has ever known.

After the service, they talk with Carl, his wife and two daughters, four of their closest church friends. Andy hugs Thelma, Nora and Elsie and shakes Carl's hand. Carl says, "Andy, you put a real beating on Ball State, but I'm glad for you and Purdue. Keep on winning; I always root for you."

Andy shakes his hand again and says, “Thank you, Carl. I’ve always thought a lot of you.” They walk back to their car, and Andy thinks about how much the church and the loving and caring people mean to him. On their way back to Mahican, Andy says, “It was great seeing everyone again. When I come back, I realize how much I miss them.”

Davina says, “Life is like that. I lost my favorite aunt a few years ago, and the more time goes on, the more I realize how much I miss her.”

Andy says, “Sometimes I dislike going back to school, because I leave my friends and family behind.”

Davina says, “Andy, that’s part of life. We travel on and miss some of the stops behind us. I even miss my childhood at times, because I have such loving parents and pleasant memories.”

Andy says, “I know what you mean. I’ve also been fortunate at Purdue. Jack and Larry are already good friends. I have a good coach, and Dr. Krause has been a great professor. It’s hard to say how much Lydia already means to me.”

Judy says, “I would love to get to know her.”

Andy says, “You will.”

As promised, they get Andy back to Purdue by 5:00. Owen gets out of the car and says, “Son, I can’t tell you how proud I am of you, and how much I love you.”

Andy says, “I feel the same about you, dad. You have always shown how much you care.” Andy hugs his mom and sister. He hates to see them drive off, but at the same time, he feels blessed by being back on campus.

Andy goes to his room to check the game schedule. His first regular season game is at Wisconsin on November 8th. He wonders when Dr. Krause will get the call from the State Department. He goes to the phone room to call Lydia and tells her that he will meet her at 7:00 at her dorm.

He has a brief but pleasant time with Lydia. He’s back in his room by 8:30, since he has two hours of study before he can go to bed. He continues to enjoy his classes, and Dr. Krause is exceptionally friendly. He’s so busy that he has difficulty keeping up with his weight-lifting and running regime. He's glad that the team is getting stronger.

The first three games of the season are all wins. The Boilermakers won at Wisconsin and Notre Dame, and they beat Michigan State at home. They play Indiana University next month. Andy feels that game will be their first, real big challenge.

Two weeks before Thanksgiving, Andy finally hears from Dr. Krause about the meeting with the State Department. Dr. Krause says, "Andy, the State Department official has a meeting in Chicago early next week. On Wednesday he wants to leave Chicago and meet you in my office around 6:00 Wednesday evening.

Andy says, "That's good news, but 6:00 cuts it a little short with the end of our team practice."

Dr. Krause says, "Don't worry about that. Coach Brown will let you hit the shower early. I'll tell him that you have to finish practice thirty minutes early, so you can make a required meeting."

Andy says, "Thank you. Do I need to dress up or bring anything?"

"No, he expects to meet a college student, and he knows you'll be coming to the meeting from practice. Just bring a notepad and a pen to take any needed notes."

Andy says, "Thanks again, Dr. Krause. I'll be at your office by 6:00 next Wednesday."

Dr. Krause says, "You're welcome. By the way, congratulations on your victories for Purdue. You've become a campus all-star."

"I enjoy it. Thanks for calling."

The American Association of Sports Writers have Purdue ranked fifteenth in the nation. They mention Andy McGraig as their lead player.

Even before practice on the day of the meeting, Andy feels a little anxious. The coach dismisses him early, and Andy guesses that he'll be at Dr. Krause's office a few minutes early. When he arrives, there are two healthy men in dark grey suits and black ties outside Dr. Krause's door. Andy instinctively feels he should identify himself, "I'm Andy McGraig. I have a 6:00 appointment."

One of the men in an unemotional voice says, "Go on in."

Dr. Krause is behind his desk and in front of the desk is a man that Andy thinks he recognizes. He's a big man, about 6 foot tall, overweight and distinguished looking. He says, "Good to meet you, Andy. I'm Jonathan Abernathy."

Andy is surprised and shakes his hand, "Good to meet you, Mr. Abernathy. I recognize you from your pictures. I had no idea that I would get to meet the Secretary of State."

Mr. Abernathy lets out a hearty laugh. "We really didn't want you to know, and it is confidential that we met under these circumstances."

Andy says, "Yes, sir. It's confidential."

Dr. Krause says, "I'm going to let you talk. I'm going to the Student Center to get some coffee and catch up on some reading. Jonathan, do you want me to call before I come back?"

Secretary Abernathy says, "No, Herb. About 6:45 could you bring us two coffees?"

Dr. Krause says, "Be glad to."

The head of the State Department goes around to Dr. Krause's chair and pulls out a note pad. He says, "Have a seat, Andy. How is Purdue doing in the standings?'

Andy says, "Right now, we're ranked fifteenth in the nation."

"Excellent. I'll be blunt, Andy, since we don't have a lot of time during this meeting. We don't have routine meetings like this with college students. The State Department and I are interested in you, because Dr. Krause told us about your high IQ, your work ethic and your academic achievements. He also said that you're a strong athlete. You're certainly bigger than a lot of our security men. Herb also said that you seem to have a proclivity for discernment. Can you tell me about it?"

Andy says, "Most of my life, I've had a sense about some things, that weren't apparent to most people. I can't explain it. I just know."

The Secretary says, "That's fine. You don't need to explain it. If you have special insight, you would be an excellent asset to the State Department. Even without that, we would still be interested in you. I have thought about how we could use your talents. I understand you want to graduate before you choose a career?"

Andy says, "Yes, sir."

The Secretary continues, "We would compensate you well. I understand that the NBA will be interested in drafting you. If we offer you the right employment package, do you think you would choose government work over the NBA?"

Andy replies, "Yes, I would probably choose the State Department over most opportunities, because of my interest in national and international affairs."

Mr. Abernathy says, "I'm glad to hear that. I've been Secretary three years, and I think I may be serving longer than a lot of Secretaries. One of my main assistants is a career State man, and he will also know about you. Like I said, I'll be blunt. I have in mind an important advisory position for you. I'm thinking that your situation will be different, because of your talents. If you're interested, we will train you as a security agent, who will actually be an undercover advisor."

Andy says, "I believe that is a good plan. I believe that is a good fit for me."

"Your athleticism will be an excellent background for the agent training. Do you have any problems with learning martial arts or handling guns?"

Andy says, "No."

"I'm going to review these things with my career assistant, and I will be getting back with you. We will try to make a decision before the end of the year, because I would want you to do agent training for four weeks this summer. It begins the second week of June. Are you willing to do the training?"

"Yes, sir. I hope there would be time for me to do weight lifting and running there."

The Secretary says, "Yes, there is required running, and I will tell the head trainer you need time for weight training. Is an hour every other day enough time?"

Andy replies, "Yes, sir."

"Andy, you will be well paid. It might run just a few days longer than four weeks, because my assistant or I will want to work with you on some non-classified political scenarios. In less than five weeks, you will make more than most summer jobs in three months. To give you an idea, I could have $250 per week budgeted for you, plus your travel expenses."

Andy says, "Thank you."

"Also, after your four weeks of training, we can classify you as a deputy security agent, which is an agent in training. The training we will give you the following summer will classify you as a part-time security agent for the State Department. The training you'll receive is very similar to the Secret Service Training."

Andy says, "It all sounds good. If I go with the State Department after graduation, can they match the NBA entry level salary?"

The Secretary says, "I'm sure we can. If you stay with us, you will also get more than adequate raises. Take care of yourself, Andy. There is a possibility that you will play a major role in the security of your nation."

As Andy says, "I will be looking forward to hearing from you by the end of the year." There is a knock on the door, and Dr. Krause comes in with two cups of coffee.

Mr. Abernathy says, "Perfect timing, Herb. We were just finishing. Andy, its good meeting with you. I enjoyed our talk."

Andy replies, "It's my honor, Mr. Abernathy. Thank you for your time."

After Andy leaves, the Secretary of State says, "Herb, it looks like things will work out with Andy. I want to thank you for your time and input. Do we still have you on retainer as an advisor?"

Dr. Krause says, "Only a nominal annual retainer."

Mr. Abernathy says, "Is that the meager $300 retainer?"

"Yes."

The Secretary says, "You've been a great help by telling me about Andy. I would like to put you back on the monthly advisor retainer. Could you stay in touch with Andy while he is at Purdue? Maybe invite him over to dinner every two months, and his girlfriend, if he has one."

Dr. Krause says, "I would be glad to."

Mr. Abernathy says, "Good. I'll tell our budget department to send you the $300 per month retainer. Be sure to let me know, anytime you have good advice."

Dr. Krause says, "Thank you for meeting with Andy. He will do an excellent job."

9

Martial Arts and Liberal Arts

After Thanksgiving the Boilermakers step up their practices. They have a heavy schedule from now until Christmas break. Their game with IU is just two weeks away. Coach Brown got word that it will be nationally televised. Scouts are already beginning to look at Andy for the NBA.

On Monday evening after Thanksgiving, Lydia and Andy have supper together. Lydia asks, "Are you excited about the IU game?"

Andy replies, "I am. Coach Brown says the game will be nationally televised."

Lydia says exuberantly, "You'll become a household name!"

Andy whimsically says, "Yes, I know; me and Beaver Cleaver."

They both laugh, and they're both thinking, "If we were outside in a more secluded area, we would kiss right now."

Andy would love to spend more time with Lydia this evening, but he has a lot to study tonight, and he has to get enough sleep to stay in proper condition. They walk back to her dorm, and they find their sitting bench just a few yards from the dorm's back door. The evenings have gotten even cooler by the end of November. The Thanksgiving rains have past, and now the cold weather is starting to set in; all the more reason that that have to sit closer together. One kiss leads to another, then Andy stops and looks at Lydia and says, "We'll have to stop before we get to kiss #30."

Lydia laughs and says, "Who's counting?" They get up and Andy walks her to the door and with kiss #30, they say goodnight. As Andy walks off in the late autumn darkness, he thinks, "I'm getting to like this better than basketball practice."

Back at his dorm, he just misses Huntley and Brinkley, but he thinks, "I have to hit the books anyway. From 7:20 until 10:30, he does an assignment for every class; mostly reading the next chapter and taking notes. He also completes studying for a Biology quiz tomorrow. He makes sure another blanket is on the bed, and he turns the lights out a few minutes after 10:30.

He has another disturbing dream about violence in the streets, as well as violence from certain countries. Just before he wakes up at 6 am, in big letters he sees the word, S-E-P-T-E-M-B-E-R. He lies a few minutes and thinks about what he saw in the dream. He has the very same dream three nights in a row. On Thursday morning, he feels compelled to make an appointment with Dr. Krause after class ends.

He walks up to his professor's desk, and waits for him to finish his note. Dr. Krause looks up at Andy, and says, "Andy, how has your week been?"

Andy says, "It has been good, but for three nights in a row, I have seen something that I need to tell you about."

Dr. Krause says, "If you want to share it with me now, I have a two hour break before my next class. Please close the door, and pull up a chair."

Andy sits down by his desk and says, "Every morning for the last three mornings, I've had the same dream that ends at 6 am, when I wake up."

Dr. Krause reaches for a notepad. He opens it up and has pen in hand, "Okay, Andy, go ahead."

"The violence in the dream is more intense than the original dream I shared with you. It Is more like a violent battle, than protestors committing violence randomly. I see mortars going off and a profusion of automatic gun fire. People are killed and others are maimed and bleeding. Then the dream shifts; I see soldiers from Russia, Iran and North Korea, and they're standing at our southern border. As I see the foreigners at the border, I see masses of people with weapons walking from countries in Latin America. At the border, many of them are holding banners and signs that say, New Age Socialist Party. At the end of the dream, I see big letters that say, "S-E-P-T-E-M-B-E-R". Dr. Krause continues to write quickly but conscientiously after Andy finishes.

Andy waits for him to finish writing. After he finishes, he says,

"I believe I got everything, Andy. Let me read it back to you." As he reads his notes, only a couple times does Andy add a word or two. After the professor reads the notes, he leans back in his chair, and says, "Wow, what a report. With your permission, I'll leave a message for Mr. Abernathy. If he is not real busy, he'll probably call me back after five today."

Andy gets up and says, "Thank you for your help, Dr. Krause." Andy has two other classes, then practice at 4:00. Practicing with his team gets his mind off of other things. He has supper with Larry and Jack, then he rushes to his dorm to call Lydia.

Mr. Abernathy calls Dr. Krause at his home after supper. Mr. Abernathy says, "Herb, do you have anything from Andy?"

He says, "Yes, Jonathan. Just a second, and I'll get the information that Andy gave me today." He reads his notes, and there is no answer. Dr. Krause speaks louder, and says, "Jonathan are you there?"

In a few seconds, Mr. Abernathy says, "I'm sorry, Herb. What you read stunned me for a few seconds. Since our team has checked your lines at home and at your office, I can tell you in general that our intelligence is reporting the same type of information that Andy gave you. Our intelligence report is so serious that we are thinking about drafting qualified men, age 18 and over, by this summer. We're amazed about all the ramifications that the Socialist Party is connected to. I can't tell you anymore at this time, because it's classified."

Dr. Krause said, "I was astounded after Andy shared it with me."

"Herb, I want to think about flying Andy into D.C. during semester break. It will give us over a month to follow up on our intelligence. Don't say anything to him yet. If he asks about our conversation, tell him I appreciate him staying in touch with us. I want to talk with two of my assistants, and possibly the President. We might need Andy sooner than planned. I will probably get back with you by the Christmas holiday. When classes start again after your Christmas break, we'll probably talk to Andy. It would give him about three weeks to plan for the D.C. trip."

Dr. Krause says, "Okay, Jonathan. I'll stay in touch with Andy, and I'll wait on your call before I tell him anything."

By the first of December, the first snowfall of the season brightens the Purdue campus. One evening after supper, Lydia and Andy go outside to take in their own winter wonderland. Andy asks, "Do you get a lot of snow in Holland?"

Lydia says, "I've heard that central Indiana gets more snow than we do, but we have more mild weather. The hottest month is July, and the average high is 63 degrees. The coldest month is January, and the average high is 37 degrees."

Andy says, "Wow, the weather is mild there. You really don't have any hot weather."

Lydia says, "That's right. It's unusual to have a day that is over 80 degrees. Not to change the subject, but isn't the IU game about a week away?"

Andy jokingly says, "Don't remind me. I should get my beauty sleep between now and the game."

Lydia says, "Yes, you should. Those big muscles need their rest as well."

Andy says, "You think they're big?" He picks her up and spins her around. On the wet sidewalk, he almost loses his balance. They laugh, then they just look at each other before they start kissing."

Lydia stops and says, "We're not in our secluded spot, and you need your beauty sleep."

Andy says, "You're right, Miss Van Winkle."

Lydia says, "Oh, no; that's not my new nickname, is it?"

Andy replies, "No, that's just a reference to a lot of sleep; you know, Rip Van Winkle."

Lydia says, "Yes, I like the story. I think it is by Washington Irving. Rip Van Winkle lived in a Dutch village in America."

Andy says, "Yes, that's right. It's a great story."

The Boilermakers complete all of their practices before the IU game. The evening before the game Coach Brown says, "Okay, men, the big game is tomorrow, and you've done well in practice. Only do stretching between tonight and tomorrow night's game. I want your muscles loose, and your energy focused on the game. As you know, the game is televised. Does anyone have stage fright or camera jitters? If so, let's talk about it now. I don't want you to be distracted tomorrow night."

Coach Brown gives them a minute to collect their thoughts, when one of the players says, "What if we aren't worried now, but we get nervous when the game starts?"

The coach says, "If you start to get nervous tomorrow, I'll have the three biggest men on the team smack you around until you come out of it. Does that help?"

The player says, "Yes," then everyone laughs.

The coach says, "Alright, you men have worked hard, so get plenty of rest and protein. Tomorrow evening concentrate; work together as a team and enjoy the game. Report to the locker room at 6:15. We'll dress; shoot the ball; stretch and go to the bench by 7:20. Game starts at 7:30." The coach shouts, "Go, Boilermakers!"

The team in unison responds and shouts, "Go, Boilermakers!"

The next evening, by 7:15, the arena is packed out. The Boilermakers are at their bench by 7:20. The coach says, "Guys, it's a sold-out crowd. Go out there and show them what we're made of." The game is back and forth with the number two team in the nation. They have Don Bonan, Andy's old nemesis, and three of the best seniors in the nation. At half time it's IU 48 and Purdue 45.

The second half is also back and forth. Andy hits two points at the buzzer, and the game goes into overtime. During overtime, Larry fouls out, and IU wins 102 to 101. Andy is high scorer of the game; thirty-three points and fifteen rebounds. In the Boilermaker's locker room, you could hear a pin drip. Coach Brown says, "You played a well fought game. We'll get them next time."

After they shower, Jack says to Andy, "Well, next year, they won't have their three seniors. I know we'll beat them by then."

Andy says, "We'll beat them handily."

Jack asks, "What are your plans after the game?"

Andy replies, "My family didn't make the game, so Lydia and I are going to relax and take it easy for a couple of hours."

Jack says, "I hear that. Larry and I are going to "After Hours" in the Village and talk with some co-eds."

Andy smiles and says, "Will she be blonde, brunette or red-headed?"

Jack laughs and says, "I won't worry about that until I get there."

As they get ready to leave, Andy taps Jack on the shoulder and says, "Good game."

After the nationally televised IU game, all of the NBA scouts start watching Andy play.

When Andy picks up Lydia, they find they're both dressed in flannel and blue denim. They laugh and Lydia says, "Two blondes in blue". They both have green and blue in their flannel shirts.

Andy says, "They're the right clothes for a cold, snowy night."

As they go out the door and take hands, Lydia says, "You had a great game."

Andy says, "I have to admit that it felt good."

Lydia asks, "Where are you taking me?"

Andy replies, "Good question. Do you remember seeing the small café about a block from the movie theater?"

Lydia says, "Yes, I noticed it."

Andy says, "Larry and I went there one time, and found that it's a neat, comfy spot. The food is also good. Don't laugh; I had hot chocolate and a grilled ham and cheese sandwich, and it was delicious."

Lydia's blue eyes light up as she looks at Andy and says, "Believe it or not, I like the same thing. Don't laugh, and I'll tell you how to say, "hot chocolate" in Dutch: "warme chocolademelk".

Andy says, "That makes sense; sort of a cross between English and German. You probably know that the English language came from the Germans."

Lydia replies, "Yes, I've heard that."

When they open the café door, a small bell rings at the top of the door. The owner/waitress, an older rotund lady with a smile from ear to ear, rings out, "Good evening, friends. Pick the table of your choice. What can I bring you to drink?"

Andy says, "Two cups of hot chocolate with marshmallows."

About three minutes later she brings the drinks and says, "My name is Annie, and I'll be serving you tonight." Annie looks at Lydia and says, "Where did you find such a big boyfriend?"

Lydia smiles and says, "He's on the Purdue basketball team, and he's spoken for."

Annie lets out a loud laugh and says, "Honey, I would be too much woman for him!"

They all laugh, and Andy orders two grilled ham and cheese sandwiches with dill pickle and mustard."

As Annie lumbers back to the kitchen, Andy says, "She's a hoot."

Lydia says, "She reminds me of some of our older Dutch women."

Andy says, "I spoke to my mom about Christmas vacation. We want to know, if you have any plans for Christmas break?"

Lydia says, "No, I won't see my parents in until this summer."

Andy says, "My dad is going to pick me up for Christmas break. Would you like to spend Christmas with us?"

Lydia reaches out and touches Andy's arm and says, "I would love to."

Andy says, "You'll get to see the metropolis of Mahican, Indiana, and Judy has been wanting to spend some time with you. Mom will fix a bed for you in her room."

Lydia says, "You're sweet." She leans over and kisses him.

Annie brings the sandwiches with potato chips. "There you are my young friends. Do you need anything else?"

Andy says, "A little later, we'll get some more hot chocolate."

Annie says, "Okay, sweetie; that will be on the house."

A few seconds later, Lydia says, "I think she likes you."

Andy is amused and says, "I wouldn't know where to hide her."

After two rounds of hot chocolate, Andy pays Annie and gives her a good tip. Lydia says, "Thanks, Annie, for being a sweet hostess."

Annie says, "Anytime, my young friends. Come back soon."

Outside Andy says, "My young friend, this cold weather wakes us up fast."

Lydia says, "When we get back to the dorm, I better go right to my room, because you've had a busy day and a big game."

Andy says, "Right now, I'm wide awake, but I am tired." He looks at his watch and says, "Wow, its 11:30 already. Annie must have stayed open for us."

Andy walks Lydia to the front door and gives her a good night kiss. He says, "I'll call you tomorrow, and I'll see you in church Sunday." He stops talking a second and just looks at her.

Lydia says, "What's wrong?"

Andy replies, "I almost said, "I love you."

Lydia smiles; gives him another kiss and says, "You can tell me that, anytime."

Andy walks back to his dorm and thinks, "Now I know what they mean by, "being on Cloud Nine".

When Christmas break begins, Purdue is ranked 11th in the nation, and their record is 19 and 3. Owen picks up Andy first, then they drive to Lydia's dorm. Andy loads Lydia's luggage, and they take off for Mahican.

On the way, Owen says, "A few days ago, one of the managers from our office said they're almost to my name on the dealer's car list."

Andy says, "That's great news. Does that mean you'll get the new car by spring?"

Owen says, "It looks that way. It will probably be a 1961 Bel Air, but I don't know about the color."

Andy says, "I told Lydia where this car is going."

Owen smiles and says, "You can count on it."

Lydia enjoys the whole Christmas vacation. Judy gets out the family album and shows her Andy as a child. She also tells Lydia about the polio she had. Lydia enjoys the times that they go to their home church. She especially admires Davina. She thinks of her as the kind and lovely lady. She also gets to meet Edward, Ella, Anderson and his fiancée, Ruth.

On New Year's Eve, they celebrate with Nehi and popcorn. Everyone is in a festive mood, and they play table games, including Yahtzee. At midnight, they blow on noise makers and give out hugs. Owen takes Davina in his arms; kisses her; wishes her a Happy New Year and says, "I can't believe its 1962 already."

During her last day with the McGraigs, Lydia says, "Judy, have you thought about what career you want, and where you want to go to college?"

Judy says, "Yes, I want to go to the Purdue Business School. I'm interested in math. I've thought about being a CPA, math professor or entrepreneur."

Lydia says, "I'm impressed. Both the brother and sister are bright people."

Andy drives the '55 Chevy back to campus with Lydia and his family. He says, "Dad, I'll stop at my dorm first, and wait on me. I'll take my suitcase to my room, then I'll go with you to Lydia's dorm."

Judy ribs Andy and says, "Don't forget, big brother, you usually study on Sunday evening."

Andy says, "Children should be seen and not heard."

Lydia laughs at both of them. Davina says, "You can see what mothers go through."

When they get to Lydia's dorm, Lydia gives everyone a hug. As they drive off, Owen honks and everyone waves.

Lydia says, "What a wonderful family."

Andy puts his arm around her and says, "I'm blessed."

They hang out at the dorm and student center for a couple hours. Andy says, "Even though it's only 7:30, I think I'll walk you back to your dorm. I don't have any studies tonight, but I would like to catch up on some of my current events reading."

Lydia says, "I understand. I know that is also part of your life."

As they walk hand in hand back to Lydia's dorm, Andy says, "You know, Lydia, I really do love you."

Lydia looks at him and says, "I love you, too."

Andy gets a serious look on his face and says, "Lydia, I realize that most college students get married after they graduate, but if circumstances change, would you be interested in marriage sooner?"

Lydia smiles and says, "Andy, I would go with you anywhere. When the right time comes, put a ring on my finger and we'll be a team."

Andy stops; puts his hands on her arms and says, "That's all I wanted to know," and he leans down and kisses her.

She says, "By the way, Andy. Do you know something I don't know?"

He smiles with confidence and says, "I might."

Back in his room for the rest of the evening, Andy reads and thinks about Lydia. He thinks and prays, "I honestly hope, Lord, I don't have any premonition dreams tonight." He has a peaceful evening.

The second week of January, Jonathan Abernathy calls Dr. Krause. He says, "Herb, this is Jonathan. I talked with my main assistant and one of the President's main advisors, who is a member of the Traditional American Party. We've made arrangements for Andy to come to D.C. during semester break. Confidentially, I wanted you to know that I will call him this evening, and his trip is from January 26th to January 28th. If he has a schedule conflict, please take of it for him."

Dr. Krause says, "Will do. I know that things are moving fast for Andy, but Uncle Sam has needs."

Mr. Abernathy says, "Yes, Herb. Andy will be well compensated and taken care of. I need a favor, Herb. I have to talk to Andy on a secure line this evening. Could you have him over for supper this evening, then I could call between 6:30 and 7:00?"

Dr. Krause says, "I think he'll be at the gym for practice. I'll go back and pick him up around 5:30, when they finish practice. Could you call closer to 7:00?'

Mr. Abernathy replies, "That will be fine. Thanks again, Herb."

At 3:30, Dr. Krause starts walking to the gym. He sees Andy just before he goes in the locker room. Andy says, "Dr. Krause, I didn't expect to see you here."

Dr. Krause says, "Andy, let's walk down the corridor for just a couple minutes. I would like for you to have supper with my wife and me after practice this evening. You'll be getting an important call about 7:00. Outside this door at 5:30, I'll be in my car, a green Pontiac Catalina."

Andy says, "Okay, Dr. Krause, but I'll be done in the locker room about 5:40."

Dr. Krause says, "That's fine, Andy. Have a good practice; see you then."

Dr. Krause pulls up at 5:30; turns out the headlights, but leaves the car running to keep the heat on. Andy walks up to the car with his gym bag, exactly ten minutes later.

When he gets in, Dr. Krause says, "Thanks for coming over."

Andy says, "It's nice to look forward to a home cooked meal. What is the call about, Dr. Krause?"

As they drive off, Dr. Krause says, "Mr. Abernathy is going to call you."

Less than a mile from campus, they pull up to an elegant home with dormers and ivy at the corners of the second story. They walk through the front door, where Mrs. Krause greets them. Dr. Krause says, "Honey, this is Andy McGraig."

Mrs. Krause says, "Good to meet you, Andy. I'm Doris."

Andy says, "Thank you for the dinner invitation."

She says, "How does pork chops, mash potatoes and gravy with green beans, and peach cobbler for dessert sound? Do you like milk, water or coffee?"

Andy says, "That's very appetizing. Could I start with milk, and maybe finish with coffee?"

She says, "It will be ready in five minutes."

Dr. Krause looks at his watch. He says, "Let's sit down here in the living room, Andy. Do you need the bathroom or anything?"

Andy says, "I'll wash my hands now, and come right back."

"The bathroom is down the hall and the second door on the right."

Andy comes back in the room about a minute later, and just as Dr. Krause and Andy start a conversation, Doris Krause comes in the living room and says, "Come and get it."

They sit at a large dining table, and Dr. Krause announces, "I'll say grace."

After the prayer, Andy says, "I have to be candid, Dr. Krause. I'm glad to see a professor pray."

Dr. Krause smiles and says, "Andy, some of us still do."

As they pass the food, Dr. Krause looks at his watch again. He says, "I was hoping we would have time to enjoy the meal. We should have over thirty minutes before Mr. Abernathy calls. When he calls, Andy, you can use the phone in my study."

During supper, they talk about Purdue's basketball season; Andy's interests in national and international affairs and their hometowns. Andy finds it interesting that Dr. Krause was from Vincennes and his wife from a farm in southern Illinois. Dr. Krause says, "Red Skelton use to be in some of the same classes I had in Jr. High and Sr. High. He grew up just over a mile from our house."

Andy says, "That's amazing. He's my dad's favorite comedian. What was he like as a kid?"

Dr. Krause replies, "He was the class clown!" They laugh, eat and talk for over forty minutes, when the phone rings. Dr. Krause excuses himself and when he comes back in the room, he says, "Andy, it's Mr. Abernathy."

Andy sits down behind Dr. Krause's desk; picks up the receiver and says, "This is Andy."

"Hi, Andy, this is Jonathan Abernathy. How are you this evening?"

Andy replies, "Right now I'm doing real well. Dr. Krause's wife just gave us a delicious, home cooked meal."

Mr. Abernathy says, "That's nice of them. I just saw that Purdue is ranked 11th in the nation: congratulations."

"Thank you. Our team does a good job, and we like to play."

Mr. Abernathy says, "Andy, you know I didn't call about basketball, but I admire what you're doing at Purdue; on and off the court. Before Christmas, Dr. Krause told me about you're feeling or evaluation of what is going on in our country. I was not only interested, but I told Dr. Krause that it confirmed what our intelligence is telling us. I didn't want to keep you waiting, but I had to talk with two important government officials and decide what I wanted to offer you."

Andy says, "That's fine. It has been busy here, and also an enjoyable season."

"Andy, the main reason for my call tonight is to see if you can come to D.C. during semester break. There is a flight from Indianapolis at 11:15 am and it will arrive in D.C. at 12:48 pm. on Friday, January 26th. Your return flight would leave D.C. at 10:20 am on Sunday, January 28th. Andy, I'm asking you to come, because I feel our meeting at this time is very important."

Andy replies, "Would this meeting lead to putting my college plans on hold after this year?"

"Yes, it would, Andy, and when we meet in person, I can tell you how critical things are at this time. At this moment I can't go into detail, but a lot of people will be putting plans on hold very soon. We will compensate you very well."

Andy says, "My girlfriend and I are talking about spending our future together. If I work for the State Department after this school year, is there a place for my girlfriend there?"

Mr. Abernathy asks, "What are her interests?"

Andy says, "She is interested in early elementary education."

Mr. Abernathy says, "That's perfect. The State Department has a facility for just that purpose. We can employ her part-time or full-time, and the building is only a few blocks from where our main building is."

Andy says, "That's good. I'll come on the trip."

Mr. Abernathy says, "With your interests, Andy, you won't be disappointed. We'll pay for all of the trip expenses and give you $125 for yourself. Since Lafayette is close to Indianapolis, I'll see if Dr. Krause can take you to the airport. I'll mail the plane tickets to him tomorrow. Andy, do you have a blazer and tie that you can bring with you?"

"Yes, I have one."

"Do you have any questions for me?"

"No, Mr. Abernathy. Thank you for calling."

Mr. Abernathy says, "Andy, it is good talking with you. I'll look forward to seeing you on the 26th. I'll talk with Herb now, and ask him about the trip to the airport."

Andy lays down the receiver on the desk, and calls Dr. Krause to the phone.

While they're talking, Andy talks with Mrs. Krause and thanks her for her hospitality.

On the way back to the dorm, Dr. Krause assures Andy that he would be getting invaluable experience. Dr. Krause says, "Mr. Abernathy wanted me to remind you that the trip and purpose are confidential. Could you tell your family and girlfriend that the trip is for a special subject you're working on?"

Andy says, "That will work, since it's not a lie."

In front of the dorm, Andy thanks Dr. Krause again for the dinner invitation. Dr. Krause says, "We want you to come over sometime with your girlfriend."

As Andy steps out into the freezing temperature, he says, "I know Lydia will like that."

Before Andy goes to his room, he calls Lydia. Lydia says, "It seemed like you disappeared today."

Andy replies, “You’re feeling is partially right. I had a dinner invitation.”

Lydia whimsically asks, “Was she a 5’10” Miss Universe with an hour glass figure?”

Andy laughs and says, “No, she was Dr. Krause. His wife cooked a great meal for our supper.”

“At a professor’s house? What is going on, Mr. McGraig?”

Andy replies, “You’ll know nothing is going on, when I tell you that I have to go out of state over semester break.”

Lydia says, “Oh, wow. Well, I trust you.”

Andy says, “You’ll trust me more after we get together. Can we meet at the Student Center for supper tomorrow evening about 5:45 or a few minutes later?’

Lydia says, “I’ll look forward to it. I’ll get there by 5:50, since you have practice.”

Andy says, “Well, babe, I have to say goodnight. It has been a long day, and I need to study.”

Lydia says, “Ok, handsome. Thanks for calling; think about me tonight.”

Andy says, “I think about you every night. Good night.”

The next evening, as Andy walks into the Student Center, he sees Lydia immediately. He kisses her and says, “Have you been waiting long?”

Lydia says, “Only a minute or two.”

Andy says, “Do you want to get in the line, where we pick our own food?”

Lydia says, “Let’s do it.”

After Andy picks a table, they say a prayer, then Lydia says, “I’m all ears.”

He takes a bite of meat loaf then says, “Were you serious, when you said that you would go with me anywhere?”

Lydia says, “Absolutely.”

Andy gathers his thoughts and says, “I picked this table, because it’s not close to anyone. At this time, there are some things I can’t tell you, but what I do share is strictly confidential.”

Lydia replies, “No problem. I won’t tell anyone.”

Andy says, "Lydia, I was told to tell you and my family that the semester break trip is for a special subject I'm working on. Since this trip and my work this summer may affect your plans, I need to tell you in general why I'm going. I'm talking with a major government agency. It's not the military, so don't worry about me being assigned overseas. Secondly, the income will be quite substantial. I'm completing my freshman year, and the agency will probably work with Purdue, so my scholarships will be available, when I return. It's a lot to take in."

Lydia says, "It sure is. Where will you be this summer?"

Andy says, "I can tell you now that I will be stateside. Even this summer, I will be making a very good income. When I agreed to take the flight for the meeting, I asked if something good would be available for you, if you're interested."

Lydia says, "I'm on pins and needles."

Andy says, "Even though we're not officially engaged, I would like to get engaged, if you would."

Lydia says, "That's so romantic, Andy."

Andy laughs and says, "I know. If you want to get engaged in the near future, I was wondering, if you would want to marry late summer?"

Lydia smiles and says, "You're just full of surprises."

Andy says, "Because it's a lot to process and a lot to consider, I want you to know that I will be making enough to buy a nice house and other things. Since this is confidential, I will tell you that the location is about 600 miles from here. It is very historical, and there is a lot to do. If you haven't guessed, some of the work is classified."

Lydia says, "I did mean it, when I said I would go with you anywhere. I would also like to marry you. I understand that we need to be more practical than romantic right now."

Andy says, "Lydia, some people have to grow up fast. Some would say it's in the cards or fate. I believe in God's plan. I believe he has a calling just for you and me. Those who went through the World War grew up fast, especially the eighteen and nineteen year olds, who served in the military."

Lydia says, "I totally understand about those who started out at a young age. My father was one of them, and many others in the

Netherlands. If I need to grow up fast, I want to do it with you. Tell me about the good news you have for me."

Andy says, "First of all, I think this agency can also save your scholarship for when you return. Secondly, I told them you're interested in early elementary education, and they said you could do that work part-time or full-time. We won't need the money, so it's up to you."

Lydia says, "In that case, working full-time or part-time would help repay my parents for their early visit to America."

Andy's face lights up and says, "You mean you'll marry me late this summer?"

Lydia smiles; nods her head and Andy takes her in his big arms and kisses her. "Is it alright, if I give you a small ring before second semester ends and a big one later in the year?"

Lydia says, "That would be fine. I need to invite my parents, so they can make plane reservations."

Andy says, "When I get back on January 28th, I can give you the dates. I will tell them I need at least a week off, so we can marry. I'm hoping it will be during the week of Labor Day. I could also help your parents with their expenses here."

Lydia says, "I'm going there around June 1st, and I'll come back with them."

Andy says, "That will work out well, because I have special training in June, July and August." Andy stops a second and looks around then smiles at Lydia and says, "Do you think anyone could hear us?"

Lydia gives him an impish smiles and says, "Only the fly on the wall."

Andy says, "I feel like taking a deep breath now."

Lydia says, "You should probably inhale your food. I'm sure it's getting cold."

While Andy finishes his supper, Lydia says, "It would be nice, if the wedding were on or near the Purdue campus."

Andy says, "I agree. We met at the church, which is right on the edge of the campus. I'm sure we could reserve a date with them."

Lydia says, "My parents would love to be with us at Purdue. It would be fairly close for your family and friends. Maybe your home church pastor could marry us."

Andy says, "We should probably try to reserve a date soon. My home church pastor has only been there a couple years. The pastor here or my family's pastor is fine with me." Andy looks at his watch and says, "It looks like we better hit the books. If you're ready, I'll walk you back to your dorm."

As Andy opens the door for Lydia, they walk into an arctic blast. Lydia says, "Even though the snow is gone, it feels like this wind is from the home of polar bears."

After a fast walk to Lydia's dorm, Lydia says, "Let's go inside by the front door before we say good night." As the front door closes behind them, Lydia gets close to Andy; looks up at him and says, "Mr. McGraig, I just want you to know that I'm very happy that we will be with each other."

Andy says, "You've also made me very happy. I love you." They embrace in a long hug and kiss, then Lydia says, "I love you. Have a quick walk to your dorm, and we'll talk soon." They kiss again, and Andy does double time to his dorm.

When he gets back to his room, he decides to call his parents tomorrow, since he has just enough time to get through his assignments.

After the last day of classes before semester break, Andy packs his suitcase for the trip to Indianapolis and D.C. He has supper with Lydia, and calls Dr. Krause to confirm the pick-up time for his trip to Indy. At the break the Boilermakers are ranked 10th in the nation and their record is 22 and 4. Their only loss in January was at Ohio State. The top ten in the country are Cincinnati. Ohio State, Indiana University, UCLA, Wake Forest, Duke, Van Buren, Butler, Kentucky and Purdue.

10

There's a Storm A-Brewin'

Andy is waiting just inside his dorm's front door, when Dr. Krause pulls up at 8:45 sharp. Andy puts his suitcase in the trunk and gets in the passenger seat. Dr. Krause says, "Andy, there's a new restaurant in town, McDonalds, and we'll go to their drive through for coffee right before we get on the highway."

As they're on their way, Andy says, "That's great. Is McDonalds only in Lafayette?"

Dr. Krause replies, "I think they're a chain. Someone said they saw one in Indianapolis."

Andy says, "If we only knew, how big a new company will become."

Dr. Krause says, "That would be a golden goose. We'll get to the airport by 10:15. You'll have plenty of time to catch your flight. I'll go in with you, and make sure everything goes smoothly during check-in. You'll probably be at the gate by 10:45."

Just before Andy walks to his boarding gate, he shakes hands with Dr. Krause and thanks him for everything. He lets him know that his parents will pick him up here at noon on Sunday.

It's Andy's first trip in an airplane. He wants to sit by a window, but with the need to stretch out his long legs, he takes an aisle seat. Just before the plane takes off, the pilot announces that weather conditions are fair, and they will land at the National Airport in D.C. at 12:48.

After they touch down on a completely overcast day, Andy heads for the baggage claim. About twenty yards ahead of him, he notices two men in dark grey suits and black ties. One of the men looks at the other one and says, "Look at the size of this guy."

His black tie companion says, "He sure is easy to spot."

They're not holding any sign that says Andy or State Department. They walk up to Andy, and the one who shows Andy his badge says, "Mr. Abernathy sent us to pick you up. He's expecting you at his office."

On the way to their car, one of the agents says, "I'm Mac and this is Bruce. I saw you play against IU. You're an excellent player. You deserve the title, "linebacker of basketball".

Andy laughs and says, "Thanks." Andy picks up his suitcase in baggage claim, and he notices their car is parked in front of the terminal with a federal tag.

In twenty-five minutes, they pull the new, black Lincoln in front of a large, seven story, column building. Bruce lets out Mac and Andy and parks the car in an adjacent parking lot. They walk into an elevator and take it to the top floor. When they walk out of the elevator, there is an agent stationed across from the elevator. They walk down the hall to a door marked "Jonathan Abernathy". As they walk into the waiting room, Andy notices another agent. Mac says, "Wait here, and I'll tell Mr. Abernathy you're here."

In a minute, Mr. Abernathy comes to the waiting room and in his booming voice, he says, "Good to see you, Andy. Welcome to D.C. Have you had lunch yet?"

Andy says, "No. Lunch sounds good."

Mr. Abernathy says, "Our cafeteria is on the ground floor. We'll go there now." Mac goes with them. The cafeteria looks a lot like the one in the Student Center. After they get their food, Mac disappears.

Andy asks, "Isn't Mac going to have lunch with us?"

Mr. Abernathy smiles and says, "He'll get lunch in a few minutes." When Mr. Abernathy picks a table, he says, "Look, two tables over." He sees Bruce already eating lunch. "Bruce will accompany us back to my office. The Secretary has security 24/7. Andy, tonight you are the guest of honor. My wife and I are taking you out to one of D.C.'s finest restaurants. We'll actually meet you there, because we've reserved a room for you tonight and tomorrow at the Hotel Tabard Inn, which has one of the best restaurants in D.C."

Andy says, "I appreciate everything you're doing."

Mr. Abernathy says, "We'll meet you in their restaurant at 6:30

this evening. After we meet at my office today for about two hours, Mac will take you to the hotel, and you'll have plenty of time to rest before dinner this evening. Tomorrow is the work day. You'll have breakfast at the hotel, then Bruce will pick you up at 8:30, and you'll be busy from about 9 to 6 tomorrow. We'll take about forty minutes for lunch."

Andy says, "It sounds good to me." After they finish lunch, Bruce goes back to the office with them. The agent on duty in the office leaves, when Bruce returns. As they go into Mr. Abernathy's office, Andy asks, "How long are the agents' shifts?"

Mr. Abernathy replies, "Good question. Bruce and Mac are my main agents, and there is also an agent at my house. The agents that rotate at my house work about fifty hours per week. They also rotate three day weekends, so they have a decent schedule. When our building closes, there is an agent on the main floor and one on this floor. They have state of the art walkie talkies, so they can communicate with each other and with a central security system. Most weeks Mac and Bruce also work about fifty hours. They also get a three day weekend now and then. Have a seat, Andy. We need about two hours to go over a few things."

Andy sits in a comfortable guest chair, and Mr. Abernathy sits behind his desk. Mr. Abernathy says, "The main objective this afternoon is to share our needs. I need to know what you need to work here, and you need to know what we need. Andy, we need to create a job for you. We've talked about you being my personal advisor, but undercover as a special agent. As a special agent, other agents may think you are like an agent adjutant assigned to me. Once you go through training with martial arts and gun handling, your size and strength will convince some agents and others that you're my body guard. In your classified record, only officials with top security clearance will know your real status. Those officials will be the President, my Deputy Secretary, William Jennings, and possibly the Vice-President."

Andy says, "I'm on the same page as you. I think my services can be best used in the way that you just described."

Mr. Abernathy replies, "Andy, that's our goal for this two hour session. When we finish, I hope we'll be on the same page with everything. We would like to have a contract with you before we end the day tomorrow. Did you talk with your girlfriend about her moving to D.C.?"

Andy replies, "Yes. We plan to marry after training ends this summer. Do you have the training dates, so we can set a wedding date?"

"Yes. Training begins Tuesday, June 5th and ends Friday, August 24th."

Andy says, "That's good. We can set the wedding date between August 25th and Labor Day, September 4th."

Mr. Abernathy says, "If you want a honeymoon, I would recommend you set the date soon after August 24th. Our intelligence, like your prediction, tells us that something major will happen this September. We're preparing the military and every avenue we can, including your first day as an undercover advisor. We'll need you as soon as possible in September, sometime between the fourth and the seventh."

Andy says, "I'll tell Lydia, this coming week."

"Andy, we'll talk about finances and your time of service today. Before we do, I can't help but ask, if you have any other special talents that we don't know about?"

Andy smiles and says, "I think you will like hearing about another one. Before I share it, I need to know that it will be confidential, and that I will not be put through any special testing or paranormal/laboratory type testing."

Mr. Abernathy says, "I guarantee it. If it's in your contract, you could not only sue the State Department, but you could also terminate your contract, if it is breached."

Andy says, "Very well, then: I know if someone is telling the truth or not."

Mr. Abernathy is flabbergasted and looks at Andy wide-eyed. In another second he says, "You're serious, aren't you?"

Andy says, "Yes, sir."

Mr. Abernathy says, "It looks like the perks of your contract just increased. Of course, I have to confirm what you're saying, but I can tell it's the truth! I can assure you that it will be top secret, and that you will not go through any extraordinary testing. I must ask the reliability of your gift of truth?"

Andy says, "100%."

"In the morning, I'll start working with you at 9:00, and Mr. Jennings will take my place about 10:30 or 11:00. He will work with you until 4:30, then you'll come to my office to review your contract. On Sunday morning at 8:00, Mac and Bruce will pick you up at your hotel and take you to the airport."

Andy replies, "Looking forward to it. I would like to talk about the scholarship situations concerning Lydia and me. As you know, Lydia is on a full foreign student scholarship. She is from Rotterdam, Holland. Her last name is Van Ark, in case you need to do a background check. My scholarships are from National Merit and the Purdue basketball program."

Mr. Abernathy says, "Yes, we talked about it briefly on the phone. In your contract, we will guarantee you and Lydia full scholarships with living expenses, if you sign a contract with the initial two years; then a three year temporary leave to finish college at Purdue and lastly, a five year commitment to begin after graduation and a two week vacation. Even if the National Merit, Purdue basketball and foreign scholarships are continued when you return, we will still give you living expenses, which will more than cover your room and board."

Andy says, "It sounds excellent. I realize that when men my age and older are drafted, they will start out at a much lower salary than I will get from the State Department. We also mutually agree that we want to use my qualifications here. People who are familiar with the NBA have indicated that I will be offered much more than $25,000 for the first year. However, I realize that a United States Senator currently has a salary of $30,000 per year. Since I'm putting my college and basketball plans on hold, I would like to know what you're considering for my salary and benefits."

Mr. Abernathy replies, "Well put, Andy. I've been considering a starting salary of $27,000 for the first year and $29.000 for the second year. You will have full health and retirement benefits. You will also have an expense account that reimburses you for all job related expenses. You will be guaranteed a full scholarship to finish Purdue, plus room, board, and additional expenses. Your starting salary for the first year you return here will be $31,000. To cover inflation, the next four years, you'll receive an increase of $2,000 per year. In 1972, you'll make $39,000, and you will be building a very comfortable retirement."

Andy says, "I agree with the compensation, and I appreciate the opportunity. In 1972, I turn 29. I doubt that I will want to be an undercover agent or bodyguard after age 29."

Mr. Abernathy laughs and says, "I wouldn't either, Andy. I realize that a lot of people in government work are lawyers, business owners and retired military. Your experience will be invaluable. After 1972, part of your record can be declassified to certain government officials. After 1972 they will know that you were a very important advisor in the State Department. With your qualifications and experience by then, you could later become an ambassador, an intelligence director or have my current job as Secretary of State. If you wanted to, you could retire in your early fifties. Another option is congress or senate, if you like politics and elections."

Andy replies, "I thought those might be my future options in government work. I'm glad you went over them with me."

"Andy, I was thinking about your gift to know truth. Tomorrow morning I would like to ask you five or six questions, so I can officially confirm your ability."

Andy says, "Five or six questions are fine. I need to hear the person that is involved with the situation. I need to see them in person or on film. If I talk with them on the phone, they have to be involved in what we're talking about. The criteria I mention is what I've had experience with."

Mr. Abernathy replies, "Splendid. I will make sure that I have a connection with what I share with you. Evidently, you will give me a true or false reply?"

Andy says, "Yes."

Mr. Abernathy looks at his watch and says, "It's almost quitting time. I don't know everything that Mr. Jennings has planned for you, but I know that he has a thirty minute film for you. It shows new agent recruits what the training is like. Your advisor work with me will be mostly on the job training, which will begin after Labor Day. Initially, we'll provide a large furnished apartment for you and Lydia. Before the end of your school year, I'll have information about Lydia's work. How much time do you need to move?"

Andy says, "It won't take long. We basically have our clothes and books. The furnished apartment will be a great help. I think we could move into the apartment within two days after Labor Day."

"Excellent. Do you have a car?"

Andy replies, "My dad is giving me his 1955 Chevy Bel Air this spring or summer."

"That's a nice one! You have a good dad."

Andy says, "He's a great dad!"

Mr. Abernathy calls Mac on his intercom. Mac comes in the office, and Mr. Abernathy gets up and shakes Andy's hand, "We'll meet you at the Tabard Inn at 6:30 this evening."

Andy says, "I'm looking forward to it."

Mac goes into the Inn with Andy to check on the reservation. The lobby looks comfortable; well-furnished and trimmed heavily in wood. Mac says, "Andy, you're all set. I'll show you the room and do a quick security check." Andy grabs his suitcase. While Mac does a quick check of the room, Andy looks at the brightly painted walls and the old fashion, iron radiator, heating system.

Mac says, "You're all set. Bruce will pick you up at 8:30 in the morning and meet you in the restaurant. Have a good night."

Andy says, "Thank you, Mac."

He locks his door and takes off his sweater and shoes. He stretches out on the bed. He looks at his watch and thinks, "Good deal. I've got over an hour to rest before I get ready to meet Mr. and Mrs. Abernathy."

To his surprise, he dozes off, then gets up and turns on the television while he freshens up and changes into his blazer and tie. He walks into the softly lit restaurant a few minutes before 6:30. It's nicely decorated and not ostentatious. He tells the waiter that he is meeting the Abernathy's. The waiter takes him to the reserved table.

Five minutes later Mr. and Mrs. Abernathy walk in. Andy thinks they look good together. He has on a suit and tie, and she is wearing a gown. She is buxom and slightly overweight and looks pleasant. Mr. Abernathy introduces Andy to his wife. Mrs. Abernathy says, "Jonathan, this is this best looking guest we've had in a long time."

As Mr. Abernathy seats his wife, Andy says, "You're a good looking couple."

Mrs. Abernathy says, "I think I'm going to like you. Jonathan told me about your fiancée. I'm looking forward to meeting her. I bet she's a beautiful lady."

Andy lights up and says, "She is a beautiful person in every way."

The waiter serves the drinks, and Mr. Abernathy orders the meal. To Andy, it's a fairly extravagant meal. He doesn't know what half of the things are. He eats some small, sweet muffins, shrimp with cocktail sauce, steamed broccoli and some kind of specially made potatoes. Mrs. Abernathy has a good sense of humor, and they have a lot of good laughs during the meal. Mr. Abernathy tells a joke about a dog that goes into a bar and tells the bartender that he is looking for the man that shot his paw.

They have a friendly meal that is totally social. When they say good night and shake hands, Mr. Abernathy says, "I thought we would both enjoy a meal without business."

Andy says, "I enjoyed it a lot. I really appreciate you and your wife and your kindness. I will see you by 9 tomorrow morning."

Mr. Abernathy says, "Have a good night."

Andy leaves a message at the front desk for a 6:30 wake up call.

In the morning, Andy catches early morning local news on television; showers and puts on his navy blazer and tie again. A few minutes before 8, he goes downstairs and orders breakfast. He finishes at 8:25, and Bruce walks in exactly at 8:30.

Bruce asks, "How was breakfast?"

Andy says, "Excellent. I finished my last cup of coffee, and I'm ready to go."

Bruce and Andy arrive at the State Department Building before nine, and Andy follows Bruce to Mr. Abernathy's office. Andy sits in the waiting room a few minutes, then Bruce tells him that Mr. Abernathy is ready.

In his office they greet each other, and Mr. Abernathy says, "Before I share the five or six scenarios with you, do you have any questions? I'll be bringing your contract in by 4:30 at the latest."

Andy replies, "As of right now, I'm not to tell my fiancée or my parents much about this trip. Of course, my fiancée will have to know why we are going to move here, and my parents will have to know something about my work."

Mr. Abernathy says, "That's right, Andy. For right now, tell your parents you will train to be a special agent for the State Department, and tell your fiancée also in confidence that you will be part of security for the Secretary of State. Right now don't tell anyone about our plans for you as an undercover advisor. It is classified, and we'll talk later about what you can tell your fiancée."

Andy says, "That seems fair."

Mr. Abernathy says, "Mr. Jennings will take you through a short orientation today about the State Department. Besides the agent training film, he will give you instruction on State Department responsibilities, procedures and security. You will have plenty of time for question and answer sessions. Mr. Jennings will also have lunch with you. He'll be here by 10:30, and I will probably be back between 3:30 and 4:30. We should be finished between 5 and 6. You'll have dinner at the hotel, and they already know to put your meals on our tab."

Andy says, "It's a short stay, but I appreciate your hospitality."

Mr. Abernathy says, "I'm glad you're enjoying it. Let's go ahead with the true or false situations before Mr. Jennings arrives."

Mr. Abernathy shares with Andy six real life situations, and he writes down Andy's true or false reply to each scenario. When he finishes, he sits back; looks at the paper and then says, "Andy, it's amazing, but like your other discernments, you're 100 %. You are going to be invaluable to the State Department and to the country. I've actually thought about having security for you, until you get here in June."

Andy says, "Of course, it's your decision, but I go to bed fairly early, and I get up early. Until June, I'll be with friends at school and with my family a few other times. If you had security for me, wouldn't that arouse suspicions?"

Mr. Abernathy says, "Yes, I've thought about that."

William Jennings arrives by 10:30. After they greet each other, Jennings talks with Abernathy for a couple minutes. Andy notices his black hair, receded hairline and dark complexion. He is six foot or a little less, and appears to be an astute, professional person.

Andy thinks that the day goes by fast with Mr. Jennings. He is a fluent communicator, very informative and witty. Andy also likes the answers that he gets to his questions. They stay in the State Department building, but on film he sees the training facilities for agents. Another film on State Department procedures is very interesting to Andy. At one point Andy has the thought that he has found his niche.

As Andy goes with Jennings to his office, Abernathy calls and says that he will be there by 3:45. Jennings look at his watch and says, "Andy we have about thirty minutes for questions or anything you want to talk about."

Andy says, "I liked what you showed me today. I would like to know what working at the State Department means to you."

Jennings says, "Good question, Andy. It actually means everything to me. I feel it's an honor to be the Secretary of State's assistant. I look at my work as more than a career. It's my life, and I try to do the best I can to help the State Department."

Andy says, "I want the same. I want to help the country, and I think the best way that I can do that is in the State Department."

Jennings says, "This is classified Andy, and Mr. Abernathy may have told you that there may be a draft this summer for military service. We're on the verge of a crisis. I'm sure you would also be helpful to any branch of the military, but I do think that this is the place for you."

Andy says, "I agree. I feel like I'm cut out for the work here."

They continue to talk, when Abernathy buzzes Jennings intercom. He asks that Andy come to his office. The men get up and shake hands. Jennings is about 30 years older than Andy, but the men admire each other.

When Andy walks into Abernathy's office, he appears to be in a real good mood. He says, "Andy, since we parted company this morning, I mostly went over your contract and caught up on my rest.

I'm pleased with the contract, but I want you to take your time and carefully study it. It's only four pages, but look over it with a fine tooth comb. We have plenty of time, and I'll be going through my paper work, while you read the contract."

In less than fifteen minutes, Andy says, "I've studied it and find it to be quite satisfactory. I have no suggestions or corrections."

Abernathy says, "I'm glad you're pleased. After we both sign it, I also have your copy that we both need to sign. It's classified, so I want you to put it in a very secure place, like a safety deposit box in only your name."

Andy says, "Yes, sir. I will."

Mr. Abernathy goes over the contract before they sign, and shares again what Andy can tell his parents and Lydia. The contract is everything that Abernathy and Andy agreed to. Abernathy says, "You already know that your TWA flight leaves at 10:20 in the morning, and you'll arrive in Indianapolis a few minutes before noon. Are your parents picking you up in Indianapolis?"

Andy says, "Yes, they'll be there by noon."

Abernathy says, "Have breakfast early at the hotel, and be ready to leave by 8:15. Bruce will pick you up before 8:30."

Andy says, "I'll be ready. Thanks again for everything."

Abernathy stands up and shakes Andy's hand and says, "It was a pleasure, Andy. I wish you well with your second semester, and I hope your team does real well in the playoffs. I will be watching some of the games."

"Thank you, Mr. Abernathy. This has been an excellent experience."

Abernathy watches big Andy, as he walks to the waiting room to meet Bruce. He thinks, "What a great guy to have on your side."

Bruce gets him to the hotel before 6:00. He says, "Andy, I'll accompany you to your room. I've been instructed to do another security sweep of your room before I leave." When he gets done, they shake hands, and Bruce says, "See you by 8:30 in the morning." Andy takes off his blazer and tie and rests on the bed before he goes downstairs for dinner."

In the morning, Andy has his suitcase in the hotel lobby and his winter coat on. To his surprise, Mac walks in with Bruce. Mac says,

"Good morning, Andy, I didn't want to miss the airport detail. How was everything here last night?"

Andy picks up his suitcase and says, "Just fine, Mac."

Bruce looks at Andy and says, "Your winter coat will feel good this morning. It's already colder than yesterday."

The three young men get in the big, black Lincoln and head to the National Airport. When they get to the airport, they escort Andy to check-in and to the boarding gate. When they sit down in the gate waiting area, Bruce says, "Andy, we had instructions to wait with you until you got on the airplane." Five minutes before the passengers board, Mac shows his badge to the boarding attendant. He goes inside and checks the airplane.

When the attendant begins to announce the boarding order, Mac goes up to Andy and says, "Andy, you're all set. I wish you the best. I'll be looking for your games in TV Guide." Andy shakes hands with Mac and Bruce, and finds an aisle seat, when he boards the airplane.

On his way home, he sees only clouds all the way from D.C. to Indianapolis. Since they land before noon, all Andy had during the flight was a soda and small bag of nuts. He thinks, "I hope the family and I stop for lunch before we leave Indianapolis." He walks out of the airplane, a little before noon, and when he gets near the baggage claim, he sees his mom, dad and sister waving at him. He walks quickly toward them, and gives his mom and sister a kiss. He shakes his dad's hand and pats him on the shoulder, and says, "It's nice to be back, and it's great to see all of you."

While they wait a few minutes on his suitcase, they ask him about his trip. Andy describes the historic inn and hotel and some of his experiences at the State Department. After Andy retrieves his suitcase, he asks, "Have you had lunch yet?"

Davina laughs and says, "We were waiting on you."

Owen says, "They've completed the 465 by-pass from the airport to the Chicago exit. We can get lunch near the airport, or if you want to wait a few minutes, we can stop at Zionsville or Lebanon for lunch."

Andy says, "You decide, Dad. Zionsville or Lebanon is fine with me."

Owen pulls into a Denny's on the outskirts of Zionsville.

Andy decides on a second breakfast. He orders three eggs, bacon, a stack of four pancakes, hash browns, toast and jelly and milk. Judy says, "There won't be enough food for our orders."

Andy laughs and says, "You and Coach Brown don't need to worry; I'm working out tomorrow."

After they leave Denny's, Andy says, "Dad, could you stop at the pharmacy between the hardware store and our house? I want to get a National Review and U.S. News & World Report before we go home."

Owen says, "Sure thing, Andy. Do you have the money for it?"

Andy says, "I have plenty from my trip."

Owen asks, "When do you plan to go back to Purdue?"

Andy says, "I want to call Lydia tonight. Classes start Wednesday, and I was wondering if mom could take me back later Tuesday morning?"

Owen says, "Davina, if you take me to work and Judy to school, could you take Andy to Purdue after 9 Tuesday?"

Davina says, "Sure I can. Andy, you can drive, if you want to. Do you want to leave around 9:30 or 10?"

Andy says, "That would be perfect, mom. I want to talk with you and Dad today before I call Lydia. Could we sit down and talk before supper?"

Davina says, "We would be glad to."

When Owen pulls into the pharmacy lot, Andy runs in for the magazines while they stay in the car.

It's after 2:30, when they get home. When they pull in front of the house Andy says, "Home sweet home". Before they get out of the car, Davina says, "Andy, why don't you and your dad and I go in the kitchen to talk, and I'll fix coffee. When we get done, I'll start supper". Judy says, "I'll be in my room reading and listening to my records."

Andy asks, "What is your latest record, Sis?"

Judy says, "Since the first of the year, I got, "I Can't Stop Loving You" by Ray Charles and "Young World" by Ricky Nelson".

Andy replies, "Good choices."

Andy and Owen sit down at the table while Davina fixes coffee. Andy says, "Before I call Lydia, I'll call Tim to see if he is home from break. If he is, maybe we can meet at our old gym tomorrow and work out." As the smell of coffee begins to fill the room, Davina joins them.

Andy just looks at them and smiles. Davina says, "It looks like you have good news."

Andy says, "I know that this is going to surprise you or shock you, but just before semester break, Lydia and I got engaged."

Davina says, "I think it's wonderful. She's such a sweet and beautiful young lady. Have you set the date?"

Andy says, "When I call her, I think we'll decide on the end of August."

Owen says, "Congratulations, son; that is good news, but how will you support her?"

"Dad and mom, I have good news about that as well. I have a contract with the State Department, and this summer I begin making four times a normal, full-time salary."

Davina says, "Wow, what powerful, breaking news!"

Andy says, "What I'm sharing with you is confidential. After I start my training, you can say I'm with the State Department. Everything else is confidential, including the fact that my work is classified."

Owen says, "I thought you were going to say that. When you say four times the normal salary, are you saying that you will make four times what a teacher makes?"

Andy replies, "Yes, and the first year, they are going to provide a nice, furnished apartment for Lydia and me."

With tears in her eyes, Davina says, "Your dad and I knew that you would be blessed this way. We just didn't realize it would be so soon!"

Andy says, "It is a great blessing. My contract also allows Lydia and I to go back to Purdue after two years, and finish college. They will guarantee us full scholarships."

Owen lightly hits his hand against the table and exclaims, "Fantastic! What great news, Andy. You're a great blessing."

Now Andy has tears in his eyes and says, "You and mom mean everything to me."

Owen says, "And you are to us. If I might ask, what is the basketball plan?"

Andy replies, "I'm not saying anything until the season is over. My salary will be more than the entry level salary in the NBA. Even though I should be eligible to play college ball in another two years, I signed a contract for another five years after college. Our room and board at college, as well as tuition, will be taken care of. I think you already knew that I was more interested in government work than the NBA."

Davina says, "Yes, we knew that. Your college fans will like it when you return. You and the fans can enjoy this season and the playoffs."

"My sentiments exactly, mom. I will also be getting excellent pay increases annually."

"Davina says, "We couldn't be happier for you, Andy."

Owen says, "I know that you would have a lot of fans in the NBA, but helping your country is more important."

Andy says, "I'm going to start on the second cup of coffee. Do you want to talk anymore about my plans for the next year?"

Davina says, "We'll have plenty of time to talk tonight or tomorrow evening. Why don't you go ahead and call Tim and Lydia."

Andy goes into the living room and calls Tim. He finds out that he is home for semester break. They make plans to work out at their old gym tomorrow. Andy calls Lydia at Tracy's house. Tracy answers and tells him to hold on.

When Lydia answers, Andy says, "Hello, angel."

Lydia replies, "Is this heaven calling? How was your trip?"

Andy says, "My family picked me up in Indianapolis at noon, and the visit in D.C. went real well. I can tell you more, when we get together. Do you think Tracy could bring you to campus around noon Tuesday?"

"Hold on; let me check." Lydia comes back to the phone and says, "She does want to get back to the dorm early. She has a two hour drive, and she said we could be there by 1:30."

Andy says, "That's good. I'll get back by 11:30. I'll work out and get a light lunch. Why don't I meet you at your dorm by 2:30? We'll walk around campus, then I'll buy supper for us."

Lydia says, "That will be nice. You'll have to tell me about D.C."

Andy says, "I spent my time at a major government building, and they made reservations for me at an historic hotel and inn. I enjoyed it as well. It was a quick rendezvous. I had just enough time to miss you."

Lydia says, "That's sweet. I missed you too, big Andy."

Andy says, "I have good news for our wedding plans. We'll have the last week of August and a little longer for our wedding and honeymoon."

Lydia replies, "That worked out well. I'll tell my parents, so they can make their plane reservations."

"Let me know the total cost on the airfare in August. When I see them, I'll give them a check for part of their expense. We'll need to move to D.C. the second day after Labor Day."

Lydia says, "I'm glad to know. It will help us with plans. Are you tired?"

Andy says, "I feel good. I won't stay up late. Tim and I are going to work out at the gym in the morning."

Lydia says, "I think they're going to have an early supper here. You know that Hoosiers have supper instead of dinner."

Andy laughs and says, "Oh, yes, I know. I'll let you go. I think we're having supper in about an hour. I love you, angel."

Lydia says, "I love you, big Andy."

In the evening, the McGraigs have a good time playing board games and watching the first part of Walt Disney and all of The Ed Sullivan Show. Andy retires at 9:30 and reads most of the two magazines he bought at the pharmacy.

In the morning, Owen leaves for work by 6, and Judy leaves for school by 8. At 8:30 Andy is enjoying coffee and breakfast with his mom. Davina asks, "What time are you working out with Tim?"

Andy says, "We'll meet at the gym by 10. I'll borrow the car, if you don't mind."

Davina says, "Not at all; soon it will be yours."

Andy says, "I'm looking forward to it. I want to have breakfast with dad in the morning. Does he still start breakfast at 5:30?"

Davina says, "Yes, I have it ready by then. I'll get you up before its ready."

"I'll take him to work and Judy to school, if you don't mind."

Davina says, "That's a good thing."

Tim and Andy are both at the gym before 10. Tim says, "Just like high school practice; we're both early." First, they start working out in the weight room.

After Tim spots Andy on the bench press, Andy asks, "How are you and your Wabash team doing?"

Tim says, "Not bad. The coach said this is the first time in five years that the college has had a winning season. We've won over 60% of our games. Our wins include games against Depauw, Wheaton, Oberlin and St. Mary's."

Andy says, "Very good. How are you doing?"

Tim replies, "I'm their leading scorer; I'm averaging 21 points."

Andy says, "Excellent!"

Tim says, "We have a good team, and I appreciate the full basketball scholarship. How does it feel to be one of the best players in the country?"

Andy says, "It feels good. You know me; I enjoy the game. We'll see how we can do with one on one in a few minutes."

Tim says, "You still have the size advantage."

Andy says, "I do, but you're sly, and speaking of that; how are you doing with the girls?"

Tim laughs and says, "Greencastle is not far from Crawfordsville. Some of the Depauw co-eds know me from my games there and at Wabash."

Andy says, "I bet they know your game alright. Anyone special?"

Tim says, "Not yet. Right now I'm concentrating on the dean's list."

Tim and Andy have a good time with their one on one to 21, and they like getting together again. They don't even think about being in their glory days. They just know they're good friends, and they enjoy the game of basketball.

Tuesday morning, Andy feels something special about taking his dad to work. Before Owen gets out of the car, he says, "It's great being with you again, Andy. Have a great tournament. We will let you know what games we can attend."

As his dad steps out of the car, Andy says, "Have a great week, dad. Love you."

After he returns home, he takes Judy to school. He's glad he has almost an hour to talk with his mom, while they have coffee in the kitchen. Andy says, "Mom, I know it's obvious to you that I'm doing something more for the government than being a special agent in the State Department. I can't say what it is, but God has led me into an important position."

Davina says, "Yes, Andy. I assumed that. Your dad and I won't give any details about your work, including the wonderful pay that you're blessed with."

Andy says, "I know dad has a good retirement plan at the plant, but I also know that I can help Lydia, you and dad and others, as time goes on."

Davina says, "You've always had a good heart. I'm proud of you."

Davina locks up the house, and Andy holds opens the car door for her, and he gets behind the wheel. As Andy starts up the car, he says, "Mom, even though it's a cold day and we're not seeing the sun right now, I've felt a warmth just being back home with you, dad and Judy."

Davina says, "Me too, Andy."

Andy pulls the Chevy in front of the dorm. He unloads his suitcase, while Davina gets in the driver's seat. He goes to her window and says, "Have a safe trip, Mom. I love you." He notices how angelic she is. He watches her drive off and thinks about how fortunate he is to have such a beautiful and thoughtful mother.

After he changes clothes in his room, Andy decides to run on their indoor track, since he lifted weights yesterday. As he runs, he thinks about how quickly the season is ending now. He is taken back about it almost being tournament time. After he runs, he practices shooting from every position on the floor. He finishes with practicing different lay-ups. He takes a shower and takes his time dressing, since he hasn't seen Lydia for almost a week. He thinks, "It seems like I haven't seen her for a month."

When she meets him in the lobby of her dorm, it's like seeing her for the first time. He says, "You're beautiful. It seems like I haven't seen you for a month."

Lydia says, "Wow, you seem really romantic. I think I'll marry you," and she hugs him and kisses him. As they walk, they hold hands. After walking over ten minutes, Andy says, "It's so cold that our breath is going to turn to icicles. Do you want to talk at the Student Center?"

Lydia says, "That's a good idea. My fingers and toes are already cold."

Andy says, "I thought about going to Annie's for supper, but it's so cold."

Lydia replies, "I agree. We can go there, when it warms up a little. After we have supper here, why don't we talk in my dorm's lobby, so you can warm up before you go to your dorm?"

Andy says, "Good idea. The cold walk between the two dorms wakes up the body real fast."

They talk about a good day and time for the wedding; her parents; when they will know about her job in D.C. and their move to D.C. After supper, they walk to Lydia's dorm, as quickly as possible. When they get to her dorm, Andy says, "There's a smell of snow in the air."

By the time Andy leave's her dorm, it's snowing. It's only 6:00, but it has been dark for thirty minutes. He walks as quick as he can, then watches Huntley and Brinkley. He relaxes by reading in his room. He thinks, "Second semester begins tomorrow already, and practice starts again at 4:00."

They have ten more games in the season; the Big Ten Tournament and the NCAA Tournament. At the end of their season, Andy is named Division I Rookie of the Year. During the season, he averaged 29 points, 15 rebounds and 8 assists. The Boilermakers season before the tournaments is 25 wins and 5 losses. They're a solid number two seed in the tournament, and Purdue is ranked eighth in the nation.

Before the Big Ten Tournament is over, Andy hears that Tim happens to be Rookie of the Year in the North Coast Athletic Conference of Division III. He calls Tim and congratulates his longtime friend.

Andy, Jack, Larry, Coach Brown and the rest of the team are fired up for the NCAA tournament. After the Big Ten Tournament, their practices are long and hard but beneficial. All of the players feel that they're in top condition. In Louisville they play the first round of the tournament against Van Buren and win 98 to 69. In the second round at Louisville, they play against Earlham and win 95 to 73. In the first two rounds, Andy averages 32 points and 19 rebounds. Jack is also on fire and averages 23 points and 12 assists. Larry averages 18 rebounds and 5 blocks.

The Sweet Sixteen Tournament is in Indianapolis, and Andy is able to get tickets for his family and Lydia. Andy sends the tickets to them and makes arrangements for Lydia to sit with them.

By mid-March the weather is a lot better in central Indiana, and the Sweet Sixteen Tournament is in the third week of March. Coach Brown and his team take a bus from campus to Hinkle Fieldhouse in Indianapolis; it's only seventy miles. Their first game is in the evening, and if they make the elite eight, their next game will be the following evening. At 2:30 they check into their motel, and they have an early dinner at 4:00. They go to the locker room at 6:00 and have a team meeting. At 6:30 they go out on the floor and have a brief shooting and lay-up practice. They return to the locker room for a short time of prayer and play strategy by Coach Brown.

At 7:10 they return to the floor and find the fieldhouse filling up with fans. At 7:25 the announcer introduces the Purdue Boilermakers and the Duke Blue Devils. Right before they huddle, Larry, Jack and Andy all agree to win this one for the Purdue fans and all Hoosiers. Larry gets the tip against the Duke center. The game is back and forth during the first quarter, then Purdue gradually pulls ahead. At the half it's 45 to 39, and when the final buzzer goes off, Purdue wins 92 to 84.

After the game, Andy meets Lydia and his family in the concession area. He hugs everyone, and says, "Where are you staying tonight?" Davina says, "Since we're less than an hour away, Lydia is staying with us tonight, and we'll be back for the game tomorrow evening."

Andy says, "I know it gets late after the game, but the restaurant the team goes to is near our motel. Why don't you follow us tomorrow night, so we can all visit at the Big Boy restaurant? Owen looks at Lydia and nods, and Lydia says, "It's a date!"

The next evening the Elite Eight game also begins at 7:30. When the fieldhouse fills up with fans, Andy and his teammates have never heard so much noise. Andy says to Jack, "If this isn't Indiana basketball, I don't know what is." Villanova and Purdue are evenly matched and have the same season record. The whole game is back and forth, and Hoosier Hysteria is at its finest. In the final three seconds Andy hits a shot that sends the game into overtime. Larry, Jack and Andy seem to get their second wind, and they beat Villanova 89 to 84.

After the game Andy, his family, Lydia, Coach Brown and the team have a great time of celebration at Frisch's Big Boy. Coach Brown stands up and shouts, "Another round for everyone; your choice of shake or soda!"

The next few days, it's hard for Andy to keep his mind on his classes. He continually thinks about the Final Four. The morning after they beat Villanova, Andy reads that they will play Ohio State in the first round of the Final Four, which is in Louisville. There are only two teams in the nation that Andy is apprehensive about playing: Cincinnati with Paul Hogue and Ron Bonham and Ohio State with John Havlicek and Jerry Lucas.

When it's time to take the bus to Louisville, Andy thinks the time for the Final Four has arrived a little too quickly. Before they leave the locker room to play Ohio State, Coach Brown says to the team, "Men, you're in top condition. Everyone knows that Ohio State is ranked number two in the nation. We have five great starters and an excellent bench. I want you to play smart and enjoy the game. Get rid of any fear or butterfly. This is your night, and on any given night, you can beat any team in the country." The coach yells, "Go, Boilermakers!"

In unison the team shouts, "Go Boilermakers!"

They leave the locker room, and when they run out on the floor, the fans yell and give thunderous applause for the Boilermakers until the announcer tries talking over them. From tip off to every foul and time-out, Andy helps his team mates double team Havlicek and Lucas. All of the NBA talent scouts are at the Final Four to watch Andy McGraig, Havlicek, Lucas, Hogue and Bonham. Regardless of Purdue's efforts, Ohio State leads most of the game. Andy outscores and outrebounds Havlicek and Lucas, but their combined total is too much for Purdue, and they lose 90 to 94.

In the final game, Hogue and Bonham of Cincinnati, the number one team in the nation, beat Ohio State 76 to 73. Havlicek, Lucas, Hogue, Bonham and Andy are chosen as the NCAA All Tournament Team. The next day, sport writers nationwide are singing the praises of Cincinnati as well as Ohio State. They also declare that Andy is not only in the top five college players in the nation, but he may very well be the top player in the nation. The sports world is wondering, if Andy will enter the NBA draft after his freshman year.

In less than a week after the Final Four, the scouts are calling Andy. He knows what he is going to do, but he is especially interested in what the Boston Celtics scout has to say. He has watched the Celtics for a long time, and he's a big fan of Bill Russell. He sets a meeting with the Celtics scout, and Mr. Cohen of the Celtics says, "Andy, we are looking at you, Havlicek and Bonham. The Celtics owner is prepared to give you a first year salary of $40,000 with a five year contract worth $350,000. We don't have the number one pick in the first round, but we are prepared to also trade for you."

Andy says, "I appreciate your offer a lot; I'm a Celtics fan. I have to tell you up front, that I don't plan to enter the draft this year."

Mr. Cohen is somewhat taken back and hesitates before he asks, "Are you going to finish the next three years with Purdue?"

Andy simply says, "I plan to finish at Purdue."

Andy gets up and shakes the scout's hand. After the scout leaves, Andy thinks, "I hate that he came the distance for a short meeting, but with all the NBA draft attention, I felt compelled to have contact with the NBA. I probably should have asked for a ticket to a Celtics game in Boston."

To Andy's surprise, the April issue of Sports Illustrated has his picture on the cover. It says, "Andy McGraig, Purdue's freshman is top basketball player in the NCAA." Five days later Andy gets a letter from Sports Illustrated. It says, "Dear Mr. McGraig, Congratulations on being a member of the NCAA All Tournament Team. We realize you cannot receive payment in sports, since you're a college player. This letter gives you a lifetime subscription to Sports Illustrated. We appreciate running your photograph on our cover and your story in our magazine."

He shows the letter to Lydia, and she tells Andy that she has already bought five issues of the magazine. She says, "I'm so happy for you. I'm mailing one copy to my parents. I'm getting a lot of attention just being your girlfriend."

Andy smiles and says, "Speaking of that, I need to get you a ring, so we can change the "girlfriend" to "fiancée"."

Even though Andy doesn't have Dr. Krause for a class this semester, they stay in touch with each other. About every four to six weeks, Dr. Krause and his wife invite Andy and Lydia to their home for supper. They always have a good visit with them and have become friends. After supper one evening, near the end of April, Dr. Krause asks Andy, "Have things settled down now after all the activity with the NCAA tournament?"

Andy said, "Yes. Now it's hard to believe that preparation for finals is just a couple weeks away."

Dr. Krause says, "Even when you're young, time goes fast. Your agent training is just around the corner."

Andy says, "It seems like time goes by too fast."

Dr. Krause drives Andy and Lydia to her dorm. After Andy and Lydia talk a few minutes, Andy says, "I better get back. I have some assignments, and I haven't had a chance to read the new U.S. News & World Report."

Lydia says, "I haven't told you how much I enjoyed seeing your tournament games in Indianapolis. You were great, and your family was so nice."

Andy says, "Can you tell that we like you?"

Lydia hugs him and gives him a goodnight kiss. She says, "Think about me tonight."

Andy says, "I dream about a Dutch girl every night."

Lydia laughs and says, "You better dream about this Dutch girl."

While Andy walks to his dorm, he enjoys the pleasant and slightly cool evening. As the sun gets low in the horizon, he likes looking at the colorful tulips on the campus grounds. In his room he grabs the new issue of U.S. News and World Report. He looks at the table of contents first and sees an article entitled, "Illegal Immigrants; Are They Above the Law?"

He flips to the article and starts reading. It says that over 200,000 illegal immigrants have infiltrated the country through the southern border in less than three months. It reports that over one million illegal immigrants have entered the country in the last three years. Border agents say that now they're picking up illegals from countries other than just those in Latin America and South America. Last week they picked up a group of almost one hundred from the Sudan. Other groups in the past month have been from Somalia, Syria, Yemen and Libya. One illegal from Yemen was identified as one of the most wanted terrorists by the F.B.I.

Agents report that members of the Mexican drug cartel are guiding the illegals to soft entry points on the border. The article's news journalist says, "Our ancestors entered our country legally; learned our common language and made an honest living. Illegals begin their stay, whether permanent or temporary, by breaking the law. Many of them are involved with drug smuggling, human trafficking and other crimes. The illegals are bringing measles, tuberculosis, diphtheria, typhoid fever and other diseases with them. It is evident that an increased number of terrorists are entering our country through the southern border. It is time that the free press speaks out about the New Age Socialist Party hindering the country's need for securing the southern border and for harassing the Traditional American Party for trying to get the job done. It is time to address the crisis and the fact that our national security is in jeopardy."

After Andy finishes the article, he starts pondering what he just read. He thinks, "I wish my training had already started. Even though I'm over three weeks from the beginning of finals, I realize I'm on the doorstep of a calling that is much more important than the rest of the semester."

11

Growing Up Fast

Andy spends most of his last month as a freshman with studies and Lydia. Daily he also keeps abreast of world and national news. Dr. Krause calls him right before finals begin, and says Mr. Abernathy will be calling him, Tuesday May 29th at 7 pm. Dr. Krause says, "Why don't I pick you up about 6:20? We'll have a light supper at 6:30, then you can be ready for Mr. Abernathy's call. My wife wants to serve vanilla and chocolate ice cream for dessert."

Andy says, "I'll be ready then; I love ice cream!"

Andy's finals are between May 29th and May 31st. He goes outside his dorm at 6:15 on Tuesday and enjoys the warm May evening, while he waits for Dr. Krause. Dr. Krause is upbeat, when he meets him. Andy says, "I bet you've completed the questions for all your final exams; you're in an especially good mood."

Dr. Krause laughs and says, "You're exactly right! It's a good feeling to be done with everything but the grading. I don't have to teach summer school, so my wife and I are going to travel off and on in June and July."

Andy says, "I bet you don't travel to the southern border area."

Dr. Krause replies, "You've got that right. We both want scenic vacations. We're going to Niagara Falls and Mt. Washington in New Hampshire on one trip. On another trip, we're also taking a scenic route to the Badlands, Mt. Rushmore and Yellowstone."

"I wish I could schedule something like that. I have to be in D.C. for training by the evening of June 4th. Lydia has arranged to fly to Holland on the day that I fly out to D.C. My family will be able to see us off in Indianapolis at the same time."

They pull up into the drive at the Krause's hospitable home. They enjoy humor and pleasant conversation during the meal. Just as Andy takes his last bite of ice cream,the phone rings. In less than two minutes, Dr. Krause calls Andy to the phone."

Mr. Abernathy asks, "How are finals, Andy?" Andy says, "I finish Thursday. I think I'll have good results."

Mr. Abernathy says, "Congratulations on a great tournament, Andy. I saw your game with Villanova on television. My wife and I also saw you on Sports Illustrated. You already have a splendid career."

Andy says, "Thank you, but I'm looking forward to training now. I'm concerned about all of the illegal immigrants infiltrating the country along with the problems they bring."

Mr. Abernathy says, "Yes, that's a major problem. We're having quite a battle with that and many of the New Age Socialist Party leaders. We'll be needing your help. During the twelve week training, we'll get together at least two to three hours per week, when I'm in the country. If you were becoming only a special agent, you would have to complete another six weeks later. Since you are doing the other work as well, I'm getting twelve weeks approved for you as a body guard agent. In training they will be giving you a lot of martial arts and marksmanship."

Andy says, "It sounds good to me. I'm assuming you're also calling about my flight plans and arrival time."

Abernathy says, "That's right. On TWA we have a flight leaving Indianapolis at 4:05 pm on Monday, June 4th, and arriving here at 5:38. Bruce will be picking you up and taking you to the training base, which is just outside of D.C. Our recruits will be arriving that day. I've arranged for you and three other top recruits to share your own accommodations, but it will still be barrack living. Remember, your future work is classified, and you cannot share it with recruits as well."

Andy replies, "Yes, sir. Finals are almost over, and I'm looking forward to being there. Lydia and I are going to marry no later than August 27th."

Mr. Abernathy says, "That's good. Did any of the NBA scouts give you an offer?"

Andy replies, "Yes, I decided to meet with only one scout. The Boston Celtics offered me a $350,000 contract for five years.

Abernathy says, "Wow, it's a very generous offer. I'm looking forward to you being on my staff in September. We have our work cut out for us."

Andy says, "Yes, I'm looking forward to that even more than training, but we are doing first things first."

Abernathy says, "You don't need a lot for training: your bathroom articles; a few basic clothes for summer weather; your gym shoes, and about a week's worth of underwear. You only do laundry once a week. The training instructors allow three calls on Saturday evening and Sunday. They aren't as strict on some things as military training. We provide any kind of medical care; even calamine lotion and aspirin. We also provide the training clothes, including shorts, pants and t-shirts. We also have many sizes of boots for training.

Andy says, "I'll be prepared."

"Also, we provide all of the bedding like pillows and linen. Since we will get together for up to three hours a week, you'll have a little bit of a break. If you want a hamburger and shake, I'll take care of it, and you can have an extra call, if you want it."

Andy says, "I appreciate everything."

Abernathy says, "Your regular pay will start when training starts. I'll see that you get your check once a month during training. All of this information is just between us."

Andy says, "No problem. Since I will see you about once a week during training, I'll share anything then, if something comes to me. If I think it is urgent, how do you want me to contact you?"

"Your drill sergeant, Sergeant Crall, will be your contact to see the camp's captain, Captain Morrison. Go that route, only if you think it's urgent, then Captain Morrison will contact me. Bruce will take you back to the airport early Friday evening on August 24th. I'll give you the flight details later. Andy, I know you'll work hard on the martial arts and marksmanship. Even though you're undercover, you will still be my bodyguard, when we're in public together."

Andy says, "Yes, sir, I will. I'm looking forward to it. Will I have weight room time during training?"

"Yes, I've taken care of that. Sergeant Crall will see that you get in the weight room three times a week. You will have plenty of running and marching as well."

Andy says, "The conditioning is good."

"Andy, take care of yourself. Mac or Bruce will bring me to the base after your first week of training. There is an office at the base, where we can meet. I'm going to sign off for now. The best to you."

Andy replies, "Thank you, sir."

Andy thanks Mrs. Krause for the delicious meal, and Dr. Krause takes him back to the dorm. Right before they get to the dorm, Dr. Krause says, "Your first year at Purdue is almost over, Andy."

Andy replies, "The first year went too fast. I appreciate your help and friendship. I'm sure we'll be in touch at times."

As they pull up in front of the dorm, Dr. Krause says, "You can count on it. I wish you the best on your finals and training."

Andy stands by the curb a few seconds and waves as Dr. Krause drives off.

Andy goes into the dorm phone room and calls Lydia and his mom. He'll only have three full days to be with his family before he leaves for training. After he calls Lydia, he calls home and speaks with Davina.

Andy says, "How is everyone."

Davina says, "Just fine. It's good to hear from you."

Andy says, "I just got off the phone with Lydia, and I want to confirm that she will be with us from the evening of June 1st until June 4th, when she'll go to the airport with us."

Davina says, "It is all set. When do you want us to pick you and her up on Friday?"

"That's what I want to talk to you about. There is a very, sweet lady, Annie, who owns a small café near the campus. Lydia and I want to have lunch there about 1:00 on Friday, or if you and dad want to have supper there, we could go to Annie's about 5:00. I also wanted to see Edward, Ella and Anderson before I left for D.C."

Davina says, "I know your dad and Judy want to make the trip to Purdue, and I will call Ella and ask her to come to Mahican. It might be tomorrow before I know, because Ella might have to leave a message for Anderson."

Andy hears back from his mom the next day. She says Anderson has to work late Friday, but he and Edward want to buy everyone a meal at Quincy's Steakhouse in Mahican on Sunday. Davina also says that Owen and Judy are looking forward to having supper with everyone at Annie's place. Davina says, "By the time your dad gets home from work and cleans up, we can be at your dorm by 5:30."

Andy says, "That's good. We can pick up Lydia and her things by 5:45, and I can tell Annie that we'll be there by 6:00. Thank you, mom."

Davina says, "I'm looking forward to seeing you and Lydia tomorrow."

Andy calls Annie and says, "Annie, this is Andy, the basketball player."

Annie replies, "Oh, yes, Andy, the big, beautiful boy. How is your sweetheart?"

Annie says, "Lydia is doing well. Tomorrow we want to have supper there at 6:00. Can you accommodate five people?"

Annie says, "Vunderful! We have seven tables and on Friday evening we never have more than two or three tables taken. I will reserve the main corner for you and put two of our tables together. Andy, the only thing I can have ready is spaghetti and meatballs and sausage with potatoes and green beans."

Andy says, "That is plenty of variety. I'm sure that everyone would like either meal."

Annie says, "Okay, big boy. Because you bring five people and your year at Purdue is over, you get your meal free!"

Andy replies, "If you insist, Annie. I will make sure you get a big tip."

Annie says, "I like that: a big tip from a big boy! See you then!"

Andy hangs up, and he can't help but have a smile on his face. He thinks, "What a nice lady."

Andy sails through the finals, and takes the last one at 10:00 Friday morning. When he gets back to the dorm, he calls Lydia and they make plans for the afternoon. When they get together, Andy says, "I was looking at the time of my flight on Monday; departure is 4:05 pm."

Lydia says, "My flight leaves at 10:24 am. My parents have only a forty-three mile drive from Rotterdam to the Amsterdam airport. I hope my flight time is not a hardship on your parents."

Andy says, "Oh, no. We like Indianapolis, and my dad is taking a personal day from his job. We'll have less than four hours before we come back to the airport. We might go to the Indiana State Museum."

Lydia says, "That's nice. My flight takes almost twelve hours. I know when you get to D.C. you have to get ready for training."

Andy says, "I'm actually looking forward to it. Since we're having supper at Annie's instead of lunch, do you want to walk to a new restaurant for lunch?"

Lydia says, "Yes. Let's go restaurant exploring!"

They head toward downtown and find Bruno's about a mile from the edge of campus. They love the smell of pizza, and they order a medium with three meats and two salads. After the waitress leaves with the order, Lydia says, "This is a nice break from the cafeteria."

Andy says, "It sure is. I'm also looking forward to going back to Annie's this evening."

Lydia replies, "Me too. She is so funny and nice."

Andy says, "She certainly has a personality of her own. Can you tell if her accent is German?"

Lydia says, "I think it is. As you know, Dutch and German are similar to English, but Dutch and German are more similar to each other. I can understand some German, but there are differences."

Andy says, "After you talk with Annie this evening, maybe you and she can speak a few words in your native languages. I know my family would enjoy hearing that."

Lydia says, "I'll be glad to do that. We'll see what happens."

After they're done at Bruno's, Andy walks Lydia back to her dorm. They have a favorite, large white oak tree near the dorm. It's about ten yards off the sidewalk. Hand in hand, they walk under the tree. They're fond of a long kiss and hug before they say goodbye.

As Andy heads back to the dorm, he notices that it is already after 3:00. He goes to his room and changes into his jogging shorts. In the warm and humid weather, Andy goes for a four mile run at the track stadium. He times himself and completes it in just under twenty-one minutes. By the time he gets back to the dorm, he has well over an hour to shower and pack his things before his family arrives.

Time rushes by, and Andy walks outside with his luggage, and in a few minutes he spots "The Babe", the '55 Chevy, heading for the dorm. Surprisingly, Judy jumps out of the car and runs up and hugs him. Andy says, "Wow, sis, you and your leg are getting stronger. How was your school year?"

With a smile that reveals a sense of achievement, Judy says, "a 3.7 gpa."

Andy reaches down and gives her another hug as he lifts her off the ground and says, "That's great; congratulations!"

Davina steps over and gives Andy a big hug. Andy says, "I'm declaring June 1st to be the National Day of Love." Everyone laughs and tells him how glad they are to be with him.

Andy says, "Let's go get Lydia!"

By 5:45 they pull up to Lydia's dorm, and she is already by the front door with her luggage. Andy runs up the steps; kisses her on the check, and as he grabs her luggage, he says, "You're as beautiful as ever."

As Lydia tries to think of something to say, her ivory checks blush more than she can control. All she can think to do his grab Andy's arm and say, "Thank you. I love you."

Andy's in a hurry to load the luggage, and he returns his reply with a smile. Andy's family is happy to see Lydia. As Andy and Lydia get in the car, Owen says jokingly, "Andy, where is the big smorgasbord?"

Lydia laughs and Andy gives him the directions. Andy says, "It's just half a mile from here." When they get close, Andy says, "Dad, you can see the red and white sign now on your right, "Annie's Café".

Judy is talking up a storm with Lydia, when they pull up in front of the quaint, small restaurant. Andy holds the café door for everyone. Annie greets them with a hearty, "Welcome! Your tables are ready." Annie seats them and meets Andy's family. She says, "I love having all of you, and I love having big boy and his beautiful girl!"

Everyone laughs and Lydia surprises everyone by saying something in Dutch to Annie. Annie's big face lights up as she looks at Lydia; she says, "My beautiful girl,; you're Dutch! I grew up in Frankfurt, Germany."

Lydia replies in Dutch and says, "For Andy's family will you say something to me and to everyone in German." Annie obliges her and everyone loves to listen to them. After they finish, Judy says, "Lydia, can we hear you and Annie talk one more time?" Annie and Lydia honor Judy's request.

Annie then takes their drink order, "We have milk, brown and white; all kinds of soda, coffee, hot chocolate and water. Everyone but Judy orders a pop, and Judy orders chocolate milk. Owen orders a Nehi Cream Soda. Lydia says, "I've seen Andy order that; I need to try it sometime."

Andy says, "You might get hooked on all of the good, Nehi flavors."

Right away Annie brings three of the drinks on a tray, and goes back to get the other two. When she returns, she says, "Andy knows we have two meals to choose from tonight, and they are both vunderful: spaghetti and meatballs with garlic bread and sausage with sliced, boiled potatoes, green beans and rolls. On the menu, the Friday evening meals are listed at $2.99 and the drinks with refills are 50 cents. We also have sandwiches and fries.

Owen says, "Everyone probably wants a meal. Put them on my ticket."

Annie gets three spaghetti and meatball orders and two sausage meal orders. She says, "I have things started, so the meals will be ready in less than ten minutes."

As Annie walks to the kitchen, Andy says, "Interesting; mom and Lydia order the sausage meals."

Lydia says, "You might guess that the Dutch and the Germans like their sausage and potatoes."

Judy keeps looking at the juke box across the room, and Andy asks her, "Are six songs still fifty cents?" Judy says, "Yes," and Andy gives her two quarters."

Andy says, "Play "Twilight Time" by The Patters, if they have it."

While Judy selects her songs, Andy says, "My Jr. High friends and I started going to "Good Times" in 1957, and they had a Wurlitzer Juke Box just like the one here. We heard a lot of good songs on that juke box."

Davina says, "I know about those lovely memories. Your dad and I dated in the early 1940s, and there were melodic and rythmic big band sounds on 78 rpm records in juke boxes. We listened to hits by Artie Shaw, Tommy Dorsey, Glenn Miller and many others."

Andy says, "I remember in the early fifties, people like Frank Sinatra, Patti Page and Doris Day singing ballads with the big band sound."

When Judy finishes her selections, "The first song they hear is "Travelin' Man" by Ricky Nelson. As Judy sits down, she says, "I found "Twilight Time"."

Annie brings in the rolls, butter and garlic bread. She says, "Ahhhh, beautiful music. During the school year, we have many students coming in and listening to the music. Some of them are in love like big boy and his beautiful girl."

Everyone laughs and they get so tickled that their laughter becomes contagious, and Davina starts to get tears in her eyes from all the laughing. Andy watches his mother and thinks, "I can't get over how angelic and charming mom looks." Everyone continues to laugh with their loved ones for several minutes.

As the laughter dies down, Annie brings the sausage meals first. Annie says, "First, I bring the German meal to my Dutch friend and to big boy's mother." Within a couple minutes, Annie returns with three spaghetti and meatball orders.

Owen prays before they begin. He says, "Our Father in heaven, as we prepare to enjoy our fellowship over this meal, we are reminded of Christ breaking the bread and passing the wine to the disciples. We are thankful for all you have given us. Bless each one. We pray in Jesus' name. Amen."

Judy says, "I'll pass the rolls to big boy first."

Everyone starts to laugh again and Davina says, "If I get laughing again, I won't be able to eat."

They settle down to light conversation while they eat.

When they start to finish their meals, Annie comes over and says, "Do all of you want ice cream? It is only 35 cents, and I can bring you vanilla and chocolate. Judy and Andy can't resist, but everyone else says they are too full.

After Annie brings the ice cream to Judy and Andy, Annie asks Lydia, "Beautiful girl, where did you grow up?"

Lydia says, "Rotterdam."

Annie asks, "Did your parents leave before the Nazis invaded your country?"

Lydia says, "My dad was getting ready to begin seminary, when the Nazis took over. They conscripted him into service and said the alternative was imprisonment. During the occupation, he helped the underground resistance."

Annie says, "Thank God he didn't choose prison; they might have killed him. My dad had a wholesale business in Frankfurt. He knew a little about Hitler and the Nazis before Hitler became chancellor in 1933. I was twenty years old when my parents and I left Germany in 1933. From Germany we went to England and then to America. God bless America!"

Lydia said, "That's right; God led America and the allies to save the world from the Nazis."

Annie gives the tab to Owen, and Andy walks over to Annie with a five dollar tip. Annie says, "I give a big German hug to the big, beautiful boy."

It was Andy's turn to blush and everyone laughed.

Andy says, "Annie, I'm glad your parents saved you from the Nazis."

As they leave Annie's, everyone is talking to Annie and to each other. Once they hit the open highway outside of Lafayette, the conversation volume begins to die down. Both Judy and Lydia nod off. Andy talks with his parents the rest of the way home.

12

For God and Country

Saturday is filled with fun and activity. Judy wants to show Lydia her favorite record shop. Andy and Lydia enjoy looking over the latest albums and 45s. Andy also enjoys looking at some records from the mid to late fifties. Andy buys Lydia the 45 of Ray Charles singing, "I Can't Stop Loving You". Andy buys "Loco-Motion" by Little Eva for Judy.

Early Saturday evening, they go to Pizza King for Indiana's best pizza. Most everyone orders root bear with their pizza. When they get home, Owen fixes popcorn; his Saturday night special. Andy says to Lydia, "Until I started high school, we had one soda a week. Now on Saturday evening, we're having root bear, Bubble Up and Nehi."

Judy says, "We're just party animals."

Davina says, "Speaking of a party, have you set the wedding date?"

Andy raises his voice and says, "Good question! Actually we need your help with that, mom. Lydia and I want to marry at the Purdue Campus Chapel by Monday, August 24th, so we'll have almost a week for a honeymoon. Her parents would also like to have that experience on the Purdue campus."

Davina says, "I've been thinking about the dates. I know Saturday doesn't give you enough time, but I have an idea. Since we always go to church on Sunday morning, why don't I ask some ladies at the church, if we could have a rehearsal dinner after church, and right before we leave for Lafayette. We could start the dinner around 12:30, and the wedding in Lafayette could be around 4:00. On Sunday we would have a better turn out for the dinner and for the wedding."

Andy smiles at his mom and Lydia. Lydia says, "That sounds like a really good plan. I like that Mrs. McGraig."

Davina smiles and says, "I think the church will work with us, and please call me, "Davina".

Andy says, "Mom, I will leave the Lafayette church and pastor information with you. I will plan to make an initial call tomorrow or early Monday. We want Lydia's parents to go places with us. I will be well paid. I can get them a nice room near our house."

Davina says, "We should have two cars before August. I should say yours and ours."

Andy laughs and says, "Good ole, Babe. It's still hard to believe she will be my car."

Lydia says, "Is your car a "she"?

Andy laughs and says, "That's an American custom, like good ole' Betsy. It could be a car, jeep, plane or almost anything important."

Owen asks, "Where do you want to go on your honeymoon?"

Andy looks at Lydia, and she says, "I just want to see the United States!"

Andy says, "I can do my best in one week."

Owen asks, "What direction do you want to go?"

Andy says, "I've been south and east and Michigan and Canada are north. What about west?'

Lydia says, "Yes, Mr. McGraig. What could we see west of here?"

Owen says, "A lot of country is west of here, and please call me "Owen". In one week you would have time to go to the Badlands, Mt. Rushmore and Yellowstone."

Andy says, "That's exactly where Dr. Krause is going on one of his trips this summer! By the way, I'm leaving Dr. Krause's phone number here, in case you need to get in touch with me during training. He will call Mr. Abernathy's office, and they can get in touch with me at the training camp."

Davina asks, "What if he is on vacation at the time?"

Andy says, "He will have a house sitter, and he will call home regularly. He is doing part-time advisory work for the State Department."

Owen says, "If you decide on the Yellowstone trip, I think you will like it. It is beautiful country and gives you a good scope of what western country is like. The Badlands are very unique. I think you would like that as well."

Lydia looks at Andy and says, "I would like for us to consider that for our honeymoon. Do Americans call it a road trip?"

Andy laughs and says, "That's a good name for it."

Everyone is in bed by 11:00, and they get up early for breakfast. They go to their Evangelical Church in Mahican. At 12:30 they meet Ella, Edward, Anderson and Ruth at Quincy's Steakhouse in Mahican. Most of them order a 9 oz. sirloin. After they're seated, Anderson says, "Andy, I think you'll find that Dr. Krause is a good mentor."

Andy replies, "He has already been real helpful and kind."

Ella asks Andy, "How long will you be gone?"

Andy says, "Just three months, then Lydia and I will be married."

Davina says, "As soon as we get the details, I'll let you know. We're looking at Sunday, August 27th, for the rehearsal dinner at our church. After the dinner, Lydia and Andy want to be married at the Purdue Chapel Church. Lydia's parents would love to have the wedding there."

Andy says, "Anderson, I don't know wedding protocol, but I know there is a best man or men, that I need to talk to you and Tim about. I would also like to have Jack in the wedding party. He's my best friend at Purdue, and he played varsity with me."

Anderson says, "Whatever you want. Ruth and I will be there."

Lydia and Ruth talk about Lydia's wedding plans, Purdue and Holland. After their Sunday dinner, they stay awhile at Quincy's and visit. By 3:00 Owen says, "It looks like we're closing up Quincy's until their supper time."

Edward says, "Anderson and I are picking up the tab and the tip. It's wonderful being with all of you today."

Andy says, "I love all of you, and you'll be in my prayers. Lydia and I have to start getting ready for our flights tomorrow."

Ella hugs Andy and says, "Call us, when you can."

That evening, Andy tells his parents that he'll be able to call them every weekend while he's in training. Lydia and Andy go over their plans for her mom and dad, and when he can call and write her during the summer. Before bed, Andy picks up Judy and twirls her around, and says, "I'll be talking with you too. What are your plans this summer?"

Judy says, "I'm going to stay close to home and help mom. Believe it or not, I'm going to help dad with some of his house painting. I think we're going to the Smokies with Ella and Edward for a few days."

Andy says, "It sounds like you'll have a busy and fun summer."

Andy kisses Lydia goodnight, and they both think about their flights to D.C. and Amsterdam before they go to sleep.

Andy gets up early and listens to the news given by Frank Edwards on WXLW AM in Indianapolis. After the news he tunes his Admiral transistor radio to 93.1 FM to listen to classical music, while he reads the Bible and the current National Review.

Davina is up next to fix breakfast. Owen sleeps a little longer, since he is taking the day off to be with Andy and Lydia. Andy is in the shower first, while Judy and Lydia are still sleeping. Everyone has breakfast before 7:30, since they have to be at the Indianapolis airport by 9:00 for Lydia's Pan Am flight to Amsterdam. Andy packs a few news magazines, in case he can't get magazines and newspapers while he is in training.

Owen helps load everything and their off to the airport. Andy says, "Dad, have you heard when you will get the dealer's car?"

Owen says, "Real soon. When you get near the top of the list, they let you know. It sounds like I should get it within a month."

Andy says, "That's exciting, so I'll have "The Babe" for the wedding and honeymoon."

Owen looks at him and smiles, "It looks like it." (Andy rides in the front, because of his long legs.) In the back, Judy is napping, and Lydia and Davina are talking about Lydia's parents and hometown.

At the airport, everyone goes with Lydia to check in, since she has the early flight. The clerk says that her flight is on time. The McGraigs walk to the boarding gate with her. They have only forty minutes to visit before Lydia has to board. Andy's family gives him a few minutes alone with Lydia before she boards. As they say goodbye to her, they see tears in her eyes.

Davina says, "Sweetheart, Lord willing, we'll see you real soon. You're part of our family now. Lydia hugs her and boards the plane."

They watch her plane depart, then they have an early lunch

and go to the Indiana State Museum. As they get ready to leave the museum, Andy says, "My flight time is starting to get close."

Owen says, "We're sad to see you go, son, but it's only for the summer. We'll be back at the airport before 2:45."

At the TWA boarding gate, Andy is ready to board at 3:40. He hugs his sister and mom, and also his dad. Andy says, "I'll miss all of you a lot, but I'll call every weekend."

Davina says, "We'll be praying for you. I love you," and she gives Andy another hug and kisses his cheek.

They watch him board the plane, and they watch the plane until it taxis to the runway; exactly at 4:05."

Once they start cruising at 30,000 feet, Andy dozes off. The next thing Andy hears is the announcement to fasten your seat belts for landing.

As soon as Andy passes by the gate areas, he sees Mac. Mac asks, "How was your flight?"

Andy says, "Good. I was having sweet dreams about training camp all the way here."

Mac laughs and says, "After tomorrow, you'll be dreaming about marching and hearing the drill sergeant's voice."

While they wait on his suitcase at baggage claim, Andy asks, "Does the base have a PX?"

Mac says, "A small one. They open for the recruits in the evening from 6:30 to 8:00. They're closed Sunday, and on Saturday they're open from about 4:00 to 8:00. They only have basic snacks and drinks. They have some magazines and newspapers and a few books about military and government. They also have toiletries."

Its 6:00 by the time they get to the base. Mac shows his badge at the front gate. Mac takes him to the barracks, where the other three recruits will bunk. The barracks looks more like a large campground cabin.

Mac says, "The head is in the barracks and the mess hall is that large building down the main walk. Don't be surprised by an early wake up call. One of the sergeants will rock you out of your sleep around 4:00. Just have your tennis shoes and workout clothes nearby."

Andy goes inside, as Mac returns to his car.

By 7:30 all of the other three recruits are there, and they introduce themselves. There is Doug from Pennsylvania, Tony from New Jersey and Steve from Colorado. Tony says, "Andy, I recognized you right away from the NCAA tournament. You did a great job. I played varsity in high school and baseball in college."

The four recruits agree to turn the lights out at 9:00, so they can get their beauty sleep.

Sure enough, a burly and loud drill sergeant wakes them up at four in the morning with a loud and husky, "Come on you sleeping beauties; I'm getting tired of waiting on you. Can you hearrrrrr me?"

Somehow Andy is able to get out of bed; dress and be outside for formation in less than five minutes. The drill instructor shouts out the roll call. Andy counts fourteen in his training squad. The sergeant speaks briefly to each recruit, and they start marching after the roll call and instruction from the sergeant. At 5:00 they break for breakfast. They're given five minutes of personal time and thirty minutes for breakfast. At 5:35, they're back in formation and continue to march. After another thirty minutes of marching, the sergeant calls out, "At ease," and he announces today's schedule.

He says, "Men, this morning besides marching, we are going to give you a break and go on a four mile run on the base trail that goes in and out of the woods. Are any of you use to running two to four miles or more?"

One recruit, who looks a little more than six foot tall, but not more than 160 lbs. yells, "Yes, sergeant; four mile runs for cross country."

Andy's bunkmate, Tony, says, "Yes, sergeant; one to two miles for baseball conditioning."

Andy is the third and last volunteer and yells, "Yes, sergeant; two to four miles for basketball conditioning."

The sergeant says, "Very good. At least, we have three men in this puny squadron. I want you eleven babies to follow the lead of these three men. Also, men, I don't want you going slow for these babies. Do you understand ME?"

The three volunteers yell at the top of their voices, "Yes, Drill Sergeant!"

The sergeant continues, "By the way, babies, we have a celebrity on our squad, Mr. Andy McGraig from the NCAA basketball tournament. I understand that he might be teaching you something about weight lifting. Can you thank Mr. McGraig?"

The other eleven recruits yell out, "THANK YOU, MR. McGRAIG!"

The sergeant says, "And you three running leaders, you better not disappoint me. If one of the eleven babies finishes the run before you, they will replace you, and you will become part of the baby squad. Do you understand!?"

The three lead runners yell, "Yes, Drill Sergeant!"

After they march another hour, the drill sergeant yells, "At Ease. Take five minutes for water and a privy break. Starting NOW!"

In five minutes they start the four mile run. The "three men" finish first: first is the cross country runner, ; second, Andy, and a somewhat distant third, Tony. The other eleven take about one to ten minutes longer.

The sergeant says, "We have plenty of water fountains at this station. After you get water and a few minutes of rest, we're going to the supply center, the building by the PX and mess hall."

At supplies, Andy gets boots that are 13 ½; extra large socks; fatigues with 34/34 pants and a double x jacket and shirt. The sergeant tells the squad to take the supplies to their barracks, and meet at the mess hall for chow at twelve hundred hours. He announces that everyone is to shower before they go to the mess hall. He says, "Between thirteen hundred hours and seventeen hundred hours, you'll have classes on State Department training with Lieutenant DeVoe, and classes on State Department protocol with Captain Morrison. Ladies, be sure you wear clean clothes with shoes, socks, shirt and pants. Anyone dressed inappropriately will give me one hundred push-ups before breakfast in the morning, and write two hundred words for your instructor about why you're incompetent.

After the last set of protocol classes, Captain Morrison announces that dinner will be at eighteen hundred hours. The Captain says, "I wish you the best in training, and I hope you have successful careers with the State Department. You will take your books and notebooks to your barracks before you go to the mess hall. The small PX store will be open from 6:30 to 8:00. Tomorrow Sergeant Crall will give you your martial arts and marksmanship schedule. You're dismissed."

Tony and Andy walk back to the barracks together. Tony asks, "How many other squads did you notice today?"

Andy says, "I saw five different squads, but I thought there would be more than eighty-five to ninety people here for training."

Tony says, "Maybe they have another training camp here or at another location."

Andy says, "Could be. I haven't looked into the number of agents and other employees that the State Department has."

Tony says, "I assume that you, Steve and Doug are being trained as special agents also. I know we can't talk about it, since it's classified."

Andy says, "That's right."

After dinner, Andy goes to the PX and buys the latest newspapers and news magazines. He goes to his bunk and reads for an hour, then talks to his bunkmates until the required 9:00 lights out time.

By the end of the morning, Andy realizes they were blessed with a 5:00 reveille, instead of a 4:00 reveille. Morning chow was 6:00. While Andy's squad is at attention, Sergeant Crall announces the martial arts and marksmanship schedule for the day. He says, "You sissies are getting out of the four mile run today, so you better do your best in martial arts. I'll whip your butts myself, if you don't put out in martial arts."

Andy soon finds out that his size and strength is to his advantage in martial arts. He realizes the recruits are not as aggressive with him as with each other. The exception is the master trainer, who puts Andy to the test. By the end of the day, Andy gets good feedback from his three hours spent in martial arts and marksmanship.

Before evening chow, Sergeant Crall says, "Tomorrow after morning chow, I'm going to give you weaklings a rest for just three hours from your experiences in manhood. Since Mr. McGraig is experienced in running already, he will be in the weight room the whole time giving you 90 lb. weaklings pointers on building those puny muscles. Every squad member will take turns in the weight room. The one break is when Mr. McGraig needs a spotter for his workout. I will let him choose his spotter. "Sticks" will be giving you training in running. Sticks, I want you in the weight room too. Everyone better complete both training sessions. The weight room is limited to three at a time, including Mr. McGraig. DO You Understand ME!?"

The squad replies, "Yes, Drill Sergeant!"

Andy likes everything but the marching. Overall, the week goes by quickly, and on Saturday at the end of breakfast, he is told to shower at eight hundred hours. A corporal tells him, he will come to his quarters at 8:30 to accompany him to the office building near the front gate. The corporal says, "Mr. McGraig, bring your notebook."

After Andy is seated in the waiting room, John Abernathy, accompanied by Bruce, walks in before 9:00. Andy stands up, and John Abernathy's face lights up. He shakes Andy's hand and says, "It's good to see you, Andy. Let's go to the back office." Once in the office, Mr. Abernathy puts a bag on the desk, and Bruce hands him a tray of coffee. Bruce stays just outside the office door.

Andy has a seat in front of an officer's desk, and Mr. Abernathy unloads a bag of apple pies and egg, ham and cheese croissants. Mr. Abernathy says, "I know you had breakfast three hours ago, so I thought you might enjoy this. I know I will!"

Andy thanks Mr. Abernathy and says, "It looks better than the mess hall food."

Mr. Abernathy says, "The administrative secretary fixes coffee, but we'll start with this coffee. This is Captain Morrison's office. He runs the training camp. You probably had him in a protocol class."

Andy says, "Yes, sir. He was very informative."

Mr. Abernathy asks, "How is the training for you?"

Andy says, "Most everything has been good. I can't say that I enjoy the extensive marching."

Mr. Abernathy laughs and says, "I think they let up on that after the first week. Saturday for the recruits is usually a light day. By 3 or 4 they will let you off for the rest of the day. Sunday is another light day. Chapel is required in the morning after breakfast. Before they give you the day off, you and your bunkmates will probably having cleaning duties for a couple hours. There is a laundry room in the PX building, where the recruits do their laundry on Saturday and Sunday. Even though the current enrollment is about 90, the laundry room is large and has a lot of washers and dryers, so you won't have a long wait time."

Mr. Abernathy takes a drink of coffee and passes the apple pies, croissants and coffee to Andy. Mr. Abernathy continues, "Captain Morrison knows you're in special training, and he will give me weekly reports. He said you started out well in martial arts and marksmanship."

Andy says, "I like learning both arts. Our martial arts instructor isn't big, but he's powerful."

"It sounds like you've had a good week. I don't know how long our meeting will last this morning, but if it gets close to noon, you won't miss lunch. There is a restaurant a mile away, and you can have lunch with Bruce and me there. In three weeks, I will bring you your first check. If you need it in a bank, there is one just twenty minutes from here. We can take you there, and have lunch in the area. If you mail the check back home, I can deduct what you want for cash."

Andy says, "I may take you up on the bank offer. Before I finish training, I may get a cashier's check on the last trip."

Mr. Abernathy says, "Andy, your classified status officially begins today. I have a written oath for you to sign for your classified status. It starts today, because I have some serious information to share with you. I imagine with the challenges of training and the sleep you need, your mind doesn't have time to reflect on other things."

Andy replies, "That's right. The rigors of training and the rest required spends my energy."

Mr. Abernathy hands Andy a pen to sign the classified status statement. Mr. Abernathy looks at the document then looks at Andy and says, "Our intelligence and your insight about conflicts heating up in September has held true. I think our enemies don't want to maneuver in the middle of summer. Did you say your wedding is before the end of August?"

"Yes, sir. We'll return from the honeymoon before Labor Day."

"Andy, when you finish training, you will have a federal carrying permit that allows you to carry a sidearm in any state. After you leave training, I want that sidearm on you, including at the wedding ceremonies and on the honeymoon."

Andy replies, "Yes, sir, that's no problem."

"I would really like to have a special agent assigned to you after training. I haven't decided on that, but you carrying a sidearm is required. We know that insurgents are gathering close to the southern border. The CIA and other operatives are undercover at this time, and feeding us information. We can't tell yet, how big a role that Russia is playing in this, but we will deal with Moscow before early September. We're keeping your warning in mind about Russia and the others you mentioned. We know that some New Age Socialist Party leaders are involved in illegal immigration. It looks like martial law will be enforced in September. At that time, those party members will be arrested for sedition."

Andy says. "My body should adjust to the new training soon. Since we have some free time later today and tomorrow, I will try to take time to reflect on what you're sharing."

Mr. Abernathy says, "Excellent. If you perceive something, come to this office to see Captain Morrison or his assistant. One of them will call me, so we can talk on the phone. Captain Morrison will tell your sergeant that you may need to contact him."

Andy asks, "At this point, does most of the activity look like covert operations?"

"Yes, we don't have any countries threatening war. I think the countries involved want to invade on the sly. I believe they want to avoid declaring war. We know they have a network of insurgents in our country. It looks like most of them crossed illegally at our southern border. We think their main bases of operations are in sanctuary cities. We have already alerted all power and water facilities to increase their security."

Mr. Abernathy takes a sip of coffee and continues, "The military is already on high alert at all nuclear stations. Before September we will have national guards at all power grids and water stations to add barricades and other needed security. The military is already training for operations at the southern border and in sanctuary cities. We know of some large cell groups in cities like Baltimore, New York City, Chicago and several California cities. We'll heighten defenses at harbors; shipping lanes; all federal buildings; hospitals, D.C. and other strategic locations. The war we're expecting will be an invasion that is mostly internal. Our war board looks at the conflict like healthy cells fighting harmful cells in the body."

Andy says, "I see the strategy. You surround their cells and cut them off."

Exactly, "Our Canadian ambassador has already met with our intelligence and Canada's. They have committed to staying on alert and to securing the northern border. We'll cut them off from the north and from the south. Our ships and aircraft carriers will cut them off from the Pacific, Atlantic and the Gulf. Some of the New Age Socialist Party leaders are delusional. They think they can change the nation internally with their aggression and obstruction of justice. When we get done with them, this country will have traditional American values like we did under Teddy Roosevelt."

Andy says, "I've noticed how a lot of their party members attack Christian values."

Mr. Abernathy says, "Yes, that is one of their tactics. They've tried to take prayer out of schools, and they have tried to remove Christian symbols and standards from the public eye. One of their main networks, which was started by a communist decades ago, keeps the court system busy with their anti-Christian crusade. They wrongfully assume that the President will be easy on them, because he was a member of their party years ago, under their old name and platform."

Andy says, "It sounds like they didn't calculate the strength of American values and our military."

Mr. Abernathy replies, "Exactly; very well put. We better talk about some future plans for you, so we don't run out of time. There are some reasons why you'll be with me in the near future, when I talk with some ambassadors and heads of state."

Since Mr. Abernathy meets with Andy until almost noon, he goes with him and Bruce for lunch. When they return to the base, Mr. Abernathy says, "Bruce, go in the office with Andy to get a statement from Captain Morrison's assistant. Have him say that Andy had an official meeting from 8:30 to 1:30."

Bruce hands the statement to Andy and says, "Give this to your sergeant. Have a good week. Real soon you'll be joining us."

Andy thanks Bruce and the same corporal escorts Andy back to his barracks. Andy finds his squad doing a series of exercises that Sergeant Crall started leading daily after the first day. Andy hands the paper to Sergeant Crall, and he stops and reads it."

The sergeant tells the squad to be at ease for five minutes. He looks at Andy and says, "Okay, McGraig, go change and be back out here within five minutes." After Andy changes, he joins the squad for push-ups, sit-ups and jumping jacks.

Sergeant Crall blows his whistle and shouts, "Okay, squad, not bad for a bunch of sissies. At ease, we are going to do your favorite now; the four mile. I'm giving you a break by starting it after we stretch. You'll be finished early today; by fifteen hundred hours. In the morning you will be allowed to sleep in until seven hundred hours. At eight hundred hours you have chow, and at nine hundred hours you will be at mandatory chapel. After the four mile, you will have a free evening, but tomorrow after chapel you will clean your barracks inside and outside and the latrine for two hours. You will have free time tomorrow after twelve hundred hours. This evening or tomorrow you will also want to do your laundry, and you had better do it, or you'll be doing a lot of push-ups next week. In the PX building there are phone areas. You are allowed no more than three calls between Saturday evening and Sunday evening. Any questions?"

"NO, DRILL SERGEANT!"

Sergeant Crall yells, "Atten-hut! New Jersey Boy, Sticks, and Handy Andy, step forward! Okay, men, I want you to lead these babies again in the four mile. You better do your best. Do You Understand ME!?"

The three lead runners yell, "YES DRILL SERGEANT!"

After they run, Andy showers and calls home and Lydia as soon as possible. Andy gets to talk with Lydia's parents and gets updates about Lydia's summer activities. Lydia tells him about what is happening in Rotterdam and Amsterdam. She says that Judy will want to know that Ricky Nelson, The Everly Brothers and Brenda Lee have a big concert in Amsterdam this summer.

Everything is quiet on the home front. Judy continues to help her dad paint houses, and his mom is working on a bigger garden.

His dad tells him that he will have a 1962 Chevrolet dealer's car in less than four weeks. Andy reports that he has been so busy that he hasn't had time to be homesick. He tells his mom and dad that he likes training camp.

After he makes two of his three calls for the weekend, he decides to get his laundry done. He assumes that most of the recruits are putting it off, because the laundry room is almost empty. After supper he browses in the PX before he gets another newspaper and news magazine. He decides to buy a book about General Patton and the Normandy Invasion.

He's back at his barracks by 6:45. No one is around, so Andy kicks back on his bunk and enjoys a couple hours of reading. After reading, he gets out his transistor radio, and explores the AM channels in the area. In a few minutes, Tony comes in by 9:00. Andy says. "Where has everyone been this evening?"

Tony replies, "A bunch of us were at the basketball courts and volleyball courts; past the mess hall and the other barracks. What have you been doing?"

Andy says, "I called my fiancée and my family right away. Before supper I did laundry, then I got a news magazine and a book about General Patton."

Tony replies, "It's probably good for us that you didn't know about the basketball activity. We had a round robin, and you would have killed us. A couple guys from our squad thought you would be there."

Andy says, "If I had known, I would have gone after I left the PX. Evidently, there is no curfew tonight."

Tony says, "Some of the recruits are saying that lights have to be out by midnight tonight and by 9:00 tomorrow. I think the sergeant forgot to tell us about tonight."

Andy says, "I've got a transistor radio, if you want to listen to anything."

Tony says, "I appreciate the offer, but I also have some reading that I brought with me."

Andy and Tony enjoy a quiet evening. They turn the lights out by 11:00, and leave one light on for Steve and Doug.

During the night, Andy sleeps sound. About an hour before

reveille, Andy has a detailed dream about illegal immigrant subversives and other subversives. He sees them supplying each other through the United States Postal Service. They're buying military clothing and many other military supplies from Army/Navy stores. Andy sees them buying materials and products for homemade bombs from discount stores and wherever they can get a good supply.

He sees that those who are well financed are doing the bulk of the supplying. It appears that they're getting financed from several countries. Andy sees a wealthy American doing a lot of the financing. In the dream, the American is an older man with grey hair and deep bags under his eye. Andy also sees religious extremists from the Middle East joining the subversive cause.

Exactly at seven hundred hours, a bugler loudly plays reveille; Andy wakes up immediately. He remembers all of the dream, but makes a few notes before he showers and goes to the mess hall. After the 9:00 chapel, he spots Sergeant Crall.

Standing at attention, Andy unemotionally says, "Sergeant, by early afternoon I need to see Captain Morrison or his assistant at the camp office."

Sergeant Crall says, "Very well, McGraig. I'll tell them. You and your bunkmates do a good job cleaning the next hour, and I will dismiss the four of you at eleven hundred hours. Tell them I want it spic and span in one hour!"

Andy replies, "Yes, sergeant!"

Andy relays the message, and he and his bunkmates get busy cleaning. As they finish and put away the cleaning supplies, Sergeant Crall walks in the barracks. They stand at attention, and the sergeant says, "At ease, recruits. McGraig, you show me everything that has been cleaned." Their barracks passes inspection, and the sergeant tells Andy to go to the camp office now. He says, "You might still make it back to the mess hall for Sunday dinner."

With his notes, Andy walks swiftly to the office. He reports to the receptionist, and in a minute the Captain's assistant greets him, and they go into his office. The Captain's assistant is Lieutenant DeVoe. The lieutenant says, "Captain Morrison told me there might be times you need to contact Secretary Abernathy."

Andy says, "Yes, sir. I have an important message for him."

"Have a seat, and I'll see if I can reach him at home."

The lieutenant dials Abernathy's home. Someone answers and he says, "This is Lieutenant DeVoe at the training camp. Andy McGraig would like to speak with Secretary Abernathy. John Abernathy comes to the phone. The lieutenant says, "Hold on one minute sir; Mr. McGraig is here." The lieutenant holds his hand over the receiver and says to Andy, "I'll step outside the office. Use my desk, and when you finish, come to the waiting room."

Andy answers and Mr. Abernathy says, "This is a pleasant surprise, Andy. What do you have for me?"

Andy gets out his notes and reports his dream in detail to the Secretary.

After Andy reports his dream, Mr. Abernathy says, "Your information is very enlightening. What you saw them doing with the Postal Service is a great lead. I will have intelligence look into it. Hopefully, we'll find more of their main cells with your lead. Our intelligence is watching an American billionaire of your description. We know that some subversives are well financed from several countries. They're also getting a lot of drug money and black market weapons.

"We've also had a problem for many years with the so-called National Freedom Association. For decades they have operated under the guise of constitutional freedom and with the misinterpretation of separation of church and state. Their founder was a communist. Frankly, they have attacked Christian and Jewish freedom of speech for years. We have a lengthy portfolio of evidence against them. By the time this conflict is over, I expect them to be disbanded."

Andy says, "I've had a strong feeling that after the dust clears, our nation will have a renewal of traditional values."

Mr. Abernathy says, "You and your three bunkmates have different, special assignments. The normal eighteen week training period was reduced to twelve weeks for the four of you. Each of your work is classified, so none of you know right now what the others will be doing. Just between you and me, if it were up to me, I would have you in training less than twelve weeks, because of things going on nationally. Most everything in your training experience is important, but I would spend the most time in what is new to you: martial arts and marksmanship."

Andy says, "I have always appreciated your help and candor. Hopefully, the subversive element at home and the increased influx at the border won't start their front until September or later."

Mr. Abernathy says, "I agree. I was told that all branches of the military, including the National Guard, are on alert. We could cope now, but September or later would be better. Thanks again for your lead about subversives using the Postal Service. You also helped confirm what we suspect of the mentioned billionaire." Mr. Abernathy hesitates a second while he looks at his watch. He asks, "What time is your Sunday dinner there?"

Andy says, "12:00."

Abernathy says, "It's almost 12 now. If you walk to the mess hall now, you can enjoy your dinner. Thanks again, Andy. Let me know as soon as possible, if you see anything else."

Andy replies, "I will, sir. Enjoy your day."

Andy sees Lieutenant DeVoe in the waiting room and thanks him. He walks directly to the mess hall, and finds Tony, Doug and Steve just half way through their meal. Steve kiddingly says to Andy, "Thanks for not showing up last evening. You saved all of us from looking bad." Doug says, "Seriously, we'll let you know next time, if you promise to take it easy on us."

Andy returns the bantering and says, "If I don't see your best on the court, you'll owe me one hundred push-ups."

Everyone settles down and digs into the fried chicken, mashed potatoes and gravy and green beans with apple pie for dessert. When they finish Tony says, "Right now basketball and training are the furthest things from my mind."

Steve asks everyone, "What do you want to do now?"

In unison, they say, "Take a nap!"

Across the nation, Andy's absence from the NBA draft and rumored absence from Purdue in the fall has hit the Sunday papers. It's the talk of the sports world. The end of the Associated Press article is even more thought provoking when the sports writer remarks, "The greater mystery is: where is Andy?"

After Andy's nap, he goes to the PX and buys the Sunday Washington Post. When he flips to the Sports section, he sees the headline about him on the first page: "NBA and College Scouts Looking for Andy McGraig".

Andy says to himself, "They make it sound like I'm lost at sea." He takes a walk on the four mile run course and then finds a basketball. He shoots hoops for almost an hour. It's about 4:30, when he gets back to the barracks.

When he walks in, Tony asks, "Have you seen the Sunday paper?"

Andy says, "Yes, Nasa is planning to send a man to the moon."

Tony says, "You know what I mean: the sports section. They're sending men to the moon to look for Andy McGraig."

Andy says, "Yes, I read it."

Tony asks, "How do you think they'll solve the mystery?"

Andy replies, "At some point, Purdue will probably issue a statement saying that I will finish my undergraduate work at Purdue, but it will be at a later time."

Tony says, "Do you think the press will find out that you're with the State Department?"

Andy says, "I'm sure they will; after training. Someone will recognize me in public."

13

Lifeline

Before August, Andy turns 19 and for a very brief time, he feels alone. The last Sunday of July he talks with Lydia and his parents and comes out of his loneliness. He talks with Judy and his parents after everyone has had Sunday dinner. Davina asks, "How are you doing?"

Andy says, "I'm doing well. Frankly, when I turned 19, I felt loneliness for a short time."

Davina says, "I think that is a natural feeling. You're away from home, and you turn 19 while you're in training camp."

Andy replies, "I absolutely agree."

Davina asks, "At this point, what are you impressed with most from your training?"

Andy says, "The discipline is good, but I also learned a good bit of that in basketball. Marksmanship is good training, but I would have to say that I'm impressed the most with the martial arts training."

Davina says, "What do you like about it?"

Andy replies, "It's good to know that you can take care of yourself and others. Our instructor is tough. He says I'm a quick study, but I've learned a lot from him."

Davina says, "What are they teaching you?"

Andy says, "We're learning the basics of jujitsu, judo, taekwondo and karate. My instructor said he learned taekwondo from a South Korean marine."

Davina says, "Andy, God is blessing you with great experiences."

Andy says, "He is. You and dad taught me the right things. I'm very grateful that you have understood and had faith about my gifts, since I was a child."

"Andy, you are blessed, but most of all, you're my son. I love you very much."

"Thank you for your guidance, mom. I love you."

Davina says, "I'll look forward to talking with you next weekend. I'll be praying for you."

Andy says, "I'll also be praying for you, dad and Judy."

When he hangs up, he just sits a moment and feels peace. He thinks, "There's nothing like talking to mom."

As he starts a new training week, he realizes he has already completed eight weeks. He has become a good marksman, and proficient at martial arts. The weekly classes with Lieutenant DeVoe and Captain Morrison have given him a good understanding of how the State Department operates.

The hot weather continued through the entire month of July. The high has been 90 degrees and higher every day. Even a short rain is a welcome respite, but unfortunately, the rain brings higher humidity. Andy is thankful that the base has numerous water stations. Sergeant Crall doesn't overlook water breaks. Andy has noticed the camp's food has been well salted to help the men from getting muscle cramps.

When lights go out Tuesday evening, Andy thinks, "Tomorrow is August 1st. It's hard to imagine that Lydia and I will be married in less than four weeks." The next morning seems to be a typical time of training. Andy's squad gets the usual hour break for lunch. He and his bunkmates are talking at one of the tables in the mess hall right before lunch break ends. Sergeant Crall walks to their table with a corporal. They both look unusually somber.

In a restrained voice, Sergeant Crall says, "Andy, go with the corporal to the office. You need to call home."

Andy gets up and feels apprehensive as he looks at Sergeant Crall and the corporal. As he walks out of the mess hall, he asks the corporal, "Is something wrong?"

The corporal says, "I would tell you, if I knew."

Andy says to himself, "I know something is wrong. I could see it in Sergeant Crall's face."

When they walk into the camp office, Captain Morrison greets Andy in the waiting room and says, "Andy, I want you to use my office, and call home. Take as long as you like."

Andy says, "Yes, sir." The corporal escorts Andy to the Captain's office and closes the door behind him."

Andy thinks, "At this point, I'll just wait and talk to mom. He sits down at the Captain's desk, and he's surprised to hear his dad answer the phone."

Andy says, "Hi, dad. It's good to hear your voice. I didn't know that you had the day off."

There's silence for a couple seconds, then Owen says in broken voice, "Andy, please stay calm while I tell you something I would never want to tell anyone."

Andy is now shaken, and says, "Dad, what is it?"

Tearfully, his dad says, "Your mother passed away this morning."

Andy now in tears says, "Surely not, dad. She is doing so well."

"Andy, I know this is especially hard for you, but she was in a car accident."

Andy says, "What happened?"

Owen replies, "She went to the Mahican Hardware Store to get supplies for the garden and yard. She left Judy at home, so she could do laundry. She left the hardware store about 10:00 and was driving home. There was a high speed chase coming her direction, and the other car crossed the median and hit her head on."

Andy asks, "Why was there a high speed chase, dad?"

"Three men robbed the Rexall Drug Store, and just as they sped out of the lot, the police were almost there with their sirens on. The police said that it appears the robber lost control of his car."

Andy soberly says, "Who are they, dad?"

Owen says, "The police just told me that all three of them are illegal immigrants."

Andy is shaken and asks, "Where are they now?"

"The driver was killed and the other two were injured. They're in the hospital now under guard. By the time you get home, they will probably be in prison."

Andy just sits in silence with his head in his hand.

After a few seconds, Owen says. "Son, are you there?"

Andy softly says, "Yes, dad." He is silent another second then asks, "How are you and Judy?"

Owen says, "We're okay under the circumstances."

Andy gathers himself and says, "Dad, just stay home with Judy, and I will be there as soon as possible."

Owen says, "What about your ride from the Indianapolis airport?"

Andy says, "I'll rent a car."

Owen says, "Be careful, son. Mr. Abernathy wants you to call him now."

Thinking about his dad, Andy says, "I will, dad. Please take care of yourself. Judy and I need you. I will see you soon; love you."

Owen replies, "I love you, son. Have a good trip. Hopefully, they will get you a flight soon."

Andy hangs up and calls Mr. Abernathy.

When Mr. Abernathy answers, Andy simply says, "This is Andy."

Mr. Abernathy asks, "How are you doing right now, Andy?"

Andy replies, "Just hanging in there, sir."

Mr. Abernathy says, "Your dad called Dr. Krause, so he could reach me. I'm very sorry about your mother."

Andy says, "She was a great mother and person. It will take me some time."

Mr. Abernathy says, "I'm sure it will. You have a week off to be with your family. Dr. Krause already has booked a flight for you to Indianapolis. He wants to pick you up there. Your flight will be on United at 5:50 this evening. Mac and Bruce will pick you up at your barracks by 3:00. Andy, before you leave the office, Lieutenant DeVoe will issue you a sidearm with shoulder holster and a federal carrying permit. If you don't have your sport coat with you, he will have a corporal bring the right size coat for you from supplies."

Andy says, "That is fine, sir. I don't have my sport coat, so I'll be looking for the corporal at my barracks."

Abernathy says, "Sergeant Crall knows that you will be leaving at 3:00 to be with your family. Pack everything. You are being transferred to our main building to finish your training. I need you here, and we have a gym and shooting range in the basement. We keep our agents in shape, so you'll have the same instructors here for martial arts and marksmanship. Most of the time you'll be working with me.

Later Sergeant Crall will tell your bunkmates that you have been transferred for an upcoming assignment."

Andy says, "Do you know where I'll stay in D.C.?"

Abernathy replies, "Don't worry about that. We will be getting the furnished apartment ready early. It will be the same nice apartment for you and your new bride."

Andy says, "I may not have transportation there until after Labor Day."

Abernathy says, "No problem. We have plenty of cars and drivers. Mac and Bruce will also be glad you're here. It will give them a little more time off."

"Thank you again, sir. It sounds like a good plan. Everyone has been supportive."

Abernathy says, "I'll let you get ready. Tell Lieutenant DeVoe that you need the sport coat. Try to have a good week with your family. Express my condolences to them."

Andy says, "Thank you, sir." Andy meets with the Lieutenant and gets his sidearm and permit. Before 3:00, the corporal is at his barracks with his coat. Andy doesn't have time to say goodbye to his bunkmates; they're busy with training. Mac and Bruce pull up right at 3:00.

Mac says, "Mr. Abernathy told us about your loss. We're sorry to hear about your mother."

Andy says, "Thank you. It's good to see both of you."

They get in the long, black Lincoln and drive to the National Airport. Bruce and Mac stay with Andy until he boards the plane. Before boarding, Mac shows his badge, and tells the flight attendants that he needs to make a quick check of the plane and passenger list. While Mac checks the plane, Bruce and Andy continue to talk. Bruce says, "We're glad to hear that you're joining us soon."

Andy says, "Everything is a blur now, but I'm also glad that we can work together." When Mac comes out of the plane, Andy shakes their hands and boards the plane early, while Bruce and Mac stay a few minutes and nonchalantly observe the passengers.

Once the plane is airborne, Andy starts thinking about his mother. His memory flashes scenes from his early childhood until now. He doesn't know when he went to sleep, but the captain's announcement about being on time for arrival in Indianapolis, wakes him up. When they land, to Andy it seems like they just took off. When Andy gets off the plane, there's almost two hours of daylight left. On his way to baggage claim, he sees Dr. Krause. Andy is smiling by the time he gets to Dr. Krause. He shakes his hand. Andy says, "I'm real glad to see you. Thanks for coming."

Dr. Krause says, "Andy, I was so sorry to hear about your mother. I know it affects you and your family greatly."

Andy replies, "At this point, it's very hard to deal with. I appreciate you taking the time to get me home."

Andy retrieves his suitcase, and they walk out into the heat, and head for Dr. Krause's car. Andy asks, "How has your summer been so far?"

Dr. Krause says, "We went on the western road trip first. We saw Yellowstone, Mt. Rushmore and the Badlands."

Andy says, "When Lydia and I were with mom and dad, we wanted to get ideas for a honeymoon. We both thought a road trip would be fun. I said that I've been north, south and east. Dad said, "If you go west, you would have enough time to see Yellowstone, Mt. Rushmore and the Badlands."

They get in the car and head for Mahican. Dr. Krause says, "Wow, that is some coincidence. I agree with your dad. From our part of Indiana, you can bypass Chicago and go through Wisconsin and Minnesota to South Dakota. You might want to stop and enjoy the Badlands first. They're on the way to Yellowstone. As you continue west, Mt. Rushmore is not far from the Badlands. We left two days after graduation. We got to Yellowstone on June 6th or 7th. As soon as we drove into the park, there was a ten minute blizzard. The snow was blowing so hard that we had to go very slow. After ten to twelve minutes the snow stopped; the ground was snow covered, and the sun came out. It felt like late spring again, except for the snow on the ground."

Andy says, "I imagine that was a beautiful and a surprising experience."

Dr. Krause says, "It was. Do you feel like updating me on your summer?"

Andy says, "I would be glad to. Of course, you're well aware that some things I can't share."

"That's right. When in doubt, don't share it."

Andy continues, "Overall, I've liked the training. Learning more about the State Department is intriguing. Martial arts is invigorating, and marksmanship is a new and useful skill."

Dr. Krause says, "During the World War, I had a desk job. I was a professor by the time the Korean War started. I've wondered about martial arts many times. I was only shown the fundamentals of self-defense in basic training."

Andy says, "I've had good conditioning growing up, but I never took martial arts, and I hadn't handled guns. Martial Arts is an excellent discipline, if you have use for it."

Andy and Dr. Krause talk all the way to Mahican. The sun is just beginning to set by the time they get to the city limits. Andy says, "It's nice to get home before dark. It looks like it might be dark by the time you get home."

Dr. Krause says, "I'll have light part of the way, and I'm just enjoying the summer. I enjoyed our trip from the airport." As Dr. Krause pulls up to Andy's house, he says, "Andy, give your family my condolences. In our church service Sunday, I'll be requesting prayer for you and your family."

Andy says, "Thank you for your thoughtfulness and your prayers. I hope we can talk soon." Andy gets his suitcase out of the trunk, and he waves at Dr. Krause, as he drives off."

When Andy starts walking toward the front door, Judy runs up to him and hugs him. She tries to say something, but starts crying. While she cries, she says, "I'm so glad you're here."

His dad walks out and gives him a hug. By this time, Andy has tears in his eyes.

When they get in the house, Owen says, "We picked up some food for supper. Do you want anything?"

Andy says, "I would like some. I had lunch at the base, but I didn't take time for supper this evening."

Judy serves Andy supper, and they say a prayer and sit at the dining table together. After Andy starts eating, Owen says, "Andy I was thinking about the weekend and the best time to plan everything for friends and relatives. Ella and Edward are helping me with some of the arrangements. If you feel like it now, I would like to get your input."

"Sure, dad. I want to know, and I want to help you."

Owen says, "This is not easy for me to go over, but we should discuss it. The coroner took your mother from the hospital to the Palmer Funeral Home, near downtown. We have to coordinate the services with three newspapers. The local newspaper will announce the visitation at Palmer's and the service at the Garden of Memory Chapel between Muncie and Hartford City. We need announcements in the Hartford City and Muncie papers for the chapel service. I want your input and Judy's about the days and times."

Andy asks, "You probably know days and times better than I do."

Owen says, "Judy and I have talked about it, and we think visitation should be from 5 pm to 7 pm Friday at Palmer's. They have said they can have everything ready with the Garden of Memory staff for the chapel service and the commital service by late morning Saturday. Friends at our home church in Muncie and at the home church in Hartford City will want to be there. For those coming farther away, we didn't want to make it too early. We're thinking about announcing the chapel service for 12:00 and the commital immediately after."

Andy says, "I think that is good. It's not too early, and we need to think about the elderly, because the weather has been hot."

"After the commital service, Ella wants us to come to their church in Hartford City for dinner. Of course, it was also your mom's hometown church."

Andy says, "That is a good plan. If we see Carl and his family from Muncie, maybe we could invite them as well."

Owen says, "Absolutely. Ella wants us to invite anyone we want to."

Judy looks at the clock and says, "It's already 9:30. What time do you get up and go to bed in training?"

Andy smiles at Judy and says, "Most days we're up at five, while you're still dreaming, and we go to bed at nine."

Judy says, "I wish I could stay up longer. I'm just glad you're here."

"Me too, sis." Judy kisses her dad and brother goodnight.

After Judy heads to the bathroom, Andy looks at his dad and says in a softer voice, "Dad, there is something I want to share with you. The general information I'm going to tell you really isn't classified, but I can't go into detail."

Owen says, "Okay, son. Even though it's not classified, I will keep it to myself."

Andy continues, "First of all, you and mom have been wise, since I was a child, to keep my gifts to yourself, and to not overreact to them. The news media is not covering the extent and severity of the illegal immigration problem. Unfortunately, my mom and our family suffered greatly, because of the problem. Media influenced by the New Age Socialist Party cover up the great problem by acting like members of the Traditional American Party are paranoid and inhumane toward the illegals. Things are coming to a head in our country, and the whole situation, including our southern border, has reached a crisis level."

Owen says, "I'm listening closely, and I think I can also hear between the lines of what you're saying. I'm getting that we must be prepared."

"Absolutely. Just between us, I have a feeling that a statement will come out soon from a top government official for people to keep their guns. I just want you and Judy to be protected."

Owen says, "It sounds like I should get a gun for defense. What kind do you recommend?"

Andy says, "Get a .38 handgun and extra ammo. Also, get a five load shotgun, which is even better for home defense, if there are one or more intruders. Also, get extra coyote load shells for it. If you haven't handled guns, take Judy to a shooting range, so you and she can get use to the guns."

Owen says, "I will do it next week. How long can you stay?"

Andy says, "I will know by Monday, if I go back late Tuesday or early Wednesday."

Owen says, "I go back to work next Thursday. Will you go gun shopping with me Monday?"

Andy says, "Be glad to. Dad, I'm bushed. Are you doing alright?"

Owen says, "Yes, I think I'm coping alright."

Andy says, "I'll say a prayer for you and Judy tonight. I love you, dad." Andy gets up and hugs his dad.

The next day, "The Indianapolis Star" and newspapers across the country run front page headlines: "Purdue's Star's Mother Killed by Drug Store Thieves". Only some of the papers say that the accused robbers may be illegal immigrants. Andy hears about the articles, but he can't bear to read them or think about them.

The first week of August with high humidity is even hotter than most days in July. Andy goes downtown with his dad to meet with the director of the Palmer Funeral Home. They park and while they walk down the sidewalk to the funeral home, they can see steam rolling off the pavement. The director confirms the visitation time and the location and service time for the chapel service. Owen is informed that his local church is providing food for the family in the break room, before the Friday evening visitation begins. They also go over the local newspaper announcement.

They go home and Owen coordinates with Ella the newspaper announcements in Muncie and Hartford City; the service time and location and details about the dinner at Davina's hometown church. He tells Ella that he will call the Garden of Memory office to make the arrangements for Davina. Andy and Judy stick close to their dad. They can tell that the stress of the day is getting to him.

Andy says, "Dad, the rest of the day, let's rest at home, and I'll make dinner reservations for the three of us this evening."

Owen says, "Thanks, Andy. I'm calling Garden of Memory now, then I'm going to lie down for a while." Andy makes sure that his dad has everything he needs.

Friday morning, Judy fixes breakfast for them. After Judy pours their coffee, Andy says, "Lydia is use to me calling her on Saturday or Sunday, so I'll call her tomorrow or Sunday."

Owen says, "Your mom would want us to continue our plans and our work. I know she would insist that you keep all of the same wedding plans. Since we've been using your car, you probably assumed that the wreck totaled the dealer's car. Don't worry about anything. Our union steward said that they would have another car for me right away, and my insurance will take care of it. You can have your car, whenever you're ready for it."

Andy says, "Thanks, dad. You and Judy use it for now. I won't need it until training is completed. When I go back, I'll complete my training out of our main office building. They also need me for some work there. I'm sure they will give me a phone number, so you can reach me directly.'

Owen says, "Will that be in D.C.?"

Andy says, "Yes. I will give you more details later. They're going ahead and moving me into the furnished apartment, that was arranged for Lydia and me."

Owen says, "I'm proud of you, son. All of your life, you've done the right thing, and God is blessing you."

Mid-afternoon they shower and dress for visitation. They leave at 3:30 to meet with the funeral director. On the way downtown, Owen tells Judy and Andy that Ella and Edward will be there from five to seven this evening. She said that Anderson and Ruth will be with us tomorrow.

They first meet in the director's office for a few minutes. The director greets them and says, "Frankly, Andy is a local celebrity, and a lot of people know Andy and your family. We're expecting a huge turnout. We've also heard that we'll have some guests from Purdue. We might need your help to keep the greeting line moving. There are always talkative people, and we don't want to offend them."

Andy says, "Don't worry, I can handle it. We also want them to feel welcomed."

The director leads them to the viewing room, and says, "I know you'll want to be with your mother before you go in the break room for supper. I wanted you to see how we arranged things for you and your guests. You will have privacy now. When you finish, the break room is down the hall and to the left." The director goes to the lobby and parking lot to make sure his staff is ready to park and greet the guests.

Owen, Andy and Judy go up to the open casket. When Judy gets next to her mother, she starts crying. Andy puts his arm around her, and can hardly keep from crying himself. Owen touches her cheek and holds her hand. At that point, Andy cries. His dad starts crying, and he puts his arm around him. Andy thinks, "What a horrific experience for his wonderful, angelic mother." When his dad starts drying his eyes with his hankie, Andy holds her hand and silently talks with her. He concludes by saying, "Mom, I will do my best to make you proud of me. I love you."

Ella and Edward arrive by 5:00, and there is already a line waiting outside to get in. The staff opens the door at 5:00, and they direct the people to the guestbook, then show them where to go to greet the family and view Davina. Andy talks briefly and cordially to everyone. He sees the great need to keep the line moving. His church friends come; most of his high school teammates including Tim; Jack, Larry and other friends and teammates from Purdue; Dr. and Mrs. Krause; his dad's friends and co-workers; Judy's friends; many local people and a lot of people from Purdue.

Before 7:30, the funeral home director says that it was the first time we had over four hundred people and were able to accommodate them in a little over two hours. They thank him, and talk with Ella and Edward before they leave. Ella says, "We'll be at the chapel by 11:30 with Anderson and Ruth."

Owen replies, "We plan to be there by 11:30. We use to pass it many times on Highway 3 on the way to your house."

Ella and Edward hug everyone and say goodnight. Owen thanks the director, and Andy and Judy gather the leftover food to take home. Before they leave, all three go in to say goodnight to Davina.

The next day is even busier. There's a large turnout at the chapel. Most of Andy's hometown church comes to the service, and there are even more people from Muncie and Hartford City, who remember the McGraigs. Andy is especially glad to see Carl and his family. He is happy to see his old church friends. After the chapel service, the committal service is at manicured grounds, where the bronze markers are level with the ground. Before they leave for Hartford City, they visit Davina's and Edward's parents' burial sites. They too have the same type of bronze markers. Their dad lost his life while stationed in Europe after World War I. Their mother died heartbroken, when they were only twenty and fifteen.

When they walk into Davina's home church in Hartford City, Andy and his family feel peaceful about being there. Andy remembers visiting the church on special occasions before they moved to Mahican. Everyone makes them feel welcome, and their hosts offer them food and drinks for the most part of two hours. They have a good time visiting with Anderson and Ruth. Owen thanks Edward and Ella for everything they have done. Ella says, "Owen, I would like to request one thing before the three of you go back to Mahican. I know my request might be difficult, but I think it would be a good thing for the three of you."

Owen says, "What is your request?"

Ella replies, "It may have been a long time since you were there, but could we go to your mother's resting place?"

Owen hesitates and says, "Sure we can. I know that it is only two or three miles from here."

As they follow Ella and Edward, Owen says, "My mom died from tuberculosis, when I was only seven. My father abandoned me, and I was raised by my grandparents, who passed away before your mom and I were married."

When they pull into the entrance of the cemetery, Andy says, "I remember being here with you and mom, when we were young kids."

They take their time at their grandma's resting place. They hug Ella and Edward, and Andy tells them it was comforting being with them. On the way back to Mahican, Andy says, "Dad, I'm glad we went to see our grandmother."

Owen says, "Ella was right; it was a good thing to do. My mom never met your mom, but I believe they're together now."

Judy says, "Someday, we'll all be together there."

On Sunday they go to their church in Mahican. Andy greets many people, and enjoys being in the service with his friends. When they get home, Andy calls Lydia. First, he asks how she is doing, then he tells her about his mother; Lydia is shocked. She starts sobbing and asks, "When did she pass away?"

Andy says, "Wednesday morning. Visitation was Friday evening, and the funeral was yesterday." Andy tells Lydia about the accident.

Lydia says, "Oh, Andy. How are you doing?"

"I'm getting along okay. I'm concerned about dad and Judy. They seem to be doing alright considering the great loss. I wanted you to know that I'll be going back Tuesday or Wednesday, and they're transferring me to their main building in D.C. I should have a direct number. When I get it, I'll give it to you."

Lydia asks, "Do you know where you'll be staying."

Andy brightens up some, "That is good news. They're getting our furnished apartment ready by the time I return."

Lydia says, "That's exciting. When you can, let me know about it."

They talk awhile, but not long, since Andy's mind is still on his dad and sister. Andy says, "Babe, I love talking with you, but I better sign off and check on dad and Judy."

Lydia says, "I think you should. I love you."

Andy says, "I love you too."

When Andy hangs up the phone, he finds that Judy and his dad are both taking naps. He decides to sit in a quiet place to think about his mom. He silently starts talking with her, then he starts praying for her. Even though he saw her at the funeral home, it's hard for him to accept.

After breakfast, Owen and Andy take Judy to a friend's house, then they go to a local gun shop. Owen decides on a .38 caliber handgun and a 12 gauge, five load shotgun. For home defense, the store's owner recommends a coyote load for the shotgun shell.

After they get in the car, Andy says, "I should call the home office in D.C. before we pick up Judy. I want to buy lunch for us; where do you want to go?"

Owen says, "Wherever they have good American style food."

Andy says, "Tim and I went to a restaurant a couple times; that's near downtown. They have good, down home cooking."

Owen says, "Let's go there. Drive home, so you can make your call, then we'll pick up Judy."

Andy finds out that Mr. Abernathy's secretary booked a flight for him later Wednesday morning. "Dad, if you're still off Wednesday, will you and Judy take me to the Indianapolis Airport? We'll need to leave about 8:30. My flight leaves at 11:40."

Owen says, "We'll be glad to drive you there."

Owen and Andy pick up Judy, and Andy drives them to Shirley's Chaperral Café. When they get out of the car, Andy says, 'You can order from the menu, but I think you'll like her lunch bar." Andy greets Shirley, and they take a look at the lunch bar: roast beef and new potatoes; spaghetti and meatballs, green beans, broccoli, black eyed peas, pineapple, cottage cheese, salad and peach cobbler for dessert."

Owen says, "Wow, good selection."

They sit down, and Shirley takes their drink order and meets Andy's family. She says, "It's so good to meet you. Do all of you want the lunch bar?" Shirley gets a unanimous, "Yes"! By the way, Andy, on television I saw you play in the tournament. You made us proud."

Andy says, "Thank you, Shirley."

Judy says, "She's really nice, Andy."

Andy replies, "Tim and I have only been here about three times, and she is always a sweet lady."

Shirley's daughter, Marsha, brings their drinks and says, "Help yourselves to the lunch bar." They fill their plates and dig in. The food is so good, that they spend more time eating than talking. Owen says, "It feels like I ate three meals."

Andy says, "I'm glad you enjoyed it, dad."

Judy says, "I'm so full that I can't think about doing anything besides taking a nap."

Owen and Andy laugh, and they get up to leave. Andy pays Shirley and gives her a generous tip. They all wave at Shirley and Marsha, on their way out.

The rest of the day, and Tuesday go by too fast for Andy. He gets together with Tim on Tuesday, so they can work out. Tim says, "I'll be sure to mark August 27th on my calendar."

Andy says, "I haven't taken time to look at wedding planning, but I think there is one best man, and I guess the other men: Anderson, Jack and Larry, are ushers.

Tim says. "I think you're right. I haven't been married either!"

Andy says, "I want to be impartial, but we go back a good ways, and played a lot of basketball together. I officially request you to be my best man."

Tim says, "Aye, aye, sir!"

That evening at home, the three McGraigs talk about the August 27th wedding. Judy volunteers to help coordinate everything, since she doesn't return to school until after Labor Day. Owen says that he'll help Judy. Andy leaves all of the wedding information that he has, and says, "I'm sure Lydia and I will be in touch with you, so we don't leave you stranded. I know that some of the ladies at the church would help."

Judy says, "I'll definitely be talking with them."

They get ready for bed early, and Judy says she wants to get up early, so they can have breakfast together by 7:30. Andy says, "Thank you, so much, sis."

They're in bed by 10:00. Andy has a peace he doesn't comprehend. He says, "Thank you, Lord, for your peace. I don't understand how I can have peace with my mother being taken from us, and with the changes I'm going through with my new work. I trust in you, and thank you for the peace you have given me."

In the morning, Andy showers early, and he can hear Judy stirring around in the kitchen, before he gets in the shower. They're eating breakfast together by 7:30. Andy asks, "Dad, if you want me to, I can drive us to the airport."

Owen says, "That will be nice."

On the way to the airport, Andy says, "They have me flying on TWA again, and it's scheduled to depart at 11:40."

Owen says, "I think Judy and I want to wait at the airport until your plane is airborne."

Andy says, "I like knowing that you will be watching."

Judy says, "I like seeing those big birds land and take off."

It's another sad occasion for the McGraigs, when Andy is ready to board the plane. He gives his dad and sister a hug, and says, "I'll be back in less than three weeks. Mom would want all of us to be strong and to have faith." With tears in their eyes, they watch Andy board.

Before Andy is seated, a young, red-headed stewardess asks for his autograph. She says, "I'm from Rensselaer. My family and I are big Purdue and NCAA tournament fans." Andy signs his autograph on a TWA flight schedule. He thanks the stewardess for her support.

Andy relaxes before the plane taxis to the runway. He thinks of God's power, as he feels the power of the engines pull the heavy plane into the air. Once again, when they start sailing over 25,000 feet, Andy admires the sea of clouds. But Andy knows the port of entry lies close ahead. He thinks, "The tide will come in, and the ship will land".

14

Boiling Point

When Andy gets off the plane, the first thing he sees are Mac and Bruce. Andy says, "You'll have to kick your habit of hanging out at the airport."

Bruce asks, "How was everything at home?"

Andy replies, "It was sad, but it was good to be with the family and to see many friends."

Mac says, "I don't mean to hurry us, but we have a meeting with Mr. Abernathy in one hour."

Andy says, "I'm starting to get use to wearing a sport coat and tie."

As they head to baggage claim, Bruce says, "Soon you'll have a grey suit and black tie like ours."

Mac says, "Actually, we each have three grey suits and three black ties. There are always two in the closet that are clean and pressed."

Bruce takes Andy's suitcase, and Mac says to Andy, "You have a fairly simple day. We meet with Mr. Abernathy at 1:00, then Bruce will take you to your new apartment. There will be some check-in things that Bruce will help you with."

After they arrive at the State Department, they go to a ground floor office to get ready for the meeting. Bruce says, "We call this the prep room. It has desks and a supply room, so staff members can get ready for their meetings at the same time. Today, we're just going into the supply room, so each of us can get a notebook and a pen." When they enter the room, Andy has never seen so many office supplies except at the college book store.

They take the elevator to Mr. Abernathy's office. They walk into the Secretary's office complex a few minutes before 1:00. The receptionist greets them and says, "I'll tell Mr. Abernathy you're here."

In a minute Mr. Abernathy comes charging out of his office. He says, "Good to see all of you. How was your flight, Andy?"

Andy says, "Good and peaceful."

Mr. Abernathy says, "Let's go in my office; we have a lot to discuss."

Mr. Abernathy sits behind his desk, and Andy, Mac and Bruce sit in three comfortable guest chairs. Mr. Abernathy says, "I'm glad you brought pens and notebooks; you'll need them. First of all, Andy, we want to express our condolences to you and your family. At the ages of you and your family, it must be very difficult."

Andy says, "Thank you for the kind thoughts. It is difficult, but we trust in the Lord and His love in our family. I'm thankful that I'm here working with you and the staff in the State Department."

Mr. Abernathy expresses a smile of understanding and says, "Mac and Bruce, I appreciate your service here and dedication. Mac, I believe you're beginning your seventh year as a security agent here."

Mac says, "Yes, sir."

Abernathy replies, "Congratulations. Bruce, I have depended on you and Mac for several years now. As you know, your work here is classified. I wanted the three of you to meet with me, because I'm sharing something in this meeting that is extremely classified. You probably know that Andy had eight weeks of security agent training before he lost his mother. What you don't know is that Andy has other duties, which are extremely classified. Soon, he will become known as my body guard, but that is for the sake of staff and the public. Are you following me?"

Mac and Bruce reply, "Yes, sir."

Abernathy continues, "Andy gave up a stellar career in the NBA to be part of our staff. Andy is young, and he is also a very capable person."

Mac says, "Yes, sir. Bruce and I have noticed his maturity, and we have only heard respect from other people."

Mr. Abernathy says, "Andy will complete about four more weeks of training here, while he assists me with my work. He will be qualified as a security agent and as a body guard, but I want you to listen carefully now. Andy will have my back, and I know that both of you have my back. Starting today, I want you to also have Andy's back."

Mack asks, "So, Bruce and I will also be security for Andy?"

Abernathy says, "That is absolutely right. Do you have any questions or problems with that?"

Bruce and Mac answer in unison, "No, sir."

"Andy will also lighten some of the overtime for both of you. At times, you will have a little more time off, since Andy will be available to work with each of you."

Bruce says, "We appreciate that."

Abernathy says, "Bruce, after the meeting, I'm going to give Mac the rest of the day off. I haven't told Andy that his apartment is in the secured complex that is designed for government officials. I want you to take him there. The officer at the gate has the key and information that you will pass on to Andy. I want you to go in and sweep his apartment and phone. It was ordered to have a security check, but I want you to make sure it's clean."

Bruce says, "No problem, sir."

Abernathy looks at Andy and says, "I bet you'll be glad to have your own phone. Mac and Bruce also knew what training was like."

Andy says, "Yes, sir. We all miss a phone."

Abernathy looks at Mac and Bruce, "Every day that Andy works, one of you will be picking him up and taking him home. He will have his own car after Labor Day, but you will be assigned to him,"

Both Mac and Bruce reply, "No problem, sir."

Abernathy says, "Okay, gentlemen, and now, for the rest of the meeting: get out your pens and open your notebooks. Of course, the information I'm about to share is extremely classified, so make notes that only you will be able to decipher." Abernathy waits a few seconds until the three men are ready to write. He continues, "As you know the country is drastically changing: there are problems at the southern border; the New Age Socialist Party is difficult to work with; and there is a trail of other concerns. We also have some problems with a number of the aggressive countries in the world. You will be playing a bigger part than you realize in helping the country to correct these problems."

Bruce says, "Excuse me, sir. Do you mind asking your assistant or someone to bring in coffee or water?"

Abernathy says, "Good idea, Bruce." He takes the coffee and water count and calls to have it brought in. Abernathy says, "The coffee and water will be here in a couple minutes. Are there any questions, since we have a short break?"

Mac says, "This probably sounds petty, but do you know our schedule for the next day or so."

Abernathy laughs and says, "That's important. Mac, you'll be off from after this meeting until 1:30 tomorrow. You and I will have supper here at 4:30 tomorrow. You'll take Andy home, then you'll come back and pick me up here. Bruce, you'll get off about 5:30 today, and you'll pick up Andy and me between 7:30 and 7:45, we'll have breakfast together here at 8:00. Tomorrow you'll get off between 1:30 and 2. Andy, bring your gym and training gear tomorrow. After our meeting at 8:45 tomorrow, Bruce will show you the gym, your locker and the target range. You'll have martial arts training at 10:30 and target practice and gun handling by 11:45 and lunch around 12:45."

Abernathy's assistant brings in two orders of coffee and water; one order of coffee and one order of water.

Abernathy says, "Alright, men. While we enjoy the drinks, we'll go ahead with the second part of the meeting. I already mentioned the border crisis; problems with the socialist party and problems with several countries. The last three weeks of this month, we will be in preparation for expected outbreaks, and after Labor Day there will be some strategy sessions and special assignments." Abernathy stops and looks at all three men, who are all under the age of thirty.

Mac asks, "By September, is it likely that we could be gone days at a time?"

Abernathy says, "It's hard to predict. At times, our work will be here, but I have no idea how long our work might take us away from home."

Bruce says, "I know that all of our work is classified, and what you're sharing is extremely classified. Are you at liberty to tell us that something major may be happening by next month?"

Abernathy replies, "It is likely to happen that soon, or it could happen sooner. Because of the imminent problems, we will be preparing every day this month, and we will be even more active next month. You might say that this is an alert notice for the three of you. Andy will be gone a week before Labor Day. You may already know that he is getting married."

Mac and Bruce congratulate Andy on his upcoming wedding. The meeting lasts until almost 2:30. Bruce drives Andy to a tree lined street that is only about twelve minutes from the State Department building. At the end of the tree lined street is a huge apartment complex that encompasses about two square blocks. It has a high fence and a security gate with an officer present. At the gate, Bruce shows his badge and gets the keys and apartment information for Andy.

Bruce drives down a winding drive that has two lanes. Before it circles back, there is a large yard with a few trees, a walking path and playground equipment for children. There is a main entrance and an exit for each apartment building. The apartments are like condos with one entrance and exit to the apartments on the ground floor, and an elevator and stairway to individual entrances on a second floor. Andy carries his suitcase, while they get on the elevator to the second floor. Before they get out of the elevator, Bruce says that each condo style apartment building has eight apartments; four on each floor.

When they walk into Andy and Lydia's new apartment, Andy says, "Wow, these are big rooms. Bruce hands Andy the two keys and apartment brochure. While Bruce checks each room and the two phones, Andy flips through the brochure.

He's impressed that the furnished apartment has 1640 sf with two large bedrooms, two full bathrooms, a large living room, dining room and kitchen. He looks outside and notices a balcony off the dining room and kitchen, and a swimming pool between his building and three other buildings. He also notices a lawn designed for walking pets.

Bruce comes back in the living room, and says, "After I check this phone, I'll be done. The master bedroom phone is fine." Bruce checks the phone and says, "In the morning, I'll be in front of your building at 7:30. At a later time, you'll probably wonder how much maintenance crews are scrutinized like lawn care and garbage. I can tell you that they're watched like a hawk. Besides the officer at the front gate, there is an undercover agent who watches things like maintenance crews, and another undercover agent who watches the buildings and the perimeter. Brother, you have 24/7 security."

Andy says, "Even though we are security people, it's good to know that things are being watched during sleeping hours."

Bruce says, "Have a good night, Andy."

Andy is elated with the furnished apartment. He calls Lydia to share his excitement. She answers, and Andy says, "Hi, babe, guess where I am right now."

Lydia says, "How many guesses do I get?"

Andy says, "I'm in our new apartment! It is so spacious and comfortable. It also has two bedrooms and two full bathrooms."

Lydia says, "That is exciting. I wish I were there. Could my parents stay there, when they visit us?"

Andy says, "Absolutely."

Andy and Lydia have a lengthy talk, and they decide that Andy should call Judy and his dad about the wedding invitation list. After they finish, he calls home and goes over the list of wedding guests. He says, "Dad, don't worry about any of the expenses. Just let me know what they are, and I will send you a check. It has been a full day here. Did you have a good trip back from the airport?"

Owen says, "Yes, Judy and I stopped at White Castle. We had a good time. We all miss your mom so much, but we're doing alright."

Andy says, "I'm glad you are. Tomorrow, I will also get an office number for you, so you can reach me day or night."

Owen says, "I know you'll do your best. I love you, son."

Andy says, "I love you, dad. I'll call soon."

When Andy finishes with his calls, it's after 5:00, and he realizes he hasn't thought about supper. He goes in the kitchen and opens the frig, and it's filled with fruit, water, soda, cheese, luncheon meat, eggs, butter and many other things. He opens a cabinet door and finds crackers, tea, coffee, popcorn and other items. A large drawer has bread and donuts. Andy proceeds to indulge himself, then he turns on the news at 6:00.

Since his mother's funeral, he hasn't read as much or followed the news as much, but he is getting the desire to learn what he has been missing. After the news he gets out a month old issue of the National Review, and then reads in the books of Joshua and the Gospel of John. By 9:00 he tires out and gets ready for bed.

As he goes to sleep, he prays for his family and thinks about his mother. It's quiet outside, and Andy falls into a deep sleep. He doesn't get up in the middle of the night. He continues to sleep soundly and has scattered dreams, but before he wakes up, he has a longer dream. He sees infiltrators all over the country. Some are illegal immigrants, but there are many others with criminal and terrorist ties. He sees them operating in cells of neighborhoods; in towns and cities of all sizes.

Next he sees thousands of churches across the country. He sees them in small towns and large cities. He sees them in the country and in suburban developments. He sees churches and outreach centers of all sizes in inter-cities.

He sees churches near the ocean; churches in mountainous areas; churches in prairies; churches in arid areas and churches in fertile farmlands. When he sees the church buildings closer up, they all have the same word in big letters across their front doors, "MISSION".

Andy wakes up before 5:30 in a slight sweat. He immediately thinks, "I'm glad the Secretary and I are meeting early today." He gets ready early, and he is outside his building several minutes before Bruce arrives. Andy is dressed in his sport coat and tie, and is carrying his gym bag.

Bruce picks up Mr. Abernathy after he gets Andy. By 8:00, they're in the State Department cafeteria getting breakfast. Abernathy asks Andy, "How was the apartment?"

Andy between bites says, "Excellent, thank you."

Abernathy says, "Our staff did a good job preparing it for you and your fiancée."

As soon as they finish breakfast, Mr. Abernathy says, "Andy, let's get an early start with our meeting." Andy follows Mr. Abernathy to his office. Bruce follows behind and waits in the Secretary's waiting room for them.

When they get seated in the Secretary's office, Abernathy asks, "How was your first night there?"

Andy replies, "It was very comfortable; I slept like a baby. Mr. Abernathy, if you don't have anything urgent right now, I would like to share something important with you."

Abernathy says, "I had a feeling during breakfast, that you had something for me."

Andy says, "I had a detailed dream not long before I woke up." Andy describes his dream, while Abernathy is all ears. Mr. Abernathy scoots to the edge of his chair and gives Andy his undivided attention.

After Andy finishes, Abernathy says, "Very interesting, Andy." He pages his secretary and says, "Hold my calls for twenty to thirty minutes, unless it's an emergency." He continues, "Andy, I think I heard a few years ago that there are close to 300,000 churches operating in the country, including Hawaii and Alaska. With so many churches, it would be difficult to execute personnel to every one of them, but we could concentrate on urban and suburban churches in bigger neighborhoods. As we have the personnel, we could contact some of the other pastors, who we think are patriots. Very interesting, Andy; infiltrating the infiltrators."

Andy says, "My thoughts exactly."

Mr. Abernathy says, "After you complete your training and return from your honeymoon, I'm going to introduce you to the President. He and I agree that we can also confide in our Secretary of Defense, Robert Feara, and our Chairman of Joint Chiefs of Staff, John Calhoun, about you and your work. These men are some of the best patriots we have."

Andy says, "I will be looking forward to being here after Labor Day."

Abernathy asks, "Are you carrying your sidearm now?"

Andy replies, "Yes, sir."

Abernathy says, "There are very few places, where you don't carry it; like in martial arts class. Our department will be coordinating activities with the President, the Chairman of the Joint Chiefs of Staff, the Secretary of Defense and the CIA Director. Do you know the names of Will Cliffton and Wiley Mandex in the State Department?"

Andy says, "No, sir."

Abernathy says, "Will Cliffton and Wiley Mandex are two of the Under Secretaries. I didn't say this, but you can't trust them to give you the time of day. They are leftovers from a previous administration. They are radical members of the socialist party. We haven't done a thorough investigation of them yet, but we suspect they're involved with seditious activities."

Andy asks, "What do they manage in the State Department?"

Abernathy says, "Unfortunately, they're in charge of two of the six main branches in the department. Cliffton is over public diplomacy and public affairs, and Mandex is over global affairs. I've talked to the President about having them replaced."

Andy says, "I'm glad I know about them."

Abernathy says, "We can channel our defense preparations through other branches of the department that we trust. We have a lot to go over this morning, before your first training class. I'll cover the outline of concerns, then we'll go back and discuss them with what time we have left. First of all, we're concerned the most about a few countries, who might invade, when the uprising begins. First, I'm going to meet with their ambassadors, who live here. They include Russia, Iran and North Korea. Andy, I want you to be with me at those meetings. They will take place within the next two weeks."

Andy replies, "Yes, sir."

Abernathy continues, "With your help, I need to determine, if they are truthful with their answers to questions I have for them. If we suspect that any of them are lying, we will warn their country or countries, that any aggression in our country will be met with devastation in theirs. It's good that our military is on the right side. With the military behind us, we will overcome the expected conflicts."

Andy asks, "Do you think the major uprising will be at a coordinated time with the southern border activities and cells operating in sanctuary cities?"

Abernathy says, "Intelligence thinks it is the most likely scenario, including acts of terror at institutions like schools, hospitals and attacks on our power grids. Every day we're stepping up security at power stations and water stations. We are considering delaying school attendance immediately after Labor Day."

Andy replies, "It's a difficult decision to keep them out of school. Is there enough local security to protect the children?"

Abernathy says, "Everyone will be busy with responsibilities, including guarding our schools and hospitals. Local police and National Guard will be the best sources, but there is one other."

Andy says, "You have my full attention."

Abernathy says, "American gun owners comprise one of the largest standing armies in the world. In the Midwest alone, the American gun owners are still one of the largest armies in the world. It looks like our enemies haven't considered the gun owners in our country."

Andy replies, "I'm glad they haven't."

Abernathy says, "Vice-President Fairbank's office is sending a letter to the President of the NRA to tell members that he and the President request they do not give up their guns. I understand the NRA President is to confirm the request this week, then they will send all members the message by next week."

Andy says, "Excellent. Are the branches of the military already on full alert?"

Abernathy says, "Yes. The President, as Commander and Chief, is talking with the Joint Chiefs of Staff regularly. They may start a draft by the end of this month. Let's finish our discussion soon, so you can get ready for martial arts."

After their meeting, Andy goes to the locker room and changes for his martial arts class. He walks into the gym a couple minutes early, and his same instructor from training camp is waiting for him; Mr. Kim Park. They bow and greet each other. Andy says, "Instructor Park, if you have a moment before training, I wondered how you became a martial arts expert."

Mr. Park says, "I was in Special Forces with the South Korean Army, and I heard there was a need in the United States government for a good martial arts instructor. Today, we are going to execute some common sense tactics, that all agents need to know. You are a big man and strong, but what if your opponent is a hundred pounds heavier than you. He could be a very tall and heavy man, like the NFL uses. You have learned some Judo, which is helpful in this case, but let's try some moves that put a bigger man out of commission."

Mr. Park trains Andy on how to use the forearm and elbow to the head, and how to use the leg and the foot on the knees, legs and groin. He also goes over some other fighting techniques to disarm and incapacitate a bigger man.

After an hour, Andy heads to the locker room; takes off his sweaty gym clothes; gets in the shower and thinks, "Man, Mr. Park always gives me a challenging work-out."

When he goes to the firing range, he finds out that his instructor works out of the State Department building. He has never seen so many guns, including the M14 and the .45 handgun. He is schooled further in the use of the M14 and the .45. He estimates that the range has about twenty firing stations, and most of them are being used, when he starts target practice.

The weekend arrives, and Andy realizes only two weeks of training are left, and it's only two and a half weeks before he and Lydia marry. As he gets ready for Saturday morning breakfast with Mr. Abernathy, Mac and Bruce, he wonders if the country might be surprised with an early attack. He considers any coordinated attack before the second week of September as being early. He also thinks about the ramifications of Mr. Abernathy's meetings with the Russian, Iranian and North Korean ambassadors in the next two weeks.

He hears a honk outside his building. Mac is early, and Andy is glad he's ready early. Andy runs downs the stairs; takes two steps at a time and rushes out of the building to the car. Mac says, "I can tell you're raring to go."

Andy catching his breath says, "I like to be early." They pick up Mr. Abernathy next and he says, "Bruce is on duty at the department. He will meet us in the cafeteria for breakfast.'

Andy likes the choices they provide on their breakfast bar: scrambled eggs, ham, bacon, sausage, hash browns, fried potatoes, biscuits and gravy, pancakes, bagels, french toast and regular toast. As he helps himself, he thinks a chain restaurant would be popular with a country theme; a good breakfast menu; a fireplace in the restaurant and a gift shop next to the restaurant.

The four men pick out a table, and Mr. Abernathy says a prayer before breakfast. After they start eating, Mr. Abernathy says, "Andy, you should start getting the newspaper in the morning. It's delivered outside your door by the department's mail carrier. They bring the papers to him, and he delivers to department personnel within five miles of headquarters. Rod delivers papers from 4 to 7 a.m. Sunday through Saturday, and he carries our mail within the department from 8 a.m. to noon; Monday through Friday. He likes the job, so he can watch his kids play sports, and have dinner with his family."

Andy meets with Mr. Abernathy after breakfast. He says, "Bruce gets off at noon today, and Mac will takes us home after a late lunch here. We'll have lunch with Mac at 1:00. Your Saturday and Sunday schedule will be similar to your schedule at training camp, except for the rise and shine call at 5 a.m. You're technically off from 2 p.m. Saturday until 8 a.m. Monday.

Andy says, "I'll miss reveille."

Mr. Abernathy laughs and says, "I'm sure you will miss that and having to go to the community laundromat. We have a lot to cover today. We have less than four hours to go over everything, and we'll take a short coffee and bathroom break in two hours."

Mr. Abernathy meets with Andy about the agendas for the ambassador meetings; defense preparations for the possible invasion and uprising and Andy's scheduling after he returns from his honeymoon.

After lunch, Mac takes Mr. Abernathy home and then Andy. Andy asks, "Are you or Bruce picking me up at 7:45 Monday?"

Mac says, "I think Bruce has that schedule. You might want to be ready by 7:40." When they get to Andy's building, Mac says, "Enjoy the rest of the weekend."

Andy says, "You too."

The first thing on Andy's mind is catching up on the wedding news. He decides to call his dad and Judy first, so he can share those things with Lydia. He calls home and Judy answers. Andy says, "Is this the Mahican Wildcat?"

Judy laughs and says, "Are you protecting America today?"

Andy smiles and says, "Good counter. How are you and Dad doing?"

Judy says, "Overall we're fine, but I think we both get depressed from Mom not being here."

Andy says, "That's understandable. How are the wedding plans going?"

They talk about the invitations: the wedding list; the reservations at the Purdue Chapel and the plans with their church in Mahican. Andy says, "Judy, let me speak with dad. I know you'll take care of him."

Judy replies, "I sure will. I love you."

Owen comes to the phone and says, "How is your training at the department?"

Andy says, "Things are going well, dad. I'm looking forward to being there in a couple weeks. Have you made any plans about seeing the land?"

Owen says, "Yes. I told Edward about what you shared with me before you went back to training. He is excited about going with me, since the land is very close to the Smokies. He said that Anderson would like to go with us, if he can get a day off from work. We'll walk the land before you arrive for your wedding."

Andy says, "Excellent! Do you think you can walk most of the perimeter and some of the interior?"

Owen replies, "Yes, we will. Since we all like nature, we'll take notes for you."

He says, "Thank you so much. Dad, in just two weeks I'll be there."

Owen says, "I'm looking forward to it. We miss you."

Andy says, "I miss you too, dad."

15

American Summer

After Andy calls Lydia, he takes the U.S. News & World Report off the coffee table; turns on the floor lamp and sits down on the recliner. Before he starts reading, he reflects on the past week. He thinks the meetings with Mr. Abernathy were productive. He enjoyed learning more martial arts from Mr. Park. He's glad he was able to lift weights during two afternoon breaks. He decides to take time next week to find out about basketball courts and pick-up games.

After he reads most of the articles in U.S. News, he fixes a light supper and some snacks, and turns on the television to listen to the news. After the news, he watches a sci-fi movie that he saw, when he was a kid, "The Day the Earth Stood Still". He decides to turn in early. He reads the Bible; prays and thinks about his mom. He turns out the living room and kitchen lights and gets ready for bed.

As soon as he crawls in bed, he falls asleep. For a Saturday evening, the neighborhood is fairly quiet. Now and then a dog barks in the distance. The antique mantel clock, that his Aunt Ella gave him, can barely be heard ticking in the living room. After midnight, it's even quieter in Andy's apartment. If Lydia or a guest were in the house, they could hear Andy snoring now and then.

In August, daybreak arrives about 6 a.m. Andy didn't set the alarm. He's still sound asleep after 5 a.m. He starts moving some in his sleep. He looks outside and even though it's mid-morning, the clouds are very dark, and give an appearance that a powerful storm is coming. All of a sudden, he sees his mom in the back part of the yard, and it starts thundering and raining. He runs to the back door to make sure his mom can get in. Just as he opens the door, lightning strikes, and he doesn't see his mom. He quickly checks the yard and behind the garage, and it starts raining hard. He's soaked, but he is still looking. He keeps yelling, "Mom! Mom!"

All of a sudden, he's downtown, and a large gang of young men are assaulting families, children and the elderly. He hears gunfire, then rapid gunfire, and when the gang begins to disperse, he sees children, fathers, mothers and the elderly lying in pools of blood.

Andy starts running toward the hospital, which is only nine blocks from the center of downtown. One block before he gets there, he is thrown to the ground after a large explosion. When he gets up, there is smoke and debris everywhere. When he gets close to the hospital, its looks like one corner of the hospital was blown away. After he gets inside, he sees a children's ward close to the exposed corner, where some of the children are on fire. He grabs one of the children and then another to put the fires out. Some of the children are lying still on the ground. When he gets up, he sees an arm that has been blown off.

He looks for more children to help, then he finds himself in intensive care. He sees lifeless bodies lying on beds and stretchers. He looks down a long hall, and he sees a middle aged woman, who has been injured. When he gets closer to her, she says, "Andy."

Andy cries, "Mom! Mom!", and he wakes up in a sweat and sits straight up in the bed. After he takes a deep breath, he thinks, "I have to call Mr. Abernathy." Before he gets out of bed, he looks at the windows, and he can see some faint light through the blinds. He gets up and turns on a light and sees that it is 6:04. He goes into the guest bedroom and grabs his black book out of a desk drawer. He looks up "Abernathy"; goes to the living room and sits down by the phone. Before he calls, he realizes that he needs to go in the bathroom, then he gets a drink of water.

Before he makes coffee, he sits down by the phone and picks up his black book again, so he can dial Mr. Abernathy. Mr. Abernathy answers.

Andy says, "Mr. Abernathy, sorry to bother you early, but I think I have something important."

Abernathy says, "No problem, Andy. I've been up a few minutes. If you need to call me in the middle of the night, please do so."

Andy says, "I just woke up from a dream. It was a dreadful nightmare." Andy describes the dream in detail. When he finishes, he says, "I was just thinking about it being Sunday. It's the Lord's Day, and our enemies resent our faith and tradition. Also, the Pearl Harbor attack occurred on Sunday morning."

Abernathy says, "The dream is very startling. What is your interpretation of it?"

Andy says, "I think the dream is to reveal some events that are imminent. I don't think the events are part of the invasion or escalating border crisis. I think the attacks are a horrid decoy to distract us from the upcoming national crisis. The dream is about terrorism. I don't believe it is about the nationwide uprising."

Abernathy says, "Even though it's early Sunday morning, I think I'll call the President or Vice-President now. I'm concerned about getting out a high alert call to the local authorities and law enforcement." Abernathy calls the Vice-President first, and tells him that the President should be called immediately."

Even with the high alert status, some of the local authorities don't get the alert and information until late morning on the east coast. On the west coast, most areas get the alert by 7 a.m. pacific time and earlier.

By the time Andy fixes coffee and has breakfast, it's 7 a.m. He's concerned about the dream and the day's events, so he starts turning to several radio channels. At 7:30 he's dressed to go on a run, and when he opens the door, he sees his first newspaper. He thinks, "The department is right on time." Mac showed him a secured path that he can run on. He decides that he wants to run three miles.

He finishes the run in sixteen minutes. He stretches again after he runs, and then decides to enjoy a Sunday morning walk. He's back inside before 8:15. He turns on the television and grabs his transistor radio. He continues to search for any news report.

He decides to shave and shower. By 8:45, he's back to the TV and radio. Before 9 a.m. he hears a report about a church being attacked in Indianapolis. He searches for the same report on TV, and finds a channel with a breaking news announcement. The television crew has arrived on the scene of a church in south Indianapolis that has been attacked by several men with AK47s. The reporter says the men were masked and open fired on people arriving for their first service at 8 a.m. It's reported by a church member that over twenty people have been killed, and many more are seriously injured.

Andy continues to search for news reports on the radio. He finds a 50,000 watt station that is reporting on an attack at a hospital in Nashville at 7 a.m. central time. The report says that a bomb exploded on their third floor near the maternity ward and killed nineteen people: three infants, two of their mothers, four other children, four nurses and six other adults.

Andy picks up the phone and calls the Secretary. Mr. Abernathy answers and says, "Andy, we're doing what we can, but already in several cities they're slipping through the cracks. When you called earlier this morning, I was afraid that your premonition would be true. Many times I've thought about assigning more security for you."

Andy asks, "Sir, is there anything I can do now?"

Abernathy replies, "Just pray for our citizens and for our law enforcement. You've already done your job today. Try to rest today. It looks like we're going to have a busy week. I contacted the Vice-President right away, and the President called me about twenty minutes after that. They got the alert out, but there are just too many soft targets in the country."

Andy says, "Yes, sir, I will pray, and I'll be following the news today."

Mr. Abernathy says, "By the way, I let the Vice-President and the President know that you gave me the alert. They both want to meet you as soon as possible. They're already referring to you as "our Edgar Cayce".

Andy says, "I'm looking forward to meeting them."

Abernathy says, "Try to have a good day. Bruce will pick you up at 7:40 in the morning. We'll have breakfast at the department at 8:00."

Andy says, "Thank you for your promptness, sir. Take care."

Andy calls his dad and tells him to conceal his handgun, and take it to church today. He also advises him to ask a couple friends to help him watch the exits and parking lot. After he hangs up he thinks, "I need to call Lydia and find out if they have made their plane reservations for Indianapolis. I want to get their flight number and arrival time."

At 10:30 he leaves to attend the neighborhood church. It is attended mostly by department employees, including other security agents. He arrives early to look for other security agents; which he knows from the department's firing range. He finds three of them, who help him watch the exit doors and the parking lot during the worship service.

After the service, Andy talks with several people and greets the pastor. The day goes slow for Andy. He decides to stay at home and catch up on reading. He tells Lydia about the awful terrorist attacks that have been reported by early afternoon. He gets good news about their arrival time at the Indianapolis Airport on August 28th. She and her parents are arriving at 8:20 p.m. Andy thinks that he can arrive one to two hours before their flight lands.

On the 6:00 news, several more terrorist attacks are reported. In Birmingham, terrorists killed thirty-four people and injured twenty more at a suburban shopping center. Three police officers were killed in the shoot-out and four terrorists. During the worship service at a large church in Joplin, Missouri, five terrorists came in with AK47s and killed forty three children, women and men. Twenty-four others were seriously wounded.

At a hospital in Tulsa, thirty adults and children were killed by a bomb explosion. At a church in Dallas, twenty-seven people were killed on Sunday morning. At a large church in Austin, six terrorists killed forty-five people. By 7:00 Andy hears all the tragic news he can handle. He calls his dad and Judy to make sure they're alright. The attacks affect him so much that he only wants to read the Bible and pray.

After he finishes praying, he thinks about all the cities that the terrorists hit. He realizes that they only hit conservative areas in non-sanctuary cities. He thinks, "By early evening, I've heard that over two hundred adults and children have been victims of terrorism."

He tries to go to sleep early, but he lies wide awake in bed thinking about the terror attacks, the victims, his dream and his mother. Sometime before midnight, he drifts off to sleep.

Even though his alarm is set for 6 a.m. Andy wakes up before

5:30. He immediately thinks about the newspaper, he just started getting. He gets up and finds the morning paper by his door. He turns on the lamp by the recliner; opens the paper and the large headlines on the front page say, "BLOODY SUNDAY". He thinks the headline sounds more like a horror movie title, but sadly, its realty. He reads the article and the known, liberal journalist sarcastically coins the Sunday terrorism as, "American Summer". The article says the terror attacks occurred in ten cities and seven states, and took over three hundred lives.

It's the first day, since training started, that Andy isn't looking forward to the day's events. He tries to think positive and hopes that martial arts and firearms training will help get his mind off Sunday's events and the dream. He feels that getting ready for work today is mechanical.

He's outside, when Bruce pulls up at 7:40. When he gets in the car, Bruce says, "It wasn't a good weekend after all, was it?"

Andy replies, "It was very sad." They take off to pick up Mr. Abernathy. The three of them have very little to say on the way to the State Department. Bruce pulls up to the front entrance. Just getting out of the car helps lift the melancholy. Before Andy shuts the door, Mr. Abernathy turns around and says, "Bruce, we'll meet you for breakfast in a few minutes."

As they walk to the cafeteria, Mr. Abernathy simply says, "It isn't easy, is it?"

Andy says, "No. Just to keep my mind from yesterday's events, I'm wondering, if they will have grapefruit this morning."

Abernathy says, "I understand. It's hard to take when our country is attacked, and we lose innocent civilians. We'll keep our mind on breakfast for now, then we'll go upstairs and discuss what we need to."

Before they finish choosing their food, Bruce walks in. There's only about five people between Bruce and them. They wait at a table for him, then they pray for the victims and their families before they start breakfast.

Bruce accompanies them to Abernathy's office after breakfast. Andy and Mr. Abernathy take their seats, and before Mr. Abernathy starts the meeting, he takes a deep breath, relaxes and seems to clear his mind. He says, "Andy, your call to me was very important Sunday morning. As I said, call me in the middle of the night or whenever you need to."

Andy says, "I will, sir."

Abernathy says, "I was going to begin with the ambassadors' schedules, but at the moment, your welfare is on my mind. You may not want added security, but you're needed by your country and by me. I talked with my advisors in intelligence and security yesterday. They do not know that I was talking about you, but they agree with me. One agent stands out in my mind. He's intelligent and very capable. He's married, and his wife, Shelby, is also an agent. They haven't had children yet. They met after they became agents. I want him and his wife to shadow you and your new bride on your honeymoon. For example, they can stay in the motel room next to yours, and have meals at a table near yours."

Andy says, "I understand, sir. He will have my back, but not intrude on my privacy."

Abernathy says, "Exactly, I'm glad you understand. Once we get through this crisis, things will be different. You probably won't need extra security, when this is over. At night, I'm assigning him to watch your apartment, but your time off and your honeymoon will be a break for him as well, since his wife will be with him. They don't know about your undercover work; they just know they have a major assignment. I've asked Alex to come in to meet you at the end of our meeting this morning."

Andy says, "I look forward to meeting+ him."

Abernathy talks to Andy about national security and his upcoming meetings with the three ambassadors. He has two of the meetings scheduled this week, and one meeting scheduled next week. Abernathy says, "Each meeting is crucial. I don't trust any of the three ambassadors, and I trust the Iranian ambassador the least." Abernathy looks at his watch and says, "Since it's getting close to your martial arts time, I'll page my secretary, and see if Agent Werner is in the waiting room." Abernathy pages her and says, "Send him in."

When Alex walks in, Mr. Abernathy introduces him to Andy. Alex says, "I've seen you at the firing range. You stand out in a crowd."

Andy says, "Yes, I remember seeing a James Bond type there." Alex is over six feet tall; broad shouldered; handsome, dark complexioned with a natural five o'clock shadow." Andy guesses that he is in his late twenties. They seem to have a favorable impression of each other.

When Andy arrives at his martial arts training, he's glad to hear Instructor Parks say that today will be a review of what you want to improve on. After the bad weekend, he has less pressure with doing what he wants. In firearms training, the instruction is cut short because of agents involved with follow-up from Sunday. It's obvious to Andy that the department is preoccupied. Andy has lunch with Abernathy and Bruce at 12:30,

He asks Mr. Abernathy, "What time does Mac come in today?"

Abernathy says, "4:30".

Andy says, "With the department being busy with the aftermath from yesterday, I have more time today. If Bruce wants to get off three hours early, I could be the agent on duty in the office."

Abernathy looks at Bruce, and he nods his head. Abernathy says, "Okay, we'll do it. There's a couple things to cover before you go home today. By the way, you usually don't get out for dinner, so I'm calling Mac to let him know that you and he are to have dinner outside the office before he takes you home."

Andy says, "Thank you, sir."

When they finish lunch, Bruce thanks Andy for filling in for him.

At Secretary Abernathy's office complex, he has his secretary call an agent for a one hour security detail by the outside door. Abernathy says to Andy, "We'll be done within an hour, then you can go to the outer door and relieve the temporary agent. Between us, you can come in the office a couple times to get coffee. Bruce and Mac are the only two agents who shift from our waiting room to outside the door. No one is to come in our office unless they have a badge or a visitor's pass; always check with the receptionist. I'm getting an agent to relieve you at 4:30."

When the temporary agent arrives, Abernathy and Andy go in his office. Abernathy says, "Agent Werner will start his watch tonight, outside your building. He also has a pass to get into the building, but he won't bother you unless it's an emergency. He has your number in case of an emergency or an alert. His shift is during common sleeping hours from 10 p.m. until 6 a.m. If you need to contact him, put your number in this pager to reach him." Abernathy hands Andy the pager.

Andy says, "I hate to put you through this."

Abernathy says, "It is no problem; you're a valued member of the department. With your extra martial arts and firearms training, you will have a fast track security agent certification with the specialty of body guard. Of course, this a classified procedure, so we can get you working full-time as an undercover advisor. Next week you will have martial arts only two days and firearms only two days. The remainder of your training will be surveillance and body guard techniques."

Andy says, "I was wondering when the agent training will be completed, and when my flight to Indianapolis will be scheduled?"

Mr. Abernathy replies, "Your agent training will be completed by next Friday morning. We are having an in-house ceremony for you and Agent Werner at 11:30 next Friday morning. Agent Werner will be receiving an accommodation for outstanding service. His wife will be at the ceremony; as well as Agent Werner's superior; your martial arts and firearms instructors; Mr. Jennings; Mac and Bruce; Captain Morrison, head officer of our training camp and myself. I have also invited the Vice-President. He will be here, if he can fit it in his schedule. We're having lunch catered. The ceremony will be conducted right before lunch."

Andy says, "Very impressive. I appreciate everything."

Abernathy continues, "I will book your flight in the next two days. What is a good time for your departure next Friday?"

Andy replies, "Between 5 and 7. Earlier is much better than later."

Abernathy says, "Very good. I will have the reservation by Wednesday. Also, on Wednesday at 9 a.m. we have a meeting with the North Korean ambassador in our conference room on the main floor. Friday at 9 a.m. we will meet with the Russian ambassador in the same room. I know you'll be prepared for those meetings."

Andy replies, "Yes, I will, sir. Bruce or Mac said I would be wearing a black tie and dark grey suit like theirs. Wouldn't I be wearing it for the ambassador meetings?"

Mr. Abernathy laughs and says, "You're totally right. I've overlooked that. I would guess you need a 44L coat with extra broad shoulders. What is your pant size?"

Andy says, "I wear a 34x36, and you're right about the coat size."

"I will also have my secretary order a black tie, black belt, black socks and an XL white shirt. We have a local supplier, who will have it here by lunch time tomorrow." Mr. Abernathy immediately pages his secretary.

Andy thanks Mr. Abernathy, and relieves the agent stationed outside the door to the Secretary's office complex.

Mac shows up before 4:30 and says, "Hey, are you trying to take my job?"

Andy says, "No, but you can take us out to eat. Have you picked a restaurant?"

Mac starts to answer, when the fill-in agent arrives. He tells the agent he'll be back in about two hours. As he and Andy walk to the elevator, Mac says, "The Occidental Grill is well-liked, and they have a good menu."

Andy says, "I'm thinking about a steak and baked potato tonight."

Mac says, "Growing boys need to eat well. Actually, I'm thinking about the same thing."

Mac and Andy enjoy the good food and conversation, and Andy is home in time to catch the Huntley and Brinkley Report. He's glad to be getting the daily newspaper except for the New Age Socialist slant from some of their reporters.

Before 8:00, he calls Judy and his dad just to say, "hi". He would like to call Lydia, but its two o'clock in the morning in Rotterdam. He goes to bed about the time Agent Werner's shift begins. The alarm goes off at 6 a.m. and Andy thinks, "Alex's shift just ended."

He opens his door and gets the morning paper. He notices a headline that says, "Protest in Houston Foiled by Biker Club". It reads, "Two protests were conducted yesterday by masked protestors in L.A. and Houston. They seemed to be mainly protesting for open borders. They were shouting some of the talking points of the New Age Socialist Party. In L.A. a family and a young woman were assaulted by about eight of the masked protestors. In Houston, several masked protestors started assaulting a conservative journalist, when a motorcycle club rode up. The protestors, who were assaulting the journalist, were knocked to the ground, and the bikers ripped off their masks. The other bikers started ripping off the masks of other protestors. Most of them ran. The protestors that tried to fight back were also knocked to the ground. It was reported that roughly thirty protestors were masked, and about twenty bikers countered them."

Andy thinks, "Another sign."

In Tuesday's meeting, Secretary Abernathy says to Andy, "The meeting with the Russian Ambassador is Friday at 9 a.m. It's also in our conference room on the main floor. Can I help you with any preparation for the North Koran meeting tomorrow?"

Andy replies, "I would like to confirm that I will appear as your body guard."

Abernathy says, "Yes. People will assume you are on the agent staff."

Andy asks, "Will there be an interpreter, or does he speak English?"

Abernathy says, "He speaks English."

Andy asks, "Is there anything I should look for during your meeting with him?"

Abernathy looks at Andy for a second and says, "The truth. If you can, let me know if he is lying or not."

Andy says, "I should be able to do that. I will let you know whatever I decipher."

Abernathy says, "Excellent. Do you do anything special to get ready for something like this?"

Andy simply says, "Not that I know of. I'm looking forward to getting the grey suit and black tie."

Abernathy says, "Our supplier should be here by noon. I will have my secretary check on it. Andy, you will be interested in knowing that I've talked with intelligence about a surveillance and underground operation in strategic churches in sanctuary cities. They have already found a good number of churches, which will work with us; not all churches, but churches of all sizes. They're in the larger sanctuary cities, including Chicago, New York City, Philadelphia, Los Angeles, San Francisco, Phoenix, Baltimore, Detroit and Cleveland. So far, we've started working with church leadership in twenty-nine sanctuary cities."

Andy says, "That's great news. I would like to know how they're doing as things progress. Did you hear the news about the biker club that disrupted the protest in Houston?"

Abernathy says, "I was impressed with their effectiveness in dispersing the protestors. They have a good mode of transportation for combat. From undercover agents, we know that most of the biker members don't like socialism and communism. I'm checking with intelligence today to see if we can work with some of the bike clubs, as things escalate."

Andy says, "If there is an invasion, having a pact in place between the biker clubs would be helpful."

Abernathy says, "It all helps. Even though the military is our main tool, the church stations and the biker clubs will help us infiltrate the infiltrators."

Andy is still on his regular schedule with martial arts and firearms. Mr. Park is helping him prepare as a body guard, as well as a security agent. In class he trained to take away knives, guns, batons and longer poles from assailants. In firearms he's doing more work with automatic weapons, like the M14.

Before Andy finishes the day, he finds someone in the weight room to spot him. He can still press 600 lbs. but he tells his spotter, "I need to work at this more often." He finds a source where he can do one on one and basketball games, when he gets back from his honeymoon.

He fixes supper at home, and sits down to listen to the news. After he turns off the TV, he thinks, "I can't believe I feel a little apprehensive about the meeting with the ambassador." He dwells on that a second, then thinks, "Well, this will be the first time to meet an ambassador."

Six in the morning rolls around too early for Andy. As Andy gets out of bed, he says, "Wow, the martial arts and weight lifting must have made me sore. He makes coffee, and before he has breakfast, he spends time in prayer. He takes a quick shower and puts on his new grey suit, white shirt and black tie. He looks in the mirror and says, "Now, world, you know what a body guard looks like."

He's ready to go before 7:15, and Mac picks him up shortly after. When Andy gets in the car, Mac says, "Welcome to the clan!" At the department, they have a quick breakfast, because Secretary Abernathy tells Andy, "I want to go over a few things before we meet with the ambassador."

When Andy and Secretary Abernathy get seated in his office, the Secretary says, "Meetings with foreign ambassadors are virtually formal. Both sides are concerned about legalities over what is said. I will have my entourage, and the North Korean ambassador will have his entourage, which includes security and secretaries. Both sides usually tape what is said, and the recordings are classified. I will make a statement; something like, "There are problems escalating at our southern border. We know invasion is imminent. We don't want war. Is your country making plans to invade?" Of course, it would be very helpful, if I know that his answer is the truth or a lie."

Andy says, "I totally understand. I will be listening closely to the whole conversation."

Abernathy says, "We don't have much time before the meeting. We want to be in the conference room a few minutes before 9:00, and it's already 8:35."

Andy, Mr. Abernathy, Mr. Jennings (the Deputy Secretary of State), Mac, Bruce, a stenographer and two other staff members are in the conference room before 9 a.m. Exactly at 9 a.m. the North Korean delegation is announced. They have six people in their delegation. The meeting begins with formalities.

Mr. Jennings begins the meeting by welcoming the ambassador from North Korea and his entourage. Mr. Jennings invites the North Korean ambassador and his assistants to sit at the large conference table. North Korean table top flags have been placed at on one side of the table, and American table top flags on the other side. Secretary Abernathy sits across from the North Korean ambassador. On one side of the Secretary is the Deputy Secretary, and Andy is on the other side.

Mr. Abernathy opens the conference part of the meeting with pleasantries. Mr. Abernathy asks if the North Korean leader and the ambassador's family are well. Secretary Abernathy purposely begins a short, casual conversation with the ambassador. Meanwhile, Andy's full attention is on every word that is spoken.

After a few minutes, Secretary Abernathy mentions the southern border crisis and reports of a suspected invasion. When Abernathy asks the ambassador if he is aware of the border conflict, the ambassador says, "Yes."

When Abernathy asks the ambassador, if North Korea plans to invade with troops or with covert operatives, the ambassador says, "No."

Secretary Abernathy says, "We don't want war, but if you invade with troops or any type of covert operatives, your country will reap devastation. Do you understand me?"

The shaken ambassador says, "Yes, I understand. I will tell our country's leader and party chairman."

Secretary Abernathy says, "Our meeting today is necessary, because the border crisis is escalating. Also, tell your political and military leaders, that if your country invades in anyway, we will destroy your economy and your industries."

By this time, the North Korean ambassador becomes stilted and says, "I will relay your messages right away." He gets up and bows, and waves for his delegation to depart now.

After their delegation leaves, there is only silence in the conference room for a minute. Secretary Abernathy gets up and says, "I appreciate all of you taking part in the meeting. The proceedings are extremely classified. Let's resume our normal business duties. On their way out, there is very little conversation. Abernathy speaks briefly to his staff before they get on the elevator. He gives Mac the rest of the day off, and dismisses everyone else except Andy and Bruce.

After everyone leaves for their offices, Abernathy takes the next elevator with Andy and Bruce. He says, "Bruce, you're in charge of our office security today, and, Andy, I need to meet with you, when we get to my office."

Abernathy doesn't say anything else on the way to his office. To Andy, he appears to be pensive and preoccupied.

In Abernathy's office, the Secretary breaks his own silence. He says, "Andy, what is your general impression of the meeting?"

Andy says, "Their ambassador took you seriously."

Abernathy asks, "Did he lie to me at any time?"

Andy replies, "Yes. He lied about not having troops or covert operatives for an invasion."

Abernathy said, "I thought they might be part of the invasion."

Andy says, "Even though many communists claim to be atheists, you put the fear of God in him today."

Abernathy says, "That's one meeting down and two to go. You already know the meeting with the Russian ambassador is at 9 a.m. Friday. Late yesterday, I booked the meeting with the Iranian ambassador at 9 a.m. Tuesday."

Andy says, "I'll be ready for each meeting."

Abernathy gives a sigh of relief and says, "I'm glad that one is over. So, tell me, Andy, do you still find time to make plans for your wedding?"

Andy says, "Yes, my sister and dad are helping me."

Abernathy says, "With the help of Agent Werner and his wife, Shelby, I'm making arrangements for your security while you're gone. Mrs. Werner will be seated two rows in back of you; on the other side of the aisle, during your flight. Her husband is leaving earlier with one of our conversion vans, which has communication equipment in it. Alex will be meeting his wife at the Indianapolis Airport. You will have 24 hour security."

Abernathy continues, "On your honeymoon road trip, Alex and Shelby will be in the conversion van. In case of an emergency, there is a first aid kit and roadside repair equipment. In case of a crisis, the van will have three M14s and plenty of rounds for each of you. There are also a few grenades that Alex can show you how to use. Fortunately, your trip is far north of the southern border. Alex will also map an alternate, discreet route for the return trip; if needed."

Andy says, "The precautions sound thorough. Does intelligence have any speculation that the crisis could begin before Labor Day?"

Abernathy replies, "Believe it or not, intelligence has what they call "Vegas Odds" when it comes to serious events. Right now the odds of it happening before Labor Day are four to one; after Labor Day, two to one; after September five to one and after November twelve to one."

Andy says, "They are right to favor it happening in September after Labor Day."

Abernathy asks, "Have you had any further insight about when in September?"

Andy simply says, "No."

Abernathy says, "I better let you get ready for martial arts. Next week your martial arts schedule is Monday and Tuesday at 10:30 a.m. Your firearms schedule is Wednesday and Thursday at 11:30. I will also get next week's schedule to you for surveillance and State Department procedures."

Andy is ready for a break. The stress from "Bloody Sunday", and the meeting with the North Korean Ambassador have him on edge. He decides to call Lydia, when he gets home, even though it's 1 a.m. in Rotterdam.

Lydia answers and Andy says, "Sorry, I'm calling late. I just got home, and I need to talk." He explains how the terrorist events affected him. He also shares that they had an important meeting today.

Lydia says, "I heard about the terrorist attacks that happened in seven states. It's just so sad."

They talk longer than Andy intended. He says, "Honey, I'm so sorry I'm keeping you up. I am more than ready to see you, your parents and my family. Each day, I'm finding it harder to wait for our wedding day."

Lydia says, "Me too, big boy. I can't wait to see you and hold you."

Andy says, "I better let you go back to bed, or I'll want to talk with you all night."

Lydia says, "It's hard to be patient now, but we'll be together in nine days."

Andy says, "8:20, a week from Friday, is our time."

Lydia says, "See you in my dreams. I love you."

Andy replies, "See you there. I love you." He hangs up the receiver; leans back on the recliner and can only think of Lydia."

In another hour, he gets a surprise call from Tim. He says, "Andy, I've gotten calls from members of our high school team, who want to give you a bachelor party. There are four of them, and I was able to talk with a few of your teammates from Purdue, and there are three of them. With you and me, that's nine people."

Andy says, "I'm flattered. What kind of party? You know that I don't want anything wild."

Tim says, "I know. There won't be any strippers or alcohol. I'm thinking about a dinner where we can have toasting, good food and good conversation."

Andy says, "I agree. Are you thinking about Mahican?"

Tim says, "Exactly, it's good for everyone, and not far from Lafayette."

Andy says, "Let's make it an early evening, since Lydia's parents will be in town visiting us."

Tim says, "I'll make the reservations at a nice restaurant in Mahican. How about having it between 6 and 8 on the Saturday before your wedding? We'll take care of everything."

Andy says. "Tim, it sounds great. I really appreciate you and the guys doing this."

Tim says, "We think a lot of you. I'll be your chauffeur. Have a safe trip, my friend."

Andy says, "Take care. I'll be looking forward to being with you and the guys."

Andy thinks, "That was the medicine I needed; to talk with Lydia and Tim." He enjoys the rest of the R&R evening with food and television.

The next morning, Secretary Abernathy and Andy start their daily meeting by 8:45. Abernathy asks, "Are you prepping for the conference with the Russian ambassador tomorrow?"

Andy says, "Yes, sir, I will be looking forward to it."

Abernathy says, "Like Wednesday, we'll meet here by 8:30, then we'll go down to the conference room. Andy, the Pentagon is already on high alert. I haven't filled you in yet, on the classified information that I can share with you. It will remain classified."

Andy says, "Absolutely, it will stay classified, unless you want me to share something specific with Agent Werner."

Abernathy continues, "When the conflict begins, especially the invasion from the south, the whole country will be under martial law. D.C. among other areas will be a zero tolerance zone. If the country has problems with anyone, they will be arrested; including members of the New Age Socialist Party. If socialist members want to cooperate, we'll work with them. Will Cliffton and Wiley Mandex in the State Department will be replaced any day now."

Andy asks, "Are they under suspicion for anything?"

Abernathy says, "Yes, and it's possible they're be arrested in the near future. They're barred from any appointed government position. As a precautionary measure during your honeymoon, Agent Werner has routes to the Air Force Base in Rapid City, and to the Air Force Base south of Yellowstone. He also has routes to the Wyoming National Guard and to the U.S. Army Reserve, which are near Cody, Wyoming. Continue to wear your sidearm at all times during your honeymoon." Abernathy hesitates and adds, "during waking hours."

Andy smiles and says, "I'll be ready at all times; including for my bride."

Abernathy says, "As you probably know, I'm the State Department advisor to the Pentagon. They take my advice under consideration, but they make their own decisions. Many times their strategic planning is only known by the President, the admirals and four star generals. I can share that any possible invasion will be cut off at the sea by the navy. Aircraft carriers, destroyers and submarines have the Atlantic, Pacific and Gulf Coasts covered. The only likely invasion route is along the two thousand miles on the southern border. When they cross the border, they will run into our military net."

Andy says, "Is that the only description the Pentagon gave you?"

Abernathy says, "With your classified clearance, I can also share the few details they gave me. In California, Arizona, New Mexico and Texas, the Marines are already developing command centers on high ground that is relatively close to the border. In California, they have command centers from San Diego to El Centro and Blythe. In Arizona, they're setting up stations from Salome to Tucson to Duncan. In New Mexico, their centers are from Silver City in the west to Artesia and Lovington in the east. In Texas, the command centers are from El Paso to Sanderson to San Antonio to Houston to Jasper. When they are at a large metropolitan area, they set up several miles south of the city. They always look for the highest ground possible in the area. The marine scouts will be in touch with their heavy artillery, the Air Force and the Navy. Air Force, Army, Navy and Marine artillery will toast them, when they're in rural areas."

Andy says, "It sounds like it could be over in less than a week."

Abernathy replies, "It's possible, but local police specialists, CIA, FBI and the National Guard will be fighting the terrorists and other subversives in their cell groups. They will also be protecting citizens from terrorism. When needed, there are some Army Rangers available to help SWAT teams. The other Rangers, Green Berets and the new Navy Seals will be close to the border. Besides initial, heavy bombardment and platoons of Green Berets, there are companies of Marines on standby. They will be the first wave of ground troops by the tens of thousands.

If needed, the Army will have a second and bigger wave of ground troops. The Air Force will be used whenever we can pick off the enemy and their convoys in rural areas. Can you imagine being part of an invasion force in southern Texas and be facing the American gun owner? In all four border states, the invaders will have guns pointing at them from all directions."

Andy says, "Has intelligence said anything about enemy troop movements?"

Abernathy says, "Very little. Your insight and my suspicion about Iran are correct according to what troop movements I've heard about. Iranian soldiers in mass are sailing to one or more destinations in Latin America and South America; that's all I've heard. We also know that the drug cartel in Mexico is very active with illegal immigrants. Subversives are definitely stepping up their game near the border."

Andy says, "I haven't heard much about the increase in terrorism and other crime, since "Bloody Sunday".

Abernathy says, "We know that crime this week is at a high for the year, and much higher than this time last year."

Andy replies, "Another sign. Do you still think the invasion will begin in September?"

Abernathy says, "The Pentagon can surmise that better than I can. I believe it will be in September or early October at the latest. You might be the only one with an answer for the increase in terrorism before the invasion."

Andy says, "As of now, I haven't had any more impressions about imminent terrorism."

After Andy has supper and sits down in his apartment, he thinks, "The significant event remaining this week is the meeting with the Russian ambassador tomorrow. Next week, what seems to be the most significant thing right now is my graduation, so I can be with Lydia, family and friends." He has a passing thought about experiencing his current work at such a young age of nineteen. He quickly moves on, when he thinks about all the men and women in the country under the age of nineteen, who have laid down their lives, so all Americans could have freedom.

Andy thinks he can't wait to get on the basketball floor again, but he realizes he needs to focus on the important events of the next two weeks. He gets in bed early and begins to pray and think about the meeting in the morning.

Alex, Abernathy and Andy arrive at the department early. They have breakfast in their cafeteria, and Abernathy and Andy meet before the ambassador meeting.

Abernathy says, "We have to go downstairs in a few minutes. Are you ready for the meeting with Ambassador Voznesensky?"

Andy replies, "Yes, sir. I'm ready, whenever you are."

Abernathy says, "Good. Let's go downstairs and meet our delegation."

Near the elevator on the ground floor, the same members of the previous delegation meet the Secretary. They go in the conference room at 8:53. Ambassador Voznesensky arrives with his delegation one minute early. He has a venerable, but constrained appearance.

Secretary Abernathy greets Ambassador Voznesensky and shakes his hand. They sit at the big conference table with Russian table flags on one side and American table flags on the other side. While the Deputy Secretary gives the standard welcome, Abernathy arranges his notes, which are virtually the same notes that he used in the North Korean meeting. The Deputy Secretary sits at one side of the Secretary and Andy at the other.

Secretary Abernathy gives a brief welcome. He says, "We are always honored to meet with Ambassador Voznesensky The reason for this meeting was necessitated by problems at our southern border and illegals crossing into our country. We hope, ambassador, that you are empathetic toward the problem, as opposed to taking advantage of it. Are you aware of the problem?"

Ambassador Voznesensky answers directly in English, "Yes, I am."

Abernathy asks, "Is your country planning to send troops across the border or invade with covert operatives?"

The Russian ambassador appears to be somewhat uncomfortable, when he answers, "No."

Looking directly at the ambassador, Secretary Abernathy says resolutely, "If any country is part of the invasion with troops, covert operatives or other support, we will destroy their industries and ruin their economy."

Ambassador Voznesensky is upset, when he says, "We did not come here seeking provocation. Aggression will not be tolerated."

Secretary Abernathy responds, "That is correct; aggression will not be tolerated."

With a dour expression, the Russian ambassador gets up with his delegation and storms out.

Abernathy looks at all of the members of his delegation, then simply nods. In silence, they walk out of the conference room. Within a few minutes, Andy goes with Abernathy to his office. After they sit down, Abernathy takes his usual deep breath and says, "Andy, the ambassador and I had a solemn exchange."

Andy replies, "Yes, sir, you did."

Abernathy asks, "What did you see in the meeting?"

Andy says, "The ambassador gave our delegation the impression of being insulted. When you gave him a stern warning, he appeared to be angry, but it was an act. He did not tell the truth, when he denied Russian plans to send troops or support across the border."

Abernathy leans back; clasps his hands behind his head and says, "I believe that is a brilliant evaluation. I feel like your insight is correct once again. I have a report you'll find interesting. Intelligence has been working on your lead about illegals and other subversives using our postal system to build up supplies in their cell networks, including supplies for homemade bombs. Intelligence didn't share much detail, but they wanted us to know that they have arrested over twenty-five groups in mostly sanctuary city areas. They did mention Milwaukee, Chicago, Baltimore, New York City, San Francisco, Los Angeles and San Jose. They were doing exactly what you saw in your premonition."

Andy says, "Wow, those are good results. Did they say in how many cities or states?"

Abernathy says, "No. We can assume it was in well over eight cities and five states."

After Andy finishes his day at the department, he gets his mail and flops down in the recliner. He says to himself, "I hope this is a quiet weekend."

16

HONEYMOON ROAD TRIP

One thing disturbs Andy over the weekend; an article he reads in the Sunday morning paper. The report says nationwide crime by illegal immigrants has increased 300% compared to last year. It says terrorism has increased 250%; murder over 200%; assault 350%; rape over 100%: vandalism 200% and arson over 200%. Andy notices that the journalist, who wrote the article, is one of the few conservative reporters on their staff.

Andy is looking forward to his final, training week before his wedding and honeymoon. His last week of training in State Department protocol is good information, but somewhat boring. His surveillance training in his final week is just the opposite. He finds the surveillance information and training very engrossing. He finishes the last two classes in martial arts and firearms. He passes martial arts with flying colors. Mr. Park said, "Andy, it normally takes at least three years to earn a black belt in Tae kwon-do and in Karate. I believe you could be a black belt in each art within a year, if you continue with the two arts."

The meeting with the Iranian Ambassador is moved back to Thursday at 9 a.m. The meeting is similar to the meetings with the Korean Ambassador and the Russian Ambassador. Once again, the Iranian ambassador denies that his country is planning an attack with troops or with covert operatives.

After the meeting, Andy and Abernathy meet in his office. Abernathy says, "How does it feel to be one day away from graduating as a special agent?"

Andy says, "I'm looking forward to it."

Abernathy says, "Give me your assessment of the Iranian Ambassador."

Andy says, "The three ambassadors are almost like peas of the same pod. This ambassador is a cool one, but his deceptiveness didn't cover his lie about Iran not planning an attack with troops or covert operatives. He seemed to be smug about it; like we were expected to believe him."

Abernathy says, "I agree. Intelligence will tell us more about Iranian troop movements and their other intentions real soon. Even though, the State Department doesn't know a lot of what the Pentagon is doing, we are informed in some areas, because we are a major advisor to them. At this time, the classified information that I can share with you is what some of our political adversaries are doing. One of the socialist's main leaders has been in collusion with subversives coming across the border. I expect this Congressional leader will soon be arrested for sedition. Other New Age Socialist Party leaders have been connected to hate crimes. A number of leaders in the socialist party have been jeopardizing our national security with their involvement in promoting open borders."

Andy says, "Those activities and crimes don't surprise me."

Abernathy says, "On a lighter note; you finish training today with surveillance and protocol. On the last day, they shorten the classes. I'm going to tell Bruce to take you home early. Since your flight is after graduation tomorrow, the department is treating you and Bruce to an early supper tonight."

Andy says, "That's very thoughtful of you."

Abernathy says, "If you need to go to a store or to the bank, I'll tell Bruce to take you there before you go to the restaurant. You'll get off today by 3:00. Do you have everything you need from us for your flight and vacation?"

Andy says, "I think I have everything. When Bruce and I leave, I would like to go to the local bank and a local discount store like Zayre's or Kresge's."

Abernathy says, "That's fine. Have you noticed Agent Werner during his shift?"

Andy says, "I haven't seen him in person during his watch, but I've noticed the car, which I think belongs to him."

Abernathy says, "He respects privacy, but if he is concerned about anything, he'll let you know. During the graduation and reception tomorrow, you'll have time to talk with Alex and Shelby. Tomorrow will be a slow day for you here. We're still planning to start the graduation ceremony at 11:30. We'll have it in the conference room."

On Friday, Andy is able to spend more time with Mac and Bruce. After breakfast, Mr. Abernathy gets up from the cafeteria table and says to Andy and Mac, "Bruce and I are going upstairs. Both of you stay her for a while. Mac, you can tell Andy about your work and what you watch for. Bruce and I will see you a few minutes before 11:30 in the conference room."

Andy and Mac are still enjoying their second cup of coffee. Andy says, "I'm still getting use to wearing a suit and tie for work."

Mac says, "The suit and tie will probably become your main work attire. After we talk about some of my work responsibilities, I will take you to the places in the department, where I do security."

Andy asks, "How much of the time do you have outside security?"

Mac replies, "Right now, I'm here about 75% of the time, and outside the other 25%."

After they finish in the cafeteria, Mac takes Andy through the State Department building, and they arrive at the conference room about 11:20. The caterers are already setting up, and a podium and chairs have been set up for the ceremony. Deputy Secretary Jennings arrives next, then Secretary Abernathy and Bruce. Right before 11:30, Captain Morrison and Kim Park from the training camp come in; then Alex and Shelby and exactly at 11:30, Vice-President Calhoun arrives with two secret service men.

Secretary Abernathy welcomes everyone, and introduces Captain Morrison, as head of the security agent training camp. Captain Morrison says, "It is my privilege today to recognize two outstanding agents. We are recognizing Agent Alex Werner with a special gold lapel pin for outstanding, security agent service. We are also here to recognize our brand new, special security agent, Andy McGraig. Andy graduates today from training, and we recognize him for outstanding achievement during training." As Captain Morrison presents the lapel pin and graduation certificate to Alex and Andy, everyone stands and claps for Agent Werner and Agent McGraig.

After they're seated, Secretary Abernathy recognizes Vice-President Calhoun, and asks him to come to the podium. The Vice-President says, "The President and I are very grateful for our security personnel. Agent Werner and Agent McGraig are fine examples of the talented men and women we have as special agents, secret service, CIA, FBI and other federal security members. We congratulate Werner and McGraig for their achievements, and I want them to know how proud I am of them for serving their country. Because of our agents, we can do our duties in peace and safety. The President and I want to thank all of you for your service, and we remember today the sacrifices that all of our agents make."

The small group applauds the Vice-President. Secretary Abernathy says, "I understand the Vice-President can stay and have a special lunch with us today. Our food service personnel have prepared and catered a menu of garden salad, roast pork, mashed potatoes and gravy, green beans, and apple pie and ice cream. My wife and Agent Shelby Werner have made favors for everyone. Chaplain Peter Garcia has come to share lunch and grace with us." Chaplain Garcia gives the blessing, then everyone is served the special luncheon.

After lunch everyone congratulates Agent Werner and Agent McGraig, and thanks Vice-President Calhoun for coming. As the group thins out, Secretary Abernathy walks over to Andy, Alex and Shelby and says, "Alex, I know you have to leave now to catch a flight to Louisville, where we have the conversion van outfitted for you. In a few minutes, I need to meet with Andy and Shelby in my office."

When they're seated in the Secretary's office, Mr. Abernathy says, "First of all, I want you to know that you are doing a superb job with your work here. I want Andy to know that Alex and Shelby are very skilled in what they do, and I want Alex and Shelby to know that Andy is also very talented."

Shelby says, "We assume that he is from graduating as a special security agent. Alex and I saw him play on television in two NCAA playoff games. We admire him for choosing the State Department over the NBA."

Abernathy says, "It is important that the three of you respect and trust each other. Your security work during Andy's wedding plans and honeymoon is very important."

Andy says, "Isn't Lydia, my fiancée, going to realize that there is a reason she will keep seeing Alex and Shelby?"

Abernathy says, "Absolutely; we are going to cover that in our meeting. Shelby will sit directly across the aisle from you and not two rows back during the flight to Indianapolis. She will get off the plane right before you. Alex will park our conversion van at a special vantage point in the airport parking lot. He will be waiting for you and your party at baggage claim. Did you tell me that your fiancée and her parents will arrive at 8:20?"

Andy says, "Yes, the flight from Amsterdam."

Abernathy continues, "Andy, Alex and Shelby already have their motel reservation in Mahican, but they don't check in that night, because they will be doing security near your house. The van has enough room for one to sleep, while the other does their surveillance work. Do them a favor. Whether you or your dad drives home, tell your party that you want to order something to eat, so they can get some food and coffee for their night work. A drive up order would be best. Let them order first, so they can be sure to get their food."

Andy says, "No problem. It will be done."

Abernathy says, "Andy, here is what I recommend you say about Alex and Shelby to Lydia and possibly to your father. After everyone goes to bed tonight, tell Lydia or both of them about the van and Alex and Shelby. Simply tell them that it has to do with your work, but it's classified. Let them know that at your reception and wedding, they will be posing as guests."

Andy says, "Okay. Do we have a way to communicate with each other, when we can't communicate directly?"

Abernathy answers, "Yes. In surveillance class did they tell you that we use pagers to communicate at times, when we don't or can't use walkie talkies?"

Andy replies, "Yes, they said pagers are used at times, and there is a number code used. They didn't take time to give us the code to practice it."

Abernathy says, "It is fairly simple. It is only basic communication.

Shelby will give you your pager after this meeting, and she will show you how to communicate with it. I think the other main thing we need to cover are ways you can interact during the honeymoon road trip. Most of the time, you have to keep the appearance of being strangers. There may be times where you might be at the next table over at a restaurant. If you feel good about the restaurant setting, just do small talk, like you don't know each other."

Shelby asks, "Are the motel rooms reserved for the road trip?"

Andy says, "No, I'm behind on that; I could use some help. They should be made today or tomorrow, because we're leaving Monday."

Abernathy says, "Let's do this. On the road, you're not known, so we'll reserve rooms that have the locked adjoining door. The department has a staff member, who is quick at arranging things like this. He assists agents all the time with situations like this. Andy, tell me your route and daily plan, and I'll give it to him now. By the time you leave here for your flight, I can give you the reservation information."

Andy says, "Early Monday we'll drive from Mahican to Sioux Falls, SD. We'll travel I74 and I90 in Minnesota, then check in at a motel in Sioux Falls. Tuesday night we'll stay near Badlands, South Dakota. Wednesday night we'll stay in Cody, Wyoming, and Thursday night we'll stay in Yellowstone. On the return trip, we'll stay Friday night near the Badlands, and Saturday night we'll stay in the Wisconsin Dells area. On Sunday, we should get to Mahican by 5 p.m."

Abernathy says, "Very good, hold on a minute while I page my secretary with the schedule, and she'll make sure that Steve gets it right away. By the time you leave here for your flight, you'll both have your motel reservations."

Abernathy continues, "Okay, we'll be set with the reservations soon. Have we covered everything?' Abernathy thinks a moment, then says, "Andy, I just want to confirm, when you'll be back."

Andy says, "I will be driving to D.C. in a blue and white, 1955 Chevy Belair. Because of the drive, we'll get in late Tuesday after Labor Day. I can be at work Wednesday morning."

Abernathy says, "That's fine. Shelby and Alex will follow

you back. While you're gone, I'll have a staff member line up an elementary teaching job for Lydia. Do you know if she wants part-time or full-time?"

Andy says, "I think she wants to start out part-time."

Shelby says, "If we have a few minutes before Steve finishes with the reservations, I can go ahead and share one thing with Andy."

Abernathy says, "Go ahead, and I'll page Angela to see how Steve is doing."

Shelby says, "Andy, I know Mac will meet us soon, so we can leave for the airport. Since we have time now, it's about your exit from the airport parking garage in Indianapolis. Before you go through the gate in the parking garage, lower your headlights to your parking lights, as you go through the gate. Once you're through, turn your headlights back on, so Alex will spot you more easily."

Andy says, "Will do. You know about the blue and white, 1955 Belair. My dad might have his blue-green, 1962 Chevy Belair with him. Also, on the way to Mahican, there is a North Star Drive-In on the right side of the road, after you see the Zionsville sign. We'll pull in there, so we can order something to eat."

Shelby says, "Excellent. If we think of something else, we'll cover it while Mac drives us to the airport."

Just as they finish, Abernathy says, "Steve completed the reservations, and the list is at the front desk. Did Mac put your suitcases in the car this morning?"

They both answer in the affirmative.

Mr. Abernathy gets up and comes around his desk. He shakes Andy's and Shelby's hands and wishes them God's speed. When the three of them walk out of the Secretary's office, they see Mac waiting for them. Andy and Shelby pick up their copies of the motel reservations. When Mac, Andy and Shelby walk out of the building toward the car, Andy enthusiastically says, "Let's get this show to the airport!" All three of them laugh, as they head to Andy's long awaited flight.

Everything goes smoothly at the airport. Mac checks the plane, and Shelby boards right before Andy. As Shelby gets ready to take her seat, a middle-aged male passenger says to her, "You look like Elke Sommer."

Shelby replies in a reserved tone, "Thank you."

Andy takes his seat and acts like he doesn't know Shelby is across the aisle. The pilot takes off exactly at 4:40. Andy dozes off after they get airborne. Shelby stays alert to take care of surveillance and security. When the TWA pilot announces they will be landing in Indianapolis at 6 p.m. Eastern Time, Andy wakes up, and sits straight up. Shelby notices and laughs to herself about how Andy is startled out of his sleep.

After they taxi to the gate, Shelby exists before Andy, as planned. A few seconds after he walks in the gate waiting area, Andy sees his dad. They hug and Andy says, "Where is Judy?"

Owen says, "She stayed at home to give us more room in the car, since Lydia's parents are coming. I looked at the arrival board; it says the Pan Am flight from Amsterdam is on time."

Andy says, "That's good news. Let's go ahead and get my suitcase at baggage claim. When we come back to wait on Lydia's flight, I'll buy us a coffee or soda and something to eat.'

On the way to baggage claim, Owen says, "Judy and I arranged things, so Lydia and her parents can sleep in Judy's room. We have a cot for Lydia in Judy's room. Judy can sleep on a cot in my room or your room. My guess is she will choose your room to be with big brother."

Andy says, "It sounds accommodating. Lydia's parents may go out tomorrow and reserve a motel room for Saturday and Sunday night. The last time I talked with Lydia, they hadn't decided on the time of their return flight. I think they want to rent a car, and take a three week tour of America."

While they wait on Andy's suitcase, Owen says, "Do they have any special destinations?"

Andy says, "Yes, there are some scenic sights they want to see like Niagara Falls and the Blue Ridge Parkway. They want to see quite a few places from Niagara Falls to St. Augustine, including New York City and D.C.

Owen says, "Three weeks should be enough time to visit a lot of sights."

As Andy grabs his suitcase, he says, "I'm not sure I remember all the places they want to see. I think their list also includes The Smoky Mountain National Park, Jamestown and Williamsburg. I think they want to fly back home from The National Airport in D.C. With all the problems at the southern border, I'm glad they're not planning a trip near there."

Andy and Owen go to a small deli café in the gate area. They order coffee. Both of them want to order something different, so they each decide on a Reuben sandwich. All the time, Shelby has been a short distance away. Owen hasn't noticed her at all, and Andy has only caught a glimpse of her. At the deli, she also orders something to eat.

By the time they finish at the café, it's already 7:00. On the way back to the waiting area, Owen and Andy stop to look at the arrival board. The Amsterdam flight is now expected to land at 8:10. Andy says, "Wow, they'll be here soon."

Owen says, "I bet you can't wait. Hasn't it been almost three months, since you've seen Lydia?"

Andy says, "Yes, it has been way too long."

While Andy and Owen wait for Lydia's flight to arrive, just before 8:00, Alex pulls into a special parking spot for security in the airport parking lot. When he gets to the baggage claim area, he sees the Amsterdam flight will be arriving in a few minutes.

Andy can hardly wait to see Lydia, when he sees her plane has landed. He and his dad go to their gate before the passengers leave the plane. After seeing over twenty people leaving the plane and several tall men, Andy spots Lydia and her parents. When Lydia sees him, she hands her bag to her mom and runs to Andy and jumps in his arms. They kiss a long time and hug again, while Lydia's parents and Owen just stand and watch with a smile. After a minute, Andy puts her down, and Lydia's parents walk over to them. Lydia looks at her parents; laughs and says moeder en vader, you might guess that this is Andy. Andy, this is my father and mother, Conrad and Klara Van Ark. Andy shakes her father's hand, and Lydia's mother hugs him.

Andy says, "This is my father, Owen McGraig." They shake hands and Andy says, "You'll meet my sister, Judy, when we get home. We'll go to baggage claim, and I'll load your things in our car."

As they come into the baggage claim area, Alex and Shelby spot each other. They nonchalantly keep observing the McGraigs and Van Arks until they head through the exit doors. At that time, Shelby and Alex begin to merge together. From a comfortable distance, they watch them open their car doors, then Alex and Shelby start moving to their van, which is in a convenient parking spot.

As Andy prepares to drive his dad's Chevy through the parking gate, he changes the headlights to just the parking lights until he gets through the gate. Alex spots their car, and follows them out of the airport. Everyone is talking until they are about ten minutes from Zionsville. Andy says, "I'm going to make a food stop in a few minutes. I'm ordering some food to go for Judy. Get want you want; I'm buying."

After they park at the North Star Drive In, Andy sees their conversion van pull in a space across from them. Andy talks about the menu choices until he sees the car hop take Alex and Shelby's order. Another car hop comes up to Andy's window to take the order. Everyone orders coffee, and Andy orders a hamburger and root beer for Judy.

They get home by 9:30, and Andy and his dad carry in the luggage. Judy hugs Andy and Lydia, and meets her parent. After everyone knows where they're sleeping, they sit down for a few minutes to visit. Before Klara Van Ark sits down, she walks over to Owen and takes his hand and says, "I am sorry to her about your wife. Please let us know if we can help with anything."

Owen thanks her for the condolences, and they talk about the reception and wedding. After everyone starts yawning, Owen says, "We'll continue this over breakfast in the morning. Is breakfast at 8:00 okay with everyone?" As everyone starts getting ready for bed, Mrs. Van Ark asks Judy, "Who is fixing breakfast in the morning?"

Judy replies, "My dad and I."

Klara says, "Will you tell your dad now, that I will help you instead of him? Tell him I insist."

Judy says, "Okay."

After everyone gets settled in their rooms, Andy tells his dad and Lydia that he needs to talk with them for a minute in the kitchen.

Andy simply says, "What I'm going to tell you is classified by the State Department. You must not tell anyone."

Owen and Lydia confirm they will keep it to themselves. Andy says, "As you probably know, I have an important job with the department. I can't go into detail, but I have security, and the couple watching the house now are both security agents."

Lydia says in a soft voice, "Wow, we're being watched now?"

Andy smiles and says, "They're taking turns watching the house from a conversion van."

Owen says, "I'm glad you told me, so I don't get paranoid."

Andy's smile becomes serious again. He says, "At the reception and wedding, they will be posing as guests. You won't miss them, because he looks like a Sean Connery, from James Bond, and she looks like Elke Sommer."

Lydia says, "They must have a hard time staying under cover."

Andy says, "If anyone asks, we'll just say that they're friends of mine. It is true that they were basketball fans, and then they became personal friends. If I stay up any longer, I'll need another cup of coffee."

Owen says, "Let's go to bed. Have a good night and sleep tight."

Lydia and Andy kiss and say, "good night".

Klara and Judy are up at 7:00 to prepare breakfast. Andy jumps in the shower right after they get up. They wake up Owen and Conrad a few minutes before 8:00. Breakfast Is served; scrambled eggs, bacon, toast and jelly and coffee and juice. Since Conrad is a minister with the Dutch Reformed Church, Andy asks him to say the prayer.

During breakfast, Owen says, "We are doing things in a little different order for Lydia and Andy's ceremonies. Because of time restraints, we're having the reception dinner at our church; following a short service. Our church is providing the food, and many of the women are preparing it and serving it. The dinner will start at 12:00, and the wedding party has to leave by 1:00, because the wedding at the Purdue Chapel is at 3:00. There will be a short reception after the wedding, when the wedding gifts will be given to the bride and groom. They may not have time to open the gifts in front of everyone, but they will be there to greet all of the guests."

Andy says, "It sounds like you and Judy have been busy preparing everything."

Lydia says, "Andy and I want to thank both of you for your kindness and hard work, and Andy can they visit us anytime in D.C.?"

Andy says, "Absolutely! Dad and Sis, when you come to D.C. you'll be staying with us, and we will provide any excursion you desire!"

Lydia says, "Moeder en Vader, Andy and I want you to visit us before you fly back to Holland. Andy insists on buying your plane tickets to depart from The D.C. National Airport to Amsterdam!"

Conrad says, "You're too kind."

Klara gets up and kisses both Lydia and Andy on the cheek and says, "Thank you, so much."

Andy says, "Tim, who some of you know well, gave me fairly short notice on a bachelor dinner tonight. It's at a local restaurant with my peers, and the celebration is just food and non-alcoholic toasting. It's from just 6:00 to 8:00 this evening, and I should be back around 8:30."

Judy says, "Lydia and I trust you." Everyone laughs and talks long after breakfast is over.

After they visit, Klara and Conrad get ready to look for a car to rent and a motel for Saturday and Sunday nights. Andy fires up his 1955 Chevy and takes Lydia, Conrad and Klara to the Mahican Holiday Inn. Klara and Conrad look at a room with a full bed, and they reserve it. Near the Holiday Inn is the Hertz Car Rental Store. The salesman shows them a 1962 Buick LaSabre; a 1962 Oldsmobile 88 and a 1962 light blue Chrysler New Yorker. They rent the New Yorker, and Andy finds out they can return the car at the D.C. National Airport.

Conrad asks, "Does your dad have any plans for lunch?"

Andy says, "I haven't heard of any."

Conrad says, "We've heard about a Colonel Sanders with a white beard who started and advertises Kentucky Fried Chicken. Do they have the Kentucky chicken in Indiana?"

Andy laughs and says, "It's right here in Mahican."

Conrad says, "Vunderful! I would like to see their establishment. Klara and I want to try their chicken recipe and their American mashed potatoes and gravy and green beans. We would like to buy some for everyone."

They pick up the Kentucky chicken and sides and take it to Andy's house for lunch. Conrad and Klara follow Andy in their rental car. Without Conrad and Klara knowing, Shelby has been following them, while Alex sleeps after the night shift.

During lunch, Owen says, "While Andy is at his bachelor's dinner tonight, I want to take you out to our favorite steak restaurant."

Klara says, "That is so nice of your; we love steak."

As Andy leaves for his bachelor's party, his family and guests get ready to go out for dinner. When he arrives, he greets several of his old teammates, including Tim, Jack and Larry. After dinner, his friends and teammates toast him. Jack toasts Andy and says, "To the best freshman basketball player in the NCAA and one of the top five players in the whole NCAA!" There's cheers from everyone. Tim toasts him and says, "To the best friend I have ever had!" There's more loud applause. Larry toasts him and says, "To the best white friend, I've ever had!" He gets a big laugh and applause.

After a few more toasts, Andy gets up and says, "I toast all of you for being faithful to your team and for being good friends. I think a lot of every one of you. To you Larry, I toast the best black friend I have ever had!" Andy gets a good laugh and thundering applause.

After the party starts breaking up, Andy asks Tim, Jack and Larry, if they got their tuxedos, that he rented for them. He says, "Good. Be at the church by noon for your Sunday dinner. If you can, wear a coat and tie. We'll change into the tuxedos, when we get to the Purdue Chapel." He thanks every one for coming.

As he drives back home, he notices the conversion van following. He assumes they checked into their motel. He remembers Shelby telling him that they would have to rent a car in Mahican, so one of them at a time could sleep in the motel room and shower.

Andy is glad to finally see Sunday, August 26th, arrive. Klara and Conrad come to their house in their rental car, so they can follow them to church. They attend the worship service together. When the organist starts playing, "Great Is Thy Faithfulness", Conrad says, "Ahhhh, one of my favorite hymns."

After service, they go to the fellowship hall, where Larry, Jack and Tim have already arrived. They all have on a coat and tie. Andy says, "You all look good; thanks." As they watch the women of the church set out the bowls and platters, they see chicken, ham, potato casserole, fried potatoes, sweet peas, broccoli, sweet potatoes, peach cobbler, chocolate cake, as well as garden salad.

Conrad says, "Wow, this is like a holiday celebration in Rotterdam!"

Lydia, who looks like an angel in her yellow and white dress, says, "Fader, this is your daughter's holiday!"

Conrad looks at her and smiles and says, "Yes, pumpkin, I know this is your special day, and I wish many, many more for you and Andy." Lydia hugs him, and they sit down for her wedding dinner.

Before Andy leaves, he thanks all of his church friends for their kindness and hospitality. As Andy and Lydia pull away in the '55 Chevy, they have a small convoy: Owen and Judy in the '62 Chevy; Conrad and Klara in the New Yorker; Larry, Jack and Tim in a Studebaker and of course, Alex and Shelby in the conversion van. Their timing is good, when they arrive at the Purdue Chapel. They have thirty minutes to get ready before the wedding. Lydia's friend, Tracy, and Judy, meet in a small, private room, so the bride and her bridesmaids can dress. Andy, Tim, Jack and Larry find another private room to change into their tuxedos.

Most of the guests are seated by 2:55. The McGraigs invited the whole Purdue basketball team, which are already seated with Coach Brown. Dr. Krause and his wife are seated, as well as Edmund and Ella McCollister, and Anderson and Ruth. Klara is seated on one side of the aisle on the front pew, and Owen is seated on the other side.

Andy, Tim, Jack and Larry are in place, when the organist begins the "Bridal Chorus" by Wagner. Exactly at 3:00 Conrad walks his daughter down the pristine aisle of the capacity filled chapel. Andy thinks Lydia is absolutely beautiful in her long white gown. He thinks, "I must be dreaming."

The pastor asks, "Who gives the bride away?" Without thinking, Conrad says, "Ja .... I mean, I do." Lydia's face turns red, and she looks at her father and smiles. When Conrad takes his seat, Klara is trying to keep from laughing.

Before Andy realizes it, he kisses the bride and is married to the woman he loves, Lydia Van Ark McGraig.

The wedding guests go to the large fellowship hall for the reception. On three long tables, the gifts have been collected for Mr. and Mrs. McGraig. After an official introduction of Andy and Lydia McGraig, it is announced the bride and groom want to greet everyone. The guests are instructed to form a line and to try to be brief out of respect for the other guests. When they start to form a line, Lydia notices Alex and Shelby. Lydia whispers to Andy, "I just spotted them; they do look like Sean Connery and Elke Sommer." Alex watches each person as they get close to Andy, and Shelby walks to the other side of the newlyweds. Cake is served after the guests greet Andy and Lydia.

When Coach Brown greets Andy, he says, "Beautiful wedding, Andy."

Andy says, "I was amazed that the chapel was full."

Coach Brown laughs and says, "I guess they didn't tell you. The chapel seats two hundred, and Purdue had close to a thousand students and staff members who wanted to attend. Your dad and sister invited 132 people, including our basketball team. We had to do a type of lottery by announcements and mail-ins with birthdates. We drew birthdates until we had the 68 vacancies filled."

Andy replies, "I'm stunned. I had no idea. If you have the opportunity, thank everyone at Purdue for me."

The coach says, "I will get the word out. I just hope I'm still the coach, when you return to Purdue. I'm very proud of you."

Andy says, "Coach, you mean a lot to me. Thank you for everything."

In a rare display of emotion, Coach Brown hugs Andy.

After they greet everyone, Lydia throws the bridal bouquet away. When Lydia turns around to see who caught it she thinks, "I know her; its Larry's six foot girlfriend!" When Lydia tells Andy, he goes over to Larry and tells him to get ready to find a ring.

Judy comes up to Lydia and Andy and gives Lydia all of the wedding cards. Judy says, "I know you don't have time to look at all of the gifts. If you have room, take some with you. Dad and I will keep the rest at home for you." Lydia and Andy hug Judy. When Judy finishes hugging Andy, she has tears in her eyes.

Andy says, "Okay, sis, what will it be; something nice for you from the Badlands, Mt. Rushmore or Yellowstone?"

Judy smiles and says, "Yellowstone."

Standing by Judy, Owen says, "Son, this is one gift that you and Lydia can take with you." Andy opens a small card, and finds $500 in cash in it."

Andy hugs his dad and thanks him. Lydia hugs Owen; kisses him on the cheek and says, "We love you". You will be in our prayers and thoughts every day."

Conrad and Klara come up and say goodbye. After Klara hugs Andy, she says, "Let us know where you will be."

Klara says, "We've been working with AAA. Here is our itinerary." She hands Andy a folded sheet of paper with locations and dates.

When Andy gets a chance to just talk with Lydia and his dad, he says in a low voice, "Dad, you remember the guests I told you and Lydia about on Friday night at the house?"

His dad says, "Yes."

Andy says I need to talk with them for just a minute in this classroom behind us. Will you wait here with Lydia?" His dad nods.

The crowd has thinned out to just a few people, and Andy walks over to Alex and Shelby, like he is going to greet them. He lowers his voice and says, "Could we meet a minute in that small room on the other side?"

They say, "Sure," and they follow him to the room and close the door behind them.

Andy turns on the light in the room and says, "Lydia and I were planning to leave on our road trip in the morning from Mahican, but we packed a suitcase at the last minute, in case we could leave after the wedding reception. Right now, we're ninety minutes closer than Mahican to our destination. If you are able to leave with us, we talked about driving until 10:00 tonight, so we could spend a couple hours at the Wisconsin Dells in the morning."

Alex says, "No problem. We never leave our things in a motel room. We have a department agent working in the Louisville and Indianapolis area right now. I'll ask him to square things with our motel and rental car. He can get another key for the rental car by showing his badge. Getting a room near Wisconsin Dells is no problem. On Sunday night, there are a lot of vacancies. When we get there, I'll go in and check Shelby and me in. I'll say that a friend will be here in a minute to check in the next room, so we'll have an adjoining door."

Andy says, "Great! The Chevy is packed and ready to go. We told our families before we left, that we might be able to leave from the chapel." When Andy comes out of the room, he looks around, then gives Lydia a smile and a thumbs up. He goes up to his dad and says, "We'll be able to start our trip now. Here is the check for the pastor. Will you also thank him for me?"

Owen says, "Sure, son. I'll go look for him now; wait on me."

"I will, dad."

Andy puts his arm around Lydia, and gives her a kiss. He says, "Are you ready to get our trip started?"

Lydia smiles and says, "I'm ready, big boy."

While Andy waits on his dad, he and Lydia talk with Judy, Conrad and Klara. Tim, Jack and Larry come over to Andy and Lydia to tell them they're leaving. Andy says, "It's tradition for the groom to give a gift to the best man and ushers. I got each of you a card." He hands them the cards. Andy says, "Go ahead and open them and see if you like the gift." Each thank you card has a hundred dollar bill in it. All three of his friends are surprised, and they hug Andy. Tim says, "You're the best." They give Lydia a kiss on the cheek. They congratulate Andy and Lydia and wish them a safe trip. After they leave the building, Lydia says to Andy, "You should have seen Tracy's and Judy's expressions, when they opened their cards and saw the hundred dollar bill."

Andy says, "I'm glad they like their gift." He turns to Judy and says, "Did you like your gift, sis?"

Judy hugs him and kisses him, and gets tears in her eyes. Andy says, "Sis, no matter how much you cry, you can't come with us on our honeymoon."

Judy says, "If you insist, but you better bring a real nice gift from Yellowstone."

Andy picks her up; kisses her and says, "You can count on it."

Owen returns and says, "I think you're all set. We'll see you off, then Judy and I will load the gifts. When you get back next Sunday, we'll watch you open them."

Andy says, "Thanks, dad. I love you," and he gives his dad a hug. "I'll call you after we get to Cody or Yellowstone."

Conrad and Klara hug their daughter and son-in-law, and everybody waves, as the blue and white Chevy takes off for the honeymoon road trip.

After the Chevy goes just a block, the conversion van pulls out. While Alex follows Andy out of Lafayette, Shelby takes inventory of first aid, surveillance and car equipment and weapons. Alex says, "Shelby, one of us should probably ask Andy, if he has a box of 50 rounds for his handgun."

Shelby says, "Do you have any idea where we're staying tonight?"

Alex says, "No, we'll wing it. It's Andy and Lydia's honeymoon. I'm guessing he'll stop within an hour of the Dells. I'm sure he'll stop at a hotel like the Holiday Inn or Ramada Inn."

After they get on I90/94 in Chicago, Andy says, "Lydia, are you awake? You can see the Chicago skyline now."

Lydia wakes up and says, "Wow, it's impressive. What is the tall building?"

Andy says, "The Chicago Board of Trade Building."

They take in all the sights from the freeway. Andy says. "We'll stop for gas soon. In a few minutes, Andy pulls into a Sinclair gas station in Rosemont, Illinois. He asks the attendant to fill it up. Andy says, "You don't need to check the oil, but look at the tires and clean the windshield please." Alex and Shelby are at the next pump having their tank filled with regular gas.

Lydia says, "I need to use the bathroom."

Andy sees Shelby getting out of the van. Andy says, "It looks like you'll have company." Andy gets out to stretch, and yells out to Alex, "It looks like gas has gone up to 28 cents." Alex says, "It's usually higher here; we're near the O'Hare Airport." Andy looks around and heads to the bathroom. When the ladies come back, Alex takes his turn.

When Andy comes back to the car, he pays the attendant and waits a couple minutes on Alex. When they pull out, it's after 7:30, and they have about an hour of light left. Andy asks Lydia, "How are you doing, babe?"

Lydia says, "Pretty good, since I got a nap; when did I fall asleep?"

Andy says, "Before we got to the Illinois state line. I think you slept about thirty minutes."

Lydia asks, "Do you know, when we'll stop for the night?"

Andy says, "We have about two hours before we get to Madison, Wisconsin. We can probably find a good motor lodge there."

After a quiet ride, Andy says, "Are you awake?"

Lydia sleepily says, "I think I dozed off again."

Andy says, "We're getting close to Madison, so we'll start looking for a place to stay."

About five minutes before the Madison city limits, Lydia says, "I'm seeing small motor lodges and some cabins."

Andy says, "We'll probably stop at a bigger motor lodge." After they pass the downtown area, Andy says, "Bingo! There's a Howard Johnson's Motor Lodge with their restaurant as well."

As they pull in, Lydia reads the sign, "Ice cream, twenty-eight flavors."

As Andy parks the car, he says, "You'll love their ice cream." Andy and Alex park between the restaurant and motor lodge rooms. Alex walks up to Andy's car window and says, "I will go ahead and register Shelby and me, and will tell the clerk a friend is going to check into the adjoining room."

Andy says, "We decided to get some ice cream before we check in. After you check in, why don't you and Shelby join us at the next table?"

Alex says, "I think we will. It looks slow in the restaurant and the motor lodge, like a typical Sunday evening."

Lydia and Andy get a table, while Shelby waits on Alex. Lydia orders a water with a double scoop of butter crunch, and Andy orders water with a double scoop of pecan brittle. Right after they get their ice cream, Shelby and Alex sit down at the next table. Alex orders chocolate, and Shelby orders strawberry.

Andy says, "Come on; they have twenty-eight flavors."

Shelby laughs and says, "You can order the other twenty-six."

After they finish the ice cream, everyone realizes how tired they are. Andy quickly checks in, and both couples waste no time getting locked in their motel rooms. As soon as they get in, Andy taps on the adjoining door, and tells Alex he'll set the alarm for 6:30. They decide to leave about 8:15.

Alex and Shelby go through their bedtime ritual. Andy and Lydia begin theirs.

17

THE WILD WEST

After a shower and breakfast, Andy buys a morning paper, and they load the van and car. Andy says to Alex, "We're a little over an hour from the Dells. We just want to do some scenic driving for a couple hours. We should be back on the road before noon. Do you want to have a light lunch about 11:30, before we leave the Dells?"

Alex says, "Sure."

Andy opens the car door for Lydia and hands her the newspaper. When they start down the road, Andy says, "Will you scan the main news headlines for me, and read some highlights of any article that is of national importance?"

Lydia says, "Be glad to." She takes a few minutes to go through the news section of the Milwaukee Journal Sentinel. Lydia says, "I think you would be most interested in two of the articles. One article says they are hearing government rumors of massive troop movements from the Middle-East to South America and Latin America. The journalist has sources that say the troops are Iranian, and they are headed to Venezuela and Guatemala. The article also says there is an American military buildup near the southern border."

Andy says, "Just between you and me, the rumors are correct. Anything else?"

Lydia says, "There is another article about an escalation over the weekend of crimes committed by illegal immigrants. It basically says that crimes including theft, assault, murder, rape and vandalism have increased three hundred per cent by illegals."

Andy says, "Wow, that's terrible. You are finding what I need to know. I will go through the paper this evening."

Lydia gets out a brochure from her purse. She says, "At the restaurant I picked up a brochure of routes around the Wisconsin Dells."

Andy says, "That's great. You're wonderful. Do you see anything that might be a good scenic drive for us?"

Lydia looks over the brochure. She says, "Right before or right after Mirror Lake, we can turn right off of I90/94, and take a loop around part of the Dells and Lake Delton. The route comes back to I90/94. On the way back to the highway, it looks like there are plenty of restaurants."

Andy says, "Perfect; let's do it!"

They turn right on the scenic loop before they get to Mirror Lake. Along the route they view rocky cliffs that get as high as one hundred feet above the Wisconsin River. They go around Delton Lake and stop for lunch before they get on the highway. They wait on Alex to park. Alex comes directly to Andy's car window with a paper bag. Alex says, "I got you and Lydia some pretzels." Alex looks around and says in a whisper, "Look under the pretzels."

Andy peers under the pretzels and sees a box of fifty .38 caliber rounds. Andy says, "Thanks for the pretzels. We're going inside to look at their lunch menu. We're talking about eating a salad in the restaurant and getting a sandwich and drink to go."

Alex says, "Good idea; Sioux Falls is six hours from here."

Lydia and Andy get a table, so Shelby and Alex can sit at the table next to them. They each order a salad for the restaurant, and a soda and sandwich to go. Shelby and Alex do the same.

By the time they're back on the highway, only two hours have gone by, since they turned off by Mirror Lake. Three hours down the road, they make a pit stop and get gas. In another two hours they stop for supper. They get out of the car and van and stretch before they go in the Frisch's Big Boy Restaurant. Andy and Lydia walk in a few seconds before Alex and Shelby.

Inside Andy can hear Alex telling Shelby, "We should be in Sioux Falls by 6:30." Again they're able to get tables next to each other.

Andy says to Lydia, "Evidently, we can check into the motel about 6:30. What are you thinking about ordering?"

Lydia smiles and says, "I think I'm in the mood for a Big Boy, big boy!"

Andy laughs and says, "I think we'll order two of them. What else?"

Lydia says, "I would like some fruit with it."

While they order their food, two college aged men keep looking at Andy. After the waitress turns their order in, one of the men walks over to Andy and says, "Are you Andy McGraig from Purdue?"

Andy smiles and says, "Why do you ask?"

He says, "We would like your autograph."

Andy says, "Sure; what are your names?"

He says, "I'm Richard, and that's Aaron, my friend." He waves Aaron over, and Aaron carries two books with him."

Andy looks at them, "Bio chemistry and analytical geometry; good subjects. Are you going to college?

Aaron says, "We're headed back to Madison."

As Andy signs each book, he asks. "University of Wisconsin?" They both nod their heads and watch Andy as he signs, "Andy McGraig – Purdue/NCAA playoffs 1962."

They thank him and Andy says, "Good school. Where are you from?"

They say, "Cheyenne, Wyoming."

Andy says, "I hope you have a great year."

As the college men walk back to their table, they don't realize they have been watched closely by Alex and Shelby. Lydia says, "Wow, you're quite a celebrity."

Andy smiles and says, "As long as I'm a star in your eyes." Lydia smiles and leans over and kisses him on the cheek.

After they leave Big Boy, they're at the Sioux Falls Holiday Inn within an hour.

Alex checks in and gets the adjoining rooms again. He inspects his room, then Andy's after Lydia and Andy check in. After they bring their luggage in, everyone is ready to rest and watch some television. Andy sits down; watches the Huntley- Brinkley Report then reads his newspaper. Both couples go to bed before 10 p.m.

At 8 a.m. Alex knocks on their adjoining door and asks if they're dressed.

Andy opens the door and says, "We're showered and dressed and almost done with packing."

Alex says, "It's only four and a half hours from here to the Badlands. Do you want to get breakfast, before we leave Sioux Falls?"

Andy looks at Lydia and asks, "What are you in the mood for?"

Lydia says, "Pancakes!"

Shelby comes in the room and says, "That sounds good to me."

Alex says, "A pancake restaurant should be easy to find."

Andy says, "Let's go! We'll get our stuff out of the bathroom, and we'll be ready." When they get in the Chevy and van, Alex says to Shelby, "This is the first time that Andy and Lydia seem like they're nineteen and recently out of high school."

Shelby says, "I know. Andy is very mature and serious for his age." She looks at Alex and says, "Don't forget about my pancake restaurant."

Alex laughs and says, "Right now you seem like you're sixteen!"

They only get five blocks from the motel, and they see a big sign that says, "Granny's Pancake Restaurant". Everyone in the restaurant looks at the handsome couples, as they all enjoy a small stack of pancakes and maple syrup with an egg, bacon and coffee.

Soon they're back on the road again, and cruising the wide open prairie with the 55' blue and white Chevy leading the way. As they see the badlands ahead from the flat plains, Lydia and Andy hear a "thump" against the front of the car. They pull into the first scenic view parking area, and they both get out and walk to the front of the car. Alex gets out of the van and says, "Are you having car trouble?" Andy says, "No, we thought we would do a little hunting."

Alex walks toward them and says, "Hunting?" He stands by Andy at the front of the car and says, "Wow, you caught a ring necked pheasant in the grill of your car!"

Andy says, "Let's put him in a natural setting. My cousin, Anderson, is into wildlife and nature. I think that's what he would do."

Alex says, "I have some gloves with me." He comes back from the van and pulls the pheasant out of the grill. Andy and Alex walk off the parking lot and place it behind some rocks and brush. Alex says, "It's a beautiful bird."

As they walk back to the parking lot, Andy says, "I've heard that on a clear or partly sunny day, we can get some great pictures of the badlands during sunset."

Alex says, “Lead the way.”

Andy says, “We can check into the motel at Wall by mid-afternoon; have an early supper and have the rest of the time for sightseeing and photography.”

Alex says, “You and Lydia are also making this a nice business vacation for Shelby and me.”

Andy says, “We're here to protect and serve.”

They pull back on the highway, but before they get to Wall, Lydia says, “Andy, we have to stop here and look at this landscape. It looks like something from Mars.”

Andy pulls over and finds a parking place. He says, “It is something else; like Mars or the lunar surface. I wonder if the President has seen this. He said about a year ago, we would send men to the moon before the decade ends.'

Lydia says, “Maybe the astronauts will get some surface training here.”

Andy says, “Its only early afternoon, but I want to take some pictures with dad's Argus 35mm. These strange formations seem like they're out of this world. Rod Serling should film some of his Twilight Zone episodes here.”

Lydia says, “I wonder why the soil erodes in such an odd way?”

Andy says, “I think I heard that the make-up of the soil and rocks are different and that a constant wind blows through this area.”

After Andy takes some pictures of the odd formations and colors, they get back on the highway. Lydia reads a big billboard, “Wall Drug Store – Ice Cream and Free Ice Water – Turn right in two miles.”

Andy says, “Paradise in the prairie; Wall is where our motel is. We'll find Wall Drug Store before we check into the motel. I'm already thinking about butter pecan, butterscotch or praline.”

Lydia laughs and says, “I'm already thinking about vanilla with caramel topping! I think Shelby and Alex will enjoy our surprise stop.”

Andy says, “I'm glad they're enjoying the trip, while they do their work.”

There's a lot of people at the Wall Drug Store, so Andy, Lydia, Alex and Shelby sit together. Everyone enjoys their favorite ice cream. Lydia says, “Look at the sign, “Feed the Prairie Dogs”.

Andy says, "Let's check it out, when we get up."

They go through a door, where they can view and feed the prairie dogs. Shelby says, "How cute!"

When they walk out of the store, Andy and Alex look around from the sidewalk. Andy says, "Check that out; it's our motel, Sunshine Inn. It looks like it's about a block away. Its 3:30 by the time they get in their rooms. After Alex checks their room, Andy says, "We're going to take a short nap, then we'll knock on the door. How about supper by five, then we'll have about two hours for sight-seeing and taking pictures."

Alex says, "Its fine by me."

After supper, they take a loop through Badlands National Park that goes back to Wall. Andy and Lydia are interested in looking at a dozen scenic overviews. Andy takes longer at the stops during sunset. At one stop they view a lot of pinnacles that have a yellow cast from the setting sun. Andy raises his long arm and waves. With his other hand he takes a picture of his long, waving shadow that is cast on a large pinnacle.

Andy and Lydia get back in the car, and Andy says, "The last picture was my artistic creation for the evening."

Lydia says, "I get the message loud and clear. I'm ready to turn in too."

Andy replies, "Let's round up the doggies, and lay our heads on the lone prairie." Alex and Shelby follow them along the prairie trail.

When Lydia and Andy wake up at dawn, Andy says, "Wednesday morning already; we'll be in Cody tonight and Yellowstone tomorrow night."

Lydia turns over and kisses him on the lips and says, "And you'll be with me every night."

I better tell Alex that we should leave early; Cody is seven hours from here, and we'll probably stop for breakfast and lunch. We may need to view Mt. Rushmore from the road or just stop for a few minutes. If we do want to see Mt. Rushmore, it will add an hour to our driving time.

Lydia says, "Let's see it! We should still get to Cody between five and six."

Andy says, "Okay, we'll let Alex and Shelby know, so they can get ready."

Before they pull out of Wall, they stop and get some breakfast sandwiches and coffee to go. Just before they get to Mt. Rushmore, Lydia and Andy decide to stop at a scenic view to take some pictures.

After they take pictures at the first scenic spot they come to, Andy talks with Alex about their plans in Cody. Alex says, "Our travel planner at the department thought you and Lydia might enjoy staying at Irma Hotel, which was founded by Bill Cody and named after his daughter, Irma. They also have a number of historic rooms. If you want supper in Cody, two of the historic restaurants are Cassie's Supper Club and the Silver Saddle Saloon, which is at the Irma Hotel."

Andy says, "Let's go to Cassie's Supper Club before we check in. We should be in Cody by late afternoon."

Andy gets back in the car and Lydia says, "Even though it's cloudy right now, I think we'll have good pictures of Mt. Rushmore."

As they get back on Highway 14, Andy says, "The pictures should be fine. Alex and I were talking about where we're staying, and where we'll have supper. They're both historic places. The hotel was founded by Buffalo Bill, and Cassie's Supper Club has history that we'll learn, when we get there."

Lydia starts dozing off, while they start the long trip across Wyoming. She wakes up when they stop for gas, but soon she is dreaming again about wide open spaces. After seven hours, they're close to Cody. They see a mountain range ahead of them and a number of horse and cattle ranches. Large, white clouds are slowly gliding across the bright, blue Wyoming sky.

They hit the wide roads of Cody, Wyoming, and Andy stops to get directions to Cassie's Supper Club. When they pull into their parking lot, Cassie's already has on their bright lights, advertising: "Live Music – No Cover". The front of the building is designed like the old western style store front, including a wide, boarded floor along the front of the building.

It's almost 6:00, when a friendly waitress in a plaid shirt and blue jeans, seats Lydia and Andy at a table near the dance floor.

A minute later, Shelby requests a table close to Andy's and Lydia's. While they wait on their drink order, Lydia and Andy talk about the large pictures above the dance floor. They show Buffalo Bill and the virgin Wyoming lands of those days.

The waitress brings their water, coffee and soda, and they order two steak dinners. The restaurant tables are filling up fairly fast. Two men on stage in cowboy hats are singing country and western. They're playing guitar and fiddle. Andy recognizes, "Hello Walls", and the beginning of "I Fall to Pieces".

There are four men at a table near the music stage, just two tables away from Andy and Lydia. Everyone notices them getting louder than the music. One of the men is taunting the waitress, and it looks like they had been drinking heavily. Andy, Alex and Shelby start watching the men closely.

The man that has been taunting the waitress, gropes her. The man closest to Andy, stands up and starts to pull something out of his belt. Andy jumps up, and his massive 6'5" frame heads toward him, like he's driving to the basket. When Andy reaches him, he deflects the gun and lands a karate kick on his chest that sends him flying against the upright piano, next to the wall.

The man that groped the waitress tries to get to Andy, but Alex is there, and he lands an upper cut that knocks him out cold. Another man comes at Andy, and before he can get close to him, Andy's long arm reaches out, and with his big fist, Andy hits him with a crushing blow to his jaw. The last man standing holds his hands up, as Shelby points her handgun at him.

The manager has already called the police, and soon everyone hears the sirens approaching the building. Three men are out cold on the floor, and Alex pulls his gun, in case any of them come to. In walk three police officers and a sheriff's deputy. Alex, Shelby and Andy immediately show them their State Department Security Badges.

The officers handcuff the four men. Three officers start taking statements, and the fourth one calls the office with a description of the four men. He also goes outside and finds their tag number. Another squad car arrives with two police officers, and they load the prisoners in two squad cars.

The senior officer starts taking statements from Andy, Alex and Shelby. When the senior officer finishes, he looks at Andy and says, "I saw you on the cover of Sports Illustrated. Aren't you Andy McGraig from Purdue?" Andy and Alex look at each other, and they ask the officer to go over to a vacant corner of the dance floor with them. Shelby stays with Lydia.

Andy says to the rotund and friendly officer, "Officer, our work is classified. Since we're Feds, we have to tell you to keep our names from the public."

The officer says, "I will be glad to. I thought you were Andy, and it's a pleasure meeting you."

Andy says, "It's a privilege meeting you."

The officer admiringly says, "Buffalo Bill would be proud of you. It looks like both of you brought some action of the old west back to Cody." He looks at Alex and says, "By the way, you look like James Bond." Alex laughs and pats him on the shoulder.

The officer, who called in the identities of the prisoners and the car, comes up to his senior officer and says, "The Minnesota State Police are looking for these hoodlums. They stole the car and robbed two gas stations before they left Minnesota. The Minnesota State Police think all four are illegal immigrants."

The senior officer shakes hands with Alex, Shelby and Andy. The restaurant manager comes up to the two couples, and says, "It looks like you haven't had your steak dinners yet. It's on the house. Our singers want to know, if you have a request."

Andy says, "I Walk the Line."

The two couples sit together, and their waitress brings four steak dinners. The musicians come back to the stage, and the lead singer says, "Our heroes this evening, who delivered us from acts of violence, have requested us to sing, "I Walk the Line". We would like to think that Buffalo Bill is looking down with a smile." Everyone cheers and applauds for their heroes.

After dinner, a lot of people come over and shake their hands and thank them. Andy goes up to the two man band and gives them a tip. As the four go out the door, Andy says, "We're back in the saddle again."

Lydia says, "And I'm ready to hit the hay."

At the Irma Hotel, Lydia and Andy start to check in, and the desk clerk says, "Mr. McGraig, we heard about the calamity you encountered at Cassie's this evening. We have given you Buffalo Bill's historic suite at no extra charge, and your friends will be in the next room in Annie Oakley's historic room." Andy thanks him, and Alex finishes the registration.

After the bellman brings their luggage in, Lydia says, "They might give you the sheriff's job, while you're here."

Andy says flippantly, "They would have to offer me the marshal job of the Wyoming territory."

Lydia hugs him and says, "You're definitely my hero."

Andy says, "We'll have to sleep closer tonight. It felt like it will get down to fifty degrees."

Lydia says, "Well, okay; you talked me into it."

Lydia and Andy are up early. They decide they need to get to Yellowstone as early as possible. Thursday is the only day they have to see the park, and they need to head back Friday morning. Andy calls Alex and Shelby. They decide to head out by 7:30.

They load the car and van, and Andy says to Alex, "You know, I'm going to miss Cody."

Alex says, "I know what you mean. It's a stop we'll never forget." They go to Albertson's grocery store to stock up on some food and drinks. Before they start through the mountains, they fill up at the Conoco Filling Station in Cody.

When they're ready to head down the highway, Andy says, "We hope to arrive in Yellowstone around noon. We may stop a couple times on the way to get some scenic pictures."

Shelby rolls down her window and yells, "Head 'em up and move 'em out!"

They drive through the Absaroka Range of the Rocky Mountains. Along the valley, they see herds of buffalo and herds of elk. They see some of the most beautiful mountains and glaciers in the world. Andy stops several times to take pictures of mountain lakes bordered by wild flowers. At times they drive along the Shoshone River on Highway 20. Along the entire route, there are majestic spruce, pine and fir trees.

During one scenic stop, all four explorers get out to be refreshed by the cool air from the mountains. While they're enjoying the beauty of the earth, they hear an unusual and eerie song. They look in a field just twenty yards to their left, and they see a Western Meadowlark enjoying the moment, as much as they are.

After they enter the east entrance to Yellowstone, they drive just a few miles before going around the serene Yellowstone Lake. As they drive to Old Faithful, elk are grazing in the tall green grass and sauntering in the valley at the base of the splendid mountains. There are groves of yellow aspen with their distinctive white bark.

They cross the Continental Divide at two points on the Grand Loop Road. As they crest the steep hill at the second crossing, they look up at a bald eagle soaring against the clear, blue sky. When they come to the next scenic overview, Andy says let's stop here and look at the map the ranger gave us. When they stop, Alex and Shelby pull beside them. As Andy looks at the map, Lydia, Shelby and Alex get out to stretch.

Shelby says, "Have you ever seen anything so beautiful?"

Lydia says, "The country between here and Cody Is heaven on earth."

Alex says, "We should pay Andy and you for being tour guides."

Lydia says, "Nonsense, we're glad you're with us."

Andy steps out of the car with the map. He puts it on the hood of the car and says, "Gather round and see what you think. We're right here, and Old Faithful is here: near our hotel, the Old Faithful Inn. We have five to six hours before supper. We can go directly to Old Faithful, and then hike a 3.5 mile trail on the Little Firehole Loop. It takes us to Mystic Falls and the Fairy Falls and Creek. With sightseeing and picture taking, the hike would be about two hours. We would still have time to drive to the Upper and Lower Geyser Basins. I'm guessing we would be checked in and ready for supper by 6 p.m."

Lydia says, "It sounds like a good plan." She looks at Shelby and Alex and asks, "What do you guys think?"

Alex nods his head and Shelby says, "It looks like it will be a fun excursion."

They get back in their vehicles, and after Andy pulls out, Alex looks at Shelby and says, "We'll have to be careful that we don't get too caught up in the moment. Even as we hike, we need to be looking out for their safety."

Shelby replies, "Absolutely, that's a good reminder."

Before they get to Old Faithful, Andy makes an unplanned stop near the Natural Bridge. They get out to stretch and breathe in the fresh cool air. Andy says, "Who wants to go with me for a short walk. The map says we can walk along the Yellowstone Lake and the canyon.

Alex asks, "How long will we be gone?"

Andy says, "About thirty minutes."

Shelby says, "Let's do it."

The hike is invigorating, and Lydia says, "I'm glad we got some blood circulating."

As they get ready to leave, Shelby says, "I'm looking forward to Old Faithful and the next hike."

When Lydia and Andy get out to look at Old Faithful, Alex and Shelby are nearby doing some of their own sightseeing. Lydia and Andy walk as close to Old Faithful as the park allows. Lydia says, "So this is the famous geyser known the world over."

Andy says, "Yes, Old Faithful and her fellow geysers. We're standing on a super volcano. In our lifetime it could blow its top and affect a big part of the world."

Lydia says, "Wow, do you think we'll make it out of the park in the morning?"

Andy laughs and takes her hand. He says, "Let's tell Shelby and Alex that we're ready to find the Little Firehole Loop trailhead."

They walk the 3.5 mile trail, and as it goes along a wide, rocky creek bed, they see a black bear and its cub foraging by the creek. When they finish over half the hike, they come to a woods of mostly pines. They all notice the pleasant scent of pine in the air. Andy says, "Let's walk just a few yards into the woods. As a young kid, I loved the thick bed of soft pine needles like this woods has."

When they get in the woods, they can easily see the trail. Andy says, "Sit down a minute and check out the soft bed under you."

Lydia says, "This would be great to have in a back yard!"

The four explorers get up and get back on the trail.

Near the end of the trail, Alex asks, "What's next?"

Andy says, "Before we drive to the Lower and Upper Geyser Basins, let's check on our room reservations. We're real close to Old Faithful Inn."

The Inn is an impressive and massive structure of logs and planks. Inside the Inn, they're amazed at how immense the stone fireplace is. Alex and Andy check in, and Andy tells the desk clerk, they will bring their things in later.

After they get in the '55 Chevy and the converted '61 Ford van, they take off for the geysers. When they finish their geyser tour, they head to the Old Faithful Dining Hall. As they get ready to order, Andy looks at his watch and says, "Can you believe that for timing; it's 6:04." Before they go to their rooms, Andy gets the daily newspaper from Jackson Hole, Wyoming.

Once Lydia and Andy get settled in their cozy log room, Lydia says, "It's going to get down to thirty-four degrees tonight. We'll have to snuggle a lot to stay warm."

Andy smiles sheepishly and says, "I'm looking forward to it!"

While Lydia gets ready for bed, Andy sits down and reads the main news articles in the paper. He finds out that it is no secret that over 100,000 Iranian troops have landed in Venezuela. He guesses that the number is closer to 150,000. He wonders how many Venezuelan troops have been committed to the invasion. It also makes him think about how many contacts they have to terrorist and illegal immigrant cells in the country. Andy thinks between Iranian and Venezuelan troops, there could be a force of over 300,000 with those in the drug cartel and other radicals in Mexico.

Before Lydia comes out of the bathroom, he also reads an article about current crimes committed by illegal immigrants, and another article about two terrorist attacks in the country since yesterday. Oblivious to the dark subjects on Andy's mind, Lydia comes out of the bathroom with all smiles and the utmost appeal.

As she gets in the full size bed, Andy puts up the paper and goes in the bathroom. He changes and finishes in the bathroom as fast as he can. He turns out the light, and gets in bed beside Lydia. They quickly warm up the cool sheets. Andy thinks, "It's wonderful to be young and married to the one you love."

Morning comes around too fast. Andy has the alarm set for 6:00. Lydia is only half awake after the alarm goes off. She asks, "When are we leaving?"

Andy says, "8:00. Our drive from here to Wall, S.D. is the longest drive we have the next three days. It will take about eleven hours. Saturday we'll drive about nine and a half hours from Wall to Wisconsin Dells and we'll have about a seven hour drive on Sunday from the Dells to Mahican. I should have told you, that I talked with Alex yesterday about making the reservations. Tonight, we'll stay at the same motel in Wall. We'll stay at the Holiday Inn near the Dells, Saturday night, and we should be home by 3:30 on Sunday."

As Lydia begins to wake up, she says, "That's fine. I appreciate everything you've done to make this a wonderful honeymoon. I knew the first four days would be the main part of the vacation, and I understand that we have to put in the miles on the way back."

Andy walks over to Lydia and kisses her. Andy says, "Thank you, honey, for being a great wife and traveling companion. I hate to say it at a time like this, but I have to shower, so you can have the bathroom. If we get ready fast enough, we'll have breakfast before we leave."

Lydia says, "That will be nice."

Both couples are ready and packed by 7:30, so they eat breakfast in beautiful Yellowstone, Wyoming.

As they drive from the west side to the east entrance, they are mesmerized by the beauty of the park. The early morning hours are even more picturesque. They will never forget enchanting Yellowstone, and all of its wonders of nature. As they exit the park, they have another fifty miles of some of God's greatest handiwork.

When they drive through Cody, they wish they could stop again, but they have to keep on the road. They realize that not only do they want to get back to Mahican to be with family, but they now have a new life in the nation's capital.

Andy gets a daily newspaper in Wall and also a paper at their stop in the Dells. Each day he shares a little with Lydia about what's on his mind concerning national events.

Once again, they love the scenic drive through the Badlands and through the Dells, but the rest of the drive back is a little mundane and tiring. At their last gas stop, Andy and Lydia thank Alex and Shelby for everything they've done. They don't even mention that Alex and Shelby have two more nights of surveillance in Mahican. Andy knows the professional and kind couple will be following them back to D.C.

On Sunday afternoon, Andy and Lydia are glad to be back in Mahican. Judy and Owen are excited to see them, and they insist on carrying their luggage into the house.

Owen says, "Andy, Edward told me that he could walk the two hundred acres with me next weekend."

Andy says, "What great news to get at the end of a wonderful honeymoon! Dad, I appreciate you and Edward doing that. If you like the land, tell them that I will sign a contract, and mail them a thousand dollar deposit. Ask for a first right of refusal in writing, and try to bring it back with you. If it works out, his family and ours will have a lot of nice nature excursions on our own land."

Owen says, "I'm looking forward to seeing the land. I will stay in touch with you next weekend."

18

America Under Fire

Judy fixes a light supper. Andy and Lydia share the highlights of their honeymoon during and after supper. Andy asks, "Dad, what are the plans for Labor Day?"

Owen says, "Judy and I thought it would be nice that the four of us spend some quiet time at home. You've been traveling a lot, and we would like to spend as much time as possible with you and Lydia. We have all the food we need for a cook-out."

Andy says, "Good idea. It will be nice to rest for a day."

About 9:00, Judy says, "I think I'll get ready for bed."

Lydia says, "I think I will turn in early also."

Andy says, "I want to talk with dad for a while. I'll get ready for bed in about an hour."

Judy looks at Lydia and says excitedly, "Why don't you come in my room, while you wait for Andy?"

Lydia smiles at Judy and says, "I would like that; just us girls can visit."

Owen says, "I'll fix some more coffee."

While Owen prepares the coffee, Andy asks, "Dad, how are you doing?"

Owen says, "Considering what we've been through, I'm doing alright. Judy has been a big help. Having Judy here has helped me cope better."

Andy says, "I'm glad to hear that, and I totally understand. Lydia has helped me cope as well. It seems like Judy is doing alright."

Owen says, "She's incredible. She has one of the best attitudes of anyone I've known. She misses your mom a lot, but we support each other."

Owen takes his seat at the kitchen table while the coffee brews.

Andy looks serious as he says, "Dad, I can't tell you about some of the things happening in the nation, because of my classified work. I do want to share some general things that you might guess, because of the news.

Owen says, "I was hoping we would have a chance to talk about the nation's problems. Since the coffee is almost ready, I'll serve it, then we can talk. You might like to know that I have the handgun and the shotgun for home protection."

Andy says, "Good, I'm glad you got both. Did you buy extra ammo?"

Owen says, "Yes, I bought plenty, and next weekend, I'm taking Judy to a target range, so she and I can get use to both guns."

As Owen gets up to pour the coffee, Andy says, "That's a good thing to do."

Owen sits down after he brings the coffee to the table.

They each take a sip, then Andy says, "You have probably noticed from the news, how defiant most of the New Age Socialist leaders have been."

Owen says, "Yes, I have. They seem to be unremorseful of their actions."

Andy says, "Yes, it just gets worse. We are headed for a major conflict, and I want you and Judy to be prepared, in case things get bad. Since you're in Central Indiana, it might not get real bad, but there are people living in this country, who have no good business here, and some will cause problems nationwide."

Owen says, "Like everyone, I'm aware of more terrorism and other crimes in our country. Everyone knows about the 100,000 Iranian troops that landed in Venezuela. Even though the Venezuelan leaders claim they need help fighting the rebels in their country, most people I know believe there is something else going on."

Andy replies, "There is something else going on. You might tell your friends and close neighbors that it would be good to stay in touch with each other. Maybe let them know you have a hunch that they will need each other in the near future. If a conflict starts soon, be very careful where you go and how you go. I believe you and your friends will need each other."

Owen says, "I'm not surprised by what you're telling me. I'm taking your advice."

Andy says, "Stock up on whatever you can, including food, water, and medical supplies. I would recommend buying wood and nails and any other building supplies that would help you secure things, when something happens. Do you think Judy will have a clear head under those circumstances?"

Owen replies, "I have no doubt; she is mature for her age, like you."

Andy says, "Excellent! Dad, it was a long drive. I'm ready to saw some logs."

Owen says, "Me too. We won't have breakfast early, so we can all sleep in. I will be up before 8, so when you and Lydia get up, Judy and I will start breakfast."

Andy says, "Dad, I'm glad we'll have the whole day together. I wish I could be here more often."

Owen says, "We love being with you." Owen gets up and rinses out the coffee cups."

Andy says, "Good night, Dad. I love you."

Owen turns and looks at him and smiles. He says, "I love you too, son."

Andy and Lydia are still asleep at 8:00, and soon Andy wakes up to the smell of bacon. When Andy stirs in the bed, Lydia wakes up and says, "Is your dad cooking bacon?'

Andy says, "It's a pleasant wake-up call."

After breakfast, Lydia thanks Owen and Judy for making their breakfast. While Judy and Lydia talk a minute, Judy notices Andy just starring at her. She looks at him and says, "Well?"

Andy just smiles and doesn't say anything for a couple seconds, then he says, "Did you forget to ask me something?"

Now it's Judy's turn to stare, then a light comes over her face, and she says, "My Yellowstone gift!"

Andy hands her a small gift box that is wrapped.

Judy quickly unwraps it and exclaims, "It' a charm bracelet with all the charms! There's a bear, a mountain, an eagle, the word, "love", the Old Faithful geyser, an elk and a buffalo. I love it, Andy!" She jumps up and hugs her big brother.

As Judy pours more coffee for everyone, Andy asks, "What's on the cook-out menu today?"

Judy looks at her Dad, and Owen says, "Tell him what we picked up."

Judy says, "We'll have grilled hamburgers with all the trimmings, green beans with bacon, red potatoes, strawberries and vanilla yogurt, watermelon, chocolate and vanilla ice cream with caramel topping."

Andy says, "Wow, that's quite a menu for Labor Day."

Judy says, "It's also to celebrate your honeymoon road trip."

Lydia says, "Thank you; that's sweet."

Andy says, "There's a lot of pictures that need developing. We'll have to have a follow-up party and look at all the pictures. We'll also have a meal that will be on me."

Owen is done grilling by early afternoon, and Judy starts setting the picnic table. It's getting close to autumn, and the rain has taken its annual respite. The grass is brown and dry, and it's already ninety degrees. Andy says to Owen, "Even though it's dry, your tomatoes are still doing well."

Owen says, "It looks like they'll be plentiful this year. We may just want to have the main course outside. By that time, we'll want a break from the heat and flies."

After the cookout, Judy and Lydia volunteer to do the dishes. They know Owen and Andy want to spend some time together. They go in the living room, and catch up on friends and church activities. Andy asks, "Do Carl and you stay in touch?" Owen says, "We do. Sometimes Carl invites us to a special service or activity in Muncie. After you started your government training, we met Carl and Thelma at their house. Several churches in Muncie sponsored a great gospel sing with The Happy Goodman Family, The Florida Boys, The Blackwood Brothers and The Cathedral Quartet.

Andy says, "Wow, it would have been some gospel sing. I would have loved to seen George Younce and The Cathedrals."

Owen says, "He was so entertaining like always. It was great music and very inspirational. What are Lydia's plans in D.C.?"

Andy replies, "She goes to a teacher's orientation Thursday. She is going to teach some special classes part-time. We don't know her schedule yet."

They visit for a long time. Lydia and Judy go in the back yard after they visit in the kitchen. Judy shows Lydia what she and her dad planted in the garden. Judy tells Lydia about how her mother loved gardening and anything to do with nature. Judy says, "We loved going to the Smoky Mountains in Tennessee; especially Mom and Andy. I know they always hated to leave. We would hike; look at the early settlement cabins and farms and camp part of the time. Mom loved observing nature, especially trees, birds, plants and animals."

Lydia says, "I know she was a very loving and beautiful person."

Judy says, "Let's go inside, so I don't start crying."

Lydia puts her arm around Judy while they walk to the back door.

They go in the living room, and Owen says, "This evening we'll put the leftovers on the table, and everyone can help themselves. You can snack on the food all evening, if you want to. Andy and I were talking about playing a game of Monopoly this evening, if everyone is up for it."

Lydia says, "That would be fun."

Owen says, "Before we put the food out, tell me about your travel plans for tomorrow."

Andy says, "As you know, dad, it's an eleven hour drive. Lydia and I think we should leave by 7 or 7:30. I have to be at work Wednesday."

Owen says, "I took the day off. I want to fix breakfast for everyone. I'll have it ready by 6:30, so you can leave, when you want to. What do you want: pancakes, eggs with bacon or anything we have?"

Andy says, "Let Judy decide. She has been a big help."

Judy says, "I like what we usually have: two eggs, bacon and toast and jelly."

They have a great evening together; laughing, sharing stories, making deals with houses, hotels and Park Place and snacking on the tasty Labor Day food.

When Andy's alarm goes off, he thinks, "Mornings like these always come too early." As he gets out of bed, he has an unusual melancholy feeling. He wants to stay longer, but he knows he has to leave for D.C.

Over breakfast, everyone hates breaking up the good time they had together. Owen and Judy are outside, when Lydia and Andy get in their car. Andy rolls down the window, and looks at his dad and sister. He says, "Both of you are welcome anytime at our new home. I hate to leave, but you're in my prayers every day. I love you."

In unison, Judy and Owen say, "I love you."

Judy looks over at Lydia, and says, "I pray for you and Andy every day."

Lydia says, "I will be praying for you too, Sweetie."

As the old, but nice looking Chevy goes down their road, Owen puts his arm around Judy, and feels a sadness in his heart.

They have a good drive back to D.C. Andy is more quiet than usual, and Lydia takes naps off and on. Lydia is surprised that the route to D.C. goes through a small part of Pennsylvania and West Virginia. They make quick stops for an early lunch and an early supper. Alex and Shelby park the conversion van near their car at each stop. For lunch they get a carry out, and for supper Alex and Shelby sit near Andy and Lydia's table. Andy pulls up to their new home by 7 p.m. They're both bushed.

They unload the few things from the car. When Andy opens the door, he carries Lydia across the threshold. When he puts her down in the living room, Lydia says, "Oh, Andy, its beautiful!"

In jest, Andy says, "Do you like it better than the college dorm?"

Lydia says, "In Holland, it's like a home that a successful, middle-aged couple might have."

After an hour, they get things put away and decide to shower after the long drive. The phone rings and Andy answers. Lydia's mother says, "Andy, this is Klara. How are Lydia and you doing?'

Andy says, "Just fine. We got home about an hour ago."

Klara says, "I called your dad's number today, and he told me when I could reach you. Before you put Lydia on, Conrad and I want to know if we could stay at your house on September 13th and 14th, that's a Thursday and Friday. On September 15th we have to go to the National Airport early to catch our flight."

Andy says, "You can stay as long as you want to. The 13th and 14th are fine. Let me get Lydia on the phone."

Lydia's mom tells her that she and her dad are having a great time sightseeing. They're staying in Nashville tonight, and in the morning, they're driving to the Smoky Mountains and Cherokee. They're planning to get on the Blue Ridge Parkway outside of Cherokee. They're going to the Biltmore Estate near Asheville, then they're taking I-26 through Columbia, S.C. so they can take I-95 to Florida. She tells Lydia they plan to go to St. Augustine and Daytona.

On the way to D.C. she says they plan to stop at Savannah, Charleston, Roanoke Island, Kitty Hawk, Jamestown and Colonial Williamsburg. Lydia asks, "Can you do all of that in the next eight days?"

Karla says, "Probably not. We've had to drop a few stops before now, but we have enjoyed all the places we've seen. I do know we'll go to the Smokies, Cherokee, St. Augustine, Charleston, Jamestown and Williamsburg."

Lydia says, "I'm glad you have a feasible option. Andy and I had a great time out west. I'll give you the details later. I will give you my work number the next time we talk."

Karla says, "I will plan to call you Sunday."

Lydia says, "I'm sorry you only have two days here. It will be nice to see you by the 13th."

After they hang up, Lydia says, "Don't you think they will give me a contact number by Friday?"

Andy says, "If they don't give you the number Thursday, just ask for it before you leave. I know we're both tired. You can shower first and go to bed, whenever you want to. I have a meeting with Mr. Abernathy in the morning. This evening I need to prepare for it."

Lydia says, "I really would like to go to bed soon. Give me a minute, then I'll shower and get ready for bed." Lydia walks over to Andy and sits on his lap for more than a minute. After kissing and hugging for several minutes, Lydia says, "I know you have work to do. I love you."

Andy shows he loves her with one more, long kiss, then he starts thinking about his meeting with Secretary Abernathy. As Lydia goes in the bathroom, Andy starts making notes for the morning meeting.

From the bedroom, Lydia says, "Goodnight," and Andy is still thinking about the meeting and national situation, when he is not dozing. When he wakes up, he realizes that he feel fast asleep. It's almost midnight. He thinks, "I need to go to bed now, and shower before six in the morning. I know Bruce or Mac will be here by 7:20."

It's very quiet when he goes to bed, and Lydia is sleeping soundly. About 4:30 in the morning, he starts stirring in his sleep. He sees Lydia's parents boarding a plane, then the plane takes off. The fumes from the plane are surreal. The fumes look like they contain a hoard of troops that extend farther than the eye can see. After he sees the vast number of troops, he hears explosions and sees fire from every direction. He sees schools, hospitals, churches, water stations, power grids, houses, factories and government buildings on fire. Before 5:00, he wakes up in a sweat. Lydia says, "Honey, are you alright?"

Andy says, "Yes. I think I'll lie here a couple minutes, then take a shower."

Lydia says, "I heard you yell out. What time is it?"

Andy says, "It's almost 5:00. I had a disturbing dream, but I'm okay."

After Andy showers and dresses, he's glad it's only 5:30. He thinks, "I'll have plenty of time to drink coffee; pray; read the Bible and think about things."

Before he leaves, he goes in the bedroom to see Lydia. He thinks, "She's so beautiful and peaceful." He says, "Babe, I hate to wake you up, but I'm leaving now. Stay in bed as long as you want. You have the whole day to rest. My work number is by the telephone."

Half awake, Lydia says, "Okay, honey; have a good day."

Andy goes outside to a cool, refreshing morning. Mac pulls up, and they take off for the State Department. On the way, they pick up Mr. Abernathy, and they're in the cafeteria having breakfast by 8:00.

Mr. Abernathy says to Mac and Andy, "Men, we're facing perilous times. I want you to stay in close contact with me and each other, including Bruce, Alex and Shelby. Let's also look out for Lydia's safety. It's all new for her, and I want her to feel secure here."

After they finish their second cup of coffee, they take the elevator to the Secretary's office. Mr. Abernathy says, "Mac, when does Bruce relieve you today?"

Mac says, "4:00."

Abernathy says, "Call him when we get to the office. Tell him to come in at 3:30. Take Andy home at 3:30, so he can be with Lydia. She has teacher orientation tomorrow, and will be coming in with Andy.

Mac, I'm ordering four carry out orders at the cafeteria for you, your wife, Andy and his wife for your supper.

I'll ask the cafeteria supervisor to have them ready for you by 3:30."

Mac says, "Thank you, sir."

After they enter the Secretary's office complex, Andy follows Mr. Abernathy to his office. Secretary Abernathy says, "Andy, the assistant principal of our school operation is going to meet Lydia in our outer office at 9 in the morning. Lydia can have breakfast with us. Mrs. Alberton does a good job for us. She'll take Lydia through orientation and have her back here by 4:00 tomorrow. I think they're going to ask her to observe classes on Friday."

Andy says, "She'll like that."

Mr. Abernathy asks, "I'm glad to hear you had a good honeymoon. Are you glad to be back at work?"

Andy says, "Yes, I am glad to be back."

Abernathy has a slight smile on his face, when he says, "Andy, as you know, agents are required to report any incidents that have to do with the public or with the law. I have to admit that I was somewhat amused, when Alex told me about the type of Wild West encounter you had."

Andy says soberly, "Yes, sir, that was something else. My training was helpful."

Abernathy says, "I have to admit that I wish I could have been there. Alex, Shelby and you did an excellent job. Alex said you took out two of them."

Andy says, "I felt like I had no choice."

Abernathy says, "I'm proud of you; that's one story you can tell your children and grandchildren. Well, we better get down to business. Before I catch you up with reports I've received, do you have anything for me?"

Andy says, "Yes, sir, I do. Early this morning, I had a disturbing dream. First of all, you need to know that Lydia's parents are flying back to Holland on Saturday morning, September 15th. With that information, I can tell you the dream. The first thing I saw was Lydia's parents boarding a plane. I saw the plane taking off, and as it left a trail of fumes, I saw this massive array of foreign troops that seemed to extend for miles. After I noticed the great number of troops, I heard explosions and saw fires at schools, churches, houses, power grid stations, water stations, hospitals and government buildings. I have to say that it not only woke me up, but it was very troubling."

Abernathy appears to be contemplating what Andy just shared. Finally, he says, "It would shake me up too. Give me a couple minutes to look at one report." He shuffles through a small stack of papers that are near him on his desk. He takes out one paper and studies it for a minute.

He looks at Andy and says, "I found what I wanted. Our southern border is over three thousand miles from Venezuela. Intelligence has already reported sporadic troop movements from Venezuela by many kinds of boats and ships. It would be too obvious for a great number of troops to travel only by land, which would be through Panama, Costa Rico, Nicaragua, Honduras and Guatemala. Today is September 5th, and I received this report on Friday, August 31st. Logistically, I'm guessing that they could get a large number of troops to the border by September 15th."

Andy says, "I think it means the invasion and the signal to their terrorist cell groups will be soon after the flight leaves. I wish I could say that it will happen that day or shortly after that day."

Abernathy says, "Your information, as is, should prove to be very helpful. We have an alert system, and I will ask the military to be on their highest alert by September 14th. I need to check something else before we continue." Abernathy gets out some kind of book that looks like a large calendar book or expense book.

He says, "Here it is. At this point, it looks like we're going to be invaded at the southern border. When we are, I need you here until we decide on our next plan of action after the invasion begins. Besides helping the military and our citizens, where we can, we are responsible for keeping our staff as safe as possible. I was looking to see who will be doing your surveillance on the weekend of September 14th. Friday through Sunday, the 14th through the 16th, Alex is on duty. Shelby will be on duty the two days after that."

Andy says, "Now I see where you're going. If the invasion happens late at night, you want the agent on duty to bring me in."

Abernathy says, "Exactly. I will call the agent on duty, then you. After I call you, I'll call Mac or Bruce and have one of them replace the agent on surveillance. In case of a national emergency, the government has several agencies that will alert the institutions they oversee. For example, all of the governors of the fifty states are on alert. When something happens, we have a staff to call all of the governors, and in turn, their staff will call all of their school superintendents to close the schools."

Andy says, "I'm glad to know that. What about hospitals and nursing homes?"

Abernathy replies, "Of course, some people have to be there, and they will depend on the National Guard to protect them. There are a lot of concerns, and a lot of organizations to help us. For example, if there are chemical or biological threats, the Army Reserve works with the National Guard, the Army and the Red Cross to help any locality in the nation."

Andy asks, "In this crisis, will the National Guard be the main defense for homeland security?

Abernathy replies, "Yes, they will be in any crisis. Every crisis has its own peculiarities. The imminent crisis has a large, offensive military that is presumably well coordinated with terrorist cell groups. I have no doubt that our military can handily defeat the invasion force. With the strike force of the Navy and Air Force, the invaders will be overwhelmed. Nevertheless, they will cause havoc, destruction and death. I'm concerned about the National Guard and Army Reserve being able to quickly wipe out the terrorist cells. I believe they will defeat the terrorists, but I have no idea how much devastation the terrorists will cause before they're defeated." Andy asks, "Do you think our role during the crisis will be limited to our building or do you expect any travel?"

Abernathy replies, "It's hard to predict, Andy. If the president wants me somewhere, there will be travel, whether it's at home or abroad. Of course, you're my designated body guard, even though I also need your input. If there's travel, you will probably be going with me. In the past, Mac or Bruce would go with me. Since you need security also, I'm sure one of them will still go."

Andy says, "Two weeks from tomorrow, Thursday September 13th, Lydia's parents will be with us before they return to Holland on the 15th. Could I have that day off, so I can show her parents the local sites?"

Abernathy says, "Yes, that's fine. I need to give Alex and Shelby the same day off. I'll have Mac do security detail with you, and since he'll have an easy day, I'll assign him to surveillance at your place that evening."

Andy says, "He doesn't have to be there until 11. We'll go out for an early lunch, then we'll see the sites. We'll have dinner around 5:00, then we'll return home."

Abernathy says, "I might be jumping the gun by telling you that our school is going to schedule Lydia's classes on Monday through Wednesday. I'm sure they will be sharing the details about her classes tomorrow."

Andy says, "I'm sure she'll like her schedule."

Both Abernathy and Andy pause for a second, then Abernathy pages his secretary for two cups of coffee. Abernathy looks at his watch and says, "It looks like our morning meeting might run until lunch time. About thirty minutes before lunch, I need to make a couple of calls. At that time, you can give Mac a break. Remember that Bruce is taking Mac's place at 3:30, so you and he can pick up your carry out supper in the cafeteria."

"Yes, sir. We appreciate you thinking of us and our wives."

"Andy, you probably realize there are times you will be working overtime and traveling. I do try to make it up to my staff, when I can."

Abernathy's secretary brings the coffee, as well as a thermos of coffee. When Abernathy's secretary leaves his office, Andy says, "I've been thinking about how defiant and foolish Iran is, since you gave them the ultimatum through their ambassador."

Abernathy replies, "Iran has been dead set on a confrontation for years. They keep bellyaching about death to America. Evidently, they've convinced themselves that this is the time to act."

Andy says, "Russia and North Korea took our warnings seriously. I wonder, if Iran thinks we won't decimate their industry."

Abernathy says, "It's a mystery. I don't know what they're thinking.

They have some weird beliefs. It's obvious that they have doubts about us destroying their industry. It looks like they plan to invade, and when they do, we'll immediately destroy their industry, including their oil fields and refineries. They must not realize that their economy will be left in ruins. Maybe it's fate that their rhetoric and crimes will finally get the best of them."

Andy says, "Sir, I know Mac and Bruce work a lot of hours. Is it alright, if I go ahead and relieve Mac until noon?"

Abernathy says, "Sure thing. If nothing comes up by lunch, we'll go down to the cafeteria."

As Andy does security watch outside the Secretary's outer office complex, he sees the dates September 6th and September 16th in his mind. He realizes tomorrow is September 6th, and he also perceives that September 16th is the day of the invasion.

During lunch, Andy tells Mr. Abernathy that he has important information for him, when they get back to his office. When Andy tells Mr. Abernathy what he believes about Sunday, September 16th, Abernathy says, "I think I will call the Pentagon and tell them we think the invasion will begin early morning on the sixteenth of the month."

When Andy gets ready to meet Mac, he feels a burden about the next eleven days. He wonders if they're going to go fast, like a speeding car trying to brake for a stop light. He feels like the stop light is September 16th.

The next day, Lydia says she likes her schedule. She tells Andy that she teaches three classes per day, Monday through Wednesday. She is going to teach Dutch and German to several gifted students. She also has a sociology class for college prep students, and a non-credit class about preparing for college.

On September 13th, Andy and Lydia enjoy taking Lydia's parents to the Lincoln Memorial, the Jefferson Memorial, the Smithsonian and other popular sites in D.C. After they see off Lydia's parents at the airport on the fifteenth, Lydia says, "It seems like my parents had to leave, right after they arrived."

Andy says, "I know. I've had the same eerie feeling about the last ten days." As they leave the National Airport, Andy says, "Let's go out for lunch. Maybe we can order extra as a carryout for supper this evening."

Lydia spots a Chinese Restaurant right away. They stop and try it out. After they finish and get in the blue and white Chevy, Andy says, "I didn't know you like Chinese noodles so well."

Lydia laughs and says, "I didn't know you like Chinese shrimp so well."

Andy smiles and says, "Touche!"

That evening Andy says, "There's a good possibility that I might get a call from work about going in tomorrow."

Lydia asks, "Is something important going on?"

Andy says, "It could be real important. I can't say much about it, but if the call is early, Alex will take me in, and Shelby, Mac or Bruce will relieve him. I don't want to alarm you, but if I go in, please stay inside and stay close to the phone."

Lydia replies, "Wow, it does sound kind of scary."

Andy says, "I can tell you more tomorrow. I'm glad one of the agents will be on duty. If there is a problem, they will come to your door. At least, you know who all three are. Also, I have an extra loaded handgun and ammo in the bedroom."

Lydia follows Andy into their bedroom, and he shows her where he keeps the extra handgun. Andy goes through the fundamentals of loading and unloading, and aiming and firing.

Lydia says, "This is scary, but I know you. I realize something significant is happening. I know you want me to be safe."

Andy takes a deep breath and says, "Babe, I'm glad we shared this. It's about an hour before bedtime. Let's just relax and enjoy the moment."

Lydia goes up to Andy, and gives him a long, warm hug. She looks up at him and says, "I love you so much; you make me feel good."

She takes his words away, and he just stands there and cherishes their precious time together.

They're in bed early and soon, they both fall into a deep sleep.

Just before 5:00 in the morning, the phone rings, and Andy sleepily answers it.

Abernathy says, "Andy, the invasion started twenty minutes ago, just after 4:30, eastern standard time. They're coming across our southern border. I've already called Alex. As soon as you can get ready, he'll bring you in, and Shelby is on her way to cover for him."

Andy says, "Okay, sir, I think we can be there about 6 a.m."

Lydia starts waking up, and Andy says, "It was Mr. Abernathy, and I have to go in right away. I'm going to take a quick shower. Can you make some coffee and something?"

Lydia says, "Sure. We have some muffins that I'll get ready for you."

Andy says, "Thanks. I'll have just a little time to fill you in, while we have the coffee and muffins."

Lydia gets up right after Andy, and starts brewing the coffee. After he gets out of the shower, she toasts some muffins and fixes them with butter and strawberry preserves."

Andy comes to the table right after she finishes. She sits down with him, and he explains that the government expected Iran and some recruits from Venezuela and Mexico to invade at our southern border. He says, "We believe we can stop the invasion near the border, but we don't know how extensive their terrorist cell network is. The National Guard has been on full alert nationwide. Right now, in our area, dad's area, and everywhere in the country, the National Guard is in action. Now you know why I want you to stay inside."

Lydia says, "I totally understand. I know you and Alex will be taking a hard look around, as you go to the State Department."

Andy looks at his watch. He says, "It's getting close to 5:30. I need to leave in a minute or two." He makes a quick trip to the bathroom and puts on his handgun and coat.

Lydia meets him at the front door, and says, Be careful; I love you." They kiss, and as Andy walks outside, he sees Alex waiting for him. After she watches Andy and Alex leave, she turns on the television to look for a news report.

Alex and Andy go immediately to Abernathy's office. Bruce is outside the office complex, when they arrive. When they go inside, Deputy Secretary Jennings and Secretary Abernathy's personal secretary are already there. Abernathy's secretary pages him. Mr. Abernathy comes out of his office and greets them. He says, "Alex, go home and get some sleep. We'll be needing you and Shelby a lot this week." He tells Andy to come in his office.

When they sit down, Abernathy says, "Andy, things are going to be hectic here today. While we go over several things, I will be getting calls, and I'll have to stay in touch with my secretary and the Deputy Secretary. Right now, security is our number one priority. There is an attachment of fifty National Guardsmen to guard the State Department. They're on the way over, and they will be setting up barricades around the perimeter of the building. Mac is on his way in, because we need him to set up our own security inside. As you know, we have an arsenal under lock and key. It includes gas masks, night vision goggles, rifles, grenades and a variety of survival equipment. Bruce will meet the Deputy Secretary at the target range downstairs. He'll unlock the arsenal area for Bruce, and they with two other agents will bring us the equipment we might need.

Abernathy's phone starts ringing. Andy sits and waits until the secretary comes in to ask Andy to help Bruce unload the equipment that Mac has brought up. In a conference room between Abernathy's office and his secretary, they unload two M16s, three M14s, a five load shotgun, two .38 revolvers, twenty grenades, a large supply of ammo and other equipment. After Andy, Mac and Bruce unload all of the equipment, Andy says, "We have enough supplies for a small squadron."

Mac says, "We may need it."

When the other two agents leave, Bruce returns to his post, and Andy and Mac report to Abernathy. When he gets off the phone, Abernathy says, "Mac, you set up our own arsenal; check all the guns and be sure they're loaded. When I get busy, I'll send Andy in to help you. You and he organize the equipment like we're going to be under attack."

Just fifteen minutes after Andy sits down in Abernathy's office, he gets a call from the National Guard. When he gets off the phone he says, "Andy, the National Guard captain, who is over the platoon assigned here, just arrived with all of his troops and barricades. I need Mac to go down and work with the Captain to make sure the Department is secured as well as possible. I need you to relieve Mac, so our weapons are ready in case of an attack."

Andy says, "Yes, sir. I'll tell Mac now."

Andy has all the weapons loaded, and all the supplies organized in less than hour. Mac hasn't returned yet, so Andy locks the door knob to the Secretary's personal conference room. He checks with Abernathy's secretary to see if Abernathy is available. He returns to Abernathy's office and tells him he locked the door knob, since he doesn't have the dead bolt key. Abernathy says, "That's fine. Bruce checks everyone before they come in. Have a seat, Andy. It's almost 9:00. Did you have breakfast?"

Andy says, "I had a muffin and cup of coffee at 5:30."

Abernathy says, "The kitchen has a skeleton crew right now, but I can call an order in, and have an agent bring it up. I'm going to get some eggs and toast, and we have our own coffee."

Andy says, "Two eggs over medium with toast and jelly is fine. Can you also get me a glass of milk?"

Abernathy says, "You've got it. With everything going on, it will probably take thirty minutes or longer. Since you haven't had a chance to listen to the news or read a paper, I want to read the press release that the White House sent out after six this morning."

Andy says, "That's the one thing I've been antsy to hear."

Abernathy says, "They have the press release typed as, "From the White House on Sunday, September 16, at 6:00 A.M. EST. At 4:30 EST our southern border was breached by invaders. Our Armed Forces have been anticipating an invasion, and they are prepared to swiftly answer the invaders with the full power of our military. Our intelligence tells us that they have a lot of terrorist cell groups in our country, including cells in many neighborhoods. Do not overestimate your safety by going out in public. Our public transportation systems will be very limited. The National Guard has operating public transits under surveillance. As of today, the nation is under martial law. A curfew of 6:30 p.m. in each time zone begins today. As of 5:45 e.s.t. this morning, war was declared on Iran and Venezuela.

All church services and meetings are cancelled today and this week. All schools are closed, and extra-curricular activities are cancelled this week. The federal government orders all public and private meetings to be cancelled until further notice. Our nation is on high alert and under invasion. Stay in your homes and protect your families and neighbors. There is a very high risk of terrorist attacks in every city and small town in the nation. Be on high alert of any activity in your home area. From the President of the United States and the his Cabinet"

Abernathy continues, "Andy, one of my jobs during the crisis is to keep you informed, in case you perceive something that will help our military or the safety of the public."

Andy says, "Yes, sir. I will stay focused, and let you know if I have something."

Abernathy says, "Right now, military reconnaissance at 4:30 this morning estimated that the invasion force from the border in California to Texas is 300,000 to 350,000 troops. We have more troops than that stationed in the four border states, and we have 500,000 back-up troops ready for action. Initially, our Navy in the Gulf and in the Pacific and our Air Force have delivered a stunning blow to the invaders in just the first two hours. Our surveillance estimates that our bombing has already eliminated fifteen percent of the invading force. They estimate that we have killed or seriously wounded over 50,000. We have many Marine battalions spread from San Diego to Corpus Christi. There are nine main border sectors from San Diego to the Rio Grande Valley. There are 8,000 Marines in outposts in the Rio Grande Valley with heavy artillery and heavy defenses. So far, we have had close to forty Marine casualties from mortar and machine gun fire and over seventy wounded."

Andy asks, "Where is the Army stationed?"

Abernathy says, "The Marines have taken the front line. They try to take high ground, but they are also trying to protect the border towns that are close to Mexico, including San Diego, Nogales, Arizona; El Paso, Laredo and Brownsville. The Army is stationed not far behind the Marines, who have over 130,000 soldiers on the front line. The Army has over 250,000 troops spread out in the southern parts of California, Arizona, New Mexico and Texas.... Just a minute, Andy; another teletype is coming in from the Pentagon."

Abernathy stops and reads the Pentagon report. "The Pentagon says the Navy and Air Force have continued to heavily bomb the insurgents in the rural areas. They have killed and seriously wounded another 15 to 20% of the original invasion force. The have eliminated from action over 105,000 enemy troops or almost a third of the invasion force."

Andy says, "Those are staggering results for the first five hours."

Abernathy says, "Unfortunately, over two hundred civilians have been killed in border towns."

Abernathy and Andy sit in silence for a minute, as though they are remembering the victims. Andy breaks the silence and says, "Sir, I have been focusing on how I might help the government with the crisis. First, I need to tell…" Abernathy's secretary calls and says their breakfast is here."

Abernathy says, "Sorry, Andy. Our breakfast is here. An agent is bringing it to us now. After we start breakfast, continue with what you were saying."

The smell of fresh coffee and the sight of eggs and toast is enough to sidetrack Andy for a couple of minutes. Once they enjoy the first few bites, Andy says, "Sir, there is something that is standing in my way, before I can totally focus on trying to help our military and civilians. We have briefly discussed dissident leaders in the New Age Socialist Party. For about a week, the Speaker of the House has been coming to my thoughts. I've been reflecting on that, and I believe the Speaker is involved in a conspiracy to overthrow the President and Vice-President, so the Speaker can be sworn in as President. It has come to me that the Speaker has a close relative working in Venezuela; possibly a first cousin. I believe the relative is involved with some assassins from or in Venezuela. Their objective is to assassinate our President and Vice-President. I don't know what route they're taking to Washington, but they're using the invasion as a cover to get in the country. I don't know if the Speaker knows details about the assassination plans, but the Speaker is involved in the conspiracy."

Abernathy is amazed at what he is hearing. He says, "Wow, Andy, it is some revelation. Did your thoughts about it develop throughout the week?"

Andy replies, "Yes, sir."

Abernathy say, "I need to share this with the President and the CIA Director.

Andy says, "Sir, before you make the calls, let me share a scenario. There is little doubt this team of assassins is using the invasion as a distraction. There's a number of ways they could enter the country with false IDs. Since the Navy is watching the west side of the Gulf closely, they could land on the east side of the Gulf in Florida. It's possible they could come from the Cancun area or Cuba and dock somewhere like Fort Myers. With false IDs, they could rent cars or trucks and drive to D.C."

Abernathy says, "I haven't gotten word, if the president is operating from a bunker. In a national emergency, he could do business from a bunker and stay in touch with the Vice-President at the White House. It's up to the CIA and the President's cabinet to advise him on a safe base of operation. I will go ahead and leave a message for the President and talk with the CIA director."

"Sir, while you're doing that, is it alright to check on Lydia?" Andy goes to a vacant office to call Lydia. When Lydia answers, Andy asks. "How are you doing, babe?"

Lydia says, "I'm glad to hear from you. I've stayed inside, but it's scary. How are you doing?"

"I'm doing fine. Shelby is doing surveillance there now, because of the invasion and other conflicts. Do you have my pager in case you need to page Shelby there?"

"Yes, I know where it is. When I hang up, I will check on it. Have you gotten the reports on the terrorism?"

Andy says, "No, we've been busy with the building security and with updates on the invasion at the border."

Lydia says, "The television station just started reporting some of the terrorism incidents. It's ironic that the biggest devastation is in sanctuary cities. Several big cities have been hit at public transportation and at government buildings. In San Francisco, 260 people have been killed who were taking buses and involved with bus transportation. In Baltimore, terrorists killed 83 people and burned down the train station. Other cities have also been hit by terrorists."

Andy replies, "It's a terrible time. Mr. Abernathy is busy with something right now, but I'm sure he will update me soon with the terrorist attacks. I would like to talk with you longer, but I will need to go soon. Do you need anything?"

Lydia says, "I have everything I need. Your dad called with good news on your land. He said you will like the land a lot. He has in writing your first right of refusal. The realty company wants you to call them about the deposit and the contract. They will want you to mail the thousand dollar deposit. The down payment balance of $9,000 is due by December 15th. They will mail the contract to you for your signature. The thousand dollar payments begin January 15th, and your last payment will be on December 15th, 1963."

Andy says, "That's welcomed news at such a dreary time. Will you call dad now, and thank him for me? Tell him that it is great news! You have my number here, so don't hesitate to call, if you need anything."

Lydia says, "Yes I will call him now. Be careful. I love you."

Andy says, "I love you too."

Andy checks with Abernathy's secretary to see if he is still busy. She says, "He's still making calls for another twenty minutes or so. He told me not to page him unless it's an emergency." Andy opens the outside door to see how Bruce is doing.

Bruce says, "I could use ten minutes for a pit stop and coffee."

Andy says, "Take twenty. I have to wait on Mr. Abernathy. Would you see, if the little shop by the cafeteria has today's newspaper?"

Bruce says, "Sure thing."

Andy looks at his watch and thinks, "It's already late morning. I hope within the hour I hear reports on terrorism and the reprisal on Iran."

Bruce brings Andy a paper in twenty minutes. Andy returns to the outer office and waits on the Secretary.

He gets to read the paper for about fifteen minutes before Abernathy's secretary says, "Andy, Mr. Abernathy can see you now."

After Andy sits down in Abernathy's office, he says, "Andy, I've had some new teletypes in the past hour. I'm sure you want an update on the terrorist attacks and our military action on Iran."

Andy says, "Yes, sir."

Abernathy reads the teletype and says, "As of 7:18 a.m. eastern standard time, AGMs (air to ground missiles) were launched against Iran to take out their air defense systems. By 8:07, A3 bombers and F4 Phantom fighters from airport bases in Israel and from the carriers in the Arabian Sea, Kitty Hawk and Independence, bombed all of Iran's major industries, especially in Tehran, Mashhad, Isfahan and Karag. All of their major oil and gas fields and refineries were bombed. At 8:54, their remaining industries and defense systems, including their aircraft, were destroyed by a second round of AGMs."

Abernathy looks at Andy's reaction, and they're both satisfied with America's swift justice. Andy says, "God has used America to stop a terrorist nation."

Abernathy says, "I had no doubt that our military leaders meant business."

Andy says, "You might say that their cities have been destroyed behind them." Abernathy starts looking over another teletype. He says, "We finally got a report on terrorist activities. The teletype says, "We know of fifty-six acts of terror committed or attempted between 5:00 a.m. e.s.t. and 9:45 e.s.t. So far, there have been 631 victims killed and approximately 400 wounded; 232 terrorists have been killed and approximately 97 wounded. Identities of terrorists include Iranians and Venezuelans with visas and illegal immigrants. Large cities and small towns have been hit. Hospitals, public transportation, power grids, water stations, and government buildings have been targeted. The United States Immigration Service building was attacked as well as the White House. National Guardsmen thwarted the attacks In D.C. but five national guardsmen were killed and eight were wounded."

Abernathy stops and looks at Andy solemnly, "The report is not much longer, but I had to take a breather from such an overwhelming report." He continues, "Power grids and water stations were attacked in six major cities. The terrorists were not successful. They were carrying chemicals to put in water supplies. The worse disaster was at a hospital in Los Angeles that was bombed and caught fire. Sixty-three patients lost their lives plus three doctors, five nurses and fourteen other employees of the hospital. A major subway in New York City was bombed, and there were fifty-eight killed and nineteen wounded. Other major cities hit included San Francisco, Seattle, Chicago, Cleveland, Baltimore, Atlanta, Houston, Boston and Philadelphia."

Andy says, "It's a sad report, but it could have been much worse."

The deeply touched Secretary says, "Yes, that's right." Abernathy is silent. Andy doesn't say anything, so the Secretary can reflect on the state of affairs.

As Abernathy gathers his thoughts another teletype comes in. Abernathy says, "It's an update on the front. The teletype says, "By 11:30 e.s.t. the large array of invading troops overran the border towns of Calexico, California; Columbus, New Mexico; Nogales, Arizona; Laredo, McAllen, and Brownsville, Texas. Cities that have been penetrated by the invaders are San Diego, Tucson, Las Cruces, New Mexico; El Paso and Corpus Christi. Over three hundred Marines have lost their lives and over four hundred have been wounded. Twenty Army Infantry Divisions have moved in to support the Marines."

Abernathy scans the next part and says, "Here's a good sign. It says, "Air Force reconnaissance reports that over 20,000 enemy troops have deserted and gone south of the border. They appear to be Venezuelan and Mexican recruits. The enemy forces have dwindled to less than 175,000. Our twenty Army Division reinforcements number over 250,000 soldiers. The Navy and Air Force continue to inflict heavy casualties on the enemy."

Andy says, "By noon on the day of the invasion, we can begin to see light. I had a chance to read an article by a local journalist in today's newspaper. Evidently, he was in touch with a correspondent on the front this morning. He quoted the reporter in his article, who said, "The invading troops appear like a huge swarm of invading locusts darkening the landscape of the Rio Grande. The Phantom Jets with a deafening roar appear suddenly from the sky like a heavenly judgment, ready to eradicate the plague."

Abernathy says with a sigh of relief, "That's quite a report. Later we're going to see some remarkable photographs from the military and press. Andy, the teletype has been so busy that I haven't had a chance to tell you that I heard from the C.I.A. director and the

President's Chief of Staff. They are following up on your report about the possibility of an assassination attempt on the President. I was told the President is running the country from a secure bunker."

Andy says, "It looks like it could be one of the shortest wars in history."

Abernathy says, "I agree. We will all be thankful, when it's over. We need to take a break." He pages his secretary to have an agent relieve Bruce, so he can go to lunch with them.

19

Battles Before Victory

After Bruce and Andy sit down for lunch with Abernathy, he says, "Men, we're not out of the woods yet. Even though our military is making great headway, we are still under martial law, and the public has curfew at 6:30 p.m. Our staff will be working overtime. Bruce, after lunch, Alex is coming in to relieve you. I will need you to relieve Shelby at Andy's complex by 8:00 this evening. Andy, I will need you and Alex to watch our office complex and arsenal until 9 tonight. Mac will relieve both of you, and Alex will take you home this evening. Bruce will have you here by 9:30 in the morning. You have your badges, if you're stopped due to the curfew. We have to be on high alert here because of the terrorism."

After lunch Andy calls Lydia. He finds out that she is reading and watching the news reports. Andy says, "I'm sorry you're tied down there. I'm tied down at work, when I'm not with you."

Lydia says, "I'm fine here. I feel safe and comfortable. You're the protector now; helping the country and me. I called your dad back."

Andy asks, "Thank you. How is our food supply?"

Lydia says, "We have most things we need. Can you get some small containers of milk from the cafeteria?'

Andy says, "No problem. I'm working with Alex until 9 p.m. this evening, then he'll bring me home. When we have supper, I'll get extra food and milk from the cafeteria."

Lydia says, "It will be nice to have you here after nine. I know you and Alex will be careful on the way home."

Andy says, "I'm looking forward to being there. I love you."

Andy hates being away from Lydia for over twelve hours, but he is thankful he'll see her tonight. Before 5:00, Mr. Abernathy tells Andy that Bruce will pick him up at 9:00 in the morning. Abernathy says,

"We have a television on rollers in the storage area, next to the Deputy Secretary's office. I know you like to keep up with the news, so after 5:00 we'll have it in the reception area for you. The outer door will be locked, and Alex can be behind the locked door in the conference room with our arsenal, while you watch the news.

After 5:00 Andy shares with Alex what Abernathy said about security, while he watches the news at 7:00. Alex says, "That's standard procedure in a situation like that. We have an agent near the main reception desk after hours. The doors to the building are locked, and he can see who is near the doors, but they can't see him. He has a main alert button that signals all the agents in the building. He can also reach us individually with his pager. Before and after the news, we can have the arsenal door unlocked, as long as one of us is inside the room and the other is near the room."

Andy says, "I haven't been outside since 8:00 this morning. How are things organized with the National Guard?"

Alex says, "Day and night, they have fifty troops and a commander surrounding the building. They're guarding every entrance, including the parking lot. Our badges have to be shown to get in the parking lot and the building. On our way out, I'll introduce you to the commander, so he and some of his men will know you."

Andy is able to watch Huntley and Brinkley, and the evening is uneventful. Alex and Andy leave when Mac arrives. They go to the cafeteria, then check out with the agent in the reception area. When they get outside, Alex asks the closest guardsman if Captain Jeffries or Nelson is on duty tonight. The guardsman says, "Captain Nelson. You'll find him in the shelter at the edge of the parking lot."

On their way to the parking lot, Andy notices how well the building has been barricaded. They show their badges to the guardsman on duty outside the shelter. The guardsman announces their presence to the Captain. Alex says, "Captain Nelson, this is Special Agent Andy McGraig. He works with me and is the Secretary of State's body guard."

Captain Nelson says, "It's good to meet you, Agent McGraig. Are you the basketball star I saw during the playoffs?"

Andy says, "Yes, I was with Purdue in the playoffs."

The burly captain says, "You did a fine job. I'm glad to see you serving your country. I'm sure you're a good agent."

Andy says, "I try to be, sir."

Alex says, "It has been a long day, sir. We appreciate you being here."

The Captain says, "Let me or Captain Jeffries know, if we can help you."

In unison, Andy and Alex say, "Thank you, sir."

When Alex is close to Andy's house, Andy says, "I know we'll both be glad to get home to our wives."

As Alex pulls over to let Andy out, he says, "You're so right, Andy. We both need the rest."

When Andy walks into his home, he and Lydia hug for a long time. Andy finally looks down at her and says, "I think we can let go of each other now."

Lydia laughs and says, "You know, big boy, you were enjoying the hug, as much as I was."

Andy puts his bag in the kitchen and says, "I brought some food and milk for my little lady."

Lydia says, "Thank you. How long do you think we'll be under martial law? I was just getting ready to go to work."

Andy says, "Yes, it was quite a coincidence, as well as your parents leaving the day before the invasion. Right now, it looks like it will be a swift victory, but the problem is getting the enemy out of the towns and cities near the border and at the border."

Lydia asks, "Do you think that will take days, weeks or longer?"

Andy says, "I don't know, but I hope it takes a week or less. We also have a terrorism problem, which could take longer to contain. In the morning, I don't have to leave until 9:00."

Lydia says, "That's good news. We can sleep in until 7:30."

When they go to sleep, it is so quiet that all they can hear is the clock ticking in the background. Early in the morning, sometime before 4:00, Andy hears gunfire and explosions and sees a great war being waged. It is almost like he has a bird's eye view of large cities and small towns from San Diego to Columbus, New Mexico, to Brownsville, Texas. After he sees extensive and intense battles and carnage, he sees a large number, "7". The number appears over miles of landscape. The dream wakes him up. He goes in the bathroom, and as he goes back to bed, the clock says '4:07'."

Bruce picks up Andy right before 9:00. When Andy gets in the car, He notices Bruce is in a good mood. Andy says, "You appear to be happy, considering the circumstances."

Bruce says, "I think you're right. I got up this morning, and for some unknown reason, I had a good feeling about how things are going to turn out."

Andy says, "I agree. Things look ominous now, but I also believe it will turn around soon."

Bruce says, "Secretary Abernathy is already at work, but he told us to get some breakfast, when we get there."

Andy says, "Lydia and I had breakfast an hour ago, but I'll get a muffin and coffee and join you."

Bruce and Andy immediately report to Abernathy, when they finish in the cafeteria. Bruce takes his post, and Andy meets with the Secretary.

Abernathy asks, "Did you have a good night?"

Andy says, "Yes, I did. I think I have something for you."

Abernathy sits up in his chair and says, "Go ahead."

Andy says, "Early this morning while I was sleeping, I could see the war that is now being waged from small towns to big cities near the border. I could see the fierce fighting and the carnage. After I saw the horror of war, I could see a very large number seven, that stretched for miles across the landscape. I think the "7" means the war will be over in seven days or within 7 days."

Abernathy appears to be very pensive after Andy shares his dream. He seems to be staring at his desk, but when he looks up at Andy, he says, "What you just shared, Andy, parallels a teletype I received from the Pentagon almost two hours ago. Since the main battles are now in the towns and cities, we're experiencing a lot more military and civilian fatalities. Even though the enemy has lost vast numbers, they have dug in and now have better defenses. I'm guessing they still have a lot of their better trained troops. I hate to tell you or anyone that our estimated military death toll is over 2,000 and our civilian death toll is over 1,200."

Andy says, "That is tragic news. I know our citizens will be heart broken, when they hear the report."

Abernathy says, "The good news is that a large number of army battalions in combat teams with M60 tanks and infantry were deployed later yesterday. The Pentagon reported that 4,000 tanks with over 225,000 army personnel are descending now on forty-five occupied towns and cities from California to Texas. Once the tanks make their statement, the Marines will be the first ones in. Their plan is to overwhelm the enemy and drive them from the populated areas to south of the border."

Andy asks, "Have you heard anymore from the CIA about leads on an assassination attempt?"

Mr. Abernathy says, "I received a call from the President's Chief of Staff, and he said the CIA and the FBI are working on it." Abernathy receives another teletype. He reads it, and becomes preoccupied with the message.

Andy waits several minutes after Abernathy reads the teletype and says, "What is it, sir?"

The message I just received is about the magnitude of the terrorism activity. Acts of terrorism have been perpetrated from Los Angeles to New York City and from St. Paul, Minnesota, to New Orleans. It also updates the approximate death toll from the terrorism; it's a staggering 950 fatalities. The amount of sick and wounded form the terrorism is a shocking estimate of 36,000.

Andy is perplexed and asks, "Why so many sick and wounded?"

Investigators think terrorists dumped a mixture of chemicals in the Missouri River; not far from where it flows into the Mississippi, which is just north of St. Louis. From that one act of sabotage, over three hundred people died and over 32,000 became seriously ill."

Andy says, "Iran and Venezuela are going to have a heavy price to pay."

Mr. Abernathy continues, "Last evening the enemy bombed a power grid in El Paso, and 93,000 customers in the south part of the city lost power. They invaded homes through the night and killed approximately 225 civilians, men, women and children, and they wounded over 300. El Paso gun owners battled with the invaders, and they estimated killing 150 of the enemy. Near the end of the report, it says that gun owners, especially in southern Texas, are battling with the enemy in occupied neighborhoods. At the end, it says that terrorists are still targeting hospitals."

Andy says, "Even though that is a tragic and dismal report, we have to remember that we're making progress, and eliminating a great portion of the enemy."

Abernathy replies, "You're right, but it's just very depressing. I know that war is a nasty business." Abernathy starts looking over some paperwork. He says, "Andy, I have a lot of calls to make. Will you guard our arsenal and relieve Bruce, so he can take a break and have an early lunch?"

Andy stands up, and says, "I will."

Abernathy says, "You may be able to go home early today. You and Alex had a late night. Mac will take you home, and he'll do surveillance at your place tonight, instead of Alex."

After Andy relieves Bruce, he mentally settles into being a security guard. He thinks, "I'm glad to take a break from the distressing war news."

Before Bruce returns, Mr. Abernathy steps out of his office and says, "Andy, let's go to lunch, when Bruce relieves you."

During lunch Abernathy says to Andy, "Right before I left my office, I received another teletype I want you to hear, when we get back to the office. It's not as stressful as some of the messages, but it's something you will want to know."

When they return to Abernathy's office, he says, "Listen to this report from the Pentagon. Beginning at 6:30 this morning, Eastern Standard Time, many A3 bombers and F4 fighters flew four missions over Venezuela. They destroyed Venezuela's main industries, especially in Caracas. Their oil fields and refineries were also destroyed. The atrocities that Venezuelan troops have committed upon our citizens in occupied towns could not be left unanswered. Any surviving Venezuelan troops will not be returning to the same country they knew before their invasion."

Andy says, "They've taken a resound pounding for their aggression."

Abernathy says, "Like Iran, they will terribly regret what they've done."

Before 2:30, Andy relieves the agent stationed outside the office complex. When he goes back to Abernathy's office, Mr. Abernathy says, "Mac is coming in at 4:00 to take you home. I've called the cafeteria to give you and Mac the food and beverages you need. Take what your wife will need at home."

At 4:00 Mac and Andy carry out all the food and drinks they need. Andy calls Lydia right before they leave, and she thanks Andy for bringing the food. Lydia says, "I made some chili for us this evening."

When Andy hangs up, he thinks, "I can't wait to see her."

During supper, Lydia shares some of the news she has heard today. Andy says, "The press has already gotten a lot of the reports we received from the Pentagon."

Just an hour after Andy watches the Huntley and Brinkley report, they're both ready to hit the sack.

Andy and Lydia have a pleasant night. Andy is up by 6:00 and showers, while Lydia fixes him breakfast. Before Andy steps outside to wait for his ride, they hug and kiss. Andy says, "I wish I had more time to cuddle with you, but Lord willing, we'll pick up this evening, where we left off."

When his ride arrives, Andy gets in and says, "I'm surprised to see you, Alex. Are you pulling extra duty?"

Alex says, "Mr. Abernathy has something for me to do this morning. We're picking him up next, and he has something to tell both of us."

Just before they stop to pick up the Secretary, Andy thinks, "This is Day 3 of the invasion."

As soon as Mr. Abernathy gets in the car, he says, "Men, we need to be quick about picking up something like coffee and donuts from the cafeteria. We need to meet in my office by 8:15. I have a special assignment for both of you."

In the cafeteria, the three men move like machines in an assembly line, and Andy carries a blueberry muffin and coffee to the office. After Abernathy, Alex and Andy are seated, Abernathy says, "This morning at 6:00, I received a call from Special Agent Peterson at the FBI. I need both of you to leave for the FBI building by 8:30. Andy, you'll have a good understanding of what it's about after you meet with Agent Peterson. Alex, as always, you watch Andy's back. Andy, if you're asked about Alex, just tell them that the two of you work together."

When they get close to the FBI building, they see that the National Guard is guarding the building like the State Department building. They show their badges to the National Guardsman at the parking lot gate. Once they get inside the building, Andy has never seen so many checkpoints in any building. Andy and Alex are finally led to Agent Peterson's office. Andy introduces himself and says, "This is Agent Alex Werner. Agent Werner and I work together."

Agent Peterson shakes their hands and says, "It's good to meet both of you. Call me Wyatt. In a few minutes, we have an assignment that I want you to go on. Andy, because of your lead, you will be glad to know we arrested the assassination team late yesterday. We checked on certain individuals who rented a truck or truck and car between the coastal areas of Miami and Clearwater. The CIA already had surveillance on the Speaker's cousin. They also had surveillance on a Venezuelan male, who was connected with him.

An employee of a rental agency in Fort Myers identified them by their pictures. We picked them up along with four other Venezuelan nationals in Williamsburg, Virginia, as they were headed for D.C. They had rented a moving truck and a car. They had military rifles, handguns, grenades, a sniper rifle and homemade bombs with them. We arrested them and brought them back for interrogation. They were separated before and during interrogation. To get a lighter sentence, the Speaker's cousin blew the whistle and implicated the Secretary. We'll be leaving soon to arrest the Speaker of the House for conspiracy, sedition and treason."

Andy says, "You're right, Wyatt. I am glad to know. We're honored to accompany you."

Agent Peterson says, "Right now, my partner is organizing the arrest team and the logistics. Even though the House begins their session soon, we had a meeting set up between the Senate Majority

Leader and the Speaker at 9:30 this morning. When we arrive at the Capitol Building, we'll be going to the Speaker's office to make the arrest."

Peterson's partner comes in the room and says, "Wyatt, we have confirmed that the Speaker is getting ready to meet with the Majority Leader in the Speaker's office."

Peterson says, "Excellent." He looks at his partner and says, "Lloyd, this is Agent Andy McGraig and Agent Alex Werner from the State Department. This is Agent Lloyd Cohen."

They shake hands and Agent Cohen says, "I understand you're going with us. Agent McGraig, I think I've seen you in the NCAA playoffs."

Andy says, "Yes, sir; you did."

Three FBI agents get in a long, black sedan, and Andy and Alex get in another black sedan with Agent Peterson. Andy and Alex are impressed with all of the military security that the Capitol Building has. The National Guard directs them to a parking area near the South Wing. As they get out of their cars, it's a few minutes past 9:30. They enter the Rotunda area then proceed in the South Wing to the Speaker's office.

As they enter the Speaker's reception room, the receptionist is surprised to see six men and four of them with FBI on their jackets. Agent Peterson says to the receptionist, "I'm Agent Peterson with the FBI. We have to interrupt the Speaker's meeting without announcement." Before the receptionist can reply, Agent Peterson and the other five agents walk into the Speaker's office.

The Speaker and Majority Leader get out of their chairs, and the Speaker yells, "What is the meaning of this?"

Agent Peterson addresses the Speaker and says, "You're under arrest for conspiracy, sedition and treason against the United States." While Agent Cohen reads rights to the Speaker, Andy observes the agitation and anguish on the Speaker's face. Another FBI agent handcuffs the Speaker, and the Speaker is ushered out of the Capitol Building and taken to FBI headquarters. Andy finds out later through Mr. Abernathy that the Speaker is denied bail, because of the security risk.

On the way back to their own building, Alex says, "To say the least, we just witnessed a significant arrest. It sounds like you were a major part of exposing the subversives."

Andy looks at Alex and says unemotionally, "Like Sergeant Joe Friday says, "Just doing my job."

Alex humorously says, "Sergeant Friday, on the way back to the office, we'll pass a Dairy Queen. I think we deserve to celebrate with a milkshake."

Andy laughs and says, "Home, James, to Dairy Queen."

Before they order the milkshakes, Alex calls Mr. Abernathy. Alex says, "The arrest went well, and we're on our back."

You've been on official business, so you and Andy have lunch on the way back, then report to my office. They decide to still order the milkshakes. Alex says, "There's a steakhouse nearby, where we can order a 9 oz. sirloin. You can get any side you want or none at all."

Andy says, "it will make a complete lunch: steak, green beans and a milkshake!"

Alex laughs and says, "Add a cup of coffee to that order."

When they return, Mr. Abernathy tells Alex to relieve the agent outside their complex for an hour. Abernathy says, "In about an hour, take Andy home and relieve the agent on duty there. Shelby is going to relieve you at 7: 00 this evening. You and Shelby will be off during the day tomorrow."

When Alex leaves the office, Abernathy says, "Andy, I'm letting you off early today, because you might be needed a lot the rest of the week. I want you to know that your service here has already been invaluable. Since you've been with us, you have provided a lot of helpful information for the security of our nation."

Andy says, "I appreciate your gratitude. It's an honor to be with the Department and to work with you."

Abernathy lowers his voice and says, "Just between you and me, how did the Speaker react, when arrested?"

Andy says, "The Speaker reacted like a kid being taken to the wood shed."

Abernathy shakes his head and says, "I can only imagine."

The Secretary looks down at some papers, and says, "I've received several teletypes, since you've been gone, but the one I want to read verbatim is from the Pentagon about our tank offensive."

Abernathy puts on his reading glasses and begins to read the teletype, "By 9:00 this morning, our M60 tanks, accompanied by the Marines and the Army in California, Arizona, New Mexico and Texas, have made significant progress. Tanks have already entered the northern edges of San Diego, Tucson, El Paso and Brownsville. Fierce fighting is taking place in all four cities. Tanks have either entered or are ready to enter the other forty-two occupied towns and cities, including Chula Vista and El Centro, California; Nogales and Sierra Vista, Arizona; Silver City, Las Cruces and Columbus, New Mexico and Rio Bravo, McAllen and Laredo, Texas. Casualties are heavy on both sides."

Andy says, "It's mind-boggling. It has been a hundred years since the Civil War. Who would have thought we would be fighting a war at home in this century?"

Abernathy says, "It wasn't expected to happen at home. There has been a lot of tension from the cold war. I guess we shouldn't be totally surprised that rogue nations like Iran and Venezuela would do something absurd. I blame the New Age Socialist Party for making rogue nations think that we've let our guard down."

After the meeting, Andy prepares to leave with Alex. Before they leave the building, he calls Lydia. He says, "Hi, babe. Do you feel like getting out of the house for supper?"

Lydia says, "Are you kidding! I would love to get out of the house!"

Andy says, "I just got off work. We'll go to dinner early, so we'll be back home before the curfew. Alex will be working surveillance, then Shelby is replacing him this evening at 7:00. The restaurant is a surprise. It' an iconic place that you'll enjoy. I'll tell you on our way there. We'll leave by 4:00."

Lydia, says, "Okay, big boy. I'm looking forward to it."

On their way to Andy's house, Andy says, "I'm taking Lydia to the Old Ebbitt Grill at 4:00. It's a surprise until we leave for Old Ebbitt's. I know you'll be following us. It would be nice, if Shelby could meet you there."

Alex says, "I might just do that. I can page her by code and have her meet me at your place by 4:00. She can leave her car there, and she'll be all set for surveillance duty tonight. We can do like we did on the Wild West road trip: sit two tables over."

Andy says, "That will be great, if you can both be there."

After Lydia and Andy get in their car, "The Babe", Andy says, "We're having dinner near the White House.

Lydia is intrigued, "What restaurant?"

"It's called Old Ebbitt Grill. They say it's the oldest restaurant in D.C. It has been in business since 1856. Everyone says they love the atmosphere."

After they're seated, Alex and Shelby come into the dining area; they sit two tables over and one table back. Andy says, "It's everything that people said it is."

On their way home, Lydia says, "You don't know how much that meant to me. I did want to get out of the house, but having dinner with you there was extra special."

Andy says, "I love you all the time, but there are only shorter periods of time that I can show you how much I love you."

Lydia says, "Wow, your expression is really deep and beautiful. What came over your logical mind?"

Andy says, "I think I felt a breeze of inspiration."

Lydia smiles and says, "When we get home, I need to hit the record button on the tape recorder."

Andy says, "Since the war started, I haven't said much about the two hundred acres of land at the foothills of the Smoky Mountains. It means a lot to my family and Uncle Edward's family. You know how beautiful the land is, where we hiked in Yellowstone. The land I just bought has its own beauty. There's nothing like the Smoky Mountains. As you hike on our land and visit the Smokies, I think you will come to love it as well."

Lydia replies, "I'm sure I will. I think you're wise in investing in the land. It is a great blessing for us and the two families. I believe we'll enjoy all the nature that we experience there."

Andy says, "I know our children and grandchildren will love it also."

Lydia says, "You're full of surprises. I didn't know you were already thinking about children and grandchildren!"

20

A New Spirit

"This is Day 4 of the invasion," Andy says out loud, as Bruce drives him to work.

Bruce says, "It's an awful catastrophe."

Mr. Abernathy has breakfast with Andy and Bruce. He says, "The department has a schedule today in the gym and target range for all the agents, who are not too preoccupied with the war effort. Every Wednesday, Department heads would like to have four agents at a time in the firing range, and four agents at a time in the gym; working on martial arts."

Andy thinks, "Good; when I work with an agent on martial arts, I'll try to get him to spot me in the weight room. When the war is over, I need to get on a basketball schedule in a gym close to the department."

Most of the day is depressing with horrific news from teletypes on casualties and the wounded from terrorism across the country and battles near the 1,954 miles of the southern border. For Andy, the one stimulating break from the grave reports are the workouts in the gym and target practice at the firing range.

Andy is relieved to go home by 5:00. He's not looking forward to working the weekend, but he hopes his premonition of the number "7" means the war will end Saturday.

When Andy and Lydia go to sleep, Andy thinks, "I'm thankful our neighborhood has been quiet and peaceful."

In the morning, Andy meets with Mr. Abernathy by 8:30 in his office.

Abernathy says, "It looks like I've received several teletypes, since I left yesterday."

As Abernathy begins to peruse the reports, Andy says, "It's day 5 of the invasion."

Abernathy looks up at Andy studiously, and says, "That's right. Do you still think the war will end by the seventh day?"

Andy replies, "Since I've had the dream, I believe it's a good possibility."

As Abernathy looks down at the teletypes, he says, "I sure hope so."

After Abernathy goes through the new teletypes, he says, "There's a lot to go over, but I want to read the best news first; it's from the Pentagon. It says, "Later yesterday, the Marines and Army specialists with the tank offensive began to flank the enemy, especially in the larger cities, including San Diego, Tucson, El Paso and Brownsville. In most of the cities with a population of over 40,000, the new offensive has virtually cut off the enemy from supplies and troop replacements. In these cities, the enemy is boxed in, and cannot escape. Since early this morning, they have been surrounded. Soon we hope to hear of mass surrenders."

Andy says passionately, "Excellent!"

Abernathy says, "What a relief!"

Abernathy says, "There are more reports to look at, but first, I want to hear your input."

Andy replies, "Yesterday, I read William F. Buckley's column in the newspaper. Buckley has a great mind, and I'm glad a lot of people follow his comments. I've been reading The National Review for several years, and I read his books. "God and Man at Yale" and "Witness". I brought a copy of the article: it says, "After the invasion began at our southern border, the New Age Socialist Party leaders became strangely quiet. I wonder if they're regrouping about border security. As my entrepreneurial Uncle Matthew would say, who use to quote that popular American idiom, "They're a day late and a dollar short". Most recently the Speaker of the House was arrested for conspiracy, sedition and treason. The Speaker was the Socialist Party's standard bearer. Who might they turn to now, to replace their fallen leader? We hope whoever it is; they may be a new and improved version of their party." Andy puts the article back in his coat pocket and looks at Mr. Abernathy.

Abernathy nods his head and says, "Very interesting; how true it is! Buckley is something else. He's so polished and to the point. The article makes me wonder again about their party's chairman of the House Intelligence Committee, Cain Cliff. He and the Speaker have tried to dethrone our President, ever since he took office. Now I wonder, if he'll be arrested for sedition and possibly more charges."

Andy says, "I think he will; especially for sedition."

Abernathy says, "Really? Do you have a strong feeling about it?"

Andy says very simply, "Yes. I think we'll see it soon."

Abernathy says, "I wouldn't doubt it. We may see it happen to more than just Cliff."

Andy says, "It could. It's sad that their party leaders attack their opposition with vindictiveness and false accusations."

Abernathy says, "We better get back to these teletypes. I have to call several ambassadors and the Prime Minister of England."

After Andy and Abernathy finish with the teletypes, Andy thinks, "The good news was hearing about our great offensive. The bad news was the big increase in the casualties."

Abernathy asks Andy to rotate on security detail with Bruce and Mac, so the three of them can have lunch at separate times.

Andy looks forward to seeing Lydia and hearing the evening news. He's wanting to hear, if any of the forty-two cities have been freed from the invasion forces.

On day 6 of the invasion, Andy is up at 5:30 to shower, so he can watch the 6:00 news. Since he learned last night that eight of the smaller towns have been liberated from the enemy, he is anxious to hear if the military has freed any of the bigger cities.

Mac picks up Andy for work, then Mr. Abernathy. When Abernathy gets in the car, he says, "I just heard on the radio that we've freed three more towns; that number is up to eleven now. The casualties are heavy, but I thank God, we're making progress."

Andy says, "I hope it's no more than a seven day border war."

After the three men have breakfast, Mr. Abernathy and Andy go to the office to get the latest teletypes. After Abernathy scans them, he looks at Andy and says, "You're going to be pleased, when I read this message from the FBI. It says, "At 8:05 this morning,

Friday, September 21, FBI agents arrested the chairman of the House Intelligence Committee, Cain Cliff, and five other leading congressmen of the New Age Socialist Party on charges of sedition and conspiracy."

Andy replies, "It might be trite to say, but they didn't escape the long arm of the law."

Abernathy replies, "I have to say that I'm as pleased, as you must be."

Andy says, "Yes, sir. I'm relieved to hear it. They abased the President and his party to the point of obsession. We've seen the power of truth work against the misguided convictions of the socialist party. Abraham Lincoln said, "Truth is generally the vindication against slander."

Abernathy says proudly, "Yes, Abraham Lincoln; a great American hero. Truth is one of the greatest virtues. In this war, we have truth and strength on our side. I have great expectations about the outcome of day 6 of the invasion."

Andy says, "Yes, indeed. I'm praying that the enemy is driven from most of the towns and cities today."

Abernathy says, "Between the intensity of the fighting and battles won, we should stay tuned to the news today. I'll have our portable television brought in here, before we get back from lunch."

During lunch, both Andy and Secretary Abernathy are preoccupied with thinking about what the upcoming new reports might be.

When they return to Abernathy's office, there are more teletypes, and the television is in the office. Before Abernathy turns on the TV, he looks at the latest teletypes. Abernathy says, "You'll want to hear this teletype from the Pentagon. It says, "We have updated the estimates for casualties and wounded from this conflict, that we have begun calling, "The Border War". Estimated American military casualties (including The National Guard's battles with terrorists) is 5,340; the wounded estimate is 7,200. Estimated American civilian casualties is 2,950; the wounded estimate is 3,670. The enemies' estimated casualty count is 102,000. Their estimated wounded count is 96,000. We have now freed seventeen of the forty-six towns, and El Paso is close to being liberated.

Today the enemy has begun to surrender in large numbers. So far, there is an estimate of 20,000, who have surrendered."

Andy says, "It's possible that it could be over tomorrow."

Abernathy replies, "It sounds like it."

With the ground the Marines and Army gained, the personnel at the department seem to be calmer. Andy thinks he may get off at 5:00, because the military and government can sense victory.

At home, Lydia watches the 7:00 news with Andy. The fighting in San Diego, Tucson and Brownsville is still fierce, but even the news reporter is hearing from the military that the enemy is trapped.

For the second morning in the row, Andy wakes up at 5:30. "Day 7 of the invasion," is his first thought, as he gets out of bed. Even though it's Saturday, he still has to leave for work. After he showers, he watches a live news broadcast of the border war. The news reporter says, "We are in southern Texas near the border, where it is 4:00 a.m. Mountain Time. The southern border stretches west into Pacific Time, where it is now 3:00 a.m. Most of the border area is dark at night, but you can see from all the artillery fire that that the M60 tanks and Phantom Jets are lighting up the sky."

The reporter stops a second, because of the ear-piercing noise from the M60 guns and the Phantom Jets. After a brief pause, the reporter says, "You can tell how deafening the Phantom Jets are, even when they're not dropping bombs. We're just south of McAllen, Texas, where most of the city had been occupied by the enemy until late yesterday. We are less than a quarter mile from the border, where you can see enemy troops running from the onslaught. Because of the light from the artillery, we can tell that many of the enemy have fallen, and a great number are walking back across the border with their hands in the air."

The reporter tries to continue, but the thundering noise from the jets and tanks overwhelms everything. In a few seconds, Andy can hear the reporter say, "We have reports that the same scene is taking place at other parts of the border, including, Laredo, Eagle Pass, Del Rio and Socorro, Texas; Las Cruces, Columbus and Sierra Vista, New Mexico; Nogales and Yuma, Arizona and El Centro, California. American Marines and Army soldiers, as well as civilians, have remained undaunted in resisting and thwarting the enemy.'

Andy turns the TV off to finish getting ready for work. He thinks, "This conflict could very well be a 7 day border war." He sits at the kitchen table and fixes some Rice Krispies with banana, when Lydia walks in the kitchen, rubbing her eye.

She says, "I'm sorry, honey, I must have overslept. I meant to fix you breakfast." She walks over to him, and he puts his arm around her.

He says, "That's okay, sweetie. I just turned off the news, and it looks like the war could be over today."

As Andy pours milk on his cereal, Lydia kisses his forehead, and says, "That would be wonderful, honey. I'm going to fix coffee for us."

Today Andy is to report to Secretary Abernathy at 9:00 in his office.

As Andy is announced by Abernathy's secretary, Mr. Abernathy opens the office door, and says, "Come in and have a seat, Andy. It's going to be a busy day. I came in about an hour ago. I got word from the President's Chief of Staff that they're expecting a surrender from Iran and Venezuela very soon. The President, the Joint Chiefs of Staff Chairman, the ambassadors to Iran and Venezuela and I will be communicating the terms today, if we get the surrender."

Andy says, "That's great news. What can I do today to help?"

Abernathy smiles and says, "While you're here, you can help us celebrate. You played a big part in the victory, as well as saving the President's neck. You can probably go home early today, but I don't know what time."

Andy asks, "Do you have any idea, when they'll finish eradicating the terrorist cells and lift martial law?"

Abernathy replies, "I'm guessing martial law will be in effect today, but it should be lifted soon. It's hard to say that every terrorist cell will be cleared out, but the FBI and CIA claim that the situation has drastically improved. If we get the surrender soon, I will probably be tied up with the communications. I want you close by, in case I need your input."

Abernathy looks at a teletype coming in from the Pentagon. He reads it out loud, "As of 9 a.m. EST, surrounded enemy troops in San Diego, Tucson and Brownsville have surrendered. From California to Texas, enemy troops have vacated smaller cities and towns, and they're trying to escape to the border."

By 11:00 a.m. EST, Iran and Venezuela surrender. Abernathy works with the President's Chief of Staff to report the State Department's input. The President with his cabinet and the Chairman of the Joints Chief of Staff with his staff dictate the terms of surrender for both countries:

1. Military flights by your country and military buildup are prohibited.
2. The United States has fly over rights and reconnaissance rights in your air space at any time. Any planes shot at or downed will bring swift retribution.
3. The United States has rights to search facilities in your country without notice and at any time; with or without NATO.
4. War Reparations: Over 9,000 military and civilian lives were lost due to your invasion of the United States. Another 2,000 civilians lost their lives due to related terrorism. Over 13,000 military and civilians were wounded. An estimated $240 billion in property was destroyed (an assessment will be taken, and this figure will be updated). As your industrial revenue and oil revenue revives, you must pay to the United State Treasury ten percent of the revenue until the human losses and property losses are paid in full.
5. Whether Iran or Venezuela breaches any of these terms, their cities will be bombed immediately. Because of Iran's and Venezuela's invasion of the United States and their criminal acts during the Seven Day Border War from September 16, 1962 to September 22, 1962, no leniency will be given in any necessary reprisals.

By the next day, Iran and Venezuela, reluctantly sign the terms of surrender. Andy hears the news at home with Lydia. Andy says, "Mr. Abernathy told me that we would catch up on State affairs Monday morning. He told me to enjoy my day off."

Lydia says, "I wonder when school will reopen?"

Andy replies, "I'm guessing they will reopen soon. The National Guard has to go back to their home stations, and the FBI and the CIA have to finish with the problems caused by the terrorist cell groups. Their work will go on for some time, but hopefully, you can start your work by the end of the week. How about we share the victory news with dad and Judy?"

Lydia says, "I would love to talk with them."

Both Lydia and Andy have a good time talking with Judy and Owen. Andy says, "Dad, are you coming to visit us?"

Owen says, "Yes, son, we'll come soon. Judy and I haven't set the date yet, but we'll let you know. I'm so thankful that the crazy war is over. We can visit you in peace."

Andy says, "Yes, peace and freedom are invaluable blessings."

Lydia talks with Judy a good while. Judy is on top of the world after talking with her new sister-in-law, who she greatly admires.

Andy thoroughly enjoys the day with Lydia, but Monday morning comes too soon. Nevertheless, he is anxious to hear the latest reports from Secretary Abernathy's teletypes.

Andy, Abernathy and Bruce have a good, filling breakfast. Abernathy looks at his watch and says, "Well, men, it looks like we won't get started until 9:00. It's nice to have a break again."

Mr. Abernathy's secretary brings Andy and Mr. Abernathy coffee, as soon as they have a seat in the office. Andy enjoys the coffee as Abernathy pours through the teletypes. Andy thinks, "Thank God we're not facing the events of war today."

In a few minutes Abernathy says, "Andy, here is one the reports that you will find interesting. It was just sent from the FBI, and it says, "Mayors in twenty-six cities in eleven states have been arrested for harboring criminals and illegal aliens wanted by the federal government. Their crimes include obstructing federal law. Some of the mayors also have charges of sedition, complicity and being an accessory. They include the mayors of San Francisco, San Jose, Sacramento, Seattle, Portland, Denver, Chicago, Richmond, Philadelphia, Boston, and Baltimore. All twenty-six mayors are members of the New Age Socialist Party, and all of the cities are sanctuary cities."

Andy says, "Wow, law enforcement is cleaning house!"

Mr. Abernathy says, "The country is much more secure with

honest law enforcement agencies. Both the CIA and FBI have told me the undercover operations in churches helped smother the effectiveness of the terrorist cell groups."

Andy replies, "I'm glad that operation was successful."

The next morning, before Andy leaves for work, he calls to Lydia from the living room. Lydia comes in the room from the kitchen. She says, "What is it, honey?" "I want to read just part of this article to you. The preliminary hearing for the former Speaker of the House was held yesterday. Listen to what the judge said: "Today, as former Speaker of the House, you are arraigned on charges of treason, sedition and conspiracy. There are a number of reasons for these charges. In general, you led your party in jeopardizing the security of the United States. You are charged with colluding with the enemy, including foreign governments and illegal immigrants, who committed acts of terror and other crimes.

You knowingly conspired to overthrow the current President and Vice-President of the United States. You also committed conspiracy with an assassination team, which planned to kill the President and the Vice-President. This hearing also needs to address the way you and many of your party committed hate crimes toward the President, his administration and the Traditional American Party. We also need to look at the way you and your New Age Socialist Party leaders incited hate crimes against the opposition. I'm surprised that a person of your former standing would abase a President of this country, the way you have with continual harassment, false accusations, collusion and obstruction of justice. Your defense attorney needs to know that you could spend the rest of your life in prison."

Lydia replies, "Wow, the judge didn't mince words."

Andy says, "I'm sure Mr. Abernathy has read this in the newspaper or from a teletype. This is one of those earth-shaking reports that he would read to me from a teletype."

When Andy arrives at work, the first news Secretary Abernathy has for him is about the New Age Socialist Party. Abernathy says, "I received a call from one of our congressional leaders early last evening. He has gotten word that the socialist party is now remorseful over their actions; especially those of fighting border security and harassing the President. The socialist party members in the House have their own meeting scheduled at 9:30 this morning. Word is out that they want to return to a former party name used in our country, Democratic-Republican."

Andy says, "That's welcomed and surprising news. The last Democratic-Republican President was John Quincy Adams."

Abernathy says, "Yes, the Democratic-Republican name began to fade out in 1829. There's more good news, Andy. They want to become strong supporters of the Constitution!"

Andy says, "If I weren't seated already, I would have to sit down before I could handle such shocking news."

Abernathy says, "We'll have to make a toast to this breaking and cheerful news with a fresh cup coffee!"

Andy smiles and says, "Hear, Hear!"

When Andy arrives home that evening, Lydia says, "Why are you smiling?"

Andy says, "I feel like a light-hearted kid again. It was a day filled with good news."

The next morning in the Secretary's office, Abernathy says, "Andy, I have some good news and sad news. I think you'll want to hear the good news first."

Andy says, "Yes, sir, I would."

Abernathy says, "I received a call late yesterday afternoon, from the President's Chief of Staff. He said that on Friday, November 2nd, at a White House luncheon, you will be receiving the Presidential Medal of Freedom."

Andy is flabbergasted. He says, "What?"

As he looks at Abernathy, the Secretary's poker face nods.

Andy says, "What a motherlode of good and incredible news! I'm starting to get overwhelmed with all the good news!"

Abernathy asks, "You're not getting tired of winning, are you?"

Andy says, "No, Sir!"

Abernathy says, "The President wants to keep your award confidential for ten years, because of your classified work. He told us to invite less than fifteen guests. I can help you with the list, but I want you to make most of the suggestions."

Andy says, "That won't be hard: Lydia, my father, my sister, Dr. Krause, Deputy Secretary Jennings, Alex, Shelby, Mac, Bruce, and you and I."

Abernathy says, "We could invite two more; what about Dr. Krause's wife and my wife?"

Andy says, "Excellent!"

Abernathy says, "In the department's budget, we can fly your dad and sister in and put them up in a motel."

Andy says, "Flying them round trip would be great, but they'll stay with us."

"Contact your father and sister right away. The luncheon begins at noon. We'll invite the rest of the guests."

Andy says, "It would be nice, if you could book the departure flight about a week before the return flight. Could I give you the departure flight date in a few days?"

Abernathy says, "Absolutely." Abernathy hesitates a second then says, "Well, here goes the sad news. The Pentagon hasn't released the updated casualty and wounded numbers to the press yet, but they sent it to me this morning. It's a difficult report to read, but here are the updates: "The estimated American military and civilian casualty count from the Seven Day Border War is 12,200, including the invasion and terrorism. The estimated American military and civilian wounded count is 14,600, including the invasion and terrorism. So far, the estimated American count for missing persons is 590. The estimated casualty count for the enemy is 109,800, and the estimated wounded count is 113,600. 54,000 enemy soldiers were captured. We are estimating that at least, 30,000 enemy soldiers escaped across the border."

Andy says, "It's just overwhelming; what staggering numbers. It's hard to imagine all the family members that are directly affected by the tragedy."

Abernathy replies, "Its difficult news to share. The chaplains and other officers, who have to break the news to the families, have a difficult job."

Andy goes home under a cloud of melancholy. He thinks, "What an extreme range of news today; from the Presidential Medal of Freedom Award to a grievous death count."

When he greets Lydia, he shares the good news. Lydia says, "Oh, honey, I'm so grateful for you. You're the best man in a lifetime that I could have married."

They kiss, and Andy says, "I need to call Dad and Judy."

When Owen answers, Andy says, "Dad, I want you to know that I will be receiving the Presidential Medal of Freedom Award."

Owen says, "Andy, that's wonderful! Congratulations, your mother and I knew God had a much greater purpose for you than the NBA."

Andy says, "Mom and you have been such great supporters. I couldn't have asked for better parents."

Owen says, "I know she's smiling in heaven right now."

Andy replies, "Yes, she is. Dad, the presentation is during a luncheon at the White House on Friday, November 2, at noon. I would like for you and Judy to spend about a week with us."

Owen says, "I will check on dates at work, and then Judy can let her school know."

Andy says, "Be sure to tell Judy that the award is confidential for now. Because of my classified status, they are not releasing the news to the public for ten years. You could say that you're going to Washington D.C. to be with Lydia and me for some special engagements."

Owen says, "That's fine. I will call you with the date in a day or two."

When Andy shares the news with Judy, she says, "Oh, Andy, I've always been proud of you. I love you more than I could any other brother or sister."

Both Owen and Judy are able to get time off from work and school to go to D.C. After they're with Andy and Lydia almost a week, it is finally time to go to the luncheon at the White House. Secretary Abernathy has Alex pick up Owen, Judy, Lydia and Andy at their home. On the way to the White House, Andy says, "Just like in Indiana, the trees are starting to get bare at this time of year. We do have a big, annual event on this day; the National Press Club Book Fair. This evening is author's night, which is attended by many popular authors."

Judy says, "I think you will eventually have a best seller."

Alex says, "I also believe he will. Andy, you could add our Cody, Wyoming, encounter."

Andy laughs and says, "I think readers would enjoy that one."

In a few more minutes, they pull into the White House drive. They arrive about ten minutes early, but when they get inside to the waiting area, everyone else is already accounted for: Mr. and Mrs. Johnathan Abernathy, Deputy Secretary William Jennings, Shelby, Mac, Bruce and Dr. and Mrs. Krause. When they're ushered into the White House Company Dining Room, the President and First Lady are already there to greet them. As Andy watches the President and First Lady greet people, he notices the First Lady is elegant, but down to earth. He notices the President is polished, but also down to earth.

Lydia and Andy are the last ones to greet them. After they say a few words, the President says to Andy, "Congratulations on your award today; you deserve it."

Andy says, "Thank you, sir."

The President says, "We have a few minutes before lunch is served. May I ask you a couple things?"

Andy replies, "I would be honored."

The President puts his hand on Andy's shoulder, and they walk several steps away from the guests. The President says, "My first question is personal, but the second one is business. I'm a NCAA basketball fan, and I know how good of a player you are. Will you be able to play for Purdue again?"

Andy answers, "Yes, sir. The first part of my State Department contract is for two years. The NCAA gives a player four years of eligibility after his freshman year. After my first two years with the department, I'm going to get my degree at Purdue. I will be playing my sophomore and junior years."

The President says, "Excellent. I'm sure Purdue will have a great team those years, since they know you will be with them. Secondly, I give an annual Christmas Eve day address to the nation. It will be at 4:00 EST. I will be honoring the sacrifices that many people gave during the Seven Day Border War. I want to quote one of the many people, who sacrificed for the country. Even though your information is classified, I want to quote you anonymously about your suggestions for the well-being of the nation."

Andy thinks a few seconds before he answers. He says, "I would be glad to share that with you. I think I know what I want to say. I will write it down, and give it to you before I leave."

The President says, "Andy, you're already a great American, and you have a great future with the government. Not only could you be an ambassador, a Secretary of State, a Congressman, and a Senator, but you could eventually become a President."

Andy replies, "Thank you for your confidence, Mr. President. I will remember your words. They shake hands and sit down for the luncheon."

After lunch, the President, who is seated between Andy and the First Lady, stands up and welcomes everyone to the presentation of the Presidential Medal of Freedom to Special Agent Andy McGraig. The President says, "Agent McGraig aided the military, FBI, CIA and State Department significantly before and during the Seven Day Border War. Our country is thankful and proud of the dedication of its citizens like Agent McGraig. He deserves to be presented with the Presidential Medal of Freedom." Everyone gives Andy lengthy applause.

Andy stands up and says, "Thank you. It is a great honor to receive the award. I serve, because I love God and country. I don't blush often, but I think I blushed just now. Thank you, Mr. President."

Everyone laughs and applauds again.

The President starts thanking everyone for coming. During the conversations, Secretary Abernathy works his way over to Owen. He shakes his hand and says, "Mr. McGraig, you've raised an honest and industrious son."

Owen says, "Thank you, Mr. Secretary. I thank God for him. His mother had a lot to do with his background."

Mr. Abernathy says, "I can tell she was a splendid mother. I want to share something confidentially with you, that I notice or feel about Andy. It appears to me that truth makes Andy stronger, like rain in a desert."

Owen says, "You're right. I believe it's the anointing of God."

Abernathy replies, "Very interesting. I would not doubt that at all. Thank you for being here. I wish you and your family the very best."

Owen says, "It's a privilege to meet you."

Abernathy walks over to Andy; shakes his hand and congratulates him. He says, "Andy, I'm still getting teletypes about the aftermath of the war. You will want to know that the communist founded, National Civil Freedom Association disbanded, because they were facing federal charges of violating freedom of speech and undermining civil liberties. Congress is about to pass a bill to make it illegal for any group to harass any individual, group or institution for expressing their religion publicly or for observing American traditions."

Andy says, "I'm glad you let me know; that's great news. I've been thinking about how Iran and Venezuela overplayed their hand; believing their ties with the terrorist groups and some illegal aliens would have a greater outcome than they did."

Abernathy replies, "Exactly. The enemy not only overestimated the strength of their invasion and terrorist ties, but they underestimated the power of our military and armed civilians."

The Secretary shakes Andy's hand again and wishes him a good night.

November, like every month, passes swiftly, and everyone, including the government, starts preparing for the Christmas season. Andy gets two weeks off, and with Lydia, they spend the two weeks with their family in Mahican. They only have a little over two days to shop, since Christmas falls on a Tuesday. Owen, Judy, Lydia and Andy shop together for a Christmas tree on Christmas Eve morning. They decide on a seven foot Scotch Pine Tree. They put a blanket on the roof of the car, and tie the tree down. They take it to the fire station to be dipped, so the tree will be fire resistant.

When they get home, Owen says, "Let's have an early lunch and get the tree decorated before the President's address at 4:00. Andy and his dad have the job of putting the tree up, and placing the lights on it. Lydia and Judy help with the rest of the Christmas decorations. On a prominent limb, Judy places a bulb that says, "Mother, 1962". Judy hands the angel to Andy, and says, "You're the only one here, who can reach the top of the tree."

As Andy places the angel on top of the tree, he says, "The angel said, "Today in the town of David, a Savior has been born to you: he is the Messiah, the Lord." (Luke 2: 11 NIV) Andy then says, "I just remembered that we need to set up the nativity scene."

They finish with all of the Christmas decorations about fifteen minutes before the President's message. They're all seated in the living room with a soda and popcorn, and Owen turns on the television. The black and white broadcast of the President's Annual Christmas Message begins exactly at 4:00. The President is seated in the oval office with a Christmas tree in the background.

The President says, "Christmas greetings. Thank you for inviting me into your home. I thank God our nation is experiencing peace at this time. We have come through a great political struggle, and a war on the home front. I say with great hope and faith, that our nation now has two parties, we can be proud of: The Traditional American Party and the Democratic-Republican Party. We look forward to a bright future with our new bi-partisan efforts.

As a united nation, we overcame an enemy that invaded our homeland. It reminds us of the struggle between good and evil in the world. I am extremely proud of our military and of our civilians, who took the fight to the enemy. Many of our military personnel and many of our civilians sacrificed their lives for our nation. We remember today the families, who lost loved ones, and who have injured family members from the Seven Day Border War. We will rebuild stronger than ever in the war zones, and our full support goes out to the families, who made great sacrifices.

In our past, truth has been like a rare commodity with many politicians. We believe we can improve on our past. I wish we had the time today to hear from several of our American citizens, who made sacrifices during the war. I had the honor of talking with one of those young people. Like so many of you, he has made sacrifices for his country. I asked him what he would like to say to you on Christmas Eve. I quote one of our many dedicated Americans, "I was taught by loving parents and my faith to always be honest. My prayer for each of you is to love in deed and truth. One of the great leaders in history, the Apostle John, taught us to love God and to love one another. Permit me to quote the Apostle John, "When I saw him, I fell at his feet as dead. And he laid his right hand on me, saying to me, Fear not; I am the first and the last." (Rev. 1: 17 NIV) My Christmas wish for you is that I hope you allow God to lay his hand on you and to guide you in all things".

"My fellow citizens, as your President, I wish you a very, Merry Christmas. God bless you."

Owen gets up and turns off the TV. Owen proudly looks at Andy with a loving smile and asks, "Who do you think the dedicated American is that the President quoted?"

The other family members look at Andy in silence. Andy smiles and looks at his dad and Judy and puts his arm around Lydia. Andy says, "Each one of you is very special to me. I love each of you: Dad, Judy, Lydia and Mom."

About the Author

William Clark has a unique ability to draw from his background in history, political science, ministry and counseling-psychology and give the reader a realistic view of the importance of traditional American values. "Seeing Beyond the Shadows" is a panacea that could help bring healing to the division in America. For inquiries about reviews, comments or books, please contact William Clark at: bill.clark@inumc.org